RECOVERY

THE SECOND MANUSCRIPT OF THE RICHARDS' TRUST

BY

W. J. CHERF

Foxbat Publishing
ISBN: 978-1-7329779-8-3

Cover art. Hieroglyphic insert adapted from the Inventory Inscription of the Medinet Habu Mortuary Temple of Ramesses III. Front cover's reversing clock image is adapted from the apple.com time machine logo. Back cover image is of the author before the Sakkara Bird in Room 22 of the Egyptian National Museum.

The Manuscripts of the Richards' Trust

Bow Tie
Recovery
Children of Ptah
Imhotep
Maat-ka-re. Memoirs of a Time Traveler
Iron from the Sky

The Adventures of J.J. Stone

The First Soul
The Lictor of Magic
I Am the Storm
Dark Blade

Adventures in Paranormal Archaeology

The Magician's Tomb
Netherworld's Gate
Dhampirica
Hallowed Promises

Twenty-Fourth Century Mercenaries

I Am Jonathan
I Am Gregory
I Am Krait
I Am Peter

"Any sufficiently advanced technology would appear indistinguishable from magic."

Arthur C. Clarke

ABBREVIATIONS

AFSPC — Air Force Space Command. Organization tasked with the monitoring and cataloging via powerful radars and optical sensors objects within the Earth's near space envelope.

ALSEP — Apollo Lunar Surface Experiment Package. NASA technical term for a collection of technical experiments that were deployed on the lunar surface by the Apollo XII lunar survey team. These included experiments in soil mechanics, solar wind composition, passive seismic observations, surface magnetism, and ion and gas detection. All were powered via a nuclear power cell known as the Radioisotope Thermal Generator or RTG.

AU — Astronomical Unit. The average separation distance between the earth and the sun (1.496 x 1013 cm.), approximately 150,000,000 kilometers or 93,000,000 miles.

Borghouts — J.F. Borghouts. *Ancient Egyptian Magical Texts*. Leiden, 1978.

C — Shorthand symbol for the speed of light. Approximately 300,000 kilometers per second or 186,000 miles per second that calculates out to about 700,000,000 miles per hour.

CSM — Command and Service Module. NASA technical term of the Apollo series that refers to the primary exploration vehicle, which carries their human cargo from takeoff, to lunar orbit, and return to Earth.

ETB — Equipment Transfer Bag. NASA term for a handy bag that can carry several objects. It is used in conjunction with the LEC (see below) and is attached to the LEC's line.

Faulkner — R.O. Faulkner. *A Concise Dictionary of Middle Egyptian*. Oxford, 1976. English dictionary of the ancient Egyptian language. A very abbreviated and selective collection of the Egyptian language's volcabulary.

Hannig — R. Hannig. *Großes Handwörterbuch Ägyptisch-Deutsch (2800-950 v. Chr.)*. Mainz, 1995. A reasonably good German dictionary of the ancient Egyptian language. Additionally, it is a valuable resource for most aspects of the ancient Egyptian language and includes handy lists of gods, kings, weights and measures, abbreviations, toponyms, and maps.

HR High Resolution. As in high resolution imagery produced by an orbital camera package.

Kees H. Kees. *Das Priestertum im Ägyptischen Staat vom neuen Reich bis zur Spätzeit.* Leiden, 1953, 1958. Invaluable source on the priests and priesthoods of ancient Egypt.

JPL Jet Propulsion Laboratory, Pasadena, CA.

LEC Lunar Equipment Conveyor. NASA technical term for a hand-over-hand laundry line-like device for the easy movement of equipment from the storage area on the LM to the lunar surface.

LM Lunar Module. NASA technical term for the exploration pod that would detach itself from the CSM (see above), land on the moon, and then rejoin with the orbiting CSM. Once the transfer of the survey crew was complete, the LM was commonly jettisoned.

MR Medium Resolution. As in medium resolution imagery produced by an orbital camera package.

NEA Near-Earth Asteroid. Term assigned to asteroids whose paths cross near to the Earth's orbital plane.

NEAT Near-Earth Asteroid Tracking. Civilian scientific organization tasked with the detection of Near-Earth Asteroids (NEAs), comets, and their subsequent assessment as to whether they may represent Potentially Hazardous Asteroids (PHAs).

NORAD North American Aerospace Defense Command. Military information and command nexus located deep within Cheyenne Mountain, Colorado, whose purpose is the observation of the skies and space above continental North America.

OSA Optical Scanning Anomaly. NASA technical term for an unexpected or anomalous artifact captured on either photographic film or video magnetic tape.

RUTI *Rukovodnie Ukazania dlya Temporalnogo Isledovaniya* (*The Guidelines for Temporal Exploration*). Time travel protocol authored in former Soviet Union in 1941 by the famous Hour Glass Seminar. Chaired by the philosopher Gregor Sururov, its members included: Victor Latysev, a Byzantine papyrologist, who is credited with first expressing his concern for "the preservation of the delicate fabric of reality;" theoretical mathematicians Nikolai Fedorov, Alexandr Koslov, and Dmitry

Giga; and Pyotr Borov, theoretical engineer and quantum physicist. This document made no reference to any political or governmental body whatsoever. The *RUTI* states that all temporal decisions must occur within the framework of an international, scientific forum outside of, and free from, any religious, political, or ideological control. This apolitical and neutrally ideological stance would prove to be the Hour Glass Seminar's greatest achievement.

VOX — NASA technical term for private radio communications between individual astronauts that are not routed through any of the onboard systems, nor are taped, archived, or monitored from Earth.

Wb — A. Erman, H. Grapow. *Wörterbuch der Ägyptischen Sprache*. 4th ed. 7 vols. Berlin, 1982. Primary lexicon for the ancient Egyptian language that includes context, sources, and a reverse Egyptian-German word list. Essential, but is considered dated. Should be used in conjunction with more recent philological sources.

FOREWORD

The realm of fiction allows extraordinary personalities the ability to mold the very landscape of their age; whereas history is that crucible wherein individuals are shaped by their times.

Without question this is a work of historical science fiction. As a consequence, it represents a blending of the above sentiment. While extraordinary personalities indeed populate its pages, they are not the dominating element; rather the story itself is what is truly important.

As one might expect within such a genre, much contained within this book is without question factual in every respect. Much is also the product of the author's imagination. As with any work of historical writing, actual events and personalities are described, do appear, and are referred to by name. As with any work of fiction, any similarity either to events or individuals, either living or dead, is purely coincidental.

J.W. Richards

EDITOR'S NOTE

Allow me to introduce myself. My name is Paul Silas. I am both the editor and executor of the so-called Richards' Trust. So-called because the name behind the trust is a fiction. Nonetheless, I can assure you that the dynamic personality that lurks behind the *nom de plume* of Professor Joseph William Richards was a living and breathing individual of breathtaking capacity. You may accept this judgment based upon some twenty-nine odd years of association.

Per the instructions of the Richards' Trust, I was instructed to publish three manuscripts. It is my task, as editor, to make sure that this ardent desire of my colleague comes to fruition. As an editor of a university press, I do have some connections; however, due to the subject matter of these manuscripts I cannot justify their publication under our house banner. So I sought out the good graces of a nonacademic publishing house. As a result of that collaboration you now hold the second manuscript of the series.

The Richards' Trust was quite specific regarding the publication of these manuscripts, the schedule to be followed, and what would set the entire into motion. Put simply, Professor Richards wished, in the event he could not be contacted for a continuous period of six months, that I, as his executor, was to begin the publication process on his behalf. Additionally, I have been granted full power of attorney in all matters legal.

As of this manuscript's printing, my client has been missing for some two and a half years. Naturally, out of concern, I initially instituted an informal and subsequent formal investigation after my first loss of contact. His brownstone near the university was searched and nothing had been found amiss.

As in any such proceeding a domestic trace of his credit card statements indicated that one of his last transactions included a round-trip ticket to Egypt. A quiet inquiry made with the State Department has confirmed that Richards was processed by passport control at Cairo International Airport and admitted into that country. A missing tourist investigation undertaken by the Egyptian Government uncovered that Richards had checked into the Mena House on August 30th. Here, with his splendid accommodations overlooking the Giza Plateau left untouched, the trail of Professor Joseph William Richards ends.

Since Professor Richards' sudden and untraceable disappearance, the trust has empowered me to do the following as specified below.

All advances and royalties from the publication of the manuscripts are to be deposited into the Richards' Trust, where they will be divided equally among several designated funding instruments. Once any of these instruments reaches a specified threshold, then that threshold is to be reduced by seventy-five percent and the apportioned amount is to be distributed equally in the following manner: to a preexisting offshore bank account, as seed money for the establishment of an endowed chair in Egyptian philology at Richards' home institution, and as research grant funds to a West Coast prostate cancer research institute. Once the specified thresholds are again reached, then the cycle is to begin anew with an equal apportionment of funds to the same entities. Once the copyright limitation has been reached on the publications, then all instruments are to clear their accounts to the above established entities in final, lump sum deposits, and the Richards' Trust extinguished.

The why behind all of these details is frankly beyond me, but this is nonetheless the precise wishes of Joseph William Richards, to whom I am legally bound as his executor and colleague.

CHAPTER I

The Distress Signal

It was Christmas Eve in the Year of our Lord 321.

In that year, the Emperor Constantine I, recently converted to Christianity, decreed that the day devoted to the ancient god *Sol Invictus*, Sunday, become a day of Christian worship and rest. Luminaries of the period included: the philosopher Iamblichus, St. Eusebius, the Arian heretic Ulfilius, Ephrem the Syrian, and Constantine's advisor, Lactantinus. Meanwhile, in the Far East, the Eastern Jin Dynasty held a tenuous sway over a politically tumultuous Chinese region and during the brief reign of the Emperor Yuan, the first accurate depiction of a horse stirrup graced the interior of his tomb. A reunited India was thoroughly enjoying its "Classical Age" during the Gupta Empire. With peace came extensive dividends in science, technology, engineering, art, philosophy, religion, astronomy, mathematics, logic, and literature. To the West, the many independent city states of Mesoamerica were experiencing the "Classic Era" of art, architecture, pottery, lapidary, and relief carving.

It was now, on this very date – relatively speaking of course, that the emergency distress signal finally had arrived at The Survey Institute indicating the sudden loss of the link between the first scout surveyor and its craft.

While through the course of millennia others had met their inevitable fates, a certain amount of sentimentality had grown around the adventurous career of that first scout of scouts. In many respects that fabled career embodied the Survey's most endearing qualities of curiosity, patience, and perseverance in the pursuit of knowledge. And now, it too was over.

While a deep sense of loss for that legendary first scout was palpably felt throughout the Survey community, far greater concerns were voiced about the final disposition of the scout surveyor's star craft, the Hope. After a brief discussion, a recovery team was organized and dispatched. Traveling at just below eight-tenths the speed of light, the crew of three began to settle down for their voyage that would seem to take thousands of years to those of The Survey Institute in local relativistic terms.

Meanwhile onboard the recovery craft, The Redemption, that duration would shrink considerably. Still, at least in human terms, such a journey would be difficult to grasp, but not for the recovery team. After all, their ultimate goal was a distant planetary system located within one of the outstretched swirls of the galaxy. The sheer duration to get there was an accepted given.

CHAPTER II

One Nasty Bug

Colonel Alexander Andreovich Piankoff's first tunneled sense of consciousness was framed by the dirty yellow, blotchy, and rust stained squares of an acoustical tile ceiling. While his body was still very groggy from the heavy cocktail of administered antibiotics, the Russian's mind nonetheless was free to carry on a lively commentary.

My God! Here I struggle, no scramble, to get back to my own time to prevent a potential temporal paradox. Am flown posthaste by those soft-hearted Americans to my mother country. Am admitted into the Institute for Tropical Diseases. And here I lie numb under their filthy acoustical tile ceiling!

It's as if that Egyptian court physician Ankhmes had made me drink some of his damn opiated raisin wine! At least that tasted good!

At this point the Russian's initial railing ended as he began to reconstruct in his foggy mind just how he had got himself into this present predicament in the first place.

Fieldcraft Alexander! You forgot your basic fieldcraft! Even worse you forgot your basic survival skills! And then how could you shamelessly ignore your own body's messages?

A short pause and then he began berating himself again.

How could you go off into the desert without having first gorged yourself with water?

You stupid imbecile! You mentally lazy, stupid imbecile! You doddering, lazy, stupid imbecile!

For the next few moments Piankoff allowed himself to stew in his own juices. When he had exhausted by his count no less than an additional nine adjectives that described his poor decision making abilities, his temper finally began to cool. What followed allowed him to move on and confront the facts.

Damn it all! The water from that polluted well had indeed tasted divine! As dehydrated and delirious as I was, it was a miracle I had even found it.

Face it, Alexander. You are one very lucky man to be lying here, especially the way that young pup Richards took care of you.

My young lion...

At this point Piankoff clearly drifted off into another direction as the American came to mind.

That young bastard! That young, bright, and wonderful American bastard! What philological skills, what a loyal temperament, what sound judgment for one so green. And what a quietly calculating killing machine.

My first field assistant. I his teacher. But truly, my dear Sasha, just who taught whom the most?

A blissful mental sigh.

For the first time in my career never had I felt so whole and so secure with another's assistance. Without ever feeling threatened by it. He is so accomplished. My young Mayneken has come so far, so fast, so well . . .

A mental pause of reflection.

Sasha, I serious doubt that you could have even made it back without his aid. Face it, Sasha, you were delirious most of the time. Young Richards got you back and then deftly covered for you during your absence.

I am so proud to have been his mentor. What a fine temporal field agent he has become . . .

Another mental sigh, but this time one of resignation.

He will be more than an adequate replacement for this old and tired warhorse. Richards has already surpassed me in so many ways. But there remain just a few more rough edges for me to smooth out . . .

At this point Colonel Alexander Andreovich Piankoff, the Philology Annex's first temporal field agent, recipient of the Lenin Cross for valor and achievement in his service to his mother country, honorary member of the Russian Academy of Sciences, and special operations officer of Karlov Drazinzka, the Director of the Special Projects Directorate, quietly and painlessly expired.

As with so many things, the devil is always in the details and Piankoff's passing was only further proof of that dreaded maxim. The Russian had the bad luck of ingesting the parasitic vectors directly into his large intestine, instead of their more typical mode of invasion. Usually, acute *schistosomiasis* occurs about five weeks after the worms have burrowed through the epidermis, hitched a ride via the body's capillary system, and made their way to the large intestine. The Russian's onset of fever, nausea, headache, and diarrhea were a direct result of a parasitic ingestion versus invasion.

At the site of his recovery in Luxor the American corpsman did precisely what he had been trained to do whenever faced with a dangerously dehydrated soldier in the field: start a saline drip and administer two aspirins to ease the aches and heat induced fever. While the drip had sustained the weaken Russian nicely all the way to Moscow, the aspirins had really caused some damage. A powerful vasodilator and blood thinner, the *schistosome* ingestion and the effect of their energetic perforation of his intestinal lining only made matters worse.

What was so unbelievable was that the Russian medical staff had not detected the critical nature of the man's internal bleeding, had failed to note the fragility of his blood pressure, nor monitor his fluctuating pulse. Such negligent ignorance is all the more appalling as the treatment for *Schistomsoma mansoni* is not only well known and understood in the literature, but also that this particular species of *schistosome* is particular to Egypt.

Even more damning is the near 100 percent effectiveness of artemisinins during the early treatment of such infections. Instead, the medical staff's chosen course of therapy was to first stabilize the patient with electrolytes and a bolus of over-the-counter drugs, and then later deal more directly with his case on Monday. Meanwhile, during the early hours of Sunday morning, Piankoff, true to his nature, defied that medical faculty's engrained schedule of patient rounds and permanently checked out.

When Piankoff's autopsy was performed, the criticality of his condition was all too apparent, but just as clear would be the assignment of liability. The third shift's staffers, four bright internists, were all summarily fired. The three residents assigned to Piankoff's case, the very same who had admitted him and were responsible for his initial care, were retained.

CHAPTER III

Year 1 of Ankhkheprure Smenkhkare

The young coregent Smenkhkare was fit to be tied. His father, Akhenaten, with whom he shared the all-powerful throne of Egypt for the past three years, but none of its burdensome responsibilities, had turned up missing for the past eight days along with his two favorite Medjay bodyguards. As a consequence, the entire royal household was in a state of panic over the pharaoh's unexplained absence.

The chaos that ensued did not end there, for his daily offices at dawn within the Aten Temple had not been made. Neither had pharaoh made his daily observances at the Aten Temple before his faithful throng. Nor had the Aten made its customary appearance with its life-giving, healing, and curative rays.

While pharaoh's eldest son could fudge his way through the dawn ceremony that announced the divine appearance of the Aten sun disk upon the eastern horizon, it was a different matter when the young co-regent could not command the Aten-disk to appear later in the day above the solar temple. Could not command the solar disk to spread its life-giving rays upon the spiritually hungry masses.

While the mass distribution of sacrificial foodstuffs continued to feed the capital city's population of hungry and dependent stomachs, the cycle had been broken. There could be no sacrifice if the Aten did not appear. Things had seriously changed. As hard as the young coregent tried, prayed, pleaded, and even swore, he could not summon the Aten as his father had been so able to do. Whispers of doubt had crept into the royal court and harem.

The transition of royal power was not supposed to happen like this and certainly not this abruptly. What exacerbated the situation was that the framework for such transition had not been established by the heretic king. It, like the initial concept and ongoing construction of the capital city, the establishment of his revolutionary dogma, the free-form development of artistic forms, all had been a fluid, ongoing visionary process uniquely known only to Akhenaten.

As for Smenkhkare, he was not up to the challenge of commanding the court and royal harem, much less taking on the defense, care, and nurture of the Two Lands. While blessed with the genetic inheritance bestowed upon him by his alien father, Smenkhkare had squandered his time as an adolescent by playing cruel telepathic games and performing malicious telekinetic pranks that verged on outright atrocity. Ignorant, immature, and only partially the master of his powerful inheritance, the young man was not ready for the burden that was Egypt.

To date, he and his far more passive younger brother, Tutankhaten, had literally pissed away their royal upbringing, having ignored their tutors and truly bedeviled the members of their own family. Somehow, both sons had believed that their father would rule forever. Never had either ever considered his absence from the throne of Egypt.

Then there was the ever-looming issue of that queen, their father's former Great Wife, Nefertiti, the woman who had not been strong enough to bear them, but who did bear their six half-sisters. Still, this woman had somehow survived their own father's wrath and mental rape. Anyone who could survive that ordeal held the brothers' collective suspicion and fear. After all, had they not seen with their own eyes the deaths of so many at the mere disdainful glance of their father's eyes?

There remained a lingering rumor about their father, who had been last seen venturing off to the Northern Palace, to the very place of that woman. She and her household still lived, but what had become of their father? No one knew. And neither of the young royals was willing to venture to the Northern Palace and inquire.

So a convenient legal fiction was concocted between the two royal brothers to explain their father's disappearance. The story went that while praying in the Eastern Desert the Aten itself revealed to the brothers that it had taken their father so that they could reside as one. Henceforth, all prayers were directed to this divine pair, now understood as one. So they explained the missing royal personage. So was preserved the Aten cult. So was initiated the elaborate and farcical royal burial of a king without a corpse. So was manufactured some semblance of needed transition and closure to the entire affair.

* * *

In the Great Hall of Appearances the Pharaoh Smenkhkare now sat alone upon the throne of the Two Lands. All of the assembled pretended not to notice that the bottoms of his golden sandals barely touched the final step. On this day sixteen days since the mysterious absence of his father, the priesthood of the Aten had at his command anointed him as his father's successor. Now surrounded by his father's many advisors, once silent advisors whom his father had chosen and commanded, the young king felt defensive, overwhelmed, wary, and stifled by their very presence. Glancing from this one to that and gently glossing over their surface thoughts, they were easy enough for him to telepathically read. Most feared him, and for the moment, that majority opinion suited him just fine.

Let them fear me! He thought. *Better that than to show them any weakness! For I shall rule with a strong hand as my father had ruled.*

All will obey me. None shall rebel. I will not tolerate such from among these lowly animals.

But then the king caught a hint of curiosity and disdainful loathing from among the gathered. Slowly gazing about, he soon recognized the source of such blasphemous impetuousness. It was from one of the foreign ambassadors of Syria, representing a worthless hovel of a coastal town called Sumur, at the mouth of an equally obscure river.

Sumur, a once marginally held Egyptian vassal town that was lost to northern invaders during my father's reign. Well, this man must be its only survivor, or more likely, its treacherous betrayer.

The unfortunate's name was Adbi-Ashirti.

In full view of the court, the young and newly minted pharaoh fixed the ambassador with his eyes and the man paled. Sweat broke out across his brow. A great trembling began that was soon followed by a choking spasm. Falling to his knees, the helpless man looked up in supplication, loosed his bowels, and fell over dead. Lying in the center of the spreading pool of drool, urine, and feces, the court moved away in shock and horror at the pitiful victim, who only moments ago was one of their own. His crime was as unknown as the means of his execution. However, as to who that executioner was, there was no doubt, for the young king now wore a slight smile on his face.

"Dear and loyal members of the court, be mindful that while in my presence your thoughts remain true to me and to Egypt. As for now, I am tired. Leave my presence," he stated with an outward wave of his left hand.

As the court took its orders to leave, all made sure to view the unmoving ambassador left behind. The message had been sent and received. Among those so impressed with the royal display was the former royal stonemason, Paneshy. For him what he had just witnessed was more than sufficient confirmation of the rumors he had heard whispered throughout the palace.

Indeed, Smenkhkare was a monster loose among mortals.

CHAPTER IV

The Interview

One of the most secure vaults in Moscow was located deep within a warren known as the Russian Ministry of Science. Even by former Soviet standards, this rabbit hole was considered a dreary one with stale air tinged with acrid cigarette smoke that the overworked and poorly maintained ventilators could never seem to remove. The chamber itself was a visual wasteland: no windows, no artwork on its dirty tan walls, only several dirty shadowed squares where the outdated party memorabilia had used to hang. The lighting emanated from very special halogen pedestal lamps. Their harsh glare only highlighted the ceiling's wavy surface imperfections, poorly repaired cracks, and chance cobwebs. Nonetheless, the lamps served their purpose as each gave off a different, barely audible harmonic. When taken together, the harmonic overlapped at the centrally located conference table. All conversation was effectively muffled should the room be bugged. At the room's center, the focus of this aural dampening was a round conference table surrounded by five generously padded chairs. There had once been a sixth, but the blood of Comrade Foderev had ruined it.

The first to arrive, an elderly but fit man who possessed an unremarkable Slavic face, carried a thick purple file that indicated its ultra-level security status. Plunking down his burden before him with a muffled thud, his body language seemed to carry a still heavier weight that could not be so easily shrugged off. Folding his gnarled and arthritic hands before him in an overhand clasp, he waited for the others to arrive. In the dull silence of the vault, the aging Karlov Drazinzka had been granted a rare opportunity of vagrant time. During it he considered what he had accomplished while on his watch, what he had failed to do, and why he was here. It was the closest thing to a Christian examination of conscience that he had ever before experienced.

My dear Karly, he began. *You have done much. About that, there is no question. You built the directorate literally with your own hands. You nurtured it with the sweat of your own brow. You advanced its causes sometimes with your own blood, more often with the blood of others.*

But my dear Karly, the loss of your favorite son, the son that you never had. Now that was unspeakable! To permit the sacrifice of Sasel on the altar of security to satisfy those two paranoids was one thing, a very tough thing, perhaps even a necessary thing. But to have recovered dear Alexander and then lose him so quickly to a fucking fresh water parasite, while under the care of those idiots at the Institute of Tropical Diseases, after all he had done, all he had accomplished, now that is just too much to bear!

Now with tightly clenched hands and jaw, he continued on relentlessly with his personal catharsis while his shoulders quaked with emotional tremors.

That Colonel Alexander Piankoff, the son of my closest childhood friend, lost because of his rigid sense of duty, his selflessness. Such heroism requires – no, goddamn it, demands of the Rodina, *the Motherland, only her very best!*

At this point the sound of the arriving elevator blessedly allowed Drazinzka the opportunity to compose himself before the others arrived. As had always happened in the past, that transformation was successful.

"Ah, Karlov, it's so good to see you," beamed the older of the two new arrivals. "May I take this opportunity to introduce to you Academician Stefan Rosovec? Academician Rosovec – Academician Karlov Drazinzka, Head of the Special Projects Directorate."

Slight bows, murmurs of "it is a pleasure," mechanically efficient handshakes, and the exchange of cagey and measuring eye contact followed.

The presenter, Academician Vasily Ostrogorsky, the Director of the prestigious Institute of Theoretical Biology, sat next to Karlov. Rosovec, taking the hint, took a seat opposite them.

So, the newcomer thought, *it is as I suspected. Yet another interview.*

Ostrogorsky continued.

"Karlov, as you are aware, Academician Fedorov has recently retired. In his place Rosovec has been made the new Director of Advanced and Theoretical Technological Research."

Ostrogorsky then went on to describe in some detail Rosovec's impressive academic and administrative credentials, all of which

Karlov had already read and reread over several times. Nonetheless, Karlov paid respectful attention to the entirety of his old colleague's oration.

So, thought Karlov, *this is what the new pup looks like!*

As impressive as Rosovec's resume was, Karlov had to admit that his movie star presence of jet black curly hair, olive-colored skin, and chiseled appearance, was just as remarkable.

Ostrogorsky, having ended his presentation, let out a sigh, and then asked Karlov if he had any questions for the new director.

Theatrically opening his hands and slightly shrugging his shoulders, Karlov began his grilling.

"Frankly, my dear Vasily, I do not know which to be impressed with more, Academician Rosovec's resume or his good looks!"

To which Rosovec allowed a careful, closed lip smile that his eyes did not participate in, for he knew that something was coming, and he wasn't disappointed.

"I am curious, Academician Rosovec. Have you ever spent any time in the military?"

"Why no, Academician Drazinzka, my course of study did not allow for it."

"Ah, I see."

Pause.

"Well then, do you have any problem with being told what to do?"

"An interesting question, Academician. It would have to depend on the circumstances surrounding such a request."

With quiet steel in his voice, Karlov then restated his question. "Academician Rosovec, I am not discussing a 'request.' What I need to know from you now, right this moment, is if ordered to do something, are you capable of carrying out that command to the best of your ability?"

Blushing slightly, Rosovec replied with equal parts of sangfroid. "An order from my superiors is an order to be obeyed and followed."

"Yes. Good textbook answer," Karlov said with a chilling smile.

"But since the world is a place that is never quite what it seems, allow me to ask you this. Have you ever ordered the death of a close colleague?"

Ostrogorsky then broke in as was planned. "Karlov!"

Raising one hand, open palmed toward his generational twin in a sign of truce, Karlov then pressed, "Your answer please, Academician Rosovec."

Now with an ashen face and suddenly moist palms, Rosovec, feeling his confident composure melting, mentally screamed.

Now just what the hell kind of question is that! "Why, of course not! Never!"

"I see," Karlov softly replied.

"Well, Academician Rosovec, I must inform you my colleague next to me and I have had to, how shall I say, make some rather grim decisions in the past. Rather permanent decisions that sometimes, unfortunately, 'impacted' our very own colleagues. Given your pretty credentials and even prettier face, are you prepared to make such difficult decisions, Academician Rosovec?"

Pole axed by the force of Karlov's directness, Rosovec then counterpunched to buy some time to collect his thoughts.

"Academician Drazinzka, you are of course referring to the case of Academician Sasel, are you not?"

Recognizing the ploy, Karlov inwardly smiled. *He's stalling for time. He really needs to think about this. Good. Very good!*

"But of course. But again I ask, as a member of this inner circle, can we depend on you and your directorate to carry out an order no matter how *nikulturny* it may seem?"

Karlov's goad in using the highly charged Russian euphemism, which best can be translated as "totally barbaric," was calculated for shock value.

Now angry, Rosovec growled back, "Yes, you son of a bitch! I would eat my own mother's liver if I had to!"

During this exchange, Ostrogorsky remained silent, but quite alert.

Karlov, now smiling at Rosovec's reply, thought before he spoke his mind.

Ah, a bit of colorful savagery does exist behind that pretty exterior. Well. Perhaps this one does possess the needed ruthlessness, the steel required.

"My dear Academician Rosovec. I thank you for your most colorful affirmative. As for me being a son of a bitch, you are absolutely correct. I am. As for you, however, I believe that we have successfully established that you will allow nothing to get in the way of your ambitions. I believe that on that basis we have begun to forge a common ground, an understanding. May I welcome you then to join our inner circle?"

"Thank you, Academician Drazinzka, for that is my wish."

"In that case, my colleague, you may call me Karlov."

"Karlov it is then. And you, colleague, may call me Stefan."

"It would be a pleasure, Stefan."

Ostrogorsky simply beamed.

* * *

"Our next agenda item," Ostrogorsky continued, "is to recommend the award of the posthumous decoration of an unprecedented second Lenin's Cross to Colonel Alexander Piankoff. Is there any discussion?"

Looking around and seeing none, he then continued.

"Seeing that there is none, then we shall recommend to the appropriate authorities the issuing of this award with the necessary stipulation that this official state act must remain as secret as the personnel file that sits before you Karlov."

To which a head nodded in the affirmative and a grateful thought sent.

"Thank you, my old friend. Alexander would have been most honored."

"Now for our final agenda item – the recovery of the alien spacecraft. Is there any discussion?"

"Yes," Rosovec queried, "just what is the American position on this issue?"

Karlov, now feeling much more at ease around the "youngster" since their opening pissing match, allowed.

"Well, Stefan, at one time I suspect we could have negotiated quite easily for an equal share of the technology, but now, I am not so sure. The new American temporal field agent, Dr. Richards, was not only trained by our best and only temporal agent, but has developed far beyond what either dear Piankoff expected, or us. In fact, I have good information the Americans are at this moment considering the training of another temporal agent, this time on their own, to form a new team. In order to protect our own interests, I suggest we proactively approach them with a suitable candidate of our own. However, at the heart of the matter is the temporal technology itself. As you are no doubt aware, the Americans possess the Soap Bubble and we don't. What that means is that either the Americans share or we build our own."

With that stated, two pairs of eyes then turned to silently stare into Rosovec's, who replied, "Well, that's a tall order. Perhaps the real question should be, do we build our own from scratch, or do we steal it outright from the Americans?"

At that moment, Rosovec suddenly realized why he had been invited to this clique. *How deftly these two old men had steered him. It had all been nothing more an elaborate trap.*

CHAPTER V

Assault on the Moon

The American decision to successfully land a man on the Moon was neither a frivolous political challenge nor an ill-conceived, helter-skelter undertaking, even if the Soviet Sputnik had provided the goad. Instead, this carefully orchestrated and complex event was the culmination of preparations that resembled more a full military assault than a scientific adventure. The first order of business became the establishment of where, and even if, such a landing was feasible. Parallels to the preparations prior to the D-Day invasion of Normandy were inescapable. So was launched a formidable reconnaissance effort that carried the proud names of Ranger, Lunar Orbiter, and Surveyor. Little did anyone expect, however, what would be found accidentally by these probes and what the consequent ramifications would be for the American space program.

It all began with the Ranger series of probes during the mid-1960s. Nine in all, Rangers I and II were mere test platforms without cameras. Of the seven that launched moonward, Rangers III through VI failed, while the remaining Rangers VII, VIII, and IX performed admirably producing more than seventeen thousand high quality photographs.

Crude by today's standards, these expendable one-way drones were designed to simply fly by a portion of the lunar surface with their six television cameras blazing and antennas sizzling, as they transmitted back to Earth their precious data feeds right up until impact. For this unique marriage of camera and radio picture transmission, specially built Vidicon television cameras were used, which were capable of transmitting high resolution close-ups of the lunar surface during the final minutes of each spacecraft's existence. The six cameras provided both wide angle and high resolution shots that ranged from 25 to 2.1 degrees. This arrangement provided overlap and "produced a 'nested' sequence of pictures." Final resolutions ranged from 1.5 to 0.3 meters. This was how eight or so lunar landing sites were scouted. All made possible by the one-way passes of thirteen, twenty-three, and nineteen minutes of extremely expensive airtime.

Predictably, the flood of photographic data received was as remarkable as it was overwhelming, but as early as the Ranger VII data upload, NASA concluded that several lunar areas were indeed topographically acceptable as future manned landing sites. As luck would have it, during the last flight of the Ranger series, something odd appeared on the NASA monitors in the form of a tantalizingly brief reflection painted against the otherwise dull dark marl landscape of the *Oceanus Procellarum* – the Ocean of Storms. Back tracking the tape, it was reckoned in the neighborhood of Latitude 2.96 S. by Longitude 337.12 E. This tantalizing glimpse occurred on March 24, 1965. At 18.732 minutes into Ranger IX's final operational existence, its 76 mm high resolution camera captured at a resolution of 0.3 meters with good contrast and high shadowing a highly reflective oval object that measured some 2.0 meters across. With Ranger IX nearing its impact at 19.063 minutes, image motion blurring was at its most severe, rendering useless all subsequent image enhancement attempts.

Ranger IX provided NASA an anomaly. Some cogently argued "not to worry," temporizing that the anomalous bright spot was nothing more than an artifact of glare against the camera's lens, or a reflective glint off the Ranger craft itself. All and well meant, but others not so sure about such confidently voiced, quick-draw assessments, based more on pure conjecture, if not intellectual vapor. So to appease the doubting Thomases the object was officially logged as an OSA – an "Optical Scanning Anomaly." If an opportunity in the future would present itself, then another pass of the area could be scheduled to resolve the issue once and for all.

* * *

During the years 1966 and 1967, no fewer than five Lunar Orbiter missions were launched from Cape Canaveral "with the purpose of mapping the lunar surface before the Apollo landings." While the Rangers had indeed provided stunning photography, their 178-kilogram packages were nonetheless extravagantly expensive and short-lived exercises that perhaps were better remembered for their spectacularly Pyrrhic deaths. This would not be the case, however, with the Orbiter series that would, as their moniker implies, orbit the moon rather than to purposely auger into it.

Officially, NASA reported that 99 percent of the moon had been mapped to at least a resolution of sixty meters by these fine reconnaissance spacecraft. That fact in itself represented a triumph in aeronautical space engineering. That all five missions performed without a hitch spoke volumes for their reliability as well.

Initially, Orbiters I, II, and III were tasked with the imaging of some twenty potential lunar landing sites destined for the Apollo program, while Orbiters IV and V were held in reserve. As before, these sites had been selected based upon Earth-based observations and now they were to be examined at low inclination orbits. But given the success of these first three missions, Orbiters IV and V were retasked to broader scientific objectives – high altitude, polar orbital mapping of the near and far side of the moon.

The uncanny success of the Orbiter missions was due in part to their ingenious imaging system that "consisted of a dual lens camera, a film processing unit, a readout scanner, and a film handling apparatus." In short, NASA had managed to bundle together an automatic, remote Bimat film processing lab that digitally scanned each image and then transmitted it back to Earth. As if this were not enough, the dual lenses consisted of "an 80 mm wide angle medium resolution lens" and a monster 610 mm narrow angle high resolution lens. To appreciate the capability of this big lens, which had been used extensively on the U-2 spy plane, from an atmospheric height of seventy thousand feet, objects were discernible that measured less than a meter across. In the void of space free of atmospheric turbidity and cloud cover, crystal clarity to a resolution of one foot across was considered the norm with objects only six inches across being discernible. Together, the simultaneous MR and HR images of the barren moonscape were recorded on a special Eastman Kodak 70 mm thin film with sixteen high resolution shots centered within its wide angle twin for reference. The film rolls themselves were thirty-six hundred feet long.

Unofficially, never before had NASA expended so much and then claimed so little. From the very start with Orbiter I that launched on August 10, 1966, NASA claimed that only "thirteen high resolution photos were considered usable." A malfunctioning shutter on the 610 mm lens was said to have been the culprit.

Nonetheless, the craft managed to successfully map at an altitude of forty-six kilometers eight equatorial landing areas that included one set of coordinates within the Ocean of Storms of particular interest: Latitude 2.96 S. by Longitude 337.12 E. While Orbiter III would dutifully go through its paces at an altitude of fifty-five kilometers – "officially" to retrace Orbiter I's path because of "that darn stuttering shutter," NASA already knew what it needed to know from Orbiter I's download.

In this instance, the doubting Thomases were vindicated. The OSA was not an artifact of either a lens flare or reflection off of the Ranger, but a gracefully constructed object that photographed beautifully against the dark marl of the Ocean of Storms. In fact, on the basis of both the Orbiter I and III's high resolution photography, the object's nearly transparent, but highly reflective, two-meter wide array was clear to see. This curious feature became apparent when a comparison was made of the HR photos of the two spacecraft that were taken from differing aspects. Support for this gossamer, almost butterfly wing-like sail, was provided by a single strut that was embedded into the moon's surface crust. Its dimensions calculated out to about one meter high by twenty-five to thirty centimeters in thickness. While NASA was painfully aware that the Soviet's had been the first to soft land Luna IX on February 3rd of that same year, Mission Control was also positive that this was decidedly not where the Luna had landed. It certainly was not that of Surveyor I either, for it had landed on June 2nd, nowhere near these coordinates.

So who was this artifact's owner? While the initial logging of the OSA had been one thing, NASA now had a full-blown mystery on its hands. Since the OSA was confirmed as a real something, it needed a real code name, a highly rated security classification, and for whatever reason it was called SNOWMAN. In time, however, any public reference to SNOWMAN would be explained as a distinctive set of five craters on the moon that, when seen from a particular point of view, looked very much like – you guessed it – a snowman. In the end, only a precious few players knew the entire story.

* * *

Those players included: Leonard D. Jaffe, the Surveyor series project scientist at the Jet Propulsion Laboratory; A. R. Luedecke, Deputy Director of JPL; Otto Berg, Director, Naval Research Laboratory of Rocket Photography; Werner von Braun, Director, Marshall Space Flight Center, NASA; and last but hardly least, several shadowy high officials of the CIA and NSA. While the central purpose for the Ranger, Orbiter, and now Surveyor series remained intact – the detailed reconnaissance of suitable manned landing sites – an interesting subplot formed around the origin and ownership of SNOWMAN. Some believed it to be a secret, second Soviet soft landing. Others wondered if the object might even be of Nazi origin. Some flatly dared not to speculate, but von Braun, whenever the subject of SNOWMAN came up, beamed an infectious, boyish grin that only seemed to underline his twinkling blue-gray eyes. When once pointedly asked about his cavalier attitude toward this sensitive subject, whether apocryphal or not, legend records that von Braun chuckled and chided his tormentor.

"On what authority do you think we are not alone in the universe?"

He then added for effect, "No doubt by the same authority that first pronounced SNOWMAN to be a lens flare!"

In all, seven Surveyors were launched between 1966 and 1968. Their "main objectives . . . were to obtain close-up images of the lunar surface and to determine if the terrain was safe for manned landings." Initially, the throttleable Vernier engines of Surveyors 2 and 4 malfunctioned, transforming their planned soft landings into costly exercises in crater formation. Of the Surveyors that successfully soft landed, these ungainly tripods proved their worth, loaded down with sensing gear, a central television boom and camera, and mechanical arms that dug test trenches in the moon's surface. The later Surveyors even had magnets attached to their footpads and a remote sensing device that could perform a chemical analysis of the surrounding lunar material.

The central boom television camera had a zoom lens that ranged from a wide angle 25 mm to a modest 100-mm telephoto. The camera also had a variable iris with focal stops ranging from f 4 to f 22 and changeable filters that could for the first time transmit in color in addition to the more traditional black-and-white images. At maximum resolution, the telephoto lens could focus down to one millimeter at a distance of four meters. The entire setup could pivot 360 degrees in any direction and pan up over 40 degrees or depress to 65 degrees to view the craft's own footpads and immediate surroundings. 200-line video transmissions had a transmission lag of twenty seconds as did the high definition, 600-line stills. In short, the Surveyors were formidable packages capable of testing and photographing their immediate environs.

With the launch of Surveyor 3 on April 17th, 1967, NASA programmed the craft to land in the Ocean of Storms on a smooth mare area southeast of the Crater Lansberg. The entire flight had been letter perfect until the critical moment when the sensitive Vernier engines fired. And fire they did indeed, for ground control had a devil of a time shutting them down. As a consequence, Surveyor 3 earned the dubious distinction of being the first spacecraft to land on the moon no fewer than three times, or more technically, bounced three times. When it did finally settle, Surveyor 3 slid some fourteen meters before coming to rest on the gradual slope of a small crater wall at coordinates 2.94 S. by 336.66 E.

At this point, the command deck of mission control in Pasadena was cleared of all unauthorized personnel, much to the bitching of many. All that remained within the command center were Jaffe, Luedecke, Berg, von Braun, and the aforementioned shadowy officials. Jaffe, as the project's head scientist, confirmed that all was nominal with Surveyor 3 and then personally took control of the craft's boom television camera. He selected the wide angle setting.

After the obligatory pause of twenty seconds, the initial imagery received on the high definition Zenith display screens was disorienting because of the decided tilt to the horizon. All this select audience could see was the interior slope of a crater. Jaffe, expertly working the camera's remote joystick, panned clockwise to the next quadrant allowing for a ten-degree overlap. Again, nothing but crater slope. Again Jaffe panned and again nothing but crater slope. On the scientist's fifth pan, finally a sliver of horizon could be perceived in the right corner of the picture over the opposite side of the crater's rim. In the next pan nothing out of the ordinary appeared – just the vast expanse of dark smooth marl of the Ocean of Storms basin. Again when Jaffe panned, this time he did so with a nervously damp hand and sweaty brow. By the seventeenth pan, Jaffe had completed the camera's circuit and SNOWMAN was nowhere to be seen.

Frustration, defeat, and finally disgust hung silently in the air for minutes on end until someone finally shuffled their feet and drawled the obvious to the near empty command center. “Aw, crap!”

Little did that select group in mission control realize just how close they had come to practically landing the Surveyor on top of SNOWMAN. For if Surveyor 3 had not suffered from its Vernier malfunction and had stabilized at its initial landing point some fourteen meters up slope, then the craft’s boom camera would have peered down at the object a mere twenty-six meters away. While this near reality would later be calculated based upon the craft’s telemetry alone, it would be the photos taken by Eugene Cernan and Thomas P. Stafford of the Apollo 10 crew on May 22nd, 1969, some two years later, which would confirm and consummate their total frustration.

CHAPTER VI

A Comrade's Farewell

The passing of a loved one, dear friend, or colleague is a traumatic event. Depending upon the culture, the emotional release is expressed differently and in varying degrees of intensity. The ancient Egyptians, even though they had spiritually and materially prepared for the event throughout the course of their lives, still exploded with anguish, tears, hair pulling, and the tearing of clothing, even if some of the mourners among the participating throng were paid professionals. Nonetheless, the ancients had a clear notion of the gods, what the afterlife presented, what it offered, and the steps that were necessary to enjoy its many benefits. For the survivors of the deceased's family, their concerns were with the physical maintenance of the tomb that above all guaranteed the security and well-being of the deceased's corpse. If this was done, then all was in order. Additionally, this structure provided for the survivors a release point and a tangible way of being able to maintain a connection with the dead. So it went on from generation to generation, this endless cycle of preparation, maintenance, security, and thus eternal survival.

On the other hand, we moderns tend to be a mixed bag of emotional extremes when it comes to death. Some can stoically endure the public's eye with a rigid jaw, reddened and occasionally watery eyes. Others practically collapse in consuming and racking sobs of noisy grief. The reasons are many for these wide swings in expression, but one sure fact is that the skeptical modern mind does not have the sure knowledge that the afterlife exists, what it even is, much less what it may offer, let alone the steps for how to prepare for and enjoy its benefits. The fact is that faith has been replaced with science, pseudoscience, or even worse, with nothing at all. None of these cold and sterile options offer any modicum of emotional comfort or a socially recognized avenue for release. When it comes to death, we moderns do not have a clue, and if we do, then we are afraid to express our beliefs out of fear of social ridicule. That is the core of the modern dilemma when it comes to death: the issue of commitment. We moderns cannot qualitatively or quantitatively express what we believe, because we have been conditioned since birth to deny the very existence of the divine realm or paranormal. And science is a cruel, cool alternative.

* * *

Fortunately, this dire situation was not a universal. Moments of true release did occur, but rarely in public. Nevertheless, this was one of those precious moments, when five men of differing backgrounds came together to bury one of their own. What was remarkable was that none of them were related, yet all felt that they were a part of a distinct whole, forming a family of sorts. Crudely put, but perhaps more accurately stated, the quintet felt that they all had, or were responsible for, “a piece of the action.”

Karlov Drazinzka, the Head of the Special Projects Directorate – a very shadowy and indistinct organization within the morass of bureaucracy known as the Russian Academy of Sciences – proudly considered himself as the father figure of the deceased. With that position he also irrationally bore the personal burden of guilt for the deceased’s passing. His bloodshot eyes had flowed rivers of tears for his lost son. And they would do so again, soon.

Academician Vasily Ostrogorsky, the Director of the Institute of Theoretical Biology, itself a more visible part of the Russian Academy of Sciences, saw himself in the guise of the deceased’s protective uncle. While not so personally attached to the deceased as Karlov, he undeniably had his hand in the decision-making that so affected the deceased’s prematurely short, but meteoric career. Consequently, Vasily found himself hopelessly torn between bitter heartbreak and extreme pride for the deceased. Head bowed as if in prayer, Vasily unconsciously rubbed the knuckles of his hands throughout the proceedings until they had become raw. It was as if he was attempting to wash his hands of all guilt and only his own blood would do.

As for the American Dr. John Milson, Professor Emeritus of Egyptology, he had accepted the deceased as a valuable colleague-in-arms, even if at arms’ length. But in the end, he had learned to trust the deceased with his own handpicked candidate, despite his notoriously well-known and unorthodox training methods. Only great admiration for the deceased filled his man’s heart. Yet for Milson, this entire ceremony represented a fascinating glimpse into the Russian mind that he had previously not thought possible, and one that he would not have missed for the world.

Dr. Joseph Richards, also an American and a newly appointed Associate Professor of Egyptian Philology, was by far the youngest of this distinguished group. He had a powerfully emotional bond with the deceased as he had been his mentor, colleague, dear friend, and finally older brother. This young one would in the end surprise everyone.

Finally, there was Academician Stefan Rosovec, the new Director of Advanced and Theoretical Technological Research, also a part of the Russian Academy of Sciences, who had never met the deceased, but who knew of his many exploits and accomplishments. While he would not shed a tear throughout the proceedings, he nonetheless felt cheated for never having had the opportunity to meet the deceased.

So the proceedings began in great secrecy as was the wont of all those assembled beneath the red-stoned mausoleum of V. I. Lenin. In a cool and narrow corridor that was lit only by the harsh glare and shadow of caged light bulbs evenly spaced at every twenty feet, the men clustered closely before a modest niche in the brickwork wall, one of many such silent and forgotten places devoted to only the *Rodina*'s most deserving.

Clearing his throat and slightly lifting his chin, Karlov read directly from the formal decree and did so in English for the benefit of the two Americans. Given the nature of the moment, this detail was not missed by either Milson or Richards. In fact, they were a bit surprised at the deference extended to them. They were to soon find out why.

With a voice thick with emotion, Karlov began.

"On the behalf of the Federal Russian Republic and the former Union of Soviet Socialist Republics, we commit to his final rest Major General Alexander Andreovich Piankoff, posthumously promoted as such, who as an honorary member of the Russian Academy of Sciences, and as a special operations officer of an adjunct department to the aforementioned institution, during the course of his short and all too brief career, received an unprecedented two medals of the Order of Lenin for valor and achievement in his service to his country and the rest of mankind."

At the voicing of the phrase "we commit to his final rest" tears ran off the man's heavy cheeks. They noisily plopped upon the document that he was reading. Unthinkingly, his trembling left thumb attempted to brush the liquid away, partially smearing the text as a result. Vasily, seeing this, extended to him his own handkerchief, which Karlov gratefully accepted and daubed his eyes. Without skipping a beat, he continued to read.

"On no fewer than eight occasions, Major General Piankoff, as a member of the Special Projects Directorate, bravely and selflessly left his time, ventured into the temporal void as ordered, accomplished his missions, and successfully returned. Nor shall it be forgotten that he was the first ever to do so."

Karlov then paused, took a deep breath, collected himself again, and continued, but this time with a stronger voice.

"Major General Piankoff, during these extraordinary temporal missions at the behest of the Russian Academy of Sciences, the American Academy of Sciences, and their allied organizations, singlehandedly provided critical temporal calibration measurements to the scientists of the aforementioned organizations.

"Moreover, Major General Piankoff provided invaluable linguistic data from the temporal horizons investigated to the aforementioned scientific organizations and their allied colleagues.

"Furthermore, Major General Piankoff was the first to identify the potential threat that the alien life-form Akhenaten presented to the rest of mankind. When confronted with the magnitude of this threat, Major General Piankoff then singlehandedly trained resources to assist him with his duties in the field. In this decision, Major General Piankoff showed remarkable foresight and began the catalytic process of shared responsibilities between the scientific organizations of two sovereign nations.

"We here present wish and hope that such cooperation, as first initiated by Major General Piankoff's foresightedness, continues. Then Major General Piankoff, with the assistance of these newly trained resources, provided the aforementioned scientific organizations with the needed genetic evidence in support of his claims, claims that proved to be correct in all respects. Upon analysis of these data, Major General Piankoff, along with the assistance of resources, then removed this threat to mankind.

"Thus, all of mankind owes Major General Piankoff their debt of gratitude in that he preserved something far beyond our experience. Major General Piankoff preserved our very existence, our very reality. May he rest in eternal peace."

Having finished, Karlov swallowed hard and again wiped at his eyes.

"Well done, Karly," smiled Vasily with a soft pat on the shoulder, "very well done. Sasha would have blushed beet red with embarrassment."

For Richards and Milson, who had both furtively glanced at one another during the reading, both had been caught slack-jawed as the message they heard from the Russians was clear: *We want the partnership to continue. We want Piankoff's replacement to be a Russian.* Given their presence as witnesses at this unique ceremony and one spoken in English – not to mention the importance attributed to its august location – that had to be the only message they were to take back with them to the States. A quickly shared nod confirmed that both had heard what they had thought they had heard.

Rosovec noted this silent communication between the Americans and found himself inwardly pleased at the development.

Indeed, he thought darkly. *Our guests did not miss our carefully worded message. Given here, beneath Lenin's own shadow, should add further weight to our suggested future course of action. If they choose not to "play ball," as they like to say, well then, so be it. We will just have to find our own way. And I am fully prepared either to permanently "borrow" that portable unit of theirs or even go the lengths of kidnapping Borov himself in order to build our own prototype right here in Moscow!*

At that moment, rousing the Russians from their deep and varied thoughts, Richards asked Karlov if he could "say a few words on Major General Piankoff's behalf."

A bit taken aback by the unexpected American request, all that the director of Special Projects could do was mutely jerk a single nod. Then, much to his surprise, Richards produced from the interior of his suit coat a papyrus roll neatly bound with a length of royal blue yarn. Squeezing past the two aged Russians, the American then inserted the roll into a narrow gap between the niche's ceiling and the urn that contained Piankoff's remains. Then before the opening, standing erect and with his eyes closed, Richards raised his arms bent at the elbow as if he was a cheerleader imitating the letter U. With his open palms facing the sepulture's gaping mouth he began to chant in the tongue of the ancient Egyptians an abbreviated version of *The Opening of the Mouth* ceremony.

> I open your mouth, so that you may speak,
> I open your eyes, so that you may see Re,
> I open your ears, so that you may hear of your glorification,
> And I grant movement to your legs, arms, and heart, so that you can repulse your enemies.
> Long may you live, most righteous Piankhotep.

Finished, Richards then bent forward, kissed the urn, and whispered hoarsely in Egyptian.

"Safe journey, my old friend."

The Russian reaction to Richards' benediction was mixed. Karlov and Vasily were openly impressed at the dignity of the act, although they did not understand a word of it. To them, the American's body language and kiss were Russian enough even without the thoughtful papyrus memento.

Rosovec, however, remained coolly skeptical and rated the entire performance as poorly delivered theatrics.

How typically American!

But a glance at the old and now tearful American Egyptologist did force him to briefly reconsider that snap judgment.

As for Milson, Richards' act of filial piety had set off in him a gushing inundation of revelation and release that had truly surprised him. Not since the funeral of his own dear Alice three years ago had he allowed such deep emotions to burst forth. Indeed, he could now say that he had witnessed Piankoff's burial, but during which millennia?

Frankly, he wasn't all that sure.

CHAPTER VII

Year 1 of Ankhkheprure Smenkhkare (Cont.)

It was nearing sundown as the somber procession made its way from the river's western bank inland toward the raised plateau and its vast necropolis. To the north standing in silent witness of this progress towered the massive Step Pyramid of Djoser with the last rays of the sun painting an orange to pinkish blush across the smooth limestone blocks of its western angles and the vertical surfaces of its sacred wall. Ancient beyond calculation even to the inhabitants of this ancient land, this man-made mountain atop the Sakkara plateau had already become synonymous with that first primeval mound that had signaled the act of creation itself. The architect of this monumental complex, a man named Imhotep, had also become by the Eighteenth Dynasty far more than a mere mortal, and by the next millennium, would be worshipped outright as a god.

Heady incense perfumed the air as eight white-kilted *sem*-priests of Ptah with leopard skin padded shoulders bore the elegant cedar coffin that was decorated predominantly with the feathered pattern that represented the bird-like *ba*, or soul of the deceased. This feathery motif was then further augmented with an overlay of the blue and gold vulture wings of Nekhbet that embraced, wrapped around, and protectively overlapped across the lid of the anthropoid shape.

It was a classic example of what later specialists in the field of Egyptology would call a *rishi*, Arabic for "feathered." A religiously conservative style that began during the Theban Seventeenth Dynasty, it was particularly favored during the first half of the Eighteenth Dynasty as well. Its presence here, at this time, was clearly an idiosyncratic anachronism on the part of the deceased.

The formalized face on the coffin was of gold foil with inlaid eyebrows of the darkest ebony and shockingly lifelike eyes of white quartz centered with black basalt pupils. The whole was framed within a helmet-like black wig. A vertical ribbon made of inlaid ebony characters against a gold foil field ran down the center of the figure's length to the curve of its upturned base. The inscription proudly announced who the occupant was.

The venerable and noble first servant of the Great God,
The Osiris Meryptah,
Exalted among men for his wisdom,
Beloved of Maat,
Righteous of spirit,
Most worthy to sit among the gods as one.

In this case such weighty words were not a falsely stated sham, for this man had indeed lived them to the fullest and during a time of Egypt's greatest religious upheaval.

The procession snaked its way this way and that among the many and crowded lesser funerary monuments of the plateau that included long dead pharaohs of the earliest dynasties and members of their court. A powerfully muscled *sem*-priest led them. He carried before him the instruments necessary for the deceased's final ceremony of *The Opening of the Mouth*. In one hand smoked an incense burner that produced sometimes lingering, sometimes swirling, clouds of myrrh. Such heavily fragrant smoke, it was believed, purified the way for the deceased. In the priest's other hand was held a curiously shaped object called the *nua Wepwawet*, "the path-opener tool of the jackal god." This implement is often depicted as being held before the mummy's mouth as well as the nose, ears, and eyes during this ceremony, which magically gave the mummy the critically important abilities to speak, smell, hear, and see, not to mention to eat and drink in the afterlife.

While the tool's actual purpose is poorly understood by moderns, ancient Egyptian religious sensibilities relied upon its magical efficacy. While a fully intact mummy was necessary in order to properly house for eternity the deceased's *ba*, or spiritual double, a fully functional mummy was required if the deceased was to enjoy the fruits of the afterlife or sample any gifts of bread and beer placed before the tomb. The proper magical application of the *nua Wepwawet* allowed for this physical functionality. As for the tool itself, it was nothing more than a stylized version of a physician's long-handled tongue depressor. It is neither a sculptor's tool, nor agricultural adze, nor the celestial shape of the Big Dipper as interpreted by some modern scholars. Thus, we should really understand *The Opening of the Mouth* ceremony more appropriately as the "opening of the throat."

The name for the leading *sem*-priest who carried these sacred objects, Mayneken – "young lion" in the ancient Egyptian tongue – was a most appropriate appellation for this second servant of the god Ptah. Evidence of that fact was clear to anyone with eyes as he bore across his back four magnificent scars that stretched from his right shoulder blade to almost his left hip. These warrior scars, it is said, were earned while he dispatched a dying she-lion armed only with a knife.

Besides these scars, this Mayneken also wore the ambassadorial signet ring of the Lady of the Two Lands, Queen Nefertiti. As the bearer of this ring, it made the priest-warrior her personal adviser – in essence her remote eyes and ears.

Mayneken was also the journeyman assistant of a once powerful seer-priest of Ptah known as Piankhotep, who was well known for his miraculous curative powers and second sight.

As if this were not a sufficient biography, Mayneken was also the adopted elder brother of the hereditary prince of Memphis, Horemheb, and the adopted son of the deceased – hence his foremost role in the burial of that much-revered high priest of the Great God Amen Re.

With so much importance and influence placed within his grasp, this seer-priest-warrior, royal ambassador, adopted member of a noble family, and a high priest, Mayneken possessed a remarkably centered character and uncommon way. His rise to these positions of trust and influence was not through guile or mischief, but rather through his unwavering sense of loyalty and recognition of place. That he possessed considerable wisdom there could be no doubt. That he possessed a poet's quality of speech was a true joy to behold. That he possessed the speed of a cheetah and was a master of the arts of war – beware unto those who should choose to challenge him!

As this meandering processional group neared the twin entrance pylons of Horemheb's own family mortuary complex, Mayneken's eyes began to flood as they had when he had first found the elderly priest had gone West. Remembering back to that heartrending moment, the priest vividly relived finding him that early morning, having died peacefully in his sleep. Mayneken had gently stroked the stubble of Meryptah's usually smoothly shaved pate, noted the bluish hue of his cool skin, saw the lifeless sag of his peaceful face, and the dried rivulet of drool from the corner of his mouth. These were the images that had come to mind shortly followed by the crushing sense of loss, the rage, bottomless sadness, and finally the sublime feeling that Meryptah's time had finally come. This last had prompted the priest-warrior to whisper a wish of "safe journey" into his elder's left ear and caused him to place a kiss of farewell upon his forehead.

After much grunting and groaning, Meryptah's cedar coffin was carefully lowered down the eighty-foot shaft and maneuvered to its final resting place upon the magical bricks within the high priest's single-chambered tomb. Prior to Mayneken's performance of his religious duty, the high priest of Ptah, Ptahmesou, offered to his deceased colleague and older brother heartfelt words truly meant that were filled with the imagery and theology so typical of Memphis and its patron deity, Ptah. That finished and after first purifying the tomb with incense, Mayneken acting as both officiating *sem*-priest and adopted son, then led *The Opening of the Mouth* ceremony. He began by intoning the opening words of that magical ritual, while brandishing the *nua Wepwawet* before the mouth of the coffin lid.

I open your mouth, so that you may speak,
I open your eyes, so that you may see Re,
I open your ears, so that you may hear of your glorification,
And I grant movement to your legs, arms, and heart,
So that you can repulse your enemies.

When ceremony was completed, all turned to exit the tomb except Mayneken, who carefully placed on the floor before the coffin a festive meal of roasted duck, quail, pork ribs, several cheeses, breads, and sauces. These were accompanied with some forty sealed beer jars and fifteen wine amphorae of several vintages – all generously provided by the estate of Prince Horemheb. Finally, the adopted son concluded the rite by placing before the tomb's inner entrance a fragrant bouquet of the old priest's favorite flowers. To it he attached a papyrus roll bound with blue yarn that began with the following pious words.

My father, your faithful son
but not of your loins
Blesses your final journey

through the *Amduat*
May you live for eternity

Thereafter, with Horemheb and the chief guard of the necropolis as witnesses, the tomb's narrow entrance was filled in with rough masonry and plaster. As a final seal, a smoothed layer of plaster was applied and its still moist surface stamped everywhere with the seal of necropolis. Once so capped and with the laborers gone, the tomb's entrance was then cunningly hidden by more plaster by Horemheb's own foreman. That task finished, the four climbed the temporary ladder of the shaft into the starry dark of the late evening.

Tired, yet pleased with the course of things thus far, the foreman and chief guard then assured the hereditary prince and the *sem*-priest that the shaft would be filled in that very night with rubble and any evidence of its existence would vanish from sight before the appearance of Re's next appearance. While the prince remained confident of their word, the *sem*-priest did not. Although Mayneken's attitude annoyed the prince, vexed the foreman, and outright angered the guard at the implied insult, the *sem*-priest and warrior held his vigil nonetheless throughout the rest of the night and into the morning to bear witness that all was completed as promised. As the final block was carefully placed and a layer of waterproof plaster smoothed over its edges, then, and only then, did the priest-warrior begin to relax. The foreman and chief guard had indeed kept their word, for the shaft's entrance had been placed in the northwestern corner of the mortuary temple's own internal reflecting pool. To Mayneken, its placement had been perfect.

"After all," he reasoned aloud to the pair, "who in their right mind would even look for such a thing?"

* * *

"Noble Mayneken, now that the final affairs of your father have been attended to, what are your plans?" queried the hereditary prince of Memphis.

"My noble brother, I think it would be best for me to journey south to that 'other' capital, the former capital of the heretic who-has-no-name. After all, the Lady of the Two Lands still dwells there, as do the remnants of her family. Eventual preparations for their departure to Thebes must be made, and no doubt, a myriad of other details as well. Do you wish me to take to her a personal letter, some news, a greeting perhaps?"

While pinching in thought his lower lip between his thumb and forefinger, the Horemheb considered Mayneken's offer.

"Yes, my elder brother," he said with a smile. "Yes indeed, I do wish to send a letter to the queen. Allow me a few moments with my scribe in which to gather my thoughts, and then be off with you."

The prince thought to add, "And my brother, make use of my river craft for it is a swift one with broad sails, well provisioned, and," now broadly smiling, "is without lice and fleas."

* * *

As Mayneken made his way south toward the capital of Akhetaten – the center of Egypt's religious revolution and former residence of the heretic pharaoh Akhenaten – the Inundation had fully made its impact upon this parched land. The Nile's muddy brown water, saturated with fine and fertile silts transported all the way from Central Africa, had flooded both banks and was advancing inland by almost a third of their predicted extent. Once cracked mud banks were long submerged and only the tops of the dense papyrus rushes peeked above the water's surface.

Lotus tendrils stretched out in the flood's gentle current as if they were the long tresses of a goddess's hair. The trunks of date palms, submerged up to a quarter of their height, seemed to swell before your eyes as they gorged themselves on the plentiful and rich moisture. Irrigation ditches, which only days before were cracked and dry as a bone, were now in full spate as the Nile's waters flooded into them and filled their associated retention pools.

Mud brick farmhouses that were purposely built near the river's edge on low mounds now appeared as isolated islands with clusters of waving humanity crowded on their flat roofs and with farm animals penned within their courtyards. Larger animals, the oxen and cattle, gleefully wallowed in the knee deep waters occasionally flopping over, rolling, bellowing, and splashing in the slow moving and muddy slurry. Here and there displaced river crocodiles slowly moved like logs among the cattle in search of any predatory opportunities.

Birds clustered in ridiculous and precarious bunches atop everything and anything above the flood's waters. Flocks of waterfowl alternately darkened the sky with their riotous plumage before landing and creating floating carpets of color. But above all, it was the rich mucky smell of the flood waters that overwhelmed the senses. The black earth of Egypt was clearly in full renewal.

But other matters intruded upon this priest's otherwise unconscious recording of his riverine observations. They took the form of a nagging suspicion based upon a subtle shift in emphasis, a thought itching to be scratched, and all because of those enhanced skills of observation implanted within him by Doc Allen.

Mayneken deeply thought.

Yes, the northern Memphite dialect was indeed quite different from that of southern Thebes, and at times, even a bit amusing. No, that was not it. But what was it? Now I recall. It was something that the high priest of Ptah had said. Something he had mentioned at the funeral just prior to Meryptah's final entombment. Something about the god Ptah.

Ah, yes, now I remember. It was that sublime Memphite benediction so pregnant with meaning. That's what it was! The high priest obliquely referred to creation as being the authoritative utterance of a thought by the god Ptah. How different the religious perspective is of this Memphite priesthood! How cerebral in comparison with the creation theology of Thebes, where Atum and Amen Re begat creation as a mere autoerotic act.

And then there is something curious about Ptah's name itself. But just what is it?

* * *

Upon arriving at the eastern quay of Akhetaten, Mayneken noted that the level of the usual hustle and bustle had not diminished since the passing of the heretic, a secret assassination that he had successfully participated in. His coregent, Smenkhkare, who had assumed the throne shortly after his father's mysterious disappearance, did so under the most fragile of political fictions. His "reign" would only be a matter of months before unknown agents would permanently remove him from the scene.

Fortunately, little of this deadly intrigue affected the royal court and general population. The markets remained crowded with day-to-day commerce and the docks were clogged with river craft of all descriptions. River ferries crisscrossed here and there, going this way and that in dizzying patterns. The docks themselves were veritable hives of loading and unloading activity with boat captains and merchants haggling in their usual, distinctive, and time-honored ways. Products from all over Egypt were in evidence as were the distinctively painted transport amphorae from the island civilization of Minoan Crete and that of mainland Mycenaean Greece, long and narrow wine jars from the coastal city of Syrian Byblos, and even a large aromatic load of Levantine cedar wood.

With his private craft tied up near the southern limit of the long quay, Mayneken disembarked and made his way through the morning market area that was in full swing before the heat of the day. For the young priest, his sense of *déjà vu* was unmistakable as was an oppressive guilt as he wandered here and there, looking for and unerringly finding public water wells – wells that he himself had seeded only two years before with the Russian manufactured flu crystals. Rumors that had reached Thebes told of a virulent outbreak of plague that had claimed hundreds and even members of the royal family. Looking around, Mayneken could only marvel at the town's recovery. It was as if it had never happened.

Now munching on a proffered sweetbread roll that a merchant refused to accept payment for, the priest gave the middle-aged woman a short bow of thanks nonetheless, which earned him a wide-grinned smile in return.

Such generosity granted to a strange priest.

Then peering down at the rippling muscles of his six-pack, he reconsidered.

Well, maybe she thought I was just undernourished. Mothers are always mothers, no matter when, no matter where, no matter who.

More by instinct than anything else, the priest-warrior worked his way through the market district of Akhetaten's main thoroughfare. Called the Royal Highway by modern archaeologists, this generally straight, broad, and paved road coursed along a north-south orientation. The town itself was sandwiched between the Nile's course and a crescent arc of towering limestone cliffs to the east. Along the paved road's course were located the Royal Palace and its residences connected by a flyover structure that bridged the Royal Highway to the Aten Temple and its many subsidiary structures. At the northern limit of the city a cluster of impressive structures were built now known as the Northern Palace. It was these last structures that were Mayneken's goal – the household of the Lady of the Two Lands, Queen Nefertiti. As her personal advisor and ambassador, he carried a letter for her from his recently adopted brother, Prince Horemheb. Besides, Mayneken reckoned that it was indeed high time to check in with her highness before he returned to sacred Thebes and eventually his own proper place in time.

* * *

The sensation was certainly different, and Richards never, ever, seemed to get used to it, or even know what to expect next. To him, moving through the electromagnetic field of the Soap Bubble's drop ring had a sort of sticky, humid feeling to it, accompanied by either a mild case of disequilibrium, slight nausea, or at worse some muscular cramping. Fortunately, never did all three occur at once. Equally fortunate, all of these sensations passed quickly. He had discussed them with Doc Allen at Horizon Pass. Had been poked, prodded, and stuck, but nothing seemed to be amiss. As the good doctor from Norman, Oklahoma, liked to say, "If it isn't broken and I can't find it, then I have nothin' to fix."

Waiting on the other side at 2:12 a.m., August 14th, Major Charles Tuna Abraham Cartwright of the U.S. Army's Special Command Detachment stood patiently next to the floating drop ring of portable Mark V-A temporal device. The man expected a certain "big fish" to yank on the line extended into the ring's field that would be hauled on by the raw muscle of three of his team. The means of extraction was a braided hemp rope and an ancient-looking wooden pulley attached to a wooden beam on a pivot. None of these materials were conductive and neither would any of these simple implements alter the time line, if they happened to collapse and drop through to the other side.

CHAPTER VIII

First Semester

The sun was high on this crisp and cloudless day in the City of Broad Shoulders. The nearby great lake's offshore wind blessedly refreshed the sweating and grunting university football squad drilling on the green, but required at the very least a sweater for those not so physically active. The turning of the season was close at hand, but that was not hard to figure out in this Midwestern city as Jack Frost's bright paintbrush was already in evidence in the high treetops.

One of those sweater-wearing individuals was a solitary figure leaning against the practice field's barrier of chipped green chain-link fence. The observer was of medium stature and clearly of muscular build, despite the attempted professorial camouflage of a bulky tweed sweater, pleated wool slacks, and shiny new cappers. While peering through the fence, the man wore an emotionally charged and changeable face that revealed sometimes bitter regret, sometimes resignation that one's time had passed. Audibly sighing and shaking his head from side to side at the play he just saw, it was then that he heard the shrill sound of the coach's whistle to huddle up the troops at practice's end. Only then did the spectator decide to call it a day as well.

Boy, he thought. *Those nutcracker drills had been always such a bitch!*

Reaching down and picking up his stiff, still very virgin leather briefcase, the newly hooded Dr. Joseph William Richards began to make his way over to Smith Hall to teach his very first class.

While striding away from the practice field deep in his thoughts, Richards could not help but feel his heartstrings pulling and tugging at him.

Jesus! Last year I was already over a thousand yards going into that seventh game against Princeton, bemoaned the former first string halfback. *As a senior I had a shot at the Heisman Trophy! Well, at least a good shot at a runners-up*, he corrected himself. *Definitely a shot at the NFL! Maybe even with the Bears! Hell, why not! I'm much bigger and faster than Mike Adamle ever dreamed of being!*

And then BAM, I just threw it all away with that dynamite offer from John Milson, my signing up with the Philology Annex, all the grueling physical exams, the mind-blowing Ranger School training, the skull-numbing language training. Jesus, and somehow I did it all in less than six and a half months! And then Doc Borov, Horizon Pass, and all of the deployments back to Thebes with that crazy Russian Piankoff.

With a softening heart and moist eyes.

Piankoff. My dear, dear Alexander. Oh, how I miss you, my old Russian friend. How I miss your marvelously ruthless Byzantine mind, your nearly constant flirtations with the RUTI, your endearing humanity. I owe you so much, and yet I can never, ever, be able to repay you.

Still shaking his head and mumbling to himself, the pea green associate professor of Egyptian philology gingerly mounted the worn limestone steps of Smith Hall. Richards had not even realized he had covered the two blocks so deep he was in his reverie.

Upon entering the cool Gothic archway of the massive limestone building, guarded by two malevolent but age-worn griffin gargoyles, the young man tugged open one of its heavy wooden doors. What greeted him was a seemingly endless expanse of hexagonal black-and-white floor tile, when a sudden biological urge made itself clearly known. Ducking into the men's john on the right and securing the end stall, Richards settled himself in. Not thirty seconds later, the next stall was soon occupied as well, but as Richards could see with a pair of oddly familiar looking brown wingtips. Shortly, their owner identified himself.

"Well, Joseph. I see that you are all raring to go!" greeted the aged, but quite spry Professor Emeritus of Egyptian Philology, John Milson, with that ever-familiar smiling voice.

To which Richards sheepishly responded, "Ah, yes, sir. You could sort of say that."

"Nonsense, man. You are about to teach your first class and you've got the Hershey squirts to prove it!"

Cramped silence.

"Well, Joseph. For what it is worth, I still make a mad dash before each and every class that I teach. Always have, probably always will."

After a long pause of disbelief on the part of Richards that such a campus legend could be so tragically afflicted.

"Besides, your reaction is what I would have expected from you. You care and that's good. Your students are fortunate beyond words."

"Ah, thank you, Professor Milson."

"Now Joseph, don't you go calling me the professor crap anymore. I thought that we were well beyond that by now. After all, we're colleagues-in-arms, on the same team. Right?"

"Right."

Silence fell followed by a rustling of clothing in the last stall, an opening door, a splashing of water, and the shuffled departure of its former occupant.

To Milson, still ensconced with his own private business, all was amazement.

Christ John! Here's young Richards crapping his eyes out over his first lecture! What a crock! For what a marvel he truly is with that strong frame and that supremely bright mind. Who not only went back once, but five times, and three of those times solo, once as a biological weapon – a plague carrier. My God in heaven, what his post-deployment therapy must have been like! Doc Allen told me that his nightmares alone would have killed a lesser mortal, much less all of the agonizing guilt that he had to work through. And then taking part in that brutal attack on a telepathic alien life-form. What guts that took! Guts of the quantity and magnitude that no academic I know has anywhere near the capacity to contemplate, much less the raw ability to undertake, and then, damn it all, succeed. And here he is walking around as normal as apple pie.

Then he goes back solo again, but this time to officiate in the burial of Meryptah – a high priest of Amen Re, no less – as his adopted son! Such an uncommon man so clearly recognized as such in another time and place, who is adopted first by a high priest as the son that he never had and then by a hereditary prince and later pharaoh of Egypt as the elder brother that he never had. And to top it all off, he then inherits the role of personal advisor and ambassador to Queen Nefertiti herself!

And here he is, just like me, crapping his eyes out before teaching his first class – un-fucking-believable.

My Alice, you would have been proud of him. No, she would have tried to adopt him as well.

And with that thought, Professor Emeritus John Milson, now finished, began to meticulously wash his hands.

CHAPTER IX

The Recovery of SNOWMAN

The journey of Apollo XI and its landing in the Sea of Tranquility will always and forever be that one defining moment in the history of manned space flight. Curiously, it would be its successor mission, that of Apollo XII, which would always and forever confirm that we were not alone in the Universe. While the Apollo XI crew, and in particular those famous words of Neil Armstrong, became the stuff of modern legend, seemingly forgotten by the media, public, and history books were the equally historic launch, mission, and return of Apollo XII. After the media splurge over Apollo XI, the general public's interest in moon landings had been quenched. President John F. Kennedy's prophetic words of challenge had come to fruition on worldwide television. Consequently, subsequent coverage of spacecraft launches going to the moon became an almost ho-hum event and that too was by design.

On November 11th, 1969, at 11:22 in the morning EST, the massive Saturn V rocket that carried the Apollo XII spacecraft lifted off from pad 39-A of the Kennedy Space Center. That this mission would indeed be epoch-making was immediately signaled. "The Apollo XII mission began rather inauspiciously when it was struck by lightning just seconds after liftoff – not once, but twice." Furthermore, these strikes "resulted in a complete computer memory loss in the Command and Service Module (CSM) due to inadequate lightning protection." While the "Saturn V passed through a rain cloud, in hindsight, the plume of partially ionized gas created by the rocket's exhaust formed a perfect lightning channel. When the cloud discharged, all of the circuit breakers in the Command Module tripped and, although the Saturn V was unaffected and continued calmly on its way, the effect on the crew was 'electric.'" Electric indeed for during the post-flight debriefing, when asked about the lightning strikes, Conrad quipped, "We told them that that [the lightning strike] just beat all the sims [simulations] to hell." Was it a historic launch? Without question, for thereafter all U.S. launches of manned and unmanned spacecraft would only occur in clear, cloudless skies. The lesson had been learned.

Another point about Apollo XII should also be made. The craft that ferried this all-Navy crew bore valiant, almost warlike names on its Command and Service Module (CSM) – the Yankee Clipper – and Lunar Module (LM) – the Intrepid. While the CSM was named appropriately enough, what was the intent behind naming the LM the "Brave One," especially when one considers the whimsically named preceding Apollo spacecraft pairings: Gumdrop and Spider, Charlie Brown and Snoopy, Columbia and Eagle? And the same question could be asked of those that succeeded as well: Odyssey and Aquarius, Kitty Hawk and Antares, Endeavor and Falcon, Casper and Orion, America and Challenger.

The fact of the matter is that Apollo XII had a very serious mission before it – not to imply that the others had not. It was the first "planned and executed" precision lunar landing. Landing preparations were made while the spacecraft orbited the lunar environment multiple times, as it spun down in altitude above the Ocean of Storms, before the CSM and LM would separate. These degrading orbits were important for the crew, who first had to triangulate critical topographical landmarks, familiarize themselves with the landing site's neighborhood, and finally eyeball for themselves what would be their viable options. Dick Gordon, the CSM's pilot who was also handy with a Hasselblad camera, around this time was busy cleaning the camera's 70 mm lens, fussing over the batteries of its motor drive, and checking and rechecking its film pack. He was all raring to go for the first manned overflight of SNOWMAN, which just so happened to be their primary landing site as well. Having oriented the spacecraft's triangular windows toward the lunar surface, man and camera were primed and ready. But it was Pete Conrad, the salty-tongued mission commander from Philly, who was the first to get a bead on their target.

"Hey, there it is! There it is! Son of a gun! There it is!" he exclaimed with rapid, machine gun-like exuberance. "Holy cran!" blurted out Alan LaVerne Bean, the mission's LM pilot. With a west Texas drawl as thick as molasses, Bean possessed a remarkable weakness for colorful language that had caught NASA's notice. He had earned their dire warnings to "can it." (When later asked what he meant by "Holy cran!" Bean didn't have a clue. Just that he was excited and he was sure that the expression wasn't something dirty.)

"It sure is; it's something else," replied the wide-eyed Conrad. "We just flew over it. SNOWMAN stood out so clear that I just couldn't believe it."

All the while this professional exchange was playing itself out. The motor drive of Gordon's camera was seemingly continuous. Its noisy single lens reflex shutter went off like some sort of gun – click (grind), click (grind), click (grind), click (grind).

Lost in the moment and oblivious to what Gordon was doing, despite the noise of his camera's systems, Conrad called out to him, "Gordi, did you get all that?"

"Yeah," he sighed, "In triplicate."

"Are you absolutely sure?" a near breathless Conrad said.

"Absolutely."

And then with the passing of the moment, Conrad let out a deep groan.

"Ah shit, as if those lightning strikes weren't bad enough, I just loaded my suit again!"

Cackling laughter exploded from Bean and Gordon.

Conrad then added a bit sheepishly, "I guess that we're just going to have to let Mission Control know what OSA really stands for – 'Oh shit again!'"

* * *

Following the separation of the CSM and LM, the landing of the Intrepid occurred on November 11th, 1969, at 1:54:35 a.m, EST. That the landing was indeed a precision one is attested by the fact that the LM landed on the northwest rim of the crater that contained the Surveyor 3 probe – a scant five hundred feet away. But the visitation of that former spacecraft was of tertiary importance to the crew of the LM, for just outside their hatch windows was SNOWMAN.

In a garbled recording Bean exclaimed, "Look out there!"

Seconds later Conrad chimed in, "I can't believe it!"

Bean again. "Amazing! Fantastic!"

And Conrad agreed. "That's so fantastic, I can't believe it!

Then remembering to thumb on the VHF radio to the CSM, Conrad said, "Hey, Gordi?"

"Roger, Pete, what's the situation? Over."

"I'll bet you will never guess what we're parked right next to."

Gordon, fearing the oncoming of a much-dreaded Conradesque knock-knock joke, replied, "No, Pete. Just what are you parked right next to?"

"We're about twenty-five feet in front of SNOWMAN!"

"Roger that, Commander.

"Chalk that landing up to just flat, superior Navy luck, I suppose."

"You betcha' your bippie!"

While the next several minutes were devoted to several engineering and mechanical procedures that would ensure their safety, both Bean and Conrad were wired for that first excursion.

Could you blame them?

* * *

While struggling legs first and backwards to wedge himself out of the LM's oval hatch, Conrad's continuous jabbering only seemed to punctuate his excitement.

"I bet you when I get down to the bottom of the ladder that I cannot only see SNOWMAN, but that I can practically reach out and touch it."

To which Bean, getting wound up himself and consequently slipping into his native drawl, replied, "What are you-all? Trying to be a fancy telephone commercial?"

Conrad, giggling, said, "Here we go."

"Oh no you don't. Not so fast," said Bean.

"Okay, just a second. Don't go down yet. I've got to get my camera on you, babe."

Bean, removed his Hasselblad from his chest mount, stuck it out of the open hatch, and began shooting. Two shots captured Conrad poised on the LM's strut. The third caught Pete just as he stepped out and landed, saying, "Whoopee! Man, that may have been one small step for Neil, but that's a long one for me."

For the record, all the bets placed that Conrad would not have the guts to make this statement, which was not only a pun on Neil Armstrong's famous pronouncement, but also on Conrad's own five-foot-six stature, were not honored by anyone upon the team's safe return.

* * *

With the preliminary fun stuff out of the way, Conrad felt his way around in the dusty one-sixth gravity. He then looked up to Bean, who was still in the hatch.

"Well, Al. It's show time. Switching my radio to VOX."

In so doing, any further communications between the astronauts were not transmitted over-the-air to Houston, the public, or the Russians for that matter.

"Roger."

"Now Al, how about you take some shots, while I work my way over to SNOWMAN. Then we can get some more for scale."

"Roger. Shooting."

Several minutes later Bean stated the obvious. "Finished shooting. Pete. Heck, it's almost as tall as you."

"Don't push it, partner."

Several moments later.

"Okay. Time to set up the LEC so I can take some close-ups."

The LEC, or Lunar Equipment Conveyor, was a hand-over-hand clothesline-like device that could move equipment along it much like a "Brooklyn clothesline." In this instance from Bean in the LM's equipment bay down to Conrad on the surface. And like any clothesline, an Equipment Transfer Bag, or ETB, was used to transfer Conrad's camera down to him.

After having checked for dust, Conrad began to blast away with the Hasselblad securely attached to his chest at a range of only yards. Simultaneously, Bean was doing the same thing, but from the vantage point of the LM's hatch opening.

That task completed, Conrad then detached his camera, put it back into the ETB, and sent it on its way back to Bean.

Now speaking more to himself than to his colleague, he began, "Okay, that chore is done."

Pause for a deep breath.

"I'm going to start the mechanical soil experiment."

To which Bean acknowledged, "Roger. Got the old camera running, but don't you want me to send down some tools first?"

"Naw," began Conrad mimicking Bean's Texas accent. "I'm just going to mosey up here a little, without any tools, which makes it pretty easy."

Despite what Mission Control might have thought, this part of the mission, the attempted excavation and recovery of SNOWMAN, was in truly good hands. For Conrad, while he had attended Princeton and earned his BS in Aerospace Engineering from that fine institution, he had also taken several humanity electives including Classical Archaeology.

"Okay Al, turn on the site video and audio recorder."

"We're on and cranking."

"Okay. Topic One: Photographic Library. Virgin site photos overhead from CSM have been taken by Commander Gordon. Virgin site photos from LM have been taken by Captain Bean. *In situ* scale shots have been taken by Captain Bean from LM with Captain Conrad next to SNOWMAN. For the record, Captain Conrad is five feet six and one-half inches tall."

At this point in the narrative Bean stifled a laugh at the "one-half inches tall" part.

"Twelve, bracketed, 360-degree object close-ups have been taken by Captain Conrad at an approximate distance of six feet. Topic One completed.

"Okay. On to Topic Two: Visual Description. The object is golden in color. It is made up of two distinct parts, a supporting shaft or trunk and an outstretched, sail-like membrane attached to the top of the shaft or trunk. In short, it looks a lot like a golden flower in full bloom or a small palm tree. The shaft appears to be circular in cross section with a diameter of about eight inches and about fifty inches of it is visible above ground."

While this practically forensic lecture was being recorded, Conrad was carefully working his way around the object, looking for any additional or remarkable details to mention. Finding none, he continued with his description.

"The sail-like membrane looks like some kind of antenna or array or signal capturing surface. It is almost butterfly wing-like in shape, or maybe better, that of an hourglass. It is extremely thin in cross-section and about five by five feet in surface area if you overlook the slight narrowing on two of its parallel sides. Please note that this surface is not solid, but is made up of a fine mesh or membrane-like weave. I can see right through it. Also note the orientation of this antenna, for lack of a better term, is not flat, but instead is slightly dished or concave. As for signs of age or damage I cannot see anything, but it sure looks dusty in places and some small rocks are lodged in its mesh. All of that, however, could have been kicked up and put there by our own landing. Topic Two completed. Okay Al, kill the recording."

"Off."

"So, Al. Whaddya' tink of all of dis'?" Gordon mugged in his best south Philly accent.

"I haven't a clue, babe. Do you think that it's Russian?"

"Nope. It's too sophisticated – even to the point of being graceful, beauiful. Besides, I didn't see any Cyrillic characters or ugly red stars on it."

"Okay, Al. Enough of this gabbing. Start the recording again."

"On and cranking."

"Okay now. On to the hairy part, Topic Three: Excavation. Given that I am not wearing my camera, and given that the antenna array is so high above the ground, I am going to attempt to crawl under and beneath it to begin probing around the object's shaft-like base. Here goes."

It was right out of some comedy skit and Bean was getting it all. With Conrad standing some ten feet in front of the object, he began to slowly and stiffly fall forward as if he were a statue. Just before impact, the lunar archaeologist caught himself with his arms extended.

"Doing some early morning PT, are we?" queried the Texan.

"Yeah, some real, heavy-duty push-ups." Conrad answered his tormentor.

So working his way in slowly, crab-like, with his boots' toes dragging in the lunar dust creating two parallel trails, Conrad soon found himself at the object's base. Carefully, delicately, he gently dug away at the soil with two fingers of his right hand. First one trench on one side, and then switching hands, a similar trench on the other.

"Well, I have removed about three inches of surface soil from around the base of the shaft. Nothing to report as yet. Will continue digging."

But Conrad was quickly running smack into a big problem, for nervous sweat was dripping off of his balding pate, down his face and nose, and was slowly collecting drip by drip into a tiny pool on the interior of his helmet's visor. In short, if he was to continue as is, he had to tip up his head slightly to clear the pool. And for a time that sufficed.

Now with his excavation at a point where almost a foot of lunar material had been moved aside as if the astronaut was a nesting sea turtle, made unaware because of his total concentration, Conrad had slowly risen up and into the antenna array above him. Bean, was the first to note this potentially dangerous situation and said so.

"Pete! Freeze! You're drifting up into the object's array!"

But before Conrad could react to Bean's warning his helmet had gently impacted against the underside of the array, and blessedly, nothing happened. Now chastising himself for his clumsiness in words that would have made even a Philadelphia dock worker blush, Conrad grunted himself out, on his hands, from under and clear of the object's array. Standing again and clearing the sweat from his visor as a result, Conrad noticed something.

"Al, hasn't the antenna moved upward some since I so brilliantly blundered into it?"

"Well, come to think of it, babe. You might be right," Bean allowed.

"Al, I am going to try something. Just don't have a heart attack on me, okay? You ready?"

"Roger."

"Okay. Here goes."

And what Conrad did was walk forward, stop, and gently extend his arms beneath as much of the plane of the array as he could, having noted that it had uniformly pitched up as a result of his helmet's slight grazing.

"Now careful, Pete, for Pete's sake," Bean unnecessarily cautioned at what he thought his commander was about to do.

As Conrad slowly raised his arms against the underside of the array, he applied a smooth and gentle pressure. The array slowly began to rise and fold in upon itself, until it had become a solid vertical cylinder poised above the center of the main shaft.

"Man," sighed Bean, "that was real slick."

"Now watch this."

Conrad reached up as far as he could grab the now fully collapsed antenna and began to gently pull it down into the central core of its base. In no time, the entire array had efficiently disappeared into its golden, post-like base.

"Ta-da! Day call me Houdini!" mugged Conrad. "And for my next act, I will now extract this bugger whole. Just watch. Drum roll, please."

And to Bean's horror, Conrad began to experimentally push and pull on the golden post, rocking it as if it were a stubborn fence post that needed removal in the spring mud.

"Ah, babe . . . Don't ya' think tha' you-all might, kinda, sorta, wanna be a bit more careful thar?" slurred the worried Texan.

By the time that it took Bean to get that meandering sentence out of his mush-mouth, Conrad had the object loose and ready for its extraction.

"Okay, Al. It's really loose now. What I am going to do is bear hug it and heave. Are you ready, Ripley?"

"Roger that."

The first recorded grunt was a classic, but it took four progressive attempts before the object was out and laying on the surface. Conrad for his part, was totally spent. His chest was heaving mightily.

"Are you okay, babe?"

Gasping, breathing. "Yeah."

Pause.

"Just winded."

Pause.

"Give me a moment to collect myself, and then I will pass this mother up to you."

Now taking the time to scan the entire length of the exposed object. "Hey, Al! Take a look at its pointy end! It's got fins!"

"Pete, it looks just like the ass-end of a squid!"

"Yeah, you're right, it really does."

And then this tension-filled moment erupted into hacking laughter as Conrad deadpanned.

"Ya' know, Al. Do ya' tink dhat dis ting here is a Marine?"

Following the intra-service jab, Conrad gathered himself and after a quick estimation, asked, "Al, you know this thing has got to be about six to seven feet long. Do we have room for it in the LM?"

"Have no fear, Pete, I'll make room. Rest assured, never in my life have I ever thrown back a winner, and I certainly don't plan to start today."

* * *

So went the first and primary excursion of Apollo XII's planned three. While the second two are the only ones officially recorded, the setup of the ALSEP experimental array and the plundering of the Surveyor 3 spacecraft, these were dutifully undertaken purely as the cover for the first. But before initiating the next excursions, NASA thought it wise to throttle any possible accidental imagery of the recovered SNOWMAN, and so the TV camera that was to telecast the last two excursions was "accidentally" pointed at the Sun. The recorded audio of that pernicious act was hilarious.

Conrad: "Where, oh where, is Earth? Oh, there it is."

Pause.

Bean: "Here is the TV. And it's pointing toward the Sun. Oops! That's bad. Point it over here a minute."

Conrad: "Dum dee dum, Dum, DUM!"

So sang out Bean as a result of his misalignment of the TV's camera lens into the Sun. The top portion of the Vidicon tube had been permanently damaged and it took some time before Houston told the crew to give up on the camera.

As for the lunar lift off, it went without a hitch. Fortunately, there were no seats in the LM to block the loading up of the ungainly SNOWMAN. True to his word, Bean made everything fit. All the geological samples and the camera taken from the Surveyor 3 were stowed. It was just that the accommodations were a bit more cramped than anticipated.

In all, the return payload amounted to 34.4 kg of rock and soil samples and "about 10 kg of parts for later examination on Earth." The stated reason for the return of the Surveyor 3 gear was "to examine the effects of long term exposure on the lunar environment." A fair statement, however, the more likely reason was to use that data as a crude gauge to calculate the age of SNOWMAN.

CHAPTER X

First Semester (Cont.)

When he first entered, the planks of the classroom's worn and cupped oak flooring creaked noisily under his solid two hundred and five pounds. Even the stiff leather of his new shoes seemed to chime in as well with their own telltale squeaks. On cue, a dozen or so inquisitive heads rose to see who it was that had disturbed their realm. With eyes following his every move and nervous beyond his wildest dreams, Richards briskly crossed over to the safe security of the old lectern. Hiding behind it and with palms already slick with nervous sweat, Richards removed some papers from his brown leather satchel and began to organize them before him, all the while avoiding any eye contact.

His first day's class plan well memorized and his notes now before him, Richards took a deep breath, and turned to face the freshly washed slate slab that was his blackboard. He was relieved to find several whole pieces of chalk waiting for him in the wooden gutter. As he began to mare the center section of that great expanse a glimmer of inspiration came to him, for immediately below the Latin letters of his name he carefully rewrote it in the beautiful and flowing pictographic characters of an ancient language. Finished, he took another deep breath and turned to finally meet and greet his adversaries. He began in a most amusing way in the long dead tongue of the Nile Valley.

The reaction to this well-rehearsed, projected, and modulated utterance of guttural stops, oddly accented syllables, and curious cadence had caught his audience entirely by surprise. Drooping jaws and widened eyes gave Richards precisely what he desperately needed – their single, undivided attention and a legitimate opportunity to display his formidable credentials. After all, had he not just "gotten back," and was he not the only living being on the planet fluent in the tongue?

Now in command, he began with a relaxed grin. His hands casually looped behind him.

"Ladies and gentlemen. Welcome to Egyptian 100. I'm Dr. Richards, your instructor. What you have just heard are the sounds of a language that has been dead for almost three thousand years. What you just heard was a traditional greeting that a guest would typically receive from the head of a noble household. Loosely translated it means, 'Welcome to dinner. Let's party!'"

So the ice was broken.

The first part of the class was devoted to taking the attendance, putting names to faces, passing out the syllabus, answering any questions about it, fielding various cleverly posited questions that in sum asked, "How do I get an A?" In other words, the usual administrative folderol, student maneuvering and negotiating.

Once that was completed, Richards did not dismiss the class as is usually the case for the first class of a semester, but instead got down to the business at hand.

"Folks, now it's my turn to ask some questions. How many of you speak a second language?"

All raised their hands except for three sitting in the back of the classroom.

Well, he thought. *What's up with those folks in the back I wonder?*

"Okay. Now another question. Do I have any Classicists among this distinguished crew?"

In answer to this question five hands rose and among them were the three in the back. Relieved, Richards began probing deeper.

"Ah, good. Now that I see everyone has some idea of what a verb might be…,"

Good natured smiles appeared.

"I wish to begin with what some of you may consider shocking news. First, ancient Egyptian, as a language, is a very dead one. Meaning that we are not all that sure what it really sounded like, or where its accents might be assigned. Now I know that I just recited a traditional social greeting, but be advised that my pronunciation is what is called a scientific one. Meaning that it is our best guess, the best that we can know as of this time."

This revelation earned Richards a couple of eye squints and sneers of "charlatan" and an equal portion of confused, glazed eyes. Raising his hands in mock defense, he continued.

"Not to worry. For there are good and powerful reasons for the pronunciation of the recitation that I just gave you. It is just that there exist differing schools of thought on the pronunciation itself. For example, if we were in Tübingen, guess how it would have been pronounced? Or for that matter, if we were in Paris. Believe it or not, even our British cousins have their own preferences, no shock there. And if you stop and think about it, does it really matter? For believe me, the ancient Egyptians had several regional dialects of their own. In fact, we have preserved texts that indicate the language of the South was virtually inscrutable to an inhabitant of the Delta, and vice versa. Does any of this sound vaguely familiar to anybody?

Many bobbing heads replied.

"So my point behind all of this is that in this classroom, during this course, we will have to communicate in some sort of a recognizably understandable manner that may be considered a sort of generic or *koine* method of pronunciation."

To Richards' allusion to the *koine* or "common" dialect of the Greek Hellenistic period, the Classicists nodded in meaningful appreciation.

"Second, be advised that the ancient Egyptians did not write their language with vowels as we do today. Instead, their language was written in what we think of as consonant clusters. So in order to properly translate these consonant clusters, clusters that could potentially represent several words, one must always be mindful of context. Perhaps to better appreciate what we are up against, how many crossword puzzle fanatics do I have?"

So Richards' first class in Egyptian philology began.

Unknown to this green associate professor, who was in the process of finding his way and establishing a rapport with his first students, he had another student who was listening in on his class from the hallway. It was none other than Professor Milson, who had purposely arranged that day's schedule to do so. Leaning against the wall with his eyes closed and arms crossed upon his chest, to a casual eye he might have appeared to be dosing, but in reality he was pretending to be a fly on the wall. Listening intently, what he heard pleased him immensely. At hearing Richards' rendition of the traditional dinner greeting, he had to put his hand over his mouth to stifle his mirth.

Yes, yes, the old pro allowed. *Joseph will do fine, just fine indeed. As for that bawdy so-called dinner greeting, well, only that rascal Piankoff could have come up with that one!*

While Milson refocused his thoughts now around Richards' philological mentor, temporal teammate, and, indeed, now dead friend, a soft and respectful smile of memoriam creased the elderly man's face.

Yes, dear Alexander, I thank you for so much. For training Joseph so well and for bringing him safely back. In fact, we all truly owe you so very, very much.

* * *

Meanwhile, across campus there stood a well-weathered three-story brownstone. Located on a corner and nestled squarely within this university's heavily treed neighborhood on Chicago's south side, the structure shared a windowless narrow gangway with its neighbor to the east. Its once seven worn and settled concrete steps were now long since shored up and repaired. The twin industrial strength steel pipe railings that were once scarred with flaking paint craters that seemed to mark the seasons, now were scraped smooth and painted. The entrance door's brass kick plate glowed a warm invitation. Drapes of gossamer lace framed its sparkling clean windows. Beside the short entrance sidewalk to this thoroughly unremarkable structure stands a tasteful institutional sign, which announced in modest brass roman letters – Philology Annex.

The building's current owner acquired it through a real estate transaction from the university, itself gleeful to unload the vacant property during a time of fiscal hardship. Once beyond that formal purchase the structure underwent renovation and modification, especially with the addition of several sublevels. These became closely guarded secrets as was the tenant's true purpose for acquiring the property.

Nonetheless, the Philology Annex became a natural hive of campus activity, a nexus for research scholars and students alike. Its low key atmosphere provided a warm, cozy, womb-like environment liberally seasoned with the familiar scholarly smells of rich pipe tobacco, freshly brewed coffee, and above all, books. Its many reading rooms resembled archive-like, monkish cells with their slanted heavy oak tables, flat central perches, and low slung, restful reading lights.

There were nine such book-bulging rooms in all, three per floor, each devoted to a long dead, ancient Near Eastern or Western Asiatic language. At the founder's insistence, semester-long visitation rights were granted for the pittance of fifty cents that barely covered the cost of the laminated identification card. Tradition held that all street shoes were to be left in the foyer in orderly nooks on the left, and personal slippers were similarly stored on the right. Disposable hospital versions were available at the receptionist's desk for – yes, fifty cents. Padding about in slippers across the creaking old wooden floors and stairways engendered a special atmosphere and as the founder had calculated, the enforced slipper rule made for muffled movements and a considerable calming effect.

To the casual observer the sole sentinel of this philological sanctuary was the receptionist, who sat squarely in the center of the foyer in a perfect place of greeting. Behind her desk stood a single, full length, glass paneled office door with transom. Painted at eye level on its milky glass in tasteful golden letters were the words: HEAD LIBRARIAN.

While Milson was tenderly reminiscing about Piankoff, so was the receptionist of Philology Annex. Ms. Kelly fussed, he was her boss, and the chief librarian.

After all, she continued to herself, *he will have just a fit when he sees all the mail piled up on his desk! Now just where is he?* The grousing of this attractive and fit middle-aged strawberry blond caused a rare furrow to mar her lightly freckled forehead.

I haven't heard a word, not a peep, since that hunk Richards' return. And just when is he going to stop by, or at least call? He's such an interesting specimen of a man, she purred to herself.

As for Piankoff, *I'll just bet that he's back in Moscow undergoing a thorough debriefing just as Richards had here. But how can I confirm that when I am not even supposed to know that this building has three secret sublevels to it?*

Needless to say, Ms. Kelly's nosiness about the whereabouts of the head librarian was motivated by far more than just idle gossip, for Ms. Jennifer Ann Kelly had another job, and for that matter another employer as well – a rather important and very black one.

* * *

Jennifer Ann Borgensen hailed from central Minnesota. She was the middle kid and only girl of six siblings born to a loving Presbyterian family of modest means. Raised as a tomboy and more out of sheer will than inclination, Jenny turned out to be the brightest bulb of the six-pack. That fact alone earned her full ride to a private Minnesota college. That pretty Jenny was also a deft, elusive, and cunning left wing, and being the first girl on her high school's varsity hockey team did not hurt her application in that Nordic state. While some derided her coach and school because they could not find enough boys to fill out a team and hence her slot in the second line, others far wiser pointed out that her five brothers made up the bulk of the first and third lines. Consequently, for three years running, the Borgie Bombers wreaked havoc on their s athletic conference.

One note from the hometown newspaper is worth relating for it encapsulated what Jenny was all about. As was her custom when wearing s hockey helmet, Jenny wore her ponytail down her back. During an extremely close tournament playoff game in her senior year, Jenny took a prescient exit pass from her youngest brother, Todd, and went streaking down the boards with the puck. The rooting hometown fans exploded full knowing what stick magic they were about to behold. The opposing goalie, seeing her coming on strong, could only creep out of the goal's mouth in a valiant attempt at cutting down Jenny's angles and shot selection. Blasting full tilt across the blue line with her stick poised high and ready to let fly, an utterly desperate and trailing defenseman grabbed at her flowing ponytail, so foiling the shot. Jenny, picking herself up off of the ice, in a whirlwind of rage and forgetting about the puck, the game, the tournament, everything, methodically proceeded to devastate her tormentor against the boards. That epic moment was captured by the hometown newspaper writer who quipped, "To characterize the Borgensen foul as roughing was a kind understatement. Rather, it was more like a mugging, or better, the gutting of a trout. Never has so much blood been let by one so pretty."

When college came Jenny excelled in her classes and discovered that boys were really men and so majored in both. By her sophomore year, the spring job fair caught her interest. She was thinking ahead, aggressive as ever, trying to find her place and a chance to make a contribution. As she wandered about, seeing this and rejecting that, Jenny noted a lone young man in a simple blue suit sitting behind a barren card table. He had no literature to offer, had no fancy sign behind him, just an empty chair before him. Out of sheer curiosity, Jenny walked over and in so doing surprised the man, for he was reading a paperback by somebody named Clausewitz.

That first contact with the shyly smiling young man forever changed Jenny's life. She now had a purpose, a goal, and an employer who both appreciated and respected what she was at a root level. After several well-paid summer internships in the Maryland-Virginia corridor under her belt, and at the completion of her senior year, Jenny had never looked back.

CHAPTER XI

Outer Milky Way

How does one imagine, much less describe, that which is truly alien? This is not a frivolous consideration, for by definition that which is alien usually connotes that which is beyond our experience, something far removed from the first time a country bumpkin encountered a mall much less its escalator. Even more daunting is to imagine, much less understand, what an alien psyche might be like, whether it followed to a code of ethics, much less identify what might be considered a sense of humor.

Perhaps if we begin with some examples closer to home, then an appreciation for that great remove will become far more transparent. For example, what would be the *Weltanschauung* of an abysmal tubeworm, the ethical norms of a fruit bat, or what would a sperm whale find hilarious? Naturally, what all of these characteristics assume is that some form of intraspecies communication is taking place. After all, does the tubeworm need to be able to emote about its judged place in the universe to its like kind? The ethical norms of a fruit bat colony could only be based upon the accumulated habits of generations and then their transmission. Meanwhile, sperm whale humor suggests that a highly developed sense of sublime irony and expression exists among those most graceful and bulky sojourners of the ocean's depths. Who knows? But even in all of these examples of life-forms that are well known to us the taint of anthropomorphism is undeniable. We cannot free ourselves of it. Yet, how then can we begin to approach, much less understand or appreciate, that which is truly alien and beyond our ken?

* * *

The following should only be understood as a crude approximation, taken with a grain of salt, but a valiant attempt at the description of three alien life-forms.

Dispatched by an alien organization roughly translated as The Survey Institute, they were tasked to recover the lost first scout's surveyor star craft, The Hope. What was certain was the referent by which these individual species were heralded: Xoxx, Sard, and Quimbly. What was equally certain was that the first two life-forms consisted of silicate-based crystaloforms, while the latter was a sulfur-based organic.

That The Survey Institute sent these three on such an important mission suggested several things. That the recovery of The Hope was of vital importance, but the prime motivation for or reasoning behind such a recovery effort remained obscure, especially given the great distances involved and consequent expenditure of resources. So, we must infer, at a minimum, some sort of inherent value assigned to the recovery of the first scout's surveyor star craft.

On the other hand, the fact representatives of no fewer than three separate species were sent implies their compatibility, which meant a common method of communication, which in turn insinuated the acknowledged potential requirement for operational flexibility that three such entities may have possessed as a group. While the reddish-colored crystalline Xoxx and bluish-colored silicate Sard were permanently "attached" or "interfaced" into the central workings of their recovery star craft in order to best take advantage of their formidable memories and parallel cognitive computing power, the Quimbly was less so "attached" from a certain point of view.

As a powerfully telepathic, telekinetic, and organic chameleon species, the Quimbly was capable of insinuating its personality upon the intellects of lesser organic life-forms in one of two ways. The Quimbly could consciously "depart" its semi-dormant native shell and telepathically inhabit another organic's biological envelope – much the same way a hermit crab can exchange one protective shell for another. However, the preferred Quimbly method of cognitive invasion was to remotely manipulate an embryo's DNA to ensure a modicum of telepathic ability, allow it to complete its development, and then at the appropriate moment to merge with it *in vivo*. Birth and maturation then were experienced and took place within the subject's context. This tactic greatly lessened the possibility of accidental discovery. Furthermore, if the life-form hailed from a species that was short-lived, then this method was the only rational choice. Why was this so? Because the *in vivo* method of merging or partnering was preferred by the Quimbly, while the former approach was often harmful to the mature host upon the Quimbly's exit as the formerly repressed individual suffered serious and unpredictable reactions.

Regardless of which method of partnering was employed, the Quimbly always remained in intimate contact with its native flesh, and by extension with the pod's central nervous system, and its colleagues. Consequently, Quimbly have successfully walked, flown, swum, crawled, and slithered among alien life-forms undetected. This ability to blend in presented an invaluable source of data collection and the chance to actually experience the experiences of other life-forms. On the other hand, such deep immersion held great peril for the Quimbly who failed to differentiate between its host and its true self. So the mysterious loss of the first scout surveyor was doubly troubling, for that scout surveyor was a Quimbly.

Speculation within The Survey Institute and the crew of the recovery ship Redemption ranger far and wide as to what had happened to the legendary First Scout. Had it gone native? Had that curious Quimbly madness taken hold when one could not differentiate between host and self? Or had that experienced explorer been defeated by something aggressive that it had not foreseen? This last thought The Redemption's Quimbly found the most troubling and his colleagues had to agree.

Then there remained the issue of sheer longevity, given the relative transit duration from near the galaxy's core to its outer reaches. Existence or consciousness, measured in hundreds, if not thousands of years, was a dauntingly alien enough concept. The human rigors of sheer intellectual fatigue, boredom, if not outright psychosis, here did not apply. Just what did one do to occupy one's mind for such an expanse of time? Apparently, these three veterans routinely did so.

As for the ferry craft itself, The Redemption, it had to be by design a much larger craft than the usual for two basic reasons: to possess the sheer capability to physically ship – piggyback or remora-like, the lost star craft homeward, and to provide separate environments for its three passengers and potentially for the lost scout surveyor. Since both the Xoxx and Sard were silicate-based life-forms, their environmental habitats although similar were modified to each individual's specifications. Critical to them was a stable temperature and energy supply generated by the craft's electromagnetic engines. As for the Quimbly, a sulfur-based organic, a more complex habitat was required with a recycling unit and bulky nourishment stores. In short, by our sensibilities a Quimbly was a messy, smelly, and disgustingly brownish organism in comparison to its slower moving and colorful crystalline, silicate colleagues.

What joined the three together and in turn with their ferry craft was the ship's central nervous system – what we might crudely think of as the command system. But this central network was far more than that, for each of the scout surveyors were intimately embedded into its many matrices. Hence was possible the near instantaneous sharing of thought, reading of the ferry's outer sensor arrays, and of course the retrieval of data from or storage into silicate crystals.

That The Redemption's top speed of 89.0 percent C obeyed the Universe's own speed limit was revealing of the level of technology available and the endurance of The Survey Institute's own craft. Clearly, the basic laws of physics were well understood by those inhabiting the near galactic core. Equally sure was that warp drive remained a Hollywood fantasy.

But what of The Survey Institute itself? Remarkably, this was perhaps the most understandable detail of the entire puzzle, for The Survey Institute was conceived, fostered, and nurtured out of sheer curiosity. To build such a monumental institution whose sole purpose was the quenching of insatiable curiosity went a long way toward understanding our galactic neighbors. It also began to explain their rationale – if not zeal – to recover that which was lost to them.

Centrally located near the galaxy's core, The Survey Institute sent out its scout surveyors in search of knowledge, who then in turn reported back with their precious gleanings of wonders seen, intelligent species found, the course and development of cultures, and high civilizations recorded. These data were then carefully organized, collated, and studied by the Institute's "editors" – for the lack of a more precise term. Make no mistake these editors were not historians, for historians gather and interpret data, thus ensuring that each subsequent generation can interpret, reinterpret, and re-re-interpret the data of the so-called historical record. The cumulative result was a continuous rehash of opinion, interpretation, and oftentimes the original primary sources were ignored if not forgotten altogether, having been long buried by all the learned conjecture. This was firmly not the case with the editors of The Survey Institute.

That said, there existed a special synergistic relationship between The Survey Institute's editorial staff and their scout surveyors. They, the editors, unlike the scout surveyors upon whom they were so dependent for data, consisted of tens of species that both depended and thrived upon social interaction. To them the self-imposed isolation of a scout surveyor, while much admired, was in itself a totally alien concept. Yet and still, intimate relationships were painstakingly built between a given editor and its dedicated scout surveyor. Message traffic spanning vast tracks of space was quite frequent between such a pairing, as the scout surveyor literally became the sensory organs of its editor. Needless to say, the loss of one typically led to the eventual grief-stricken madness of the other, unless a skillful transition was not undertaken. Such was the strength and weakness of these "marriages."

The most cherished of issues sought after by the scout surveyors on behalf of their editorial mates was evidence for the galaxy's First Source. In many respects, this subject, the First Source – the ultimate first intelligence of the galaxy – came the closest to eliciting an emotional, religious reaction among The Survey Institute's community, for both scout surveyors and editors alike. For them this was, without question, "The Holy Grail." As with us, periodically every century or so, lively discussions took place within The Survey Institute that mulled over the latest data regarding this most sacrosanct of topics.

While every scout surveyor, who was assigned an editor and tasked for exploration, at a subliminal level they too searched for the First Source. The fact of the matter was the day-to-day workings of The Survey Institute were far more mundane. Quite often, the organization would dispatch scout surveyors on wild goose chases in search of an unclassified, deep space signal's source. So while The Survey Institute was constantly transmitting data between its many editors and scout surveyors, so too was that same institution in the business of patiently listening to the background hiss of the void. Listening for that one possibility out of a trillion, trillion, the First Source would contact them directly.

* * *

With The Redemption well on its way, its crew of three turned their sensitive sensors in the general direction of their goal. Passive listening was standard procedure, especially whenever approaching an unclassified source that required investigation, and given the unique circumstances that surrounded the first scout's automated beacon, all the more so.

Experience had long taught The Survey Institute that nascent civilizations, upon reaching a certain level of technology, tended to flood a considerable amount of electromagnetic energy into their immediate neighborhood, all of which eventually leaked to the great beyond.

In the present case, the trio decided to exercise extreme caution, for one of their own had turned up mysteriously missing. Its very pod linkage had been snuffed out in an instant. Not even a mental sigh or scream had been recorded that could hint toward the reason or cause for the sudden linkage break. This fact was made eminently clear from that last automated message of distress, a transmission they all had long ago memorized, analyzed, and discussed in depth. Just what had happened, they all wondered, that could bring about such abrupt finality? Thus explained their elevated sense of readiness and concern as their approach began to near.

When the recovery mission entered the outer edge of the galaxy's spiral, they began to detect faint radio wave emanations from the general neighborhood of their goal. This presented The Recovery's crew with their first taste of what they expected would besiege their hull's sensors like heavy seas lapping against a windswept pier. A recording was made and archived for later comparison and data analysis.

That recording was of the first radio broadcast from San Jose, California, the year, 1909. As predicted, the flood did arrive as the number and frequency of radio broadcasts multiplied during the late 1910s and 1920s. While the evergrowing amount of transmissions grew that same abundance made the translation process all the easier. Early on, the crew realized that these transmissions were encoded differently. With analysis, they surmised that the encoding was only the matter of a differentiation in communication. This fact brought into play several well-known models of planetary cultural development, several of which unfortunately supported hostile and belligerent scenarios. Then, several of the broadcasts in fact spoke of such conflict – a world war was in progress.

In the end, the recovery mission's occupants discerned seven languages, each with several dialects. In some instances complex actions and reactions could be followed practically word for word. This was the case with something called baseball, while in others the disjointed announcements remained obscure in their meaning.

After all, what was Twenty-Mule Team Borax?

Their patient observations became intriguing when the first video broadcasts were picked up. "Finally," the scout surveyors chimed in unison, yet what they perceived in those first weak signals left them perplexed. The first was a stage production from a place called Schenectady, New York, the second an educational broadcast from a place called the State University of Iowa.

While the audio encoding employed was well understood – it was locally referred to as English, the video context was not. The Quimbly was the first to suspect that the bipedal life-forms depicted were organics of some variety based upon the fluidity and speed of their locomotion. Which variety would be conjectural at this stage. Before a discussion on that subject had progressed very far, another transmission arrived, this one in the audio encoding called Deutsch. It displayed a close-up of an individual life-form with activities displayed in the background that announced the opening of something called the 1936 Berlin Olympiad. Each was amazed at what they saw, fascinated at the moving mouth parts, mind-boggled by what all the regimented imagery might mean. Organization for sure, but as with other civilizations and cultures, where was the place of the individual in such precise blocks of movement?

Ever intrigued, another broadcast appeared. This one too with an individual life-form, who at first appeared to be communicating directly to them, which caused alarm that they had been detected! But the opening words, "My fellow Americans," immediately removed that notion from consideration. Instead, what the message did imply, beyond its understood content, was that the planet's technological level now could support global audio and video communications. Also made explicit was another major war was in the making.

With the next video signal received the Xoxx was provided with many answers, but also many questions. Its initial reaction was classic.

"So that is baseball?"

* * *

So while the Xoxx was in deep contemplation immersed in decoding the esoteric nuances of baseball statistics, the Quimbly was searching the database for bipedal organics with the appropriate number of body parts. As for the Sard, it had detected the first probing and scattered energy pulses of powerful search radars.

"Now this is an important development and challenge to our mission," the Sard said. It then added, "At present, we are decelerating and are only 17.3482 light-years to our goal. We must begin to prepare for our arrival, for it must go unnoticed."

CHAPTER XII

Near Space

On February 6th, 1966, the Combat Operations Center of the North American Aerospace Defense Command, or NORAD, went fully operational within the bowels of Cheyenne Mountain, Colorado. Founded as a direct result of the Cold War on May 5th, 1958, NORAD coordinated and linked both Canadian and US ground and satellite radars to create an early warning trip wire for the defense of North America against intercontinental missile and hostile bomber attack. In many respects, NORAD's interests were consumed by a doctrine biased to focus upon what is launching and from where, what is in the air, approaching, or in danger of violating North American air space. NORAD even tracks the progress of Santa Claus every December 24th for the past forty-odd years.

The reverse of this doctrinal bias is the task of the Air Force Space Command, or AFSPC, located nearby NORAD at Peterson Air Force Base in Colorado Springs. Fully operational since 1985, this command's monitored and cataloged, via powerful radar and optical sensors, any object within the Earth's immediate near space neighborhood. Readily available online via the Internet for public consumption was the so-called Satellite Box Score. In essence, the SATCAT readout of what was orbiting the planet, who owned it, and how many of them there were. The current total is some 20,000-plus objects from fifty-three nations or organizations that range from active satellites, space probes, payloads, rocket bodies, platforms, and debris of all sorts, shapes, and sizes – spent booster canisters, two wrenches, odd nuts and bolts, even an astronaut's outer glove. Needless to say our near space would be even more dangerously crowded if it were not for mother Earth's gravitational pull and the fact that over 24,000 or so items have already succumbed to incineration upon re-entry.

As to how far out into near space the AFSPC considered its domain remains an open question. If that organization routinely tracked the meanderings of space probes, then that would suggest ground and satellite tracking radar assets of considerable number and technologies. As the military was naturally reticent about revealing its performance capabilities, one has only to look to NASA and its many scientific collaborators to get an inkling of what truly may be possible.

A good place to start was the delicate subject of near-earth comet and asteroid detection – collectively known as NEAs. Several civilian, NORAD-like detection systems have been on watch for these potential threats to mankind's welfare. After all, it would take just one such impact of sufficient magnitude to end all human life as we know it. To that end, a graduated scale has been established for the assessment of such an eventuality – the Torino Impact Scale.

One of these civilian watchdog organizations was Near-Earth Asteroid Tracking, NEAT for short. This organization focused upon the detection, calculation, and monitoring of those asteroids considered a potential hazard to Earth. Officially called PHAs, for Potentially Hazardous Asteroids, NEAT tracked their orbits in considerable detail using the massive radar observatories of NASA's Deep Space Network at Goldstone, California, and the Arecibo Observatory in Puerto Rico. In one example, Asteroid 1950 DA, an object about two-thirds of a mile across, NEAT calculated its potential close encounter with Earth some eight hundred years into the future. The radar data gathered that made this astounding estimate possible was taken from a distance twenty-one times that of the Moon's orbit, or about 5,017,029 miles out into space.

At a minimum, therefore, one can assume that the assets and level of technologies available to AFSPC must be far greater than what is available to any American civilian research organization.

"Near" space indeed.

CHAPTER XIII

Cambridge, MA

In 1969, the terms *geek* and *nerd* had yet to be coined. Nonetheless, they did exist and in profusion among the student body at the Massachusetts Institute of Technology. They were easy to identify. They were armed with their slide rules worn at the hip like the *gladus* or short sword of Rome's legions of old. Shielded with plastic pocket protectors filled with mechanical pencils loaded with the softest of leads and erasers, such minds were counted as being America's best – with the sole exception being those at Cal Tech.

Among the many distinguished technical and scientific departments on the Cambridge campus bounded by the Brookline tracks, Main Street, and the Charles River, for Roy Allen Peters, nothing could beat the Department of Materials Science and Engineering. The ugly truth was that Roy was both geek and dreamer. He represented a rare breed of individual, who thought that "stuff" was intrinsically cool. Who thought that the probing about what made stuff, "stuff," was cool as well. In translation, Roy thought of himself as a grand nexus, a sort of symphony conductor who orchestrated the various instruments of physics, chemistry, metallurgy, ceramics, and even geology into a useful harmony – a way to figure out what "stuff" really was. While always respectful of the theoretical aspects of these disciplines, the draw of materials science for Roy was that these scientific disciplines came together under materials science into one cosmically practical application.

Practicality had been something that had been drilled into Roy from an early age. Born in the town of Terra Haute, Indiana, in 1948, Roy Allen Peters worked on the family farm along with his two older brothers ever since he could remember. Talk around the kitchen table was either about the weather, which they could do nothing about, or the soil. "What's in it? What's not? And what we will put in it?" In other words, something they could do something about.

Unlike many of his friends and neighbors, however, the Peters boys had it pretty easy as their farm was a corn farm and not a dairy farm with its daily double chores of milking – not to mention the feeding and hoeing out of the stalls. That extra time meant the boys studied more than most and as a result all went to college and finished with degrees. While the two eldest returned to the farm, Roy didn't feel the calling and it was just as well as his older brothers were fixing to settle down, get married, and start building their own homes on the two remaining corners of the family's vast, triangular plot of acreage.

During the first semester of his junior year, Roy nosed about the job fairs. Initially, it was more out of curiosity than anything else, but after doing some reading and listening, he discovered much to his horror that while a BS in materials science was nice, a graduate school degree was far better. While his grades were solid A's and his student advisor, Professor Jerry Graves, thought the world of him, the junior felt a bit adrift at sea. This feeling Roy did not like one iota, so he decided to do something about it.

Knocking on Doc Graves' second floor office door in the red bricked Number 12 Engineering Building, Roy was armed with his spiral notepad full of questions. Upon hearing the friendly "Enter at your own risk," Roy did so with his trademark broad grin that crinkled his pug nose.

"Well," greeted the sandy-haired middle-aged professor, "If it isn't that corn silk smoking hayseed from Indiana. Good to see you, Roy. Grab a chair."

Inwardly pleased at Professor Graves' personal greeting, the student entered and plopped himself down. As for Graves, who as an Iowa farm product himself, although from a wheat-growing family of six, he had almost adopted the bright, clear-headed, God-fearing, and practical lad from the Midwest. When he "just stopped by to jaw," it was always well thought out, important, if not heady stuff.

Graves saw Roy's infamous notepad in hand, so he leaned forward on his elbows with sleeves rolled up and tie askew.

"Okay, Roy. What's on your mind?"

"Well, Professor Graves, I have been doing some research on what I want for a career. The problem is – despite my grades and this school and all – a BS in Materials Science doesn't seem to be good enough. At the job fair I read some of the job descriptions. It looks like I need at least a MS to even get my foot in the door. While grad school doesn't bother me one bit, how I am going to pay for it does."

Graves, with his head cocked to the left and listening, listened to his young charge, freckles and all. He sympathized with his plight, for he well remembered a similar discussion he had had with his academic advisor way back when.

"Well, Roy, let's see. You're a junior, aren't you?"

A nod.

"Well. Sometimes, what's needed is some practical experience to catch an employer's eye, something valuable to put on your resume, something that shows that you've been around the block. Also, such experience might be good for you, because then you can see for yourself whether you might like a research position in industry. Or do you see yourself going more the academic route into research and such?"

Squirming a bit in his chair at the choice, Roy decided to speak his mind.

"Professor Graves, and please do not take this personal, the academic route scares the hell out of me with all the theorizing, research, and publications. What I want to do is figure stuff out, analyze problems, fix things, and make my contribution that way. So I guess industry is it, but how do I find who I want to work for, much less make them want to hire me?"

Smiling and thinking. *Boy what a pleasure. No sugarcoated bull is going on here, no, sir.*

"Roy, how good are you at keeping your mouth shut?"

"Well, Professor, I never before thought about it, but I have pulled off some great pranks on my brothers and they still don't know just who, did what, to whom!"

He stated proudly and with an emphasis on "who," "what," and "whom."

"Interesting. I'll remember what you just said, Mr. Peters, given the coming spring semester and its usually creative chaos and mayhem," Graves intoned in mock seriousness.

"But what I have in mind, however, is a tad more serious. Have you ever heard of the Manhattan Project?"

"Sure. Who hasn't?"

"Well, for starters, plenty of people. But my point is that MIT played a big part in that particular project, as did of course the U. of C., and Princeton, Cal Tech, Stanford, and many other fine institutions of higher learning. Currently, I am aware of four such projects going on here, right now, very quietly.

This nugget of information was digested by a surprised young man with wide eyes.

"My question is: Roy, would you be satisfied spending the rest of your life working on important projects, but projects that you would never be able to talk about, not even to your dad, mother, or wife?"

When Roy's eyes glazed over in his familiar faraway stare, Graves knew that he had hit a nerve, a very deep one.

A moment later, Roy having returned to the here and now, answered, Yes. Yes indeed, Professor Graves. It would be difficult for sure, but it would be well worth it to work on important stuff and make that kind of contribution. So yes, Professor, my answer would have to be yes."

"Even when the important stuff was a boring chore?"

Looking back with a knowing, insider's smile back at Graves, Roy replied, "Look, Professor Graves, I grew up watching corn grow."

* * *

Later that afternoon, Graves picked up the phone and dialed a number with a 202 area code, which in 1969 extended into select parts of Virginia and Maryland outside of the immediate Washington Belt Way. After the usual pleasantries, Graves got down to business.

"John, I think that I have located for you a material science's type for that project you mentioned last month.

"Yeah, that one.

"Well, that's the problem, he's just a junior.

"Would you consider him as summer research intern? Perhaps put him on something not quite so sensitive?

"Well, for what it is worth, he is an extremely solid citizen, especially given the current trend these days.

"Drugs? No. Absolutely not, I would stake my reputation on that."

"An interview with one of your people? Yeah, that could be easily enough arranged.

"His name is Roy Allen Peters.

“Terra Haute, Indiana.

“That’s H-A-U-T-E.

“No, I haven’t a clue. It probably means something like ‘high ground’ or something.

“Hey! Watch that! I’m from Iowa, remember?”

“Look, John, he’s just a good kid, bright, clear-headed, and above all practical. He really needs a dash of whimsy in his life.

“Yeah, farm bred like me.

“John, now watch it!”

Chuckle.

“Yeah.

“And John, thanks for giving him a look over. I don’t think you will be wasting your agency’s time.

“Yeah. And all the best to Cindy too.

“Yeah. Bye now.”

* * *

Roy had been an excited bundle of nerves ever since Professor Graves had told him a week ago to “get his butt” over to the student union building and make sure that he was wearing a coat and tie. Never before had he been so keyed up, so primed. He even had put his under shorts on backwards, he was in such a tizzy. It was all that he could do to think straight.

Wow, an interview! Somebody wants to talk to me. I’m only a first semester junior. Wow!

Now sitting on the bench, next to the appropriate administrative office, Roy waited for the time to arrive as he was a full twenty minutes early. He didn’t care. Besides, he had his notepad secreted in his inner sport coat jacket pocket so that he could take notes if he had to.

He waited.

At about fifteen minutes before the appointed hour, another male student arrived similarly attired in a wool sport jacket, wide colorful tie, and corduroy slacks. Looking around as if he didn’t know where he was, he smiled, nodded at Roy, decided this was indeed where he should be, and sat down on the same bench.

Five minutes passed in silence between the two potential candidates. Furtive looks were exchanged, but as yet no words. Roy noted, however, that the fellow had shinier shoes then he and so he began to kick himself for forgetting something so obvious.

Another five minutes passed and still no interviewer and both candidates began to fidget. Roy would shuffle his feet, check to see if his notepad was still there, and rub his hands' perspiration off on the sides of his tan cotton slacks. Meanwhile his twin began studiously examining his nails. Roy, now peeking at his, realized that he should have cleaned them up as well. Working in the materials lab could be, no, was, often a dirty business.

Then precisely at the appointed time, the newcomer asked Roy, "Are you here for the interview for that materials science internship?"

"Well," said Roy. "I guess so. Professor Graves didn't say it was an interview specifically in materials science. He just suggested rather strongly that I show up."

"So you're one of Prof. Graves' boys!" exclaimed the other.

"Well," allowed Roy, now blushing. "I suppose. Although I'd never heard of any of us being referred to quite like that before."

"Ah, well, that doesn't matter. My name's Mike Donnelly," the other said while extending a friendly hand.

"I'm out of the Physics Department. I'm into quantum mechanics and silicates. What about you?"

"Pleasure to meet you. I'm Roy Peters. Ceramics and metallurgy interest me. That's why I'm here, I suppose."

"Oh," said the one rather diffidently.

With that the conversation died a quick death with each candidate wondering with the usual paranoia whether the other's background had some sort of imagined edge over the other.

Another five minutes passed and still no interviewer had shown up.

After another five minutes both candidates really began to squirm. Almost on cue they sighed, checked, and rechecked their watches.

Finally, Donnelly again broke the silence.

"You know what the rules are on late profs, don't you?"

"Yeah," said Roy, having memorized the "legal wait rule" during the first week of his freshman year. "Fifteen minutes for a full prof, ten for an associate, and five for a green assistant, and zero for a lecturer."

"Whaddya' think a late interviewer should get?" Donnelly queried.

"Well," Roy reasoned. "At least that of a full, maybe more."

"You're unusually generous, Mr. Peters." Donnelly smiled knowingly.

"Well, no. I guess it's more out of respect, that's all."

"Respect? Or could it be that you are blessed with something called patience?" probed Donnelly.

"Yeah. That too."

Catching himself and now taking the time to really look squarely at Donnelly, Roy asked, "Just who are you?"

"Why, Mr. Peters," again extending his hand with a warm smile, "I'm your two o'clock interview. And Roy, thank you for waiting. By the way, my name's Mike."

CHAPTER XIV

One if by Comet – Two if by Asteroid

"Given the amplitude of the multiple search radars that are emanating from our mission's goal, I strongly suggest that we discuss how we are going to approach the planet undetected."

So began the conversation aboard the recovery ferry, The Redemption.

The Sard continued, "I have already taken the initiative and blacked out our ship's hull to foil optical detection, but that will soon prove to be not sufficient. We require more."

Several moments passed in silence. Then the Xoxx piped up.

"Well, the solution is simple. We reconfigure the hull to scatter the radar waves."

"All well and good," replied the Sard, "for an individual hull. I have performed that trickery several times with great success. But alas, our current transport is not capable of configuring itself for such stealth. It is unique, a transport ferry, an emergency rescue ship. We even have a spare environment if we find the first scout recoverable. This ship is an ungainly, inefficient in form, but eminently practical for our recovery purpose. It is the first of its kind and was made ready in haste."

Again moments passed in silence, but this time the Quimbly spoke.

"So, The Redemption is practical for the task at hand, but inelegant. I totally agree. Then I suggest that we shield ourselves, camouflage ourselves with similarly ugly things in order to avoid detection. The question is, with what? What would be best? To hide within a comet's tail? Or perhaps better to surround ourselves with asteroid debris?"

"A most intriguing thought!" exclaimed both the crystalline and silicate, which warmed the Quimbly with pleasure, for what went unstated was the obvious talent of the Quimbly for making the visible invisible, or at the very least, unnoticed.

"Comets," the Xoxx continued, "are unstable, too bound to their orbits, and above all too noticeable."

Warm intellectual smiles immediately broke out over the Xoxx's choice of emphasis on the word "noticeable."

"I agree," said the Sard. "Then let us select an asteroid or two, magnetically bind them to our dorsal and ventral moorings and drift in toward our goal as if nothing were amiss."

So it was agreed, and to make things even more interesting, the Xoxx made the following suggestion.

"Gravitational dynamics being what they are, we have to mask our transport's mass and composition as well as its radar signature. So why do we not add a bit of rotation, spin, and tumble to our little nest we are about to construct? Let us elaborate on our theme of visible invisibility, the more mass we can have moving about us the better."

"Would not that be difficult if not impossible to safely arrange?" queried the Quimbly.

"Not at all. Are you forgetting your colleagues? It will only take a bit of astrogravitational computational engineering. Besides, it will be an interesting computation. Certainly a challenge worthy of us."

"But," asked the Quimbly, "how close do you intend to guide the orbits of these small planetoids?"

"Surely, it would have to be close, but of no harm. Why do you ask?" The Sard said.

"Again," cautioned the organic, "I was just wondering that once we are in the immediate vicinity of the planet, and after we shed our nest of rock, how we will approach the planet undetected?"

Again, several moments passed in quiet silence.

"Perhaps," began the Sard, "we should again do something obvious. Could we not disguise our craft as an asteroid fragment? We suddenly plunge into the dense atmosphere as a fiery blaze and then disappear once within it."

"That is an extremely risky proposal," intoned the Xoxx with a clear emphasis on the word "that."

"Yes, it is," replied his colleague. "Do you have a better one?"

"Not at the moment."

"Then," replied the Sard, "perhaps we should think on it and consider it a working hypothesis until something better comes to mind. In the meantime, perhaps we should begin acquiring some suitable nesting material."

And so it was agreed.

CHAPTER XV

Wright-Patterson AFB

Roy Allen Peters turned out to be almost too good to be true. He was a geek in the truest sense through and through. On top of that he was tight-lipped, blessed with a dogged determination, and a deep reserve of patience. The summer internship he had got through Doc Graves' machinations was at an aircraft facility in Burbank, California. There he inspected stainless steel nuts, bolts, and washers. While it had been a numbing experience for this bright and creative kid, Roy stuck it out, and in the process devised a sorting system that is one of that institution's frontline quality controls.

Now a year later, a year wiser, and a freshly minted graduate from MIT with high honors, the government came to him with an offer that he could not refuse. Roy's decision to "sign on the dotted line," however, took a bit of time as he wanted to first bounce the offer off of his dad. So during a tension-filled long distance telephone call that was rippling with excitement and expectations, father and son commenced to jaw.

"Now, son," Mr. Peters drawled. "Are you sure that you really want this?"

"You bet!"

"That's real good to hear, because I know that whenever you put your mind to something, it gets done right proper."

Mr. Peters then continued with a seldom used softness to his voice that his son had long recognized as a dose of wisdom coming head on.

"Now, son, I know that you can't tell me anything about who you might be working for in the government, or for that matter, on what. That I can easily live with because I know that you will do the right thing and you'll do a fine job. What I am concerned about is your personal future and that eventually means finding an understanding woman to take as your wife. How will you ever be able to find a woman who will respect and trust your job's need for secrecy?"

"Gee, Dad, I haven't thought much about that."

"I know that you haven't. That's why I brought it up, son."

* * *

As it turned out, Roy took the job and became a government employee. The hook that landed him was the promise he would become a part of a team of scientists who would play at the futuristic bleeding edge of his beloved field of material sciences. After the six months of clearance processing, he discovered that indeed he could not discuss anything he was involved in with anyone on the outside. That meant no patents, no publications, no textbooks, nothing. However, within his select cadre and those with the proper clearances, the sky was the limit on discussions, seminars, and presentations. Of course there were always the much-dreaded weekly reports that had to be submitted in triplicate, but given the resources available and the latest in technology at his disposal, Roy found himself in hog heaven and plans were already in the works for his MS. MIT, naturally, was selected as the sponsoring institution and Doc Graves had readily agreed to be his advisor and reader.

* * *

Working closely on a daily basis with the government's expensive scientific toys required care and consideration, but when you were allowed to use them to work on one of the government's prize secrets, now that was entirely another ball of wax. As ever, Roy was up to the rigorous security measures and sterile anti-contamination strictures required for access to the super-secret materials science laboratory at Wright-Patterson Air Force Base in Dayton, Ohio. What that meant was almost fifteen minutes and four security checkpoints just to get to his personal cube, and then two more security gates to get to the scrub and gowning room of the material sciences laboratory. Once suited up after another ten or so minutes, Roy passed through a negatively pressured airlock that automatically vacuumed him and the air envelope that had accompanied him for any stray lint or dust motes. Now finally loose in his "play pen," he had to call up from stores his next "victim" scheduled for sampling. Ten minutes or so later that victim arrived on a rubberized conveyor belt strapped to what looked like a jury-rigged ordinance rack, itself having passed through a similar decontamination airlock.

Reading his typed sampling instructions through its clear plastic envelope, Roy felt a bit like a pharmacist trying to decipher precisely what a physician had prescribed for his patient. Bending the page in his gloved hands this way and that in an attempt to remove the glare from the overhead lighting, he discovered this victim's name: SNOWMAN. Next, he had to figure out how to remove some minute samples from this curious object, for he was certain that its name was the product of random generation. The shiny golden object before him looked like anything but snow – unless of course it was made of Frank Zappa's "yellow snow." Given the current room temperature that whimsical assumption was not at all possible.

As for SNOWMAN, it looked like a very smooth cast iron pipe with funny-looking fins at one end that came to a point. The configuration was considered "squid-like," or so went the learned in-house scuttlebutt on his sampling instruction sheet. At its opposite end, the nearly two meter long object, some twenty centimeters in diameter, Roy noted an inner core of some type that made the object's outer casing less than a centimeter thick. Over all, Roy was intrigued with SNOWMAN, because it was relatively light at less than eighteen kilos, or forty pounds, but was structurally rigid and strong.

Dang, he thought. *I have to get the sample down to the lab for a full chemical analysis right quick! Maybe even get them enough for a thin section. That would be just perfect!*

But these naïve thoughts were formulated long before he had begun planning his siege of SNOWMAN's outer hull.

At first, Roy thought he would begin by grinding away several grams of material directly from the main hull and get it to the chem lab for analysis by nine that morning. That idea turned out to be overly optimistic for all that the carbide grinding wheel seemed to do was polish the outer housing's surface. Not to be denied, Roy applied progressively more and more aggressive materials to the outer shell's surface and to no avail. Finally, and after only totally ruining several diamond grinder wheels, Roy was able to dislodge a meager 0.7 grams of sample, much of which he suspected was spent grinder material that would have to be sorted out by the lab rats, and that would not make them happy.

As for attempting to remove a fragment large enough for a thin section, Roy decided to assault one of the leading edges of

SNOWMAN's two squid-like fins. Given the difficulties he had encountered with the hull sample, he stopped, and paused as to how to next proceed. As he did so, Roy began to feel more and more as if he were desecrating a hallowed artifact as he came to appreciate the subtle lines and strictly utilitarian shape of SNOWMAN.

Darn, he thought. *This is one beautifully engineered form, so graceful and yet so direct in its design. It's a real shame that I have to scar it again.*

With that last thought passed on, he began anew his assault, and after four and a half hours of carefully applied destructiveness, the lab had its fragment and the left squid fluke sported a newly acquired, but minor nick to its otherwise gently flowing curve.

CHAPTER XVI

1979 North Sakkara

Depending upon your particular point of view, Egypt can be either a glorious place or an absolute hellhole. At this particular moment, Professor Dr. Willem van der Boek was absolutely sure which he would have chosen. Breathing hard from physical exertion and sitting in the relative coolness of the tarpaulin's shade, he was glad to be out in the open air and in the breeze, instead of being in the dusty and hellishly hot underground warren that he had just wormed himself out of. Looking down at his perspiration-soaked T-shirt, his head, face, and arms were caked with sweat-congealed limestone dust. Only his mouth, nose, and eye sockets were clear due to the goggled respirator's outline. He heaved a very heavy sigh.

Willy, he began. *You are too fat, too out of condition, and far too curious for your own good. You are no longer that young and svelte soccer player you once were. And damn it, you just drive yourself too hard. There are far better, far healthier ways to pursue a career.*

Then pausing to reconsider his lot in life.

But, my dear friend, you love being out of doors and in the open desert, instead of buried somewhere in a research library, all the while acquiring a vampiric pallor. Besides, how many people can say that they are an Egyptian archaeologist? Can answer honesty, "Yes, I have dug in Egypt." Or can say "I love my job"?

Drink, Willy, drink, he commanded himself. *Otherwise you will dehydrate like a prune. And be thankful that it's only early March and not June or July.*

A few moments later, he unsnapped the leather flap that protected the face of his wristwatch and took a peek.

Well, my fifteen minutes are up and it's only 10:22 in the morning! Time to get back to work. Mustn't appear to take the role of a slacker! Mustn't let them know I have a touch of claustrophobia either, he darkly added.

With that self-inflicted mental nudge, van der Boek knocked out all the surface debris from his twin filters, donned his respirator, got down on his gloved hands and padded knees, and began to slowly descend the long aluminum ladder through the shaft's one by two meter opening.

While it was true that this middle-aged archaeologist from the University of Amsterdam had already lost a good fifteen pounds during the last three weeks in service to his beloved profession, he had also contracted a nasty stomach bug that he prayed might be only food related. Dehydration was the biggest enemy of this fair-haired Hollander with skin that preferred to burn first and tan later in the Nilotic sun. van der Boek, now in the field for five weeks, was very tanned and even the tips of his eyelashes and remaining gossamer hair had bleached out white. Accepting his minor and rapidly dwindling paunch, the ruggedly handsome and stocky Hollander was really quite fit, being broad and well muscled in the shoulders, and because of his soccer days, strong in the legs. And with the ladder climbing up and down, it was just as well.

The shaft in question that van der Boek had climbed into was designated Shaft IV, located in the Second Courtyard of a mortuary complex built by and for a general named Horemheb, a contemporary of the famous Pharaoh Tutankhamen. Today, the excavated remains of this complex can be found by driving south from Cairo to Memphis. Cross the Nile at the main bridge and ask for directions to the Step Pyramid Complex at Sakkara. Park your car at its southeastern extreme. Walk north to the broken down Pyramid of Unas and look to the south for several groupings of papyri-form columns. These should be located to the west and upslope from the Monastery of Saint Jeremiah. Adjacent to and south of the tomb of Maya, stand these proud ruins with their multiple columns and courtyards decorated with fine low-relief carvings.

This Sakkaran tomb was never finished as it was built before fate conspired to make General Horemheb pharaoh, who ruled Egypt as the last king of the Eighteenth Dynasty. During Horemheb's reign only a second wife would be interred here, one Mutnedjemet. To no one's surprise, many later intrusions had been identified within this funerary monument. Less well known, however, was that prior to Horemheb's accession to the throne of Isis as the supreme ruler of the Two Lands, a provision had been made for another burial that contained the eternal remains and effects of a dear advisor, one Meryptah, a high priest of Amen Re.

To the Dutch excavation team, Shaft IV held promise for its entrance had been carefully hidden in the northwest corner of the courtyard's pool. After having cleared almost eighty feet of packed rubble fill from the interior of this vertical rock cut shaft, a pillared hall finally had appeared.

This underground hall, called imaginatively Pillared Hall N, was about twenty-by-twenty-feet square. Four massively squat pillars arranged in a square configuration supported its low roofline and managed to gobble up most of its square footage. Its walls and ceiling were thinly coated in plaster and undecorated. Within van der Boek's team discovered yet another shaft. Presumably it led down to either another hall or burial chamber. It was this second shaft that the team was now laboriously attempting to clear.

Spelling a team member, van der Boek returned to his post, kneeling above the dust-clogged opening of the second shaft located in the middle aisle of the Pillared Hall N. To better visualize and appreciate the scene, light was provided by three brutally bright and hellishly hot halogen flood lamps. These fixtures simultaneously cast inhumanly harsh shadows with glare reflecting off of the air born white limestone dust, itself at times more like pumice than anything else. The closed space seemed airless. Any generated body heat and moisture only added to the oppressive suffering. Needless to say, working in the goggles and respirators was also a sweaty, unpleasant, but needful practice, as there was no other way to breathe. While a photographic record of the excavation's proceedings were needed and necessary, the task was a maintenance nightmare as the dust permeated and got into everything. Any delicate mechanical mechanism, if not thoroughly field stripped on a daily basis, would soon find its inner workings reduced to a mass of useless metal shavings. This occurred especially with motor-driven cameras, but as with all the reflex cameras, lens shutter mirrors became even quicker victims to scratches if they were not cared for properly.

Then a graduate student's red bandanna-wrapped head and bug-eyed respirator appeared from the shaft's opening. It was shortly followed with a grunt and a good-sized limestone block. Hefting the stone with his gloved hands, van der Boek carefully stepped away from the opening and turned the block in his hands looking for any evidence of an inscription or carving. Finding none, he held it against his chest while he began a calf- and buttocks-burning crouch-waddle over to a pile of similar stones stacked along the southern end of the pillared hall. This comical crouch-waddle, even if he did look like a big duck, was very appropriate given the hall's low ceiling that was amply attested from all the heedless dents in his hardhat.

Eventually, van der Boek thought in bitter agony, *all of this material would have to be removed up and out. Maybe I should look into some kind of mechanical lift, something like what roofers use.*

He then dutifully crouch-waddled back to his post and awaited his next load from below.

* * *

Three hours later, van der Boek was beat, but the day had been a productive one as the second shaft had been totally cleared. He was amazed. This one had only been twenty feet deep before they had reached the blocking stones of a chamber of some kind. With nearly the entire southern half of Pillared Hall N now filled with neat stacks of rocky debris, the archaeologist decided to lean up against the northern wall and collect himself before his final ascent of the day. By now an old and ingrained habit, he crouch-waddled over to the wall and noted for the first time in the halogen glare a slight depression marked by the chisel marks of some long dead workman. Intellectually, he considered the feature probably the barest beginnings of another passage that was then abandoned.

Probably begun just before Horemheb reached the throne and probably ended just as quickly, he casually thought.

Noting that it would comfortably fit the curvature of his backside, the archaeologist plopped himself against the wall with a fleshy sigh. His hardhat soon following with a dull thump that immediately brought van der Boek to full attention with widened eyes.

Vas ist hier los! He rapidly thought.

So he banged his head again against the area of the unfinished chisel work and was again rewarded with a dull thump. Now very curious, he immediately got up, turned, and kneeled down on his heavily padded knees before the area of the unfinished chisel work. Taking off his helmet, he began tapping its dented metal surface horizontally from the far right across the chiseled area to the far left and could not believe what his ears were telling him.

Tink, tink, tink, tink, thump, thump, thump, thump, tink, tink, tink, tink.

Then van der Boek, truly astounded, performed the little experiment again, but this time vertically.

Tink, tink, thump, thump, thump, thump, thump, tink, tink.

Now truly amazed, he reached into the pocket of his now baggy tan field shorts, extracted his Swiss Army knife, and began scraping at the wall's surface. What he quickly discovered was that "tink" sounds were coming from the areas of thin plaster wash over solid limestone and "thump" sounds were coming from just plaster. Taking a few more minutes of investigation to completely delineate outer the dimensions of the thumping plaster versus tinking limestone washed in plaster, van der Boek quickly realized beyond a shadow of a doubt that he had discovered a cleverly disguised entrance!

How clever! His mind rushed. *To hide an entrance to a passageway or chamber by faking it in plaster as a started, but unfinished excavation! It's brilliant! Simply brilliant!*

Then he began to laugh, and laugh some more, which wasn't all that easy to do in his respirator. For some reason, all the work, the clearing of the second shaft, and now here, lo and behold, he found yet another entrance, but this time camouflaged in plain view!

Still laughing like a hyena in his respirator, van der Boek barely could make it out of Shaft IV. All of his younger colleagues who were grouped around the opening of the shaft thought that old van der Boek had finally lost it. But much to their surprise, they would learn quite the opposite.

CHAPTER XVII

The Meeting

With almost two weeks of classes behind him, Richards felt that he was standing on top of the world. This semester's batch of students was bright and inquisitive. The faculty and staff were helpful with his few needs. During his off-hours he worked out daily in the gym and then hung out either in his office or the Near Eastern Institute's womb-like archive preparing for this, finding an answer to that, or working on his next book on the development of the Egyptian language. He had allowed himself to be consumed by his ivory tower existence in an effort to become part of it all. In short, the green associate professor had yet to experience the many realities of the academic grind: the predictable fallout of his first quiz; the jealous heat of his first academic disagreement; the grading of midterm examinations; the extreme discomfort of passing a professional adversary in the hall and being able to fake a kindly "Good day," much less survive his first departmental review.

Richards, however, forgot one important item, how he came to be where he was, when he was, for he was first and foremost the world's only surviving temporal field operative. That reality was about to intrude and complicate his carefully scheduled little world, and it all began with a knock on his door.

Looking too slowly up from his work spread out across his sparsely covered desk, Richards automatically said, "Please come in."

"Why thank you, Professor Richards, murmured a smiling and familiar voice.

Now seeing who was filling his doorway, a broad grin spread across his eager face as he rose and offered his lone visitor's chair.

"Good to see you, John. How the heck are you, anyways?"

Gently sitting down, smelling the freshly painted walls, and glancing around the still all-too-barren shelves, bereft of books, knickknacks, and even dust, the elderly scholar found himself experiencing a flood of old and sacred memories.

My, his office looks just like mine when I first began.

"Quite well, thank you. The polyps in my sinuses have cleared up and my oncologist confirms that my cancer is in remission. Now exactly what that means, I am not really sure, but frankly, I feel great, and I have even begun courting again!"

To this last, Richards had to stop, think, and translate before he formed his next sentence.

"Well, who's the lucky lady?"

Followed up with a quick, "When can I get to meet her?"

"Not on your life! I don't want to lose her once she catches sight of you!"

At the folksy remark smiles broke out all around.

"So," Milson continued. "How are your classes going?"

The needed and preparatory small talk began and lasted for a good ten minutes of pure tomfoolery complete with some tear-jerking guffaws that managed to leak into the corridor. Truly, Milson the mentor was living vicariously through Richards the protégé. The departmental scuttlebutt said that they were the "pair extraordinaire," two peas from the same pod, where if one would readily lie, the other would surely swear to it. Never had any of the old guard seen Milson so alive, so animated, since the passing of his dear Alice some three years before and his recent defeat of cancer. All judged the change beneficial and long overdue, and despite their own better judgment and sense of decorum, young Richards' exuberance had brought a certain brilliance back to the department that was sorely needed. The signs were clear. There were more undergraduates hanging around then before in the archive, coffee room, and in fact a bench had to be added outside of Richards' office as a courtesy to those who seemed to be endlessly waiting for an audience with him. As it was, some still preferred to sit on the floor. The department devoted to long dead languages was again coming alive.

* * *

Now breathing hard to catch their breath and while still wiping tears of laughter from their eyes, Milson then informed Richards what the real reason was for his visit. There was scheduled later that afternoon a meeting over at the Philology Annex that he should attend.

"I'll meet you at the front reception desk at 4:30 sharp," ordered the mentor.

"See you then," answered the protégé.

* * *

It was only as Richards was ascending the six concrete steps of the Philology Annex's three-story brownstone that a sinking feeling began to settle in his stomach. His memories of this organization's receptionist had been more than cordial and in fact they were quite special in a number of ways. It was just that since he had gotten back from Egypt, the long debriefings, his preparations for his first fall semester, getting the apartment all settled, his office, his wardrobe, all the working out, he had just plum forgotten about her. And now it was all coming to a head.

Gulp!

At entering the pleasantly warm and lightly perfumed reception area that uneasy feeling rapidly became an awkward one, for the vision of Ms. Kelly sitting there talking in an overly animated way with Doc Milson told him all that he needed to know. As their eyes met, Professor Joseph Richards' heart skipped a beat. Swallowing, he bravely extended his hand across her desk and said, "Hello, I'm Dr. Richards. I'm here for a meeting."

Milson, watching with sublime amusement this clearly contrived introduction for his benefit, positively felt his nose twitch as the estrogen and testosterone levels in the room reached critical mass.

"Ah, yes. Dr. Richards, so I see."

Ms. Kelly purred with an ever so provocative blush rapidly spreading across her face and neck. And she didn't let go of his hand all that quickly either. Then with its release, she indicated to her left.

"Ah, Professor Milson will show you the way, but ah, first, you will have to leave your shoes over there."

Turning around to the "where" indicated, Richards saw a bunch of wooden cubbyholes almost all filled with shoes. Surprised by what he saw and immediately thinking of a bowling alley, he then reflexively slipped off his shiny cappers, bent over, and put them into a nearby vacant slot. Now turning around to follow Milson, the receptionist again stopped him dead in his tracks.

"Ah, Dr. Richards, I think that you need something on your feet. Don't you?"

Richards looked confused. The receptionist then pointed at Milson's feet, which were decked out in a pair of pink, bunny-eared bedroom slippers. While Milson grinned and wiggled his toes through his slippers in fun back at Richards, the elderly professor failed to see Ms. Kelly bending over and reaching into a lower draw of her desk to retrieve a pair of disposable hospital slippers. Unfortunately for Richards, he did not miss either the exaggerated arched back maneuver or the moistening of lips that was so clearly displayed for his eyes only.

"Yes, thank you," was the best that he could muster.

"Ah, Dr. Richards, that will be fifty cents please."

"Right," as he fumbled through his pockets, "Would it be all right if I just owed it to you? I'll pay you back as soon as I can!" Richards blurted out like a six-year-old who had discovered a hole in his pocket while at the candy store.

"Ah, Dr. Richards, be assured that your credit is very good here. But I must hold you to your promise, at, say later this evening, perhaps after the meeting?"

Red-faced and nearly choking, Richards staggered to answer.

"Right. Sounds good. I'll see you then."

During this last exchange, Milson had purposely stepped away into the hallway and turned his back both in deference to those two youngsters so clearly in rut and to compose himself as well.

Damnation! That is one hot woman, he panted.

* * *

As the two academics departed for the special elevator that would deliver them to the second secured sublevel, the receptionist smiled.

Well, by the end of this evening, I should know the whereabouts of one Colonel Alexander Piankoff. And if I don't, well, then I will just have to try, and try, and if necessary, try again.

Oh, poor little me, the things that I must do for the good of God and Country!

* * *

The meeting's agitated chair was Dr. Paul Allister Young, the university's Dean of Humanities, a man who Richards had only once briefly met during a new faculty orientation meeting. Milson, however, had informed Richards that he owed the man a lot and that extreme deference and respect were in order. The meeting finally commenced only after a final straggler arrived, some physicist, who mumbled his apologies to all and then escaped the dean's wrathful glare to take a seat in the back row. Hence the source of the chair's agitation. The meeting began.

"Dear colleagues, we have a full agenda today so we must press on." All words precisely stated in a business-like and clipped British accent.

"But first I have the pleasure to introduce to our number our newest member, Dr. Joseph Richards, an associate professor at the Near Eastern Institute."

Polite clapping broke out.

"Ah, yes. Having Dr. Richards among our faculty is a great honor, all the more so that he is also the world's only temporal field agent."

Now with that obligatory introduction out of the way, the dean continued, "As to the matter of some unfinished business, there remains the issue of the recovery of the alien's craft. In short, we owe it to ourselves to make the attempt. We command the technology and we possess the remaining temporal field agent. But the real question is whether we should allow Dr. Richards here to undertake this mission solo, or should we first regroup, find and train an assistant for him, and then deploy?"

A hum of side conversations broke out along with much of the usual ear tugging, nose scratching, and jaw stroking.

Unself-consciously, Richards raised his hand, and with a smile the chair recognized it, thinking, *This Richards is a polite and interesting fellow, instead of bellowing his presence, he first requests to be recognized. How positively quaint!*

"Yes, Dr. Richards. You have something to say?"

Standing, Richards said, "Ah, yes, Dean Young, I do."

Richards began as the rest of the room quieted and turned to better hear what the newbie had to say.

"When I last left Egypt, and after I saw to the burial of the high priest Meryptah, I became Queen Nefertiti's new ambassador through a sort of naturally occurring inheritance or transition from master to journeyman. My point is, is in that time line, I did not have an assistant. While I well realize that finding and training one is a much-needed priority, their introduction into the time line will have to be a well-planned and staged event so as not to violate the *RUTI*. So, at least initially, I believe that I, acting as the queen's own ambassador, will be able to do a lot of preparatory leg work, while my future assistant is being trained."

The dean next recognized a raised hand from the back. Indeed it was that of the perpetually tardy physicist!

"Yes, Dr. Jung, you have something to add?"

Coming to his feet, the bushy eye browed five-foot-something physicist began as the rest of the room turned in their seats to see who it was. Unaccustomed to such attention, the several time runner-up Nobel Prize physicist began to speak rather nervously, clearing his throat at inappropriate moments along the way.

"Yes, I indeed do. Acchheemmm. I have recently heard from several of my colleagues in the former Eastern Bloc that there has been – acchhheemm . . . an important recent shake up within the Russian Ministry of Science. It seems that one of the gentlemen who took part in the last video conference has been – accchheeemm . . . forcibly retired or perhaps even worse."

The silence in the room became deafening with the mention of the "even worse" part.

"It now seems certain that a successor has been appointed to take the retiree's place. His name is Professor Dr. Stefan Rosovec. Perhaps some of you – acchhheemm . . . recognize the name. You should if you are in any way involved in the field of quantum mechanics. The man's an innovative genius. But the man – acchhheemm . . . is also very young by Russian standards – mid-forties, is extremely good-looking, and has a vandal-like reputation with the ladies."

Then catching himself, he amended, "Of course, ladies, I meant no offense."

Then continuing, "My point to all of this is – acchhheemm . . . that we have a new, young, clearly ambitious, Russian scientist-administrator, who is now the Director of Advanced and Theoretical

Technological Research. He no doubt means to earn – acchhheemm . . . a reputation and his spurs as quickly as possible among his elder peers. Furthermore, his accession means he has replaced that madman Nikolai Fedorov, who as you may recall, reportedly had placed a contract out on Peter Borov's own head!

"Now what I fear, my dear colleagues, is that – acchhheemm . . . if our Russian colleagues do not have a temporal agent to hold over our heads, then they might get a bit desperate, perhaps even do something really stupid – like attempt to acquire one of our Soap Bubble devices."

Gasps and outraged voices filled the room. After some gavel banging on the part of Dean Young, silence was achieved.

"Folks, let's be realistic. The Russians know – acchhheemm . . . that there is a spacecraft out there somewhere. They know it represents a technological gold mine. I believe we should proactively diffuse any questions whatsoever in our Byzantine friends' minds and that we should: a) share all that we find, and b) ask for one of their own to be trained as Dr. Richards' second."

The reactions to Jung's proposal were predictably all over the map.

Some said, "Tough luck. We have the technology. After all, had not the genius behind the Soap Bubble technology defected to the United States from the bosom of his Mother Russia?"

Others said, "The American-Russian partnership in this venture must be sustained and nurtured and not allowed to go adrift."

After two solid hours of discussion, a common ground still had not been reached, so Dean Young adjourned the meeting with the promise of shortly scheduling another.

* * *

With a growling stomach and with his head hurting from hunger and the dizzying swirl of argumentation still in his head, Richards discarded his slippers, put on his shoes, and then asked a still patiently waiting Ms. Kelly where she would like to go for dinner. As he bluntly stated the situation, "I could eat a horse."

In response, he took her up on a sensible suggestion of a local steak and ale pub within easy walking distance. But before they left, Richards begged Ms. Kelly for a couple of aspirins to help kill his crushing headache. Efficiently producing several varieties, Richards downed two that he recognized.

Then she teased, "Well, Dr. Richards, your credit account is really piling up now, isn't it? Just how do you intend to make good on your 'arrears'?"

Hearing the pun with a tired smile and a wink, Richards devilishly whispered, "While I was overseas, I learned a lot."

CHAPTER XVIII

The Teleconference

One month to the day after Piankoff's funeral, a special satellite teleconference took place. As had occurred twice in the past, a call was made to the United States Air Force, who then generously provided the secure uplink between the two parties. Why the United States Air Force? Because they owned this particular satellite and its extraordinary software package. As for why the Air Force Chief of Staff was so amenable to lending out his expensive high-tech toys, he craftily reasoned that it could be used again in the future. Besides, the man was willing to traffic in the currency of political favors for those who wished to listen in. Consequently, the zoomie boss knew how to reply with a smartly stated "Yes, sir!" whenever such unique requests for secure communication arrangements arrived on his desk from such interesting and well-connected clients.

As for those interesting and well-connected clients, which were comprised of two panels of scientists located half a world apart, the entire event still remained something of a real time technological wonder. The Air Force's simultaneous voice recognition and translation software made for considerable ease in communications. The only difference was that the software had been significantly enhanced as a result of the previous two meetings. This fact neither party would be made aware of. Just that their conversations would seem to flow smoother and without any noticeable time lags as the translation software struggled to connect the dots and decipher all the contextual idioms.

For quite some time the ability to discuss important issues face-to-face, across vast distances and multiple time zones, had been a commonplace among high powered business circles. This, however, was not the case among the scientific principals of competing nation states, who were far more accustomed to physical contact and the protocols provided by academic conferences. But as with all such physical meetings, usually planned long sometimes even years in advance, the secure satellite teleconference offered immediacy and a quick circumnavigation of such sticky issues as jetlag, security, and conflicting schedules. The only real difficulty for the panelists, and in particular the Russians, remained the starkness of the video camera's lens and its glowing red dot. This last was not so much an issue among the relatively relaxed and gregarious Americans, but for the Russian principals, individuals who prided themselves on their faceless anonymity, the presence of the video camera represented a considerable challenge and almost cultural intrusion.

On the American panel in Chicago sat three individuals. Professor Emeritus John Milson, Egyptologist, cultural and historical consultant, sat to the camera's left. Dr. Paul Young, economist, university dean, financial liaison, and *de facto* representative of the Philology Annex, sat center stage. And then there was Professor Ernest Jung, physicist and expert in quantum mechanics, who sat to the camera's right.

Hands, and what people do with them while waiting for something, whether trivial or important, reveal a lot. Milson feigned disinterest if not total boredom, while he rested his chin in the palm of his right hand and rhythmically thrummed the conference table with the fingertips of his left. Young's precisely folded hands betrayed his conservative Anglican and prep school upbringing. Jung expertly twirled his pen with his left hand, while he imagined what Fedorov's successor, Rosovec, looked like. Rumor had it that he had the young looks of a lady-killer.

Opposite the American panel sitting halfway around the world in Moscow sat the three heavy weights of the Russian Ministry of Science. Academician Stefan Rosovec, the new Director of the Advanced and Theoretical Technological Research Institute sat to the camera's left. Academician Vasily Alexandrovich Ostrogorsky, Director of Theoretical Biology for the Russian Academy of Sciences, was ensconced to the camera's right. Lastly, Karlov Drazinzka, the Head of ultra-secret Special Projects Division, was positioned dead center. Unlike their American colleagues, two of three Russians were settled back deeply in their padded chairs, exuding an air of confidence. After all, they had been through this twice before. Only the new kid, Rosovec, sat forward as this was his first such teleconference. Needless to say as the technology guru, he was very eager to see his contemporary on the other side. Would it be Borov himself? Besides, he was as curious to see how good the satellite transmission and its translation software really were, for that would give him a good yardstick of what he really was up against.

As the appointed time arrived, two monitors half a world apart suddenly sprang to life and in the process caught the Russians talking among themselves. Seeing that they were live, Dr. Young, as had become custom, began by clearing his throat to alert the Russians. Once so noted, he then started the meeting with a broad smile of greeting in his clipped, rehearsed British delivery.

"Welcome, gentlemen. It's certainly good to see you again. I am Dr. Young, and I am here to represent the general interests of the Philology Annex. To my right is Dr. John Milson, Professor Emeritus of Egyptology at our own Near Eastern Institute. And to my left is Professor Ernst Jung of the Department of Physics, also a member of our institution."

The American introduction earned a look of a shock on the Russians' faces as Young's voice boomed at them, for the technician at their end had the volume turned up quite high on their monitor. Realizing swiftly what was amiss, Rosovec quickly gestured off-camera and the volume was immediately turned down to a more comfortable level. Regaining their composure, Karlov Drazinzka responded first with the guarded smile of a hunting tiger.

"Fellow Academicians. Indeed, indeed it is very good to see you again as well. As you already know, Academician Vasily Alexandrovich Ostrogorsky, Director of Theoretical Biology for the Russian Academy of Sciences, is seated to my left. To my right, I wish to formally introduce to you Academician Stefan Rosovec, our new Director of the Advanced and Theoretical Technological Research Institute. He has been recently appointed to replace Academician Fedorov, who due to the stress of his advanced age, chose to retire from the duties of his arduous post. I, of course, am Karlov Drazinzka, the head of a subordinate division of the Russian Academy of Sciences."

During the course of these introductions six pairs of eyes stared hard at one another, measuring, calculating, and noting any new wrinkles, gray hair, or any other detail from the previous meetings. At the very same time, three very black organizations, two American and one Russian, had their in-house psychology teams watching and recording as well. All were looking for any edge or advantage.

But despite Young's carefully prepared and distributed agenda, it was Drazinzka who initiated the open discussion. He knew precisely what he was doing. He was taking control. Besides, he loved stubbing the nose of that damn Brit! And from the look on his face, he had already succeeded.

"Fellow Academicians. As you are probably no doubt aware, one month ago, in fact on this very day, Major General Alexander Piankoff was buried with full honors. Our panel wishes to thank Academician Milson and Dr. Richards for attending that memorable event. I wish to say that Dr. Richards' gift to the deceased, and by extension to the entire Russian nation, was most graciously delivered and accepted."

A brief pause ensued as the Russian coughed softly into his fist, as was his habit, and then he took the bit squarely in his teeth.

"With Major General Piankoff's passing, we believe that a need for his replacement has arisen. To address this need, we have already identified several promising candidates suitable for your review. We presume and hope, of course, that Dr. Richards will play a significant role in the candidate's preparation and training. Is that not so?"

Young's face went rigid with annoyance, while Jung appeared to be thoughtfully digesting the opening gambit. Milson could only smile, which prompted him to innocently ask, "Are your candidates male or female?"

Milson's question made all three of the Russian's sit bolt upright. Sharing quick glances among themselves, Ostrogorsky responded, "Why, Dr. Milson, they are all male." Pausing and then stating with certitude, "As it should be for such hazardous duty."

Milson began to mentally dig in for the big blow that he knew was about to happen.

"Gentlemen," he chided, "Come now. Our armed forces currently have female fighter pilots that land on naval aircraft carriers. You have female cosmonauts. But that aside, let us consider for one moment the field advantages of a male-female team."

As Milson began making his points, counting them off on the fingers of this right hand, the Russians were staring at him with a mixture of thoughtfulness from Rosovec, disdain and head-shaking mirth from Drazinzka, and goggle-eyed disbelief from Ostrogorsky.

Milson concluded, "And that gentlemen, is why a male-female field team is far more flexible and formidable, especially in the cultural context of ancient Egypt."

Rosovec, with a sly and tight-lipped smile, was the only Russian capable of finding his tongue and so he replied to Milson's logical presentation.

"Dr. Milson. I do believe that your suggestion has made quite an impression on me and my fellow colleagues. May I suggest that we adjourn for, say, fifteen minutes?"

Nods of assent were seen silently bobbing from the Chicago panel and then the feed from Moscow was abruptly killed.

Taking control indeed! That damn Milson truly is a most formidable one, thought Drazinzka with a grudging smirk of admiration for the cagey intellect of the man.

A female he wants? And the advantages he then enumerates! Well, I have just the hellion in mind to bedevil them with!

CHAPTER XIX

1980 North Sakkara

Without doubt, the vast majority of the West is nuts over anything Egyptian, be it their mummies, pyramids, tombs, temples, and even "authentically aged" Egyptian artifacts courtesy of the digestive juices of a goose's gut. But by far Egyptian archaeology is the sexiest of propositions. Yet it is one that requires a serious commitment of financial capital to underwrite a full scale excavation, its publication, the payroll for its professional field staff and that of local labor, much less the highly charged political acquisition of an archaeological permit. In short, it is an undertaking not for the fainthearted. Financially, such monies typically come from only a handful of recognized philanthropic sources. These sources have annual budgets, are deluged annually with a myriad of grant proposals, must be wooed with appropriate documentation, credentials, even personal interviews, and oftentimes depend upon "expert outside evaluators" to help determine a project's merit. Additionally, these evaluators are sometimes not objective at all – being more interested in settling an old, petty academic score or establishing some arcane, irrelevant ivory tower benchmark. Then, of course, there is the issue of the extraordinary time lag between the submission of a project proposal and the granting institution's final decision. The entire proposal process from project inception to actual go-ahead can be best described as glacial. In short, the successful acquisition of timely emergency funds for an archaeological project that is underway has all the chance of a snowball in hell.

* * *

Unfortunately, this dire financial situation was all too real to the senior staff members of the Horemheb excavation. True enough, by the tail end of the 1979 season, the team had successfully cleared the shaft from Pillared Hall N and had broken through to uncover the burial chamber of Horemheb's second wife, Mutnedjemet, who unfortunately was not found within. Nevertheless, the find was historically significant as it did contain within its disturbed debris a hieratic text in an empty wine jar that dated to the thirteenth year of Horemheb's reign.

As for van der Boek's late-breaking discovery, it was thought best to leave it well enough alone until the 1980 campaign – the last fully funded season of the excavation. In preparation for that anticipated push, van der Boek and the team did manage to fully clear Pillared Hall N of all its stacked debris by the end of March. The effort had been herculean.

With the last season about to begin, the senior staff met to discuss their options. With the surface epigraphic work completed, they decided to economize and leave those two members home, reasoning that if something significant appeared they could be readily flown in. Given that the mystery plaster was their sole focus, local labor was cut down from the previous five to two, another economy. Until needed, they would be usefully involved in the directed restoration of the complex's many papyri-form columns. In all, the staff agreed they should be in good financial shape, unless something really unexpected was encountered.

* * *

On the first day of the season and under the familiar glare of the halogen lamps, van der Boek began to pick away at the plaster camouflage before him. That he was excited and tense was an understatement. Having left this treat behind since last year had been like leaving a Christmas present unopened. In outline, the area of his investigation proved to be a rectangular ovoid roughly about a meter wide by two tall. After forty minutes of gentle poking and prodding around its parameter, the archaeologist noted a layering to the plaster in one corner. With a dental pick, he was able to tease away a palm-sized piece intact. What he found beneath the outer plaster was a second layer. Just peeking out at him were the curved edges of a cartouche-like seal that had been stamped into the once still damp plaster of the second layer!

With his heart beating at a terrific rate, he unconsciously breathed in his mother tongue, *"Mein Gott!"*

Showing what he had found to his two nearby colleagues, the electricity in Pillared Hall N rose dramatically and it wasn't coming from the floodlights.

Van der Boek stopped the work and several photographs of this first intrusion were dutifully made, while his mind and imagination raced ahead.

Could it be, he furiously thought, *that this plasterwork has not been disturbed?*

With the photos taken, van der Boek took up his position and began again at his teasing at the corner and was quickly rewarded with another clunk of plaster – this one the size of a legal pad of paper broken across its center. Holding and supporting this piece and allowing it to fall slowly away as if holding a newborn baby, van der Boek tenderly laid it aside as his colleagues gasped. Looking at the exposed section of the second plaster layer, the fair-haired Hollander could do nothing but gasp too. For before him three and a half perfectly preserved stamp seals of the Chief Guardian of the Memphis Necropolis were staring back at him.

Seals pristine in their form. Seals never before seen intact, in situ, *as they were here.*

Again all work stopped as the photographic record with scale continued, during which van der Boek dared to speak what was on his mind. When he did, he did so in an emotional way. His accent thickening with excitement, he shook his head.

"Never zince de dizcovery of Tutankhamen's tomb hat ever zuch necropolis Siegeln been found bevor und in zuch pristine kondition."

With that, van der Boek returned to his teasing of the first plaster layer. In all, the clearing of the camouflaging plaster layer took him some two hours. When he was finished, it was again photographed. In all, he counted fifty-six individual ovoid necropolis seals. All were intact and perfect. Nowhere was there in the second plaster layer any evidence of intrusion.

Stopping at this point, he and his two colleagues took a break and emerged from the entrance of Shaft IV grinning from ear to ear with success and teenage-like energy. This last immediately infected the rest of the team. Permission was granted for peeks, look-sees, and personal photos next to the find.

While those trips were underway, van der Boek and his colleagues – the Frenchman Legrand and Duncan, a Scotsman – started plotting out a scheme for the intact removal of the unique, stamped, but extremely delicate plaster layer. Making a latex mold was discarded as being too risky. Finally, after much discussion in the shade, drinking water, and just drying out in the breeze, Duncan suggested the construction of a simple, light wooden frame that would support the plaster with a layer of soft packing foam pressed up against it. It was a nice idea, but how then were they to cut out the plaster's backing to, in essence, lift it forward against the supporting foam? Deadlocked, they finally settled on a less than perfect method, but one that was practical. The trio agreed on cutting a narrow but deep channel to outline the entire field of the plaster. Then they would cut similar channels horizontally and vertically between the seal stamps to preserve them. The plan then was to carefully tease and lift out each small section as if the whole was a large jigsaw puzzle. Duncan's idea of a padded frame would be their new temporary home with each section carefully numbered and placed in its original position. And if the scheme did not work marvelously! Best part of all, Legrand, the team's principal photographer, chronicled on film the entire step-by-step process that took a day and a half of incredibly tedious work.

* * *

With the delicate plaster fragments removed, logged, numbered, photographed, packed in foam, and sealed in handy sealed containers, van der Boek now faced the real work – the breaking down of the entrance's plaster- and rock-filled plug. In the excitement of the moment, the temptation to swing away full force with a pickax came to mind, but was discarded by the sober Hollander. Instead, his handpick would have to make do. And in an effort to prevent a rubble cave-in, he began high, nibbling at first here and there, looking for an opportunistic purchase. With Legrand at the ready with his cameras and Duncan clearing away the fallen material with a large sweep brush into a canvas bucket between van der Boek's momentary pauses to rest, a clear dent was being made at about eye level. What the threesome did not and could not know was whether the thickness of the rubble and plaster plug was measured in inches or feet. All they could do was go slow.

* * *

Meanwhile, as van der Boek was busy teasing away with his handpick, another senior staff member was busy transporting the thirty-eight individually boxed plaster seal fragments to the Cairo National Museum. Backing into the loading dock on the western side of that pink structure, the driver was surprised to see that a small reception was awaiting her, all wearing big grins on their faces.

To Ingrid Bockmann, the team's surveyor, geologist, and occasional medic, the shock was almost too much, for there was the museum's director, his beaming secretary and daughter, and the museum's chief curator of restoration and preservation, Dr. Ahmed Rashid. Having depressed the safety brake and shut down the Range Rover's diesel motor, Bockmann greeted the trio in her best Arabic as several of the museum staff in white lab coats appeared out of nowhere with a trolley cart. With the fragments swiftly unloaded from the back of the Rover and whisked inside under the protection of the museum's roof, only now could the native from Leiden finally breathe a sigh of relief.

"Very well done," said the kindly chief curator to his staff at the end of the unloading, who then dismissed himself and disappeared to escort the precious remains to his conservation laboratory.

"Dr. Bockmann," the booming voice of the tall director said.

"How goes the breakthrough?"

* * *

Van der Boek had removed a foot of plaster and debris from the upper third of the entrance's plug, and still from the sound of his handpick, there was much more to go.

* * *

"Well, when I left about two hours ago, Professor van der Boek was just beginning to work at the upper third of the plug. The problem is, we do not know how thick it is, so he is proceeding slowly to prevent a cave-in that may damage whatever is on the other side."

Listening and nodding with approval at the methodology employed and van der Boek's obvious restraint, the director could not be more pleased. Then remembering where he was.

"My apologies, Dr. Bockmann, may I offer you some shade and perhaps a glass of cool juice as well?"

"Gladly!" said the thirsty and relieved geologist.

* * *

Now having removed the lower two-thirds of the plug to about a foot as well, van der Boek called for some photographs before he began again with his probing. Legrand's task completed and the removal of the debris accomplished by Duncan and three energetic graduate students, the Hollander began yet again and this time was heard an encouraging sound that distinctly sounded hollow. Turning to his two colleagues he tapped several times more for their benefit and received two big grins and one thumbs-up in return. Working on the spot in question, friable plaster and nugget-sized rock began to cascade down onto van der Boek's boots, first in a trickle and then in clumps. Stopping, he then grabbed the newly exposed end of a bread loaf-sized block and began working it gently back and forth. Then he pulled it out. More light debris spilled forth, but in place where the block had been, now a black void appeared.

"You're through, Willy!" whispered Duncan.

"You are correct. Monsieur Legrand, if you please." The archaeologist gestured with a polite pivot of his body and extended hand.

"Allow me to be the first to congratulate you, *mon ami*," Legrand whispered around his Canon camera body as he flashed three bracketed shots for posterity.

"Here, here," Duncan punctuated with enthusiasm.

Unclipping his hand torch from his wide military belt, van der Boek then breathed, "Vell, here ve go."

He peered in through the gap with the light held tightly against his right temple.

Duncan, unable to contain himself, was the first to speak. "Well, Willy? What do you see?"

Silence.

Then Legrand, "So, Willy, what do you see?"

Silence, and then the Hollander spoke softly. "Gentlemen, I see vonderful dings."

Turning to face them with a big grin and glittering eyes, van der Boek said, "Gentlemen. I have always vanted to repeat dhat famous line of Carter's, but truth be known, ve have ourselves a big problem."

Two faces totally fell at the Hollander's last statement.

"Vhat I have just seen vill probably take us several seasons to klear, much less pack off to Kairo for preservation."

"What!" Duncan and Legrand simultaneously exclaimed.

"Drs. Legrand und Duncan, if you don't belief me, dhen just look vor yourselves," said an emotional van der Boek as he extended his hand torch.

After about five minutes of ooing and ahhing, van der Boek called for an air break. As they ascended the ladder of Shaft IV, the jubilant trio emerged once again with broad grins and goofy smiles to the expectant faces of their teammates overhead. Something else was in their eyes as well, the certain knowledge that they had just made history.

Looking around among the faces now crowding him, van der Boek asked, "Vhere's Ingrid?"

"In Cairo making the delivery," someone offered.

"Vell," the Hollander smirked, "she is going to be disappointed vhen she gets back."

"Why?"

"Because dhen she vill find out dhat she vill have to make several hundret more trips!"

* * *

The next day at dawn the museum director and his daughter arrived at the site. Invited the night before to be the first to enter the chamber, van der Boek had personally removed all of the remaining plaster and rubble from the chamber's entranceway. The archaeologist had laboriously removed, while having placed his hand on the inner side of the plug's remaining debris, everything out piece by piece. The result was a text book clearing. Not a crumble of debris had been allowed to fall into the still pristine chamber.

Alighting from the museum's Land Rover, the director moved gingerly and stiffly while his daughter, dressed smartly in loose-fitting tan slacks and a matching long-sleeved shirt was clearly all business. One look at her worn boots swiftly confirmed that impression. Fluent in Arabic, English, German, and French with a fresh Cambridge PhD in Egyptian philology to her credit, Sharil's training in her first love was impeccable. Ever since she could remember, Sharil had accompanied her father on all of his digs, helped to wash pottery, joined him on many of his far-flung inspections, and singlehandedly rationalized the bureaucracy and operational management of Egypt's cultural jewel, the Cairo National Museum. In many respects she represented the leading edge of a new generation who represented Egypt's future in Egyptology and at the same time threatened the virtual stranglehold of foreign scholarship in the determination of that proud nation's heritage. Besides, Sharil Moussa, age twenty-four, was a devastatingly beautiful woman. Trim and of erect posture, confident and proud, with her shoulder-length blue-black hair trimmed in a pharaonic style with sweeping side wings and simple bangs, to say that she had presence would be an understatement. Besides, she knew it.

Following the traditional greetings, introductions of the entire staff, and handshakes, the museum director then addressed van der Boek before the entire team.

"Professor Dr. van der Boek, again, I wish to express my nation's many thanks for the privilege that you and your fine team have extended to us. The gesture was most respectful and that is something I will never forget. However, as willing as I am to personally see with my own eyes this wondrous accomplishment, I unfortunately cannot. My back will not allow such exertions. So, in my place, I will send Dr. Moussa. As most of you probably know, Dr. Moussa is also my daughter. She is my second set of eyes. So, please allow her to take my place on this most happy of occasions."

Not caring one whit and all smiles, van der Boek without further ado donned his respirator and began his descent into Shaft IV. After some helpful adjustment tips from Ingrid with her respirator, Dr. Moussa soon followed.

I cannot believe, Sharil thought, *how these poor people could stand to work in such uncomfortable headgear! I must not forget to point this out to my father.*

Then down she went.

Her father then turned to Legrand and asked about the goggled respirators.

"Sir, they are necessary as all of the underground passages are very dusty and the slightest movement stirs up veritable clouds. Any digging just makes the situation even worse."

"So," was the museum director's only reply followed by the thought, *I really must ask my daughter about these respirators. Their use still seems a bit extreme to me.*

* * *

For Sharil, just when she thought the initial descent from Shaft IV would never end, she noticed the first hint of the stark glare from the halogen lighting. Now at the bottom of the specially built eighty-five-foot aluminum ladder, Sharil immediately squatted down out of habit and hard experience to survey Pillared Hall N.

This chamber is extremely tight. How did they manage down here?

For his part, van der Boek directed the lone floodlight toward the opposite end of the chamber, while he waited for her crouched down before a black void in the whitewashed background. He had a canvas bucket at his feet. Once oriented, Sharil, being barely five feet even, soon was at the Hollander's side trying to peer into the darkness beyond.

"Now, Dr. Moussa, before we go in, I am first going to check the ceiling for any evidence of cave-in with my hand torch." As he flicked the focused beam this way and that, the pair was treated to a vast expanse of dark blue sky adorned with golden, painted, five-pointed stars.

"It is just like the stars in the Pyramids of Unas and Pepy!" Sharil excitedly exclaimed.

"Und just like die ceiling treatments at Hatshepsut's mortuary temple at Deir el-Bahri," van der Boek expanded.

"Vell, I see no damage vhatsoever." Then forgetting himself. "Dhat's damn gut."

And then remembering just who he was with.

"Ah, excuse me, Dr. Moussa. I meant no offense."

"None taken, meant, or received, Dr. van der Boek. But my name is Sharil. Let us enjoy this moment together."

A bit taken aback by his charge's relaxed and casual demeanor, all that the Hollander could do was nod his agreement.

"All right, Sharil, I am now going to start lighting dies pure bees vax candles in order to illuminate our vay. I do not vish to risk the halogen lighting or their generated heat in der chamber. Besides, dies candles, I have been assured by my colleagues, vill not leave a carbon residue. Now let me light der Erst."

As the flame caught the generous wick of the thick candle, a gloriously pure and soft light began to spread. Much to both archaeologists' delight it reflected off many artifacts before them. Carefully extending the first candle into the chamber, van der Boek peeked around to the left of the entranceway and carefully placed on the floor a numbered paper plate on which he set the candle. Then handing over to Sharil a thick bunch of similarly numbered paper plates, he said.

"Follow me."

Not two steps in van der Boek stopped dead in his tracks for right before him and spread out on the floor was a bouquet of dried flowers. Attached to them lay a roll of papyrus bound with a blue length of yarn. Now taking one step to his right to allow Sharil in as well, he pointed to this poignant testament of emotional loss and thickly whispered, "Klearly, die occupant of dies chamber vas much-loved. Und please note die papyrus. I cannot even begin to imagine vhat sort of text dhat it may contain."

Nodding in agreement, Sharil placed a paper plate to the left of these delicate remains, and van der Boek then passed over another lit candle and the chamber brightened by degrees yet again.

A few feet later, the pair encountered the dried and plated remains of a traditional last meal. In this case, the occupant must have had quite an appetite as there were three dishes in all, which held the desiccated remains of baby back ribs, several kinds of fowl, bread, along with several gummy-like smears that were probably the remains of sauces or cheeses. Next to these were placed two short jars.

"Beer," whispered Sharil.

"Ja," replied her guide in agreement.

With the lighting of the third candle the extent of the chamber was beginning to take shape, so much so that Sharil, carefully stepping to her left, began placing down her remaining paper plates and van der Boek continuously lighted candles until all twelve were blazing.

Now back to where they had started, the pair could take in the entire scene and what a scene it was. Directly in front of them and dominating the chamber that measured about thirty by thirty feet rested a magnificent anthropomorphic coffin with beautifully inlayed hieroglyphics and gilded strips. The entire coffin was a riot of lapis lazuli, gold, carnelian, ebony, and cedar wood. The whole was decorated with delicately painted blue and gold feathered wings.

"What a beautiful *rishi*-type," breathed Sharil through her respirator.

"It is simply quite exquisite," van der Boek choked out in disbelief.

Now peering over the coffin to read the text and name of its owner, Sharil sounded out, "Meryptah, 'beloved of Ptah.' That's a good name for a man buried in the Memphite area, although it is one that I am not familiar with."

"Sharil," van der Boek added. "Dies coffin vas probably not originally his. Look here at these glyphs. His name is a later insertion. I'll just bet dhat dies vas a quick burial, but a quick burial of someone very important, maybe even to the household of Horemheb."

"I agree."

They noted the coffin was elevated above the chamber's floor and that it rested upon four inscribed magical mud bricks.

"Sharil, see des bricks? Day represent die combined powers as defined by Spell 151 in der *Book of the Dead.* Day protected the deceased vom intruders."

Usually sealed in separate recesses in the tombs four walls, the fact that the bricks were in direct contact with the deceased coffin was more evidence of a hasty burial.

To their right were four wicker baskets of bread, about twenty jars of beer and ten of wine. Peering closely, but daring not to touch anything, Sheril the hieratic inscriptions on the beer and wine jars.

"Professor! This is not an intrusive burial! These wine jars came from Horemheb's estate!"

To the left of the chamber neatly set all in a row awaited six pieces of lidded cedar furniture, all inlaid with breathtaking ivory decorations of rosettes, sphinxes, and lions.

"No doubt dhose are storage cabinets of linens, unguents, und personal items," van der Boek surmised. "Literally his packed baggage for the underworld."

While the darkly blue painted ceiling with stars seemed to be absorbing the candle light, the painted light yellow walls seem to glow with a radiant subliminal warmth, walls that were decorated on practically every square inch with scenes from *The Opening of the Mouth* ceremony, *The Judgment of the Individual before Thoth*, *The Weighing of the Heart on the Scales of Maat*, and finally *The Presentation of the deceased before Osiris*, the Lord of the Underworld. But it was when they turned around and faced the fourth wall, the wall that was pierced by their entrance that they were confronted with vertical panel upon vertical panel of densely written, black hieroglyphic text.

"*Mein Gott.* Es ist a biographical text," groaned van der Boek in mixed wonder and awe.

"Indeed, and here is Meryptah's name!" Sheril pointed.

"Vell, I guess ve know who's tomb dhis ist."

While she continued to scan the panels, Sharil began to excitedly exclaim, "And there is Meryptah here, and here again! But there are several others mentioned. Let's see, the Pharaohs Amenhotep III and Amenhotep IV are mentioned as are a certain Piankhotep, a Mayneken, and here's Horemheb as well!"

"I believe dhat it ist time to let de others known vhat ve have found!"

"Yes! Yes, indeed! Let's blow out the candles so that I can tell my father the good news!"

* * *

After the flush of animated description of what the chamber contained and the absolutely pristine condition of the entire find, van der Boek took the opportunity to lead the museum director and his daughter over to their Land Rover and away from all the hubbub of excitement.

"Mr. Director," he began looking directly up into the man's eyes. "You have heard firsthand from Dr. Moussa," he indicated in her direction to make sure of her inclusion, "both of the state and condition of Meryptah's tomb. However, ve do have a rather serious problem. Dhis is our mission's last season, und I do not believe dhat I and my staff can properly klear, record, and transport the tomb's kontents to your museum in only one month's time."

"Professor van der Boek," the director replied. "Granting an extension to your archaeological permit will not be a problem. In fact, we can personally hand you that document in the matter of days for however long you think that you need, and if your estimate is incorrect, then for its re-extension. From what my daughter has told me, your team is one of the best in the field. That said, however, I believe that you face perhaps an even greater obstacle. Is that not so?"

To which van der Boek nodded and flatly stated, "Yes, Mr. Director, my mission indeed does. To be blunt, we have run out of funding, and I will not plunder the publication budget, which is already insufficient as a result of this find. Frankly, we need help."

With a small smile and tinkling eyes the director looked to his daughter, who merely nodded her head in agreement.

"Well, Professor van der Boek, I too will be blunt. Your team has delivered to the Egyptian nation a pristine moment of our history and heritage. Such a gift, for I believe it to be so, will not go unnoticed. Let it be said, clearly, before my own daughter and Allah himself, your mission will not want for funding or resources, on that you have my word."

With that the tall Egyptian extended his massive right hand, which van der Boek eagerly took, even if he temporarily lost sight of his encased in that massive mitt.

CHAPTER XX

Brown-Bag Lunch

"Folks," the departmental supervisor began. "You will note that today's Brown Bag Lunch Talk was by invitation only. For security, this presentation is for a narrow audience and for reasons that will become obvious. Further, this conference room has been reserved from noon to two o'clock, one full hour more than usual. While we will try hold to that schedule, I suspect given the subject matter that we may well go over.

"But before I introduce our special guest today, please help yourselves to the cold sodas and cookies over there on the credenza. Barbara Ann made them, so the limit is four apiece. No more," the man chided, "or I will call security."

Light and polite laughter.

* * *

"Ladies and gentlemen," the departmental supervisor began again. "It's not often that the scientific community here at Wright-Patterson is honored with the presence of someone of our guest speaker's caliber. For that matter, it's also not often that we are even told what we are working."

Raucous laughter, several "Har, hars," and one "No shit!" was voiced.

"But today, I'm told we're going to enjoy both. For Professor Jerry Graves of the Material Sciences Department at the Massachusetts Institute of Technology is with us today to, let's just say, tell a story. Needless to say, Jerry Graves has enjoyed a distinguished career at MIT and truly needs little introduction as many of us in this very room have benefited from him either as a colleague, teacher, or friend. But for the few of you who do not know Jerry Graves, or only know of him by his formidable reputation, then please allow me this delicious opportunity to embarrass the man."

Again good-hearted laughter.

"It has been calculated that if Jerry Graves' *curriculum vitae* was typed double-spaced on one side of 8.5 by 11 inch paper with one inch margins, then its mass, when dropped from the height of three stories, would be sufficient to crack the sidewalk below."

Silence.

"His many awards and medals in materials science alone are cause for reflection as to how could one do so much within the short span of a middle-aged lifetime. To wit: the International Prize for New Materials – American Physical Society; the John Jeppson Medal – American Ceramic Society; the American Chemical Society Award in the Chemistry of Materials; the von Hippel Award – Materials Research Society; and the Robert Lansing Hardy Gold Medal Award – Minerals, Metals, and Materials Society, and the list goes on and on. So, folks, please welcome Professor Jerry Graves."

All stood, cheered, and wildly clapped as the sandy-haired and middle-aged professor from the Iowa wheat belt made his way to the podium. Stopping to carefully adjust his wire-rimmed glasses and notes before him, Graves looked up, warmly smiled, and stated to his small audience of twenty-two eager minds, "Ya' know what Mark Twain used to say. 'If you can't dazzle them with brilliance, then baffle them with bullshit.'"

Another outbreak of laughter, and when it subsided, the folksy professor that did not own a necktie continued, "Unfortunately, what I am about to tell you today may sound like a bunch of dazzle mixed with a whole lot of baffle. Believe it or not, much of hard science is just that. You figure out how a thing works and then suddenly five new questions arise. Call it job security. So it is with my subject today and one way or another all of you have played a part in its analysis – no doubt unknowingly.

"Could someone please dim the lights and turn on the slide projector?"

As the comfortable conference room dimmed, twenty-two chairs creaked as one as their owners unconsciously leaned forward in anticipation.

"Today's subject is SNOWMAN."

A gasping intake of air occurred when the first color slide of a golden butterfly-shaped antennae array and its stalk sharpened into a brilliant focus.

"As you can see, SNOWMAN was found on the Moon. The actual location where it was found is unimportant, but Orbiter I back in 1966 was the first to detect it. NASA initially brushed it off as an OSA, or optical scanning anomaly. But when Orbiter III also picked it up, heads began to spin. Ever curious, NASA then specifically tasked the Ranger III Lander to film it close-up from the Moon's surface. They only missed by some twenty-five meters. It seems that the Lander settled within a small nearby crater, whose lip obscured SNOWMAN from the spacecraft's camera boom. In the end, it was the crew of Apollo XII, who actually went out, retrieved it, and brought it back to Earth for us to study.

"As to who built SNOWMAN, we don't know. What its purpose was, we can only guess at. What those statements really mean, however, is that SNOWMAN's origin is not of this Earth. It's extraterrestrial. It's clearly and unquestionably the product of an alien civilization's technology. Now it is ours to study and try to understand."

As Graves waited for those words to sink in, the room became as silent as a church at midnight on a warm summer Thursday.

"Before I dazzle you with SNOWMAN's many physical characteristics and what they might mean for the future of technology by way of reverse engineering, let's first talk about all that still baffles us.

"It is always good to start with the question: 'Just what's it supposed to do?' Frankly, we're not all that sure, but this beautifully graceful antenna array did face Earth, which suggests some sort of telemetry receiving system. For what purpose, we don't have a clue.

"What we do think we know was how it was planted in the lunar surface. From all indications SNOWMAN seems to have been shot into the lunar surface from near space. Given its size, compact nature, and curious squid-like shovel nose, this seems at the moment to be the best hypothesis. Then once planted, the antenna array was deployed and unfolded as you see in this slide, when we first found it.

"Next slide please.

"Here is NASA Astronaut Captain Pete Conrad standing next to SNOWMAN. For your reference, Pete's five feet six inches tall, give or take. The antenna array is here folded up and stowed within its protective hull casing.

"Next slide please.

"In all, SNOWMAN is almost two meters even in length. Note the shovel-like or squid-like fins at the one end. The shovels at its penetrating end mechanically prevented it from burying itself. The best analogy that I can make is that SNOWMAN was designed to impact kinda' like a toy Jart.

"The obvious next question would be: 'How old is it?' This question alone almost caused several near heart attacks.

"May I have the next slide?"

A golden colored image appeared that had a noticeable demarcation line that ran across it from the upper right-hand corner to the lower left. The upper left-hand quadrant the golden color appeared richer and its surface smoother, while in the lower right quadrant the color was more muted and its surface texture mildly eroded.

"This is a one meg magnification of SNOWMAN's outer hull surface. The diagonal line indicates the lunar soil boundary. The upper left-hand quadrant was buried, the lower right exposed to the sun, hard radiation, and micro-meteoritic impacts. By simple inspection of the hull's discoloration, SNOWMAN has been on the lunar surface for some time. That estimate was arrived at when compared the erosion of Surveyor III's camera housing. And by some time, I mean that the best estimate is several thousand years. That kinda' nixes the paranoid notion of some so-called experts that SNOWMAN is of Nazi or Soviet origin."

Brief, nervous chatter.

"Now for the dazzle part of this presentation.

"The laboratory analysis of SNOWMAN's outer hull casing tells us that it is about one centimeters thick. It was manufactured of an ingenious superlight, titanium-like, metalloceramic composite material. This hull has a definite grain to it as the material itself was deposited through some sort of spinning process – much like binding twine is spun onto a spindle, layer by overlapping layer. So in some respects the hull material seems to have been a fiber-like material that then was fused, most likely in some sort of mold. As for its durability and hardness, the hull material is near diamond-like, composed of a nonconductive, neutral, non-ferric material that does not corrode.

"Next slide please.

"As for the assumed antenna array, it too appears to have been spun and then woven of a similar fiber-like material, but gets its remarkable folding flexibility from thousands upon thousands of mini-links or joints that were found throughout its surface. Here is that array's surface at five hundred power. Magnified this close, its structure looks like a chain-link fence.

"Given that SNOWMAN's total shaft diameter is about eighteen centimeters, and that its hull is about one thick, that leaves an internal core space of some one hundred and ninety centimeters, of which the antenna array takes up only sixty. That leaves plenty of space for SNOWMAN's guts, which is tubular in shape. Upon examination of this space, we found what we think are fused silicon micro-circuitry, threaded bundles of spaghetti-like, flexible material that seem to be connecting cables of some sort, and what we think was once a small power source. One small device was even found containing a magnetic charge. One expert thinks it may represent a recording medium of some kind. In other words, at some point we might be able to rewind it and play it back.

"Needless to say, all of this is brand-new to us and will probably take us decades to reverse engineer, much less completely figure out.

"Would someone please turn on the lights and kill the projector?"

Everyone winced at the abrupt shift in lumens. As for Graves, he left the podium and stood casually before his audience with his hands buried in the pockets of his required tweed sports jacket.

"It is now I that must ask you a favor. Does anyone among this distinguished group have any ideas as to what SNOWMAN might be?"

After a momentary hush at the intellectual challenge, the ideas began to flow forth at an ever quickening pace: a beacon, a remote listening device, a weather tracking device. But it was the suggestion from the most junior member of the group, Roy Peters, which stunned both his former professor and the group as a whole. Roy, who had worked on retrieving samples from the artifact, found himself almost compelled to solve the mysterious purpose for it.

"It's probably a one-time, perhaps emergency, communication's uplink."

"How did you arrive at that conclusion, Roy?"

Graves quietly said with his familiar encouraging tone that gently egged on his former student to continue.

"Mostly because of the level of miniaturization used throughout the artifact. Its tiny power source, circuitry, and small recording device – of course, if that's what it is. All of that aces out a monitoring device that is functioning for a long period of time. It just doesn't have the capacity. But the big thing that really jumped out at me during your presentation was that you said that its circuitry was found fused. That suggested to me that this device was a single use, one-time communication's uplink. The sort of thing that would be dandy to have in an emergency. You know, just like the emergency beacon pods that nuke subs have."

Now realizing the depth of Roy Peter's snap analysis, Graves prodded for him to gone on.

"Okay, Roy. Let's say for the moment that I buy your idea. What about the orientation of SNOWMAN's antenna array? It was pointing toward the Earth's equator."

"That's simple too. Whoever planted SNOWMAN was on Earth. Their message had to first fight its way through the turbidity of Earth's atmosphere to SNOWMAN. Then SNOWMAN uplinked that message in one spasmodic surge of energy into the void of space."

Graves' eyes glazed over in deep thought at the heady ramifications of what his former student just said. Then Peters concluded, "Doc, given what you have told us, that is the only scenario that seems to fit the evidence."

CHAPTER XXI

Amsterdam

With the tomb cleared the year before and all of its contents now safely within the Cairo National Museum, van der Boek finally had the time to think. As with everything in this world, it's the details that really tell the story. In the case of Meryptah's burial there was a raft of them.

The first that jumped out at the archaeologist was the conservative iconography that was consistently displayed throughout the chamber. This theme manifested itself in the rigid adherence to traditional religious scenes. This was indeed odd, since this was a time when the worship of the Aten disk ruled supreme and the divine names of Amen Re, Osiris, and Thoth were being systematically hacked out of public inscriptions. Peculiar was the style of artwork as it too hearkened back to the classical, pre-Amarna Egyptian canon from the early part of the Eighteenth Dynasty.

The second item that the Hollander noted was the growing body of evidence that pointed to the fact that the burial had been a quick one, maybe an unplanned one as well. There were the alterations to the sarcophagus' lid, the total lack of personal or familial heirlooms, personal effects such as weaponry and scribal kits were all missing, as was the display of personal wealth that often accompanies an individual into the afterlife. In van der Boek's opinion, the burial had been a rush job.

Then there was the inscriptional data. All of the seals and hieratic inscriptions that denoted the origin and contents of the many beer jars, wine amphorae, cedar chests, cabinets of household items, and clothing all dated to the occupation of the tomb to just prior to Horemheb's ascension as general under Tutankhamen. Unique was the papyrus of farewell attached to the bouquet of flowers authored by a certain Mayneken, the man's own adopted son.

Last, but hardly least, was Meryptah's own autobiographical text, which in many respects held quite intriguing and heretofore unique information, but again expressed within a traditional and well-known documentary medium.

* * *

It was raining on that June day in Amsterdam, when, in the cozy clutter of his office, surrounded by several philological references, and his massive two-fingered coffee mug, van der Boek finally got to work on finalizing the autobiographical text of Meryptah. Before him he had arranged in sequence the photographic record of the chamber's fourth wall, with its lengthy painted inscription, as well as his own field notes. In all, the inscription took up five panels of text recorded as Panels A through E.

As was van der Boek's habit whenever he worked with a formal hieroglyphic inscription, he followed a simple three-step process of carefully first copying down all of the Egyptian characters before he transliterated them into Latin text. Then with the transliterated text, he began the actual translation into, in this instance, German. After he had learned this process while a graduate student in Munich, it had become rote.

The copying of the Egyptian hieroglyphs was relatively simple in this case as they had all been created as merely outlined figures in black paint without any internal details or added color. There had been no erasures or evidence of tampering. Between each character, van der Boek, writing with a mechanical pencil, left ample room as he spaced them out across the width of his legal pad, skipping every other line. At the top of the page, he wrote the panel's letter that he was working on and in the left margin, the line number of the figures that he was transcribing.

I must remember to note in the commentary the abbreviated style of these characters as yet another indication of the haste in which this tomb was most likely prepared, thought the archaeologist.

Next he began on the transliteration of each Egyptian character into its Latin-lettered equivalent and wrote them down next to their associated glyphs. With that chore completed, van der Boek dived directly into the text by translating all the proper names and nouns he could readily identify. With that done, next was the individual line-by-line analysis, the identification of verbs, prepositions, adjectives, and the structure of the clauses. Only when that was complete could he finally work on the inscription's flow and take on any contextual issues that may have arisen.

After two hours' work, while the last quarter inch of coffee in his mug went stone cold, van der Boek had his first rough draft. While he could identify many stock phrases, he saw that others had been reconstituted, while still others were new and so he flagged them as either rare or unique expressions. He followed an abbreviated version of the universal editorial convention for the translation of ancient documents, so any textual additions as omitted by the author he inserted with angular brackets, and any text supplied as explanatory he inserted with rounded brackets. New or rare expressions he marked with a question mark and some with academic shorthand references.

Panel A:

An offering which [the king gives and] Anubis,|
Who is upon his mountain and in the place of embalming,|
The lord of the necropolis.|
Buried is Meryptah,|
(Meryptah) acolyte (and) priest of the Great God [Amen-Re],|
(Meryptah) first servant of the Great God [Amen-Re] (since) the twentieth year of Nebmare Amenhotep [= Amenhotep III], (Cf. Kees, p. 65.)|
(Meryptah) first prophet of all the gods [of Thebes], (Cf. Kees, p. 83.)|
(Meryptah) manager of the treasury of the Great God's [Amen-Re] House, (Cf. Kees, p. 18, note 3.)|
(Meryptah) falcon flier (?) [Or better flier of falcons? A falconer?], (Rare/new expression. Not listed in either Faulkner, Hannig, or *Wb*!)|
(Meryptah who) first who soared on the winds of Re's warm breath,|
(Meryptah who) [first] who flew on the strong falcon wings of Horus,|
(Meryptah who) [first] falcon teacher (?) of men. [Better falconer of men?] (Rare/new expression. Again not in Faulkner, Hannig, or *Wb*!)|

Panel B:

Meryptah exalted companion to the great house of Neferkheperure Amenhotep [= Amenhotep IV],|
(Meryptah exalted) helper of the creation of new things with the youthful Neferkheperure Amenhotep [= Amenhotep IV],|

(Meryptah exalted) advisor to the *sia* (?) [wisdom or intellect?] of the youthful Neferkheperure Amenhotep [= Amenhotep IV].|

Panel C:

Meryptah confidant (and) advisor to Piankhotep,|
magician (and) priest (Rare/new expression. Not in Kees, Faulkner, Hannig, or *Wb*!) of the second rank to the god of the White Wall [Ptah],|
(Piankhotep) master of (?) [mentor of?] Mayneken,|
(Piankhotep) ambassador of Neferneferu Nefertiti,|
(Piankhotep who) struck down He-Who-Is-In-His-Grimness. (Note Set determinative! Cf. Borghouts, Spell 59, for parallel.)|

Panel D:

Meryptah confidant (and) advisor (and) hereditary father of Mayneken,|
(Mayneken) servant of the second rank to the god the White Wall [Ptah], (Name not in Kees,)|
(Mayneken) powerful warrior marked by the claws of a dying she-lion,|
(Mayneken) royal ambassador to the Lady of the Two Lands Neferneferu Nefertiti,|
(Mayneken who) struck down the rebels who worshipped He-Who-Is-In-His-Grimness. (Again note the use of the Set determinative! Cf. Borghouts, Spell 59, for parallel.)|
(Mayneken who) struck down He-Who-Is-In-His-Grimness. (See above.)|

Panel E:

Meryptah in his tomb, (which is) in the good Western Desert.|
(Meryptah) confidant (and) advisor to the great house of the Overseer of the Granaries of Thebes (and) Hereditary Prince Horemheb [= Djerer-Kheprure Horemheb],|
(Horemheb who) caused this tomb to be built within his own precinct,|
(Horemheb who) did so at the command of his hereditary brother Mayneken,|
[In order] to protect the form and possessions of Meryptah,|
Who has gone to his *ka*.|

(As) for any people who would enter this tomb unclean, (and) do something evil to it,|
There will be judgment against them.|

Having read and reread his draft over several times after checking and re-checking his references, van der Boek sat back with a sigh and began to think deep thoughts.

Yes, he said to himself. *Yes, indeed. This Meryptah was very well connected. But then again, why wouldn't he be as the high priest of Amen Re, whom Kees believed may have been the brother of Ptahmesou, the high priest of Ptah in Memphis and son of the Lower Egyptian vizier Thutmose?*

But would he have enjoyed much clout during the Amarna Revolution? He chided himself before his focus returned to his analysis.

What is the significance of all this detail about falconry?

You know, Willy, he again began to muse. *This inscription is not strictly autobiographical, but is more a prosopographical listing, a who's who if you will, of those important to Meryptah and by association who might have been helpful to Horemheb at the tail end of the turbulent Amarna Period. It is curious that he chooses to mention so extensively these other individuals, who by their mere association with Horemheb must each be of considerable significance in their own right. And Meryptah even lists them before mentioning his own association with Horemheb!*

So, if I understand the internal chronological organization of this text correctly, then this Piankhotep is older than Mayneken. Mayneken, meanwhile, the hereditary brother of Horemheb, commands him to include Meryptah within his family tomb. So that makes Mayneken probably Horemheb's elder brother. And so that makes Horemheb the youngster of these four, all who must be considered traditionalists, conservatives, and thus outlaws to Akhenaten's Amarna Revolution.

As for the conservative iconography of his tomb's decoration, Meryptah's status as the high priest of Amen Re easily explains that. And then there are these two mentions of ambassadorships to Queen Nefertiti herself! Now that's an interesting tidbit. Apparently, Mayneken inherited the position from his master, Piankhotep.

Now sitting back and rubbing his temples in thought, the Egyptologist asked himself, *Just who were Piankhotep and Mayneken?*

Men who are so casually mentioned in the same breath by a first servant of Amen Re in association with the Amarna pharaoh, his wife and queen, and a hereditary prince?"

And then, *Who is "He-Who-Is-In-His-Grimness?*

Just who the hell is that? Clearly, it was someone who was so reviled that their name was not even enunciated. And again, that epithet is associated with a Set determinative, implying some sort of association with that most evil of the Egyptian gods.

Well, whoever he was, he was surely hated. That is for sure.

Pause, and then a light bulb began to burn brightly.

Willy, he mentally gasped. *Could it be that "He-Who-Is-In-His-Grimness" is none other than Akhetaten himself? If so, then that would make Piankhotep and Mayneken his assassins!*

Scratching his head before he continued chewing on this mental checklist, van der Boek continued, *And what is this line about Piankhotep being a "magician and priest of the god Ptah? I just don't get that one.*

But even more to the point, why did Mayneken feel the need to have Meryptah included in Horemheb's own family mortuary complex?

In conclusion, the archaeologist's mind screamed, Mein Gott! *Just vhat did dhis man do to earn such a burial?*

CHAPTER XXII

A 1994 RAvMH

The people who name things that they discover are an ever so human bunch. For example, the Latin nomenclature for the cataloging of biological species, first devised during the Enlightenment's scientific revolution by the Swedish botanist Karl von Linné, still holds sway today. The rules are relatively straightforward. Devise a name that either describes a salient feature – such as a big nose, or the place that it was found – like the Neander Valley, or just Latinize the name of the discoverer – as with John Brown.

Naming conventions within astronomy, however, are ever so much more interesting, since much has been borrowed from man's classical past, when astronomy and astrology were one in the same. Constellations, stars, planets, moons, identifiable features on the moon and Mars, all carry on this classical heritage. But there are only a finite number of classical names available, and so occasionally famous personalities find their names affixed to celestial objects, topographical features, and the like. One can also detect from time to time playfulness among the astronomical community. A good example was Asteroid 4179 (formerly 1989 AC) that was coined Toutatis by its discoverer Christian Pollas. The whimsy here is that the asteroid is named after the Celtic or Gallic god "whose name is invoked often in the well-known comic book series *Les Aventures d'Asterix*, set in ancient Gaul." Clearly, the chuckle is very French, but other such arcane examples could just as easily be trotted out.

* * *

It began on May 13th, 1994, when a second-year graduate student from the University of Hawaii's Institute for Astronomy noted optically a possible track of a new asteroid. Working initially from a series of photographic plates taken by her thesis director from the ten meter Keck I Observatory atop Mauna Kea, three things came to mind.

What am I going to call it? Does this represent a publication opportunity? And most important of all, am I looking at a possible thesis topic?

What Becky Hildebrand did not know at the time was she had hit the veritable jackpot. After she had dutifully logged her findings in the Jet Propulsion Laboratory's database as A(steroid) 1994 RAvMH – her full initials – it would not be until five months later that two friends, one in Japan and the other in Italy, could confirm her sighting. They also were able to provide her with critical data from which she could begin to calculate the asteroid's orbital path, or establish even if it had one.

The variables to be considered and dense mathematics behind the extrapolation of a celestial body's peripatetic meanderings require powerful computers and even more powerful programming. Fortunately for Becky, she had both at her disposal. What she had to do was to connect the dots and draw a line, all while she and the object were both moving spatially and over time. Then, once this rough three-dimensional mathematical plot had been established, the next set of variables regarding gravitation had to be factored in that might perturb the course of that theoretical, mathematical plot.

Even using the big Cray II at Livermore, it took twenty-two minutes of run time – a near eternity in a world calculated in nanoseconds – to generate Becky's first plot. Now, it was up to her to interpret its meaning. After she had hovered over the data, Becky's brows began to furrow in recognition.

Wow, this sucker is really moving! Just on the basis of the three positions and five months' time, this baby has really covered a lot of ground. I wonder . . . She flipped back and forth between several pages of data output and another thought came to mind.

Given its current velocity and course, assuming nothing else perturbs it, besides its expected resonance with Jupiter, it should be in our immediate neighborhood in mid- to late-2012.

Wow, that's really cooking!

After more flipping back and forth of the green bar printout, some dismay if not disbelief began to creep into Becky's mind.

The extrapolation puts A 1994 RAvMH into a near perfect match with the plane of the Earth's orbit in 2012, but the question is – where will the Earth be when it passes by? And, of course, by how far?

Then reaching up and taking out a folder marked "Orbital Intersections," she thumbed through it and realized that Asteroid 4179 Toutatis was on a similar course, but ahead of hers. In short, hers and Toutatis would be in the Earth's neighborhood at nearly the same time. It was just that hers was closing in on Toutatis and Earth at a significantly higher rate.

At this point in her analysis, Becky knew that she needed to have another pair of eyes take a look at the data – maybe several. If she was right, and she had seen plenty of similar data elsewhere within the NEAT database, then she, Rebecca Ann von Müller Hildebrand had found herself a real live near-Earth asteroid! That meant publication, and if her instincts were dead on, a for sure thesis topic.

Heck, maybe I might even be able to beg some radar time on the Goldstone and Arecibo arrays as well!

Becky also knew she needed to come up with a name for her asteroid, something dignified, something with significance, and after some thought, the perfect name came to her. Being third generation Hawaiian, her great-granddaughter, a German trade representative who fell in love with the Big Island, settled down and shrewdly sank all of his assets into a sizable chunk of land in what is now north Hilo. This meant that the asteroid's name had to be something Hawaiian. And since she discovered her swift celestial body – virtually speaking that is – at the Keck I Observatory atop Mauna Kea, logic demanded that the asteroid be dubbed Poliahu – the Hawaiian goddess of snowy Mauna Kea.

* * *

Four months and several more observations later, Becky was urged by her thesis director to publish what she had.

"Beck, gosh darn it, don't sit on this any longer. It's just too hot. You've done your due diligence. Now have the guts to let the rest of the astronomical community in on Poliahu. Their observations will only help fine-tune your own brilliant analysis."

He then added for emphasis, "This paralysis-by-over-analysis shit has got to end now!"

* * *

“Good evening, ladies and gentlemen,” began the beautifully coiffed television news anchor.

“It is not often that we can offer you an important news story that has yet to happen, but in eighteen years’ time, in September of 2012, scientists say that the Earth will be visited by not one, but two near-asteroid flybys. The first was discovered back in 1989 by a French scientist, the second just this year by our own Rebecca Ann Hildebrand, an astronomy student at the University of Hawaii.”

Shift to a still shot of the Keck I Observatory atop Mauna Kea with the narrative continuing.

“Here, atop the volcano Mauna Kea on Hawaii’s Big Island, astronomers can see with their powerful telescopes far into the heavens.”

Shift to a split screen video interview with a smiling and tanned young face with a wall of blinking and important-looking electronic gear in the background on the right, the anchor in her New York studio on the left.

“So, Rebecca . . .”

“No, just Becky, if you don’t mind.”

The anchor, visually a bit taken aback at being interrupted during her all-important airtime, corrected with a hardened smile.

“Oh, okay, Becky. Why did you name the asteroid Poliahu?”

“Oh, that’s easy. Poliahu is the Hawaiian snow goddess of Mauna Kea. Since I’m native Hawaiian and first to discover the asteroid’s trail from atop Mauna Kea, *voilà*, Poliahu!” The attractive young woman smiled back.

“Oh, how interesting,” blathered on the anchor, who had never before considered that a native Hawaiian could connote anything other than a brown-skinned Polynesian wearing a grass skirt, much less one using a French phrase. Finally rallying, she looked down at her notes and continued, “And about this asteroid you discovered, just how close to the Earth will it come? I mean, will we be able to see it in the night sky?

“Will you be able to see it with a naked eye? Oh, no. It’s a dark asteroid. It’s not a comet,” the young smiling face corrected. “But how close it will come to Earth, well it is an NEA for sure. That stands for ‘near-Earth asteroid.’”

Gritting out a smile through her almost locked jaws, the announcer then asked, “Well, Becky, just how close is close?”

At the question, Becky's head tilted slightly and her eyes squinted in thought before she replied, "Well, that is a very good question. It could come as close to the Earth as five one-thousandths of an AU, or astronomical unit."

Upon realizing and seeing the interviewer's lack of comprehension, Becky elaborated, "In other words, about twice the distance between the Earth and the moon at perigee, or about 740,000 kilometers. That's about 460,000 miles. And in astronomical terms, that's very, very close. Very close indeed."

"Oh, how interesting," was the glazed reply.

CHAPTER XXIII

Cheyenne Mountain

Second Lt. Charles M. Perry, U.S. Air Force, reran the taped television interview of Becky Hildebrand with mixed feelings. As a member of Air Force Space Command's research staff stationed at Peterson Air Force Base in Colorado Springs, and himself a PhD geek in astronomy, his job was to stay current with the field and maintain cordial relations with his civilian counterparts. Charlie Perry played his role as an old shoe very well, who poked around at conferences, gathered all the good gossip that he could, attended the papers and socials, and occasionally made recruiting recommendations to the AFSPC. In short, he was a mole. That fact did not, however, prevent Charlie from suffering a tinge of academic jealousy with Becky's way cool discovery and the Hawaiian native's comfy billet.

It just doesn't seem fair, he thought.

As soon as he had devoured her article in *Science*, he had informed his supervisor about the object in question and had strongly recommended a deep and near space radar probe of it. To his surprise, he was politely informed that he must have been deadheading it, as a "Hot Rush" requisition was already in the works for just that. Shocked and red-faced that someone had beaten him to the punch, Perry then realized that someone out at Livermore must have flagged it. After all, Hildebrand had used their Cray.

Duh!

That duty accomplished and out of the way, Perry knew Rebecca Ann von Müller Hildebrand was blessed with brains to burn. Her two coauthors with the Japanese and Italian research addresses had supplied her with positional data only. The true legwork had been Hildebrand's and hers alone.

Brains and beauty, but so far away, he thought, shaking his head a bit wistfully. *Wouldn't ya' know. It just didn't seem fair.*

* * *

When requested, the material and technological assets available to the AFSPC could be described as simply awesome. Since the organization's inception in 1985, and with many years to work out all of the kinks, stuff happened and very quickly. Hot Rush requisitions received notice and were granted priorities that bumped, pushed, and jostled other projects aside, whether they were in process or not. As the pulses began to return from no fewer than five radar telescopes, which included those at the fully steerable Goldstone and Arecibo arrays with their southerly declination – the other three units remained closely held private facilities – the Hildebrand analysis was confirmed, expanded, and extrapolated upon.

The tracking data taken from these five points proved that Hildebrand had been correct in postulating a deep space origin for the object. Its current course was indeed as straight as a string given the known observational limitations. Drawing that line in space and time did make the asteroid's path coincident with the Earth's orbital plane, again supporting the Hildebrand analysis. What the new data indicated was that the near-Earth approach of Asteroid 4179 Toutatis and Poliahu would almost occur at the same time – late September of 2012.

This fact prompted one of the AFSPC data analysts to comment, "You know, it's almost like Toutatis and Poliahu are running down the same railroad track, except that Poliahu is the express and Toutatis is the local."

Initially, the asteroid's data was a real hash due to what was initially interpreted as the radar scattering qualities of its surface. Upon subsequent inspection, it was discovered Poliahu was not one asteroid, but five bodies, all seemingly spinning around a central axis and the whole tumbling willy-nilly through space. Several experts believed that they saw in this configuration the "remnants of the accretion of planetesimals," or a rogue planet in formation. Meanwhile, the radar returns indicated Poliahu's "density as homogeneous or its inhomogeneities mimic the inertia tensor of a homogeneous body." In other words, the asteroid's many parts appeared to be made of the same material. Judged a dark, poorly reflective S-Class asteroid, its mineralogical composition was guessed at as being similar to stony-iron meteorites. The spin and tumbling of Poliahu's five parts, however, remained "one of the strangest rotational states yet observed in the solar system" and in some respects made the previously considered exotic tumbling of Toutatis look simplistic in comparison.

CHAPTER XXIV

Cairo National Museum

If the display cases and public areas of Egypt's crown cultural jewel, the Cairo National Museum, could be characterized as overcrowded, dusty, finger-smudged, and poorly lit, then it would be fair to expect that this institution's Department of Restoration was technologically impoverished. This judgment, while harsh, accurately represented reality within that third world country in 1982.

To consider what the urgent priorities were for the Egyptian nation and its budget during the previous decades of the twentieth century was to recognize a sublime irony. Prime among that country's needs was the completion of the Aswan High Dam, and with it, the electrification of the entire valley. Once that was established, then came the digging of fresh water wells, the extension of the nation's irrigation, and the construction of a unified sanitation system for Cairo. Next came the wholesale construction of roads and the establishment of a basic telephone infrastructure. Then, wonder of wonders, the foreign importation of expensive agricultural fertilizers became necessary for the first time in that nation's long and storied history.

Why?

Because the annual Nile flood no longer occurred and with it the delivery of that river's rich and fertile silt.

Why?

The Aswan High Dam's base trapped the silt at the northern end of Lake Nassar. Finally, and this effect would not be felt for almost a generation, with the formation of Lake Nassar the water table of the North African plateau rose by some 150 meters, effectively placing Egypt's most prize cultural possessions at risk.

Why?

Because the North African Plateau is composed of highly permeable limestone that after twenty years began to hydrate. In the process, various salts and minerals were transported through the rock. The consequence was that the monuments of ancient Egypt began to crack and breakdown, and the carved and painted surfaces of many tombs began to flake away as their limestone foundations, walls, and ceilings were invaded by this damp migration of salts and minerals.

Given these monumental expenditures, the upkeep, preservation, and restoration of the nation's national treasures sadly fell to the wayside. When the Aswan High Dam neared its completion and the future watershed area of Lake Nasser began to fill, who funded and undertook the emergency archaeological salvage of the Nubian area, and for that matter, who organized the moving of the temples of Abu Simbel stone by stone, lock, stock, and barrel, and the magnificent Temples of Isis and Hathor on the Island of Philae? Certainly not the Egyptians, for they could not solely support such a burden. Instead, the world paid in donated manpower, resources, and yes, in money as well. Simply put, what was not salvaged became submerged. Is it any wonder then that the presence of a dedicated x-ray machine within the Cairo National Museum's Department of Restoration could not be justified for the study of the dead, when nearby hospitals had such technology for the treatment of the living?

Confronted with this dreary reality, the museum's careful and patient technicians did their absolute best to restore and preserve their nation's priceless cultural treasures, even if they had to employ tools and methods that were barely adequate for the task. In fact, the laboratory resources and methods available in 1982 were much the same as those employed when the monumental work, *Ancient Egyptian Materials and Industries*, was first published by the British chemist Alfred Lucas in 1926.

An additional burden placed squarely upon the museum and its thin resources was the volume of archaeological material that arrived at the museum's doorstep every year. All such material required safe and recorded storage. Some artifacts might even deserve their formal display and in the process displace others that were then relegated to the abyss of permanent storage. While many of these new arrivals required some modicum of restoration, a triage of sorts naturally developed given the constraints of the museum's budget and lack of adequate staffing.

So when the director of the Cairo National Museum offered van der Boek's troubled excavation his full support, the director did so full knowing the potential for his political peril. Such an open expression of support is as rare as it is dangerous for one's career. Once known, the persistent cries of political foul and accusations of partiality among the various foreign archaeological missions were guaranteed to turn ugly. Nonetheless, the director believed Meryptah's tomb was worth that risk and in fact considered the find a potential moneymaker for his museum. For at that very moment the Tutankhamen treasures were on tour throughout the world and earning for his museum much needed capital. He reasoned that the pristine tomb of Meryptah would shortly hit the circuit of the world's museums as well. Maybe not as splashy a collection, but a very fine one and one unspoiled. After all, even Tut's tomb had been robbed twice.

The challenge for Dr. Ahmed Rashid, chief curator for the Cairo National Museum, was to make possible what his director had promised. Rashid was known among his peers throughout the world as the miracle man of restoration and preservation. Educated in Chemistry and Egyptology at Cambridge, the man was remarkable in more than his intellect and delicate touch with some of his famous clients, who in the main were more than three thousand years old. During his school days in Britain, "Rush" Rashid had been a dashing soccer winger known for his near clairvoyant passes and marvelous ball-handling skills. But during the most recent conflict in the region, Rashid had made a supreme sacrifice for one of his profession. In a vain attempt at saving a trapped child in a burning house, he lost several fingers of his right, dominant hand. Nonetheless, with the assistance of an appliance specially built by one of his colleagues at the museum, Rashid, indomitable as ever, continued on as if the loss never had occurred. When confronted with what his director had promised, Rashid breathed a sigh of relief, as the Meryptah remains, required little, if any, restoration.

The issue of their preservation, however, was a more daunting task for Rashid and his staff, especially the exquisitely preserved floral bouquet, the attached farewell papyrus, and the textile linens, clothing, and personal effects included in the burial, not to mention the unspoiled plaster seals of the Chief Guardian of the Sakkaran necropolis.

As one might expect, included under Rashid's umbrella of responsibility fell matters of research as well, and as a result his department undertook an examination of the remaining dregs and contents of the many unguent bottles, perfume vials, beer jugs, and wine jars. The results of these tests were predictable: cedar oil, olive oil, extracts of papyrus and perhaps acanthus blossoms, a thick emmer wheat-based beer, and several grape, palm, and date wines based upon their greater sugar content.

Even more important than these was the beautifully decorated cedar coffin and the well-preserved mummy of Meryptah himself. Here is where the controversy began. On the one hand, Rashid had before him a perfectly preserved mummy of an important personage – a high priest of Amen Re that dated from the late Eighteenth Dynasty. On the other hand, the second floor of the museum possessed royal Egyptians, in essence gods, who had been unwrapped and exposed for the public to view – a godless and disrespectful act to his conservative way of thinking. So rather than performing irreparable harm to the careful bandaging and risk any damage to the mummy by exposing it to the air, he decided to follow in the noninvasive footsteps of other scholars, and x-ray the mummy of Meryptah instead.

Since his laboratory did not have such an apparatus on site and the nearby hospital did, Rashid made special arrangements and Meryptah's mummy got a ride in an ambulance, an amusing event that managed to catch the attention of the local newspaper. True to form, the chief curator insisted on accompanying his noble client in the ambulance and even walked him into the hospital's X-Ray Department on a properly white sheeted, wheeled gurney. Both activities were captured by the newspaper's reporter and splashed across the newsprint. When later asked about the publicity, Rashid shrugged and quipped, "So that's my fifteen minutes of fame? If I had known better, I would have worn my best suit."

* * *

As processes go, x-raying an inanimate object is about as exciting as watching paint dry. Nonetheless, after about an hour's time, six ventral and twelve lateral overlapping, numbered, and bracketed exposures had been carefully made. Because of the heavy wrapping, the exposures were purposely varied in duration, causing Dr. Hosny Zaaki, the hospital's chief x-ray technician, to note, "Dr. Rashid, when we are finished, this subject will glow in the dark!"

* * *

For some grisly reason, or perhaps out of a sense of pure self-preservation, forensic experts possess a wicked sense of humor. They are universally known to go full out in order to pull off a prank. With the eighteen developed x-ray exposures in hand, Dr. Hosny Zaaki considered his dear colleague Rashid at the Cairo National Museum just such a consummate prankster. With a mixture of professional anger and awe at the skillfulness of his counterpart, he again reviewed what he knew to be the state of affairs.

With his head down and leaning heavily against the lighted panorama of x-ray displays, he closed his eyes and shook his head in the solitude of the dimly lit room.

"First," he whispered, "I and I alone positioned and took all of the exposures. Second, I, and I alone processed all of the films. While I can understand the worn molars, slight curvature of the spine, and many arthritic sites all symptomatic and so typical of the aged, the rest I simply cannot accept."

Raising his head again, he then again viewed the images of the lower right arm, both laterals and the ventral. And once again, the cause of his anger and his awe stared back out at him.

Sighing heavily and coming to a decision, he reached for the phone, dialed, and got Rashid on his private line.

"Dr. Rashid, this is Dr. Zaaki," he began with a well-modulated and civilized tone that even surprised him.

"I have successfully developed your mummy's x-rays.

"Yes, they are most clear, and if I might say, quite intriguing. Do you have the proper lighting facilities at your laboratory to view them?"

Listening to the negative response, he then stated with a slight bit of strained venom in his voice, "Ah, then may I suggest my dear colleague you get yourself over to my office as soon as possible?"

With a rising volume and sarcasm he continued, "Excited? No, I am not excited."

He then fully vented.

"I'm angry! Very angry! And I want an explanation for why I pissed away the better part of my day, my department's resources, on this sick, sacrilegious prank!"

At the other end of the line, Rashid could only look in shock at his telephone's receiver and simply said in a surprised and confused voice, "Dr. Zaaki. I can assure you that I don't know what you're talking about. But I am putting on my coat right now!"

"Good!" was Zaaki's sharp reply. "I just can't wait to see you!"

And with that, the exasperated chief x-ray technician slammed his receiver into the cradle, flipped off the lighting displays, and muttered under his breath, "Goddamn governmental bureaucrats!"

* * *

By his black digital desk clock that his wife had given him on his last birthday, his fiftieth, Zaaki noted that it had taken Rashid only twenty-two minutes to arrive.

Well, he thought. *That does not bode well. If all of this had been just a joke, would he not have left me stewing in my juices for at least an hour or more?*

After his departmental secretary had announced the arrival of one clearly perplexed Rashid, the two men shook hands in a manner that could only be described as freezingly civil. Still without either having said a word, Zaaki led his colleague into the adjoining room with its four banks of walled mounted x-ray displays.

Zaaki turned to him and began with his hands behind his back in a controlled poise.

"Dr. Rashid. Until this morning I had always considered you a serious scientist, working in dreadful conditions with a poorly staffed department, who despite it all protected our national treasurers as a lioness would her own. That is why I had agreed to help your department. Yes, out of patriotism, out of pride, and yes, out of a desire to assist a highly respected colleague in need. However, given these films, I am beginning to wonder if I have made a mistake."

And with that last line, Zaaki turned on all of the displays with a flourish. Walking over to the far left panel, he then began to stonily lecture, "Here, Dr. Rashid," indicating with his left forefinger first to the ventral and then right lateral film, "we have a set of heavily worn molars. Over here, the heavily arthritic knuckles and fingers of the left hand. Here, a slight spinal curvature with a compression of the third lumbar, probably from some accident or fall. In some ways it looks like the result of a modern car accident. In sum, nothing very spectacular really. I see things like this all the time. However . . ."

Totally dismissing these past three films with a flick of the hand, he now moved over to the remaining three panels, each with their own film of the left lateral, ventral, and right lateral of the mummy's right arm – or what was left of it.

"Now, Dr. Rashid," pausing for emphasis to see if he himself had to deliver the hammer blow. "Just what do you make of these films?"

Rashid, again peering through his reading glasses, began to squint at each of the three offending films in turn. Moments passed as he looked. Needless to say, sweat began to form on his cleanly shaven upper lip as he could feel the glaring heat of Zaaki burning through the back of his head.

In a nervous panic Rashid thought to himself, *just what am I supposed to be looking for anyway?*

And then it hit him. The detail stuck out like a sore thumb. Looking back and forth between the three films he saw that the arm was missing its right hand. He was looking at an ossified stump that was remarkably regular and uncannily too even in its formation.

In a hushed voice, he said, "Can this be?"

"Not in my experience, Doctor," snorted Zaaki.

Now turning to the departmental chief with an ashen look, the shorter Rashid gasped, "What do you mean by 'not in your experience,' Dr. Zaaki?"

"That right limb amputation, Dr. Rashid, was not mechanically produced."

Stunned and dumbfounded, Rashid then asked, "What do you mean, Dr. Zaaki?"

"What I mean is that this limb was precisely removed and instantaneously seared. It was not sawed off, Doctor. There are no latent striations nor saw marks anywhere in evidence. In fact, when the amputation occurred, the bone itself was fused by the application of tremendously high, but localized heat. Here is evidence that the bone actually melted. That the subject survived the ordeal is clear from all of the subsequent layering of callus here, here, and here."

Now Rashid began to appreciate his colleague's consternation as he reviewed again the three films of the limb amputation.

"Do you know what I think, Doctor?"

Zaaki stated with acidic sarcasm, as he still was not taken in by what he thought were Rashid's attempt at flabbergasted theatrics.

Then he crossed his arms across his chest and coolly waited for an answer.

But Rashid disappointed him.

"No, Doctor, but I was hoping you would share it with me."

Shocked at the passive reaction and now with his hands on his hips and a slight tilt of his head to the left, Zaaki then challenged, "Well, Doctor, I'll tell you then. This amputation must have been performed with something like a high-powered laser, which means that this mummy is either an American or European, because I know of nowhere else that such cutting-edge industrial or medical technology is available."

At the explanation Rashid turned as white as a ghost.

"Well, at least I now know why you were so uncharacteristically rude on the telephone. Now, are you sure that you didn't mix up these films with one of your hospital's own patients?"

"Dr. Rashid, not a chance," Zaaki replied. "I took the films myself. I processed the films myself. No one else has handled your precious mummy's films BUT me!"

He emphasized this by thumbing his own chest. He then followed up with his own accusation.

"Now, Dr. Rashid, just where did that mummy come from?"

Speaking now in a soft, faraway, glazed-eyed way, Rashid began answering in mental fragments, "Southern Sakkara. A newly discovered tomb. A tomb of a high priest of Amen-Re. Dutch excavation. Late Eighteenth Dynasty. Flawlessly recovered. I myself have even visited the site."

Then recovering slightly, he probed again, "Dr. Zaaki, again I must ask you, are you sure that there is evidence of bone fusing?" As Rashid began again to examine the films even more closely.

In a huff, but also beginning to sense the genuineness of Rashid's shock and confusion, Zaaki told him, "I would stake my reputation on it."

Now wide-eyed, Rashid asked, "Are you absolutely sure?"

"Absolutely sure? Not entirely, but it is the only explanation that makes any sense. What this looks like to me is a very successful form of experimental laser surgery, probably the first of its kind, and likely a bloodless one at that. My guess is that the entire region was instantly cauterized."

Rashid's face remained a picture of confusion and deep concern.

"Is it possible this priest may have lost his hand in a kiln accident?"

Now frowning, the chief radiologist replied, "Dr. Rashid, absolutely not. This is not a charred stump, but rather an even, cleanly severed amputation."

Then after a few seconds of consideration, Zaaki continued, "You're deadly serious about all of this, aren't you?"

"Absolutely," stated the chief conservator of the Cairo National Museum as he continued to stare in disbelief at what his eyes were seeing. Then a thought came to him.

"Dr. Zaaki? You said that you and you alone know of this?"

A nodding head was returned.

"Would you mind for the moment keeping these films confidential?"

"Have no fear, Dr. Rashid. Do you think that I'm a total idiot?"

* * *

As it turned out, Zaaki was as shaken by Rashid's confusion as he was with the implication of the films themselves. To ease his mind and despite Rashid's wishes for confidentially, he sought a second opinion. He decided that it would be best to ask someone from outside his hospital's departmental staff. Fortunately, he knew just the fellow, the chairman of the Radiological Sciences Department at the Cairo University Medical School, a one Professor Dr. Ali Hassan.

"Ah, yes," Hassan murmured. "Most interesting. You were right. The fusing is quite complete. And it has such regularity to it as well. Has to be the result of a laser. Hmmm. A very nice and neat job. Where was it done? The US, Europe?"

"We don't really know," Zaaki evaded.

"Oh, come on now, just who is the lucky fellow? I would love to see such fine work in the flesh, as it were," the senior radiologist hopefully and brightly queried with a smile.

"Ah, yes," hedged Zaaki. "Well, the fellow in question is a foreigner and is no longer with us. I just wanted to confirm how his amputation was accomplished. That's all. It's just that I have never seen the results of such fine laser surgery before. Lots of bone breaks and mechanical amputations, but never before anything like this."

"Yes, Dr. Zaaki. Be assured, you were right in your diagnosis," reaffirmed the head of radiology.

"This is truly the future of medicine."

"Oh, wonderful," Zaaki murmured, then remembering his manners, "Thank you very much, Dr. Hassan, for confirming my reading. One can never be too careful now-a-days."

Rapidly shifting gears, Zaaki then suggested, "Excuse me for my lack of manners, but in return for your professional observations and appraisal, Doctor, may I offer you some lemon tea?"

* * *

"Hello? Dr. Rashid?"

"This is Dr. Zaaki at the hospital. Do you have a moment?

"Ah, good. I thought that I would let you know I just got through having tea with Dr. Ali Hassan.

"Yes, that Dr. Hassan, the chairman of radiology at the university.

"Yes, yes. Amputation was definitely performed using a laser.

"I thought that I would let you know your mummy is probably either an American or European."

"Yes, that's right.

"Why? Because those are the only places that could do such fine work.

"No! I didn't tell him who it was!

"Yes, yes, that would be fine.

"Some tea? Why certainly, Dr. Rashid. I would be delighted to visit your laboratory.

"Tomorrow afternoon? Let's see. After a momentary pause, "Ah, yes. That would be fine. Three it is.

"And good day to you too, sir."

CHAPTER XXV

Some Curious X-Rays

Dr. Hosny Zaaki was not by nature a patient man, but what overworked head of radiology ever is. Nevertheless, he was curious about this whole affair of the mummy's x-rays, but was more so with Rashid's perplexed reaction and quiet confusion. Even more intriguing was the museum curator's invitation for tea.

Now what's all that about? He stewed as he walked up the worn steps toward the monumental pink brick and stone entrance of the Cairo National Museum.

Easily finding a handy museum guard, the radiologist identified himself with great importance and asked for directions to the chief curator's office. Instead, and much to Zaaki's surprise the guard welcomed him, then informed him that Dr. Rashid had specifically instructed him to wait for his arrival. The guard then escorted him to the museum's administrative suites. Now following along after the helpful guard, Zaaki unconsciously began to berate himself for not having visited the museum for so long.

Let me see now, he mused. I*t must have been during secondary school sometime that I last set foot in this amazing cultural shrine.*

As the pair zigged and zagged through the overcrowded maze of the museum's first floor, they arrived at a semi-hidden hallway that was lined with high oak doors from another time, complete with modest gold lettering painted on each of their milky-glassed panes. Stopping before the third on the left, marked "Chief Curator," the guard respectfully knocked, listened for Rashid's greeting, opened the door for Zaaki, and stepped aside for Zaaki to enter.

Having risen from his chair and now standing by the side of his immaculate desk, Dr. Rashid greeted his guest with a slight bow and formally said, "Dear Dr. Zaaki. Thank you for adjusting your busy schedule and accepting my invitation for tea."

So Rashid directed his guest with his meticulously manicured left hand to a padded leather chair, while subconsciously hiding his injured right in his coat pocket.

With both parties seated, Rashid began.

"Well, you are probably wondering just what this is about, so I won't keep you in suspense."

To this direct opening and where it may lead, Zaaki was all for that, and so he nodded for his colleague to proceed.

"Shortly, we will be joined by this museum's director and together we can discuss the rather odd nature of the radiological results."

The museum director is in on this prank too! Zaaki paused with slightly widening eyes. *And here I thought that this meeting was some sort of peace offering. Instead, it seems that . . .*

At that moment a gentle knock came from Rashid's office door that broke Zaaki's train of thought. Shortly thereafter in came the museum director himself. Standing, because Zaaki didn't really know what else to do, he came face-to-face with what seemed to be a giant of a man, but a gentle giant with a broad smile and friendly handshake. To Zaaki's surprise, the museum director had in his other hand the back of a small wooden chair that he had dragged in behind himself. Now sitting on it backwards between the other two and leaning his mass against it, the museum director stated for the record, "Well, you must be Dr. Hosny Zaaki, the hospital's head of radiology. Is that not so?"

"Yes, sir," was the best that the radiologist could muster before the well-connected bureaucrat.

"So, Dr. Zaaki, how is your father? I haven't seen him in years. No. In fact the last time we spoke you were in Germany at, let me see now, Tübingen. Is that not so?"

"Director, I did not know that you and my father . . ."

"Dr. Zaaki, your father and I were absolute hellions when were we young. Will you please do me the pleasure of sending him and your lovely mother my best regards?"

"Absolutely, sir. Absolutely!"

Zaaki, now confused and caught off-balance as well, the museum director continued, "So, Dr. Rashid, from what you have told me, there seems to be a problem with the Meryptah mummy. Is that not so?"

"Yes, sir, indeed." answered Rashid. "In fact, on the basis of Dr. Zaaki's fine x-rays and the expert opinion of Professor Dr. Hassan, there is no question that the amputation of the right hand and partial wrist was performed by a high-powered laser. Again, according to

Dr. Hassan's opinion, he seems to think that our mummy is either an American or European."

At this startling news, the director sat back, thinking, with a look on his face that was a mixture of disbelief and wonder, and this startled reaction was not missed by Zaaki. In fact, at the news, the radiologist began to feel sorry for him and now even nervous about his diagnosis.

Recovering from his shock, the museum director looked at Zaaki with a penetrating and measuring gaze.

"Dr. Zaaki, and please do not take any offense at what I am about to say, but is there any possibility, any possibility whatsoever, that these films could have been mixed, exchanged, replaced, or mislaid with another patient's from your hospital?"

Reflexively, Zaaki actually gulped before he answered with an absolute negative.

"In fact," he continued in support of his answer, "I was the only one who took the films and processed them. They have not been seen by anyone else on the hospital staff except by Professor Dr. Hassan, and of course, by Dr. Rashid," indicating with a wave to his neighbor, and unnecessarily adding, "and of course myself."

Now coming to a decision as to what to do, the museum director then said, "I see."

Pause.

"Then in that case, Dr. Zaaki, may I request that all of the x-ray films be placed in Dr. Rashid's care? Further, may I suggest that you do not speak of this matter unless either I or Dr. Rashid is present? While I do not wish to sound melodramatic, something strange is going on, and I intend to get to the bottom of it. Also, by not discussing this matter, you will be protecting yourself and your reputation as well. I say this not to frighten you in any way. It is just that I do not know where my investigations will take me."

Then the museum director added for emphasis, "Dr. Zaaki, do we have a professional understanding regarding this matter?"

Shaken by what the director had just said, Zaaki responded, "Why absolutely, Mr. Director! I will bring over the films myself!"

"Splendid!" was the director's smiling reply as he stood to make his departure, but not before having again shaken the radiologist's hand, politely reminded him to say hello to his parents, and sending a meaningful glance toward his chief curator.

In the silent vacuum of the director's departure, Zaaki again gulped as he sat down.

On cue Rashid then asked, "Dr. Zaaki, may I offer you some lemon tea?"

* * *

An hour later after Dr. Zaaki had left, a concerned Rashid left his office and entered the museum director's suite at the end of the administrative corridor. To his surprise, the receptionist – the director's daughter – said that he was expecting him. Even his door had been left open a crack. Knocking gently and walking in after hearing his colleague's grunt of greeting, Rashid found the man pacing around his desk with a furrow-creased forehead and hands behind his back. Stopping at a respectful distance, the head of the restoration department decided to wait this one out. He knew his colleague well. Seldom, if ever, did he find him so agitated. As the pacing increased, so would the reason for it emerge. It was just a matter of time, and after a few moments, that time arrived.

"You know, Dr. Rashid, we have a big problem with that Meryptah mummy."

Nodding, Rashid responded, "Indeed we do. The radiological films are extraordinary. At least they are now in our hands, and out of professional courtesy Dr. Zaaki has pledged his silence."

"Yes, yes, I know, but it is not Dr. Zaaki that troubles me. He's from a good family and understands. What is really troubling me is van der Boek and the support that we have guaranteed. No. What I guaranteed for the clearing of the Meryptah tomb. What I have to do may cause some serious repercussions, but I cannot see any other way around it."

"I'm sorry, sir. What serious repercussions do you mean?"

Looking up at Rashid, tense eyes bored in on him.

"Ahmed. How long have we been colleagues?"

A bit surprised by the question, Rashid's eyes went momentarily blank as he calculated the years.

"Well, I suppose, if you count our days together in graduate school, some twenty-three years. It has been a long time. There have been challenges, but all in all, they have been a good twenty-three years. Why do you ask?"

"Ahmed." At the use of Rashid's first name for a second time, the man unconsciously took a seat at the chair to the left of the pacing man, for he sensed something important was about to happen.

"When was the last time I withdrew a promise? That I went back on my word?"

"Never, at least to my knowledge. If anything, your word and reputation carry quite a bit of weight, both here and abroad."

"Well, as the Americans like to say, 'all that's about to change.' I am going to embargo the publication of the Meryptah tomb material in order to sequester the mummy x-rays. They are just too controversial. I will not allow our fine nation's cultural heritage be brought into question, because of one man's odd amputation!"

Now sitting behind his desk, the museum director continued to vent his emotion due to the difficult decision that he had to make.

"Others have embargoed information, and in each and every instance the situation became extremely messy. The political fallout I can stand. What galls me the most is that I must deny that fine scholar and his team the funding and permission that I, and I alone, promised, and then sealed with my own handshake. That, Ahmed, is the serious repercussions that I am referring to. Far more importantly, I will lose face with an esteemed colleague. My credibility and that of the entire Egyptian Antiquities Organization will be put in jeopardy. That is why I am so pleased that you are here, Ahmed. We, I, must find a compromise to this dilemma."

After several moments of consideration, Rashid suggested, "Well, do we have to embargo the entire tomb and its contents, when in fact it is only some x-rays that are the problem?"

Silence.

Then came the museum director's reply.

"Ahmed can you imagine the publication of such a pristine tomb without a full and thorough forensic discussion of its mummy?"

"No, no, you're right," was the conservator's crestfallen reply.

After several more moments of silence, a gentle knock was heard. The museum director looked up and Rashid turned in his chair to see who it was.

"Please excuse me, Dr. Rashid, Father," the receptionist quietly stated. "But I believe I might have a solution to your dilemma."

"Yes, Sharil," her father smiled hopefully. "Please come in and share with us what's in your heart."

While some might think this intrusion could never happen was to deny the love that a father held for his only child. Sheril was an extremely bright one who since childhood had been her father's constant companion, in the field and the museum. This child could sight-read stock hieroglyphic inscriptions at the age of nine. By sixteen had visited most of her country's many sites. She was known by name to most foreign archaeological missions. Sheril had just been hooded in Cambridge in Egyptian philology. Not only did the museum director's daughter have a knack for running the day-to-day operations of the museum, she possessed a sensibility far beyond her years. She was, in short, the veritable apple of her father's eye. So Sharil's well-timed intrusion, due to the acoustics of the museum director's transom, left open by design, was much welcomed despite the delicate subject at hand.

"Father, I believe a compromise is available that should, at least temporarily, offer you a palatable solution."

Standing in the middle of her father's office, Sharil explained. "Basically, Dr. van der Boek's publication of the Sakkaran mortuary temple can be published and we should assist with that effort where and when needed. If the Meryptah cache is to be embargoed, then Dr. van der Boek will be able to publish most of his hard-earned field research. Then later, as developments occur, the department will be free to release the Meryptah material in part or whole. It should be made clear that if the material is released piecemeal, then Dr. van der Boek and his team should be the only ones who can publish it. While not a perfect solution to your dilemma, Father, I believe it is one that you can live with."

The daughter paused for a moment.

"You know, Father, Dr. van der Boek is a fine man and scholar. He knew you were extending yourself with that promise of support. He knew also you were exposing yourself to some potential political repercussions as well. I suspect as disappointed as he may be, he would readily understand a financial argument that we are overextended. What will cause trouble, however, would be the complete embargo of the Meryptah material. The promise of its future release will of course solve that dilemma. But then you are faced with the fact that once a promise is broken, how can the second be truly believed? It will be an emotional time, but one that is survivable."

CHAPTER XXVI

Christmas Break

Following Milson's bombshell concerning the gender of Piankoff's future replacement, Richards, with Milson's approval, e-mailed a certain Dr. Sharil Moussa at the Cairo National Museum. Given that Christmas Break would be fast approaching, Richards thought that if he could get all the logistical pieces in place early enough, then it would be possible to make a visit to let her and her father, the museum's director, in on a little known secret about the Temple of Karnak.

The next day, Richards discovered a positive reply in his mailbox. He walked over to Milson's office, informed him of the good news, and the pair booked flights for Cairo at semester's end.

* * *

The commercial flight from Chicago to Cairo via Heathrow took about eighteen hours. Going east always took its toll, but the business class accommodations aboard the German carrier really helped. Given their final destination, their baggage had been thoroughly searched, as had their persons. The six-hour layover in London, while a drag, had nonetheless offered the men the opportunity for a hot shower, shave, hot meal, and a catnap. Now somewhat refreshed, the two boarded the final leg of their flight.

* * *

The flight from London to Cairo was uneventful, but the approach was spectacular. While sitting on the left side of the plane, both in window seats, the airplane's western glide path into the Cairo airport afforded Milson and Richards a ringside seat that looked directly down on the Giza Plateau and its three pyramids. Even from this aerial vantage point, these vast monuments of stone still possessed an overwhelming visual impact.

Leaning forward Milson whispered to his former student between the edge of the headrest and fuselage, "You know, Joseph, every time I come to Egypt, the feeling is always like a homecoming, complete with a tugging at the heartstrings. I must admit that I truly envy you."

Richards, still mesmerized by the sight below, could only nod his head in mute response, for his thoughts had wandered off to a time not long ago, when he had first visited those monuments. Sharil, no Dr. Sharil Moussa, had been his personal guide first through the Cairo National Museum that she herself managed, and then during a delightful lunch, Richards caught her up on some select experiences that he had just been involved in. Thereafter, Sheril arranged for a quick trip to view the pyramids firsthand. A bright star of Egyptian archaeology and philology, she was also a competent administrator and devastatingly beautiful woman.

While Richards mind lingered on that last detail, a smile came to his face about how strong-willed Sharil could be as well. While approaching the entrance to the red granite casing blocks of Menkaure's pyramid, a guard magically appeared from the shadows. He had challenged them for entrance fees. Knowing full well that none were needed and that this was a typical archaeological shakedown, she smiled to the officious guard and asked, "Do you know who I am?"

"No," he said with a slight sneer and a distinct puffing up of his chest. "Should I?"

Still smiling sweetly and continuing to unflinchingly hold his eye, she softly suggested, "You know, you really should. That is, if you wish to keep your all-too-soft position, much less ever hope to collect your pension. Besides, demanding payment when none is due to our nation's cultural treasures is a criminal offense. Minor, but criminal nonetheless."

Now with his chest deflating fractionally, the guard had to ask the question, "And so who am I speaking that wields such influence?"

As soon as he had stated that haughty challenge, he knew that he had made a big mistake, for his eyes had just then registered a slight movement from the second member of the party. A man who now stood next to the woman with his feet widely spaced had his thick and well-muscled arms folded across his chest. His dark eyes were locked on the guard, while his mandibular jaw muscles were clearly twitching just short of full fury. He had not said a word. They were not necessary.

Sharil just then noted the threatening and protective posture of her companion and decided to quickly diffuse the situation.

"I am Dr. Moussa of the Egyptian Antiquities Organization. The director of the Cairo National Museum is my father. And this is," now turning toward her charge, "Dr. Joseph Richards, an American, and a scholar of our own ancient history."

With that she produced from her tiny purse a business card that she gave to the guard, who at this point had further deflated, and had noticeably shortened in stature by some four inches.

Taking the card with a slightly trembling hand and fearful eyes, he then studiously read it, carefully inserted it into his breast pocket, gave Sharil a slight bow, and then said, "My deepest apologies, Dr. Moussa. "Would you wish a tour of the Menkaure pyramid?"

"Why, thank you," purred the smiling woman. "That would be most kind."

* * *

After enduring for the second time the arcane experience known as international security and customs, Milson and Richards threaded their way through the throng with their wheeled carry-ons in tow. On reaching the reception area, they were greeted by a wall of people waving their hands at the recent arrivals. One of them, presumably a museum guard dressed in a light tan khaki uniform, was holding a small placard that said in large letters "MILSON PARTY" with "Cairo National Museum" printed beneath it in smaller capitals. Milson, seeing the sign, pointed the way and, upon reaching the man, announced in fluent Arabic who he was along with the identity of his companion. After first checking their passports, the guard then led the Americans to an awaiting car, stowed their baggage in the trunk, and whisked them off into the absolute bedlam that is Cairo's afternoon rush hour.

One hour later and after several hair-raising near misses, the two frazzled travelers disembarked at the main entrance of the Cairo Nile Hilton Hotel. Before checking in, Milson had turned to their adventurous driver, thanked him, and attempted to tip him for his trouble, which he politely refused much to Milson's total astonishment.

The driver then told Milson in perfect British English, "The museum director and Dr. Moussa will pick you and Dr. Richards up this evening for dinner promptly at eight o'clock. I have been instructed also to tell you to dress casually."

Then the driver added with a smile, "And by the way, Dr. Milson, your Arabic is quite good."

Milson, now flattered and a bit fascinated, stuck his head into the passenger side window and asked.

"By the way, Mr. Safir," reading it directly from his name badge, "your English is quite good as well. Just where did you come by it?"

"Cambridge, sir. And it's Dr. Safir."

"Oh! I'm so sorry. No offense meant!"

"None taken."

"A doctorate in Egyptology, perhaps?"

"No, museum conservation. I am a chemist. I will no doubt see you tomorrow at the museum. Until then. Have a pleasant dinner!"

And off sped the car with a wave from its driver.

* * *

Dressed in cool cotton slacks and golf shirts, the two Americans met in the hotel lobby at 7:55 p.m. and decided to await their dinner hosts at the curb of the hotel's circle outside. Standing silently with their hands in their pockets, while taking in all the sights, sounds, and smells of the city, Milson began to muse aloud.

"You know, Joseph, telling the Moussas about the secret entrance to the Amen Re Treasury beneath Karnak's Fourth Pylon might be a bit embarrassing for our French colleagues. After all, they have been restoring the complex since before God knows when. Then there is the issue of whether the passage's entranceway still is operational."

The broad smile on Richards' face told Milson more than he needed to know and he said so.

"And judging by that shit-eating grin on your face, just let me guess. One, you don't give a care about any bruising of the French ego. And two, you already know that the passageway is functional. Knowing you, you and Piankoff probably have already explored it. Am I correct?"

"Only partially, Doc. Major Cartwright and I checked out the area after Piankoff had taken ill with that river parasite."

"And . . ." Milson prodded.

"And . . ." Richards replied. "The pylon is currently in a ruinous state as the French were looking for any reused building material. There was none. Besides, the entire area is under reconstruction. However, Tuna and I did know where to look and what to look for. I think that the evidence is there for someone to find. Frankly, Doc, if anyone wants to have a ghost of a chance at opening up the treasury, they will need some heavy lifting machinery. But once opened up, I think that they will find that there had been some looting, evidence also of looters succumbing to some mantraps, but all in all, the museum and its conservation department will probably be busy for the next decade just clearing up all the loot. Doc, we just gotta' get them down there as soon as possible. We have been sitting on this way too long."

"I know, my boy, I know. Well, here they come! And just in time, I'm absolutely famished!"

* * *

With the main dinner course long cleared away, the four sat with their thick and sweet coffees as they leaned over the table in deep and quiet conversation. The phrase "thick as thieves" begins to capture the sense of the scene as Richards' narrative held them all in rapt attention.

"Believe it or not, much of the red sandstone core the Fourth Pylon was once hollow. The hidden entrance, now long gone, was located within a long and narrow offering chapel once faced in exquisite Tura limestone, painted, and carved in low relief. All of that is currently gone as well. About fifty feet within the chapel and on the left side, if you pushed on just the right set of stones, a portion of the wall swung inward into the pylon itself. But while this secret entrance into the pylon no longer exists, the treasury itself is actually located far beneath the temple's foundations and extends far into the limestone bedrock below it. My only hope that it is not flooded."

At this point in the story, Sharil Moussa could no longer contain herself.

"Are you sure, Joseph, of just what you are saying? My God! The French have been working in that area now for well over fifty years and have not reported the existence of such a passage. Are you absolutely sure?"

"Absolutely sure," stated the young American with a conviction that was unimpeachable.

Then the museum director spoke the words that both Milson and Richards had been long hoping to hear.

"Dr. Richards. I believe you. May I suggest that we visit Luxor the day after tomorrow? That would be a Saturday, and I will make sure that the site is cleared of all tourists. There will no doubt be some comment made about the restricted access, but as the new head of the Egyptian Antiquities Organization, I do have some privileges. Now, please continue."

"Well, from the interior of the Fourth Pylon, a sloped passage leads down past the foundation of the temple into the limestone bedrock layers below. When it finally levels out, there is a long straight corridor of some one hundred and fifty meters or so, off of which there must be at least twenty side chambers. In many respects, it reminds me very much of the layout of KV5 with its tens of individual chambers that branch off of its many corridors. By the way, the thresholds of many of these side chambers are false, being made of a thin plaster layer that camouflage deep rock-cut mantraps. I can only begin to imagine what might have been stored down there. But I do remember being told that during the Amarna heresy of Akhenaten, the priesthood of Amen Re had secreted all of their precious items down there. So, it could well be that some of that may still be there. In any case, your museum and its conservation department could well have to work overtime for the next decade clearing and preserving what may be down there."

Once finished, Richards sat back and took a sip from his already cooled coffee. The two Moussas were looking at one another with unreadable expressions, silently communicating as only a father and daughter can. Milson's eyes were glazed over, a combination of jet lag, the stirring narrative, a pleasant food coma, and what it all potentially could mean for the field of Egyptology. Then Sharil Moussa asked a question that at first seemed to come from left field.

"Joseph. You said that this was a secret entrance. That means to me that someone had to reveal it to you and Piankoff. You also just said that you remember being told that the priesthood of Amen Re hid its treasures there as well. Just who did this and told you these things?"

"A fair question. The first time that I was shown the secret entrance, there were four of us: Piankoff, myself, Prince Horemheb, and the aged High Priest of Amen Re, Meryptah. It was the ancient Meryptah who showed us the way, who told us of his preservation of the wealth of Amen Re from the plunderers of the Aten movement. It was he who made us swear to preserve the secret of the entrance and treasury."

At the mention of Horemheb's and Meryptah's names, both of the Moussas gasped in wide-eyed recognition. Looking at one another, each did not know what to say. Whether they should say anything. But the Americans now knew from their candid reactions that something had to be said. After an uncomfortable moment of silence, the museum director nodded to his daughter.

Addressing the two Americans, "Gentlemen, do either of you remember anything about a Dutch archaeological mission some fifteen to twenty years ago that was excavating at Horemheb's Sakkaran mortuary temple?"

Milson indicated that he did and added, "Why, yes, I do. I also seem to remember that for whatever reason its publication was stalled or the mission ran out of funding or something like that. I understand that it was a real shame. Then a funding source appeared. I do remember, however, a brief mention about a flawlessly executed clearing of a chamber tomb and then nothing. When the temple's publication finally reached print, there was nothing about this tomb, other than what vaguely appeared in the preliminary reports. Why do you ask?"

"Well, for one thing, Dr. Milson, your memory is as sharp as ever. And secondly, what I am about to share cannot leave this table. Is that agreed?

To which the Americans nodded as one, but Richards began to suspect something.

"Beneath Horemheb's family mortuary temple, the Dutch team cleared several shaft tombs. These were all dutifully published, although none were truly spectacular. However what was spectacular was the discovery of a very cleverly camouflaged burial chamber of none other than a high priest of Amen Re named Meryptah. I presume the very same one, Joseph, which you just mentioned. When the Dutch team found it, it was intact and its clearing was flawlessly performed as you remembered, Dr. Milson. I was even there to witness it."

Now it was the Americans turn to look at one another.

"You have just got to be kidding," stated Richards with a bloodless face and an emotional gulp.

"Absolutely not," Sheril said. "In fact, the Egyptian Antiquities Organization initially underwrote the funding for its clearing, preservation, and publication, but then because of extenuating circumstances had to rescind that promised financial support and embargo the entire publication of the tomb. While the rest of the site has reached the public domain, this tomb and its contents have not."

Milson, his interest truly piqued, then asked the obvious, "Sharil, just what do you mean by 'extenuating circumstances'?"

The director chose to field this delicate question and in his thickly accented English began to tell an amazing tale.

"You know, John, we have known one another for quite some time," he began as he examined his massive hands.

"But as the director of the Cairo National Museum and now Head of the Egyptian Antiquities Organization, I must somehow simultaneously manage both, fight for their continued government funding, and be an administrative figurehead as well, not to mention an international ambassador of our culture. Blessedly, I have my daughter here who so ably shares this burden with me. Without her, frankly, I could not have done it all, much less so well. But remember, John, this site was under investigation just as the Tutankhamen exhibit was on tour, a tour that funded much for both the museum and the Egyptian Antiquities Organization. Those funds provided the shortfall of a government budget that was still reeling from the effects of Israeli War. The richness and pristine nature of Meryptah's tomb, when it was first opened, suggested to me yet another such fund-raising tour for the museum and the EAO. However, 'extenuating circumstances' did arise of a magnitude that precluded even the publication, much less tour, of the Meryptah cache."

Milson pressed again, "And those 'extenuating circumstances' were what?"

"John, you just cannot imagine. Initially it was because of a curious set of x-rays that had been made of Meryptah's mummy. Since the mummy wrappings were in such perfect condition, we chose to pursue a noninvasive method of investigation, much as Harvey James had so kindly done for the rest of our royal collection. But what the x-rays revealed of the deceased's missing right hand, I could not allow to be published. The amputation of the high priest's right hand and how it was so precisely accomplished would have turned my museum and the EAO into a media circus of nosy tabloid reporters, television reporters, von Däniken followers, and pyramidologists. I just could not allow our national heritage to be so sullied. So I had to painfully withdraw the museum's funding and had the contents of the entire tomb put under lock and key. It was an ugly time. A time of confusion, shock, scholarly distrust – all things that I have striven throughout my career to prevent, and here I am the very author of it all! The painful result is that Willem van der Boek and I are no longer colleagues. Although I have promised him that whenever, if ever, his find is published that his name and that of his team will be the only ones to appear on its cover. Obviously, given my past record with him, he does not believe a word of that promise. And that is what hurts me most of all."

The director continued, but this time addressing another issue entirely.

"Then one might say that Allah had moved my hand. And well I did, for the names of two personalities that appear prominently in the autobiographical narrative of Meryptah, which fully covered one of the tomb's walls, were none other than a certain Piankhotep and Mayneken. Need I say any more?"

* * *

The following day, Friday, the Muslim Sabbath, both Milson and Richards paid an early morning visit to the Cairo National Museum and in particular to Dr. Ahmed Rashid, the head of its conservation department. At the museum director's insistence at the previous night's dinner, they were to examine for themselves the x-rays of Meryptah's mummy, while the rest of the department's staff was away. In short, they were there to see the very reason for the director's embargo on the Meryptah tomb.

After getting past the usual pleasantries, Dr. Rashid took the pair into a darkened adjoining room that had two panel displays. As he walked over to them, the chief conservator stated the obvious, "Gentlemen, you must understand that what I will show you must remain in this room. Under no circumstances are you to reveal to anyone what I will show you."

With a flip of a rocker switch on the vertical side of the right-hand panel, both illuminated to reveal two plates of radiographic film that were views of an arm missing a hand from the mid-wrist.

Dr. Rashid, now in lecture mode with his hands behind his back, "Gentlemen, the right arm of the Meryptah mummy is most curious. While accidental and medical amputations in ancient times were quite common, they also have certain characteristics that are missing from the example before you. Specifically, any evidence whatsoever of crushed, pinched bone, splinters, fragmentation, or bone saw markings. Instead, what we see is remarkable regularity to the amputation and a fusing of the bone at the amputation itself. This last detail, here and here, however, is most intriguing. This is callus – callus that formed after the amputation itself. Along this clearly defined boundary, you can see where the amputation occurred and the post-trauma calcification began. If I were any judge of such things, I would have to guess this medical procedure occurred early on in Meryptah's life, when he was perhaps seventeen, maybe as late as nineteen or twenty years old. That means that whatever and however this amputation occurred, he survived it and was able to finish out his long life that has been estimated at some fifty-odd years."

Following the brief presentation and after some gawking at the two plates, Milson was the first with a question.

"Dr. Rashid, clearly the fusing of the bones is your greatest concern. In your estimation, if you were asked to reproduce this fused amputation under laboratory conditions, how would you go about doing so? With a kiln, a heated plate, a hot iron, or what?"

Rashid answered the question with a straight face.

"Given current technology, there is only one way I know that such a precise amputation could have taken place. It would have been an accident, an accident with a powerful industrial laser. The sort that cuts steel plate."

The ashen faces of the two Americans replied for them. And with a flick of this finger, Rashid shut down the displays and removed and pocketed both of the radiological negatives in their separate manila sleeves. Finished, he then turned to them.

"Gentlemen, I well recognize that it is not my place to question you as to how this amputation occurred in such an ancient time. Nonetheless, the evidence before my eyes makes me curious. Do you have any ideas?"

Milson just stood with his hands in his pockets, staring at the floor and shaking his head. Richards took on as blank a stare as he could muster. After about twenty seconds of silence, Rashid, suspected that he was being stonewalled, but being too polite to press the issue, just nodded his head in resignation.

* * *

The following day, the quartet of the two Moussas, Milson, and Richards took the 7:30 a.m. Egypt Air flight to Luxor. As they were the only ones who boarded the plane without luggage, the museum director had to intervene with security and show them their return tickets for later that very day.

After the short sixty-five minute flight and a brief cab ride from the airport, the group found themselves standing before the abbreviated avenue of ram-headed sphinxes that led to the Grand Pylon of the Karnak Temple. As they walked up to the blocked and bolted entrance to the temple, a guard came out and greeted them with a slight bow.

Meanwhile, a disappointed and milling crowd of water bottle and camera-touting French tourists, having been earlier turned away, when they saw the foursome gaining entrance, rather brazenly attempted to follow them in. Stopped in their tracks by the lone guard, and in danger of being bullied aside by their native tour leader, the tall director stopped, turned, and returned to the gateway. Now standing behind the guard, whom he towered over by a good foot, the director barked over him at the troublesome tour guide. Did indeed this obnoxious tour guide have on his person his required papers? Looking up at the museum director and head of the EAO, and puffing up his chest in defiance, he proudly exclaimed, "Well,

Messieurs, I do not have them directly on my person, but they are in the glove compartment of the tour bus."

"Congratulations. However, would you be so kind and bring them to me for my immediate inspection?"

A bit shocked and then becoming even more emboldened, the guide then demanded just who was invoking such an arcane bureaucratic inspection to which the received response was simply, "The Director of the Egyptian Antiquities Organization."

Quizzical would best describe the immediate assimilation of that answer, quickly followed by a mumbled apology, and then he herding away of his charges from the entrance gateway.

The archaeological guard, turning around to take a good look at his savior, gulped and whispered a brief thanks. Now smiling broadly, the director merely murmured something barely audible in Arabic about "those damn pushy frogs."

* * *

As they now stood before the ruinous remains of the Fourth Pylon, Richards could only remember gazing upon the once beautiful raised relief inscriptions before him.

My God, what a marvelously riotous blur of color they were!

Now walking around the foundation of the pylon to the where the dark coolness of the offering chapel used to stand, the young Egyptologist stepped over some blocks and into the core of the structure. Reaching down, he began moving away some smallish blocks inward and away from one of the original outer limestone casing blocks. Bending down, Richards carefully and meticulously brushed aside with his hands all the sand and stone chips from behind the casing block. As he did so, the pylon's core floor surface behind the block was revealed. Satisfied, he then stood up and stepped over back onto the chapel's pavement. Now with his foot firmly planted against the casing block's right edge, he grunted as he pushed against its mass, which to everyone's surprise, pivoted inward several inches. He pushed again, and another several inches were gained with much stone scraping. Of importance was the stone was pivoting inwardly on an arc established by its opposite end!

Richards explained to the slackened jaws in attendance, "This limestone casing block was once the pivot point of the hidden entranceway into this pylon's core. The width of the gap was originally several times wider, but this is all that has survived. If we picked up this block, the pivot and its nipple would be clear to see."

As for his companions, who were standing beside him, Richards had performed nothing less than a feat of magic, something incredible, definitely worthy of Hollywood lore. Milson's jaw dropped in utter surprise. The museum director squinted in disbelief. Sharil, with her hand over her mouth, stifled a giggle of delight. Wide-eyed, they could only look down in disbelief at what their eyes were telling them.

Richards continued, "Please note that the approximate floor level of the pylon's core interior to that of the exterior public area. That is because the hidden entranceway swung inward, and when it closed, it did so against the public paving stones so its movement would leave no trace."

The agile young man worked his way over and around some of the larger dislodged limestone blocks and stone litter toward the pylon's core. Standing upon a particularly large sandstone block, he continued his description.

"At a point about right here, but obviously several feet below me, one should be able to find the beginning of the stepped and ramped passage. Equally obvious, if we are to gain access to the passage, we will need some serious manpower, or even better, horsepower, to clear the area."

On that assessment, the museum director, with his arms crossed across his broad chest, grunted and nodded, and then added, "Are you absolutely sure, Dr. Richards?"

"Yes, sir. As absolutely as I am standing here."

"Well. Given the clear indication of door pivot over there, I am strongly inclined to believe you."

The director stated absentmindedly as he began to look this way and that, measuring in his mind clearances, access, and potential dump sites.

"In fact, I am willing to wager that it would be relatively easy to maneuver over to this very spot a small mechanical crane and pickup truck. Yes. Yes, very easy indeed. And I know just the man to take on this clearing as well. You, Dr. Richards, of course would have to assist in the undertaking. I know you are not a trained archaeologist, but are you willing?"

Glowing, Richards exclaimed, “Absolutely, sir!”

“Good.” The director smiled with approval and then turned to his daughter.

“Sharil, you must oversee this clearing and act as my personal representative. I am sure that you can just imagine how enthusiastic the French archaeological mission will be when they catch wind of this,” he finished with a devilish smile.

Then turning to Milson and Richards. “Gentlemen, on behalf of the entire Egyptian nation, we are again in your debt.”

“Not so fast,” Milson chided. “We haven’t seen nor do we know whether the treasury even exists as yet.”

“John.” The museum director smiled. “What Dr. Richards has just showed us is more than enough for a preliminary investigation.”

While these two Egyptologists were talking, Richards, as a precaution before leaving the area, again camouflaged the door pivot’s location just as he and Tuna had done before. As he finished, the director could only say, “It’s simply unbelievable!”

CHAPTER XXVII

An NEA Update

Youth is a time for discovery. While finding, proving, getting to name, and then publishing your very own NEA is pretty cool and exciting, its periodic updates can be a real drag. Checking up on your own celestial children can be thrilling, especially if they are nearing home, getting close enough almost to see with a naked eye – albeit through a first-class deep space telescope. So it was for Becky Hildebrand, no longer a graduate student, but a PhD in astronomy and long-term research fellow attached to the Keck I Observatory.

* * *

Getting time to check up on her fast approaching asteroid on the upgraded Arecibo radio and radar telescope in Puerto Rico, despite her topic and connections, proved to be a trying process. In the end, her proposal found acceptance and a series of dates and times were scheduled for her observations.

That time had come. Sitting in the command chair, this was her chance with the new instrumentation and its super precise twin Gregorian reflector system. Becky's plan was simple. She was going to paint her NEA with as dense a radar signal she could muster from the installation's one million watt transmitter – a three centimeter wave at a frequency of ten gigahertz. Becky figured the return echo from such a blast would provide her first images of Poliahu and maybe answer some questions about its quirky nature. She reasoned the sensitivity that she was using could detect a steel golf ball on the surface of the Moon.

* * *

"Sir, this is Sergeant Duncan at the communications desk. I have some interesting news for you."

"Yes, Sergeant, what is it?"

"I have a note here that Dr. Rebecca Ann von Müller Hildebrand has Arecibo all warmed up, dialed in, and is ready to shoot Poliahu."

"Oh, really?"

"Yes, sir. And from what the folks out there say, she's going to microwave it."

"So she's really going to fry its ass, is she? Well, good for her. What frequency is Hildebrand gonna' be using?"

"Full shot, sir, ten gigahertz."

"Jesus! She means business. Has anyone on the outside used that high a setting yet?"

"Nope, she's the first."

"Well, when she's done cooking that NEA, be sure to send me a copy of its returns. They should be interesting to say the least."

"Yes, sir."

* * *

Approximately two hours and twenty-four minutes later, relatively speaking of course, an alarm triggered aboard The Redemption. Its crew, shocked at the intense magnitude of the radar signal's probing beam, at first thought themselves under attack, but the Xoxx quickly discounted that concern.

"No, that was not an attack. That was, however, full and positive confirmation that the species is aware of us. While their curiosity is laudable, their awareness is not. As you know, this is not the first time that they have looked our way. I fear, my colleagues, that we may need more of a diversion than a collision with the asteroid ahead of us. Given their current interest and technological level, perhaps we should contemplate a further diversion, one that significantly dampens their sensor capability and hobbles their communication's grid as well."

"Well, what have you in mind?" asked the Sard.

"Conjuring up a space storm," the Xoxx replied.

* * *

At 12:07, the first return data were received by the massive one-thousand-foot dish at Arecibo. For Becky, it had been a long four and a half hour wait before those first echoes came back from Poliahu. It would be another couple of hours of numbers crunching before any of it would make any sense and whether she even had an image that she could pin the name Poliahu on.

Three hours later, Becky had her data on Asteroid 1994 RAvMH as well as twelve images. Looking excitedly for those, the astronomer came to two collage-like printouts of six images each, all taken and reproduced in their numbered sequence due to their time delay and line-of-sight velocity, or Doppler frequency. Calibration marks appeared on those sheets, with the vertical hatching indicating time in microseconds between images and the horizontal radial velocity differences, which in this case were nearly zero.

Even at this great remove, Becky could see that Poliahu was not an asteroid, but rather a cluster of them, all revolving around a central mass. While she would have to consult her data to more accurately assess what she was seeing and in what proportions, Poliahu looked very much like a high schooler's model of an atom. The central mass, however, was barely visible as there always seemed to be one of its satellites in the way. As to how many satellites there were, Becky provisionally counted seven or eight. The fact that Poliahu and its constituent parts were very dark and poorly reflective did not help.

"Most likely an S-Class asteroid," she whispered to herself. "And if so that means that their composition must be similar as well. But with all of these spinning and tumbling pieces and parts, Poliahu must represent some kind of record in asteroid complexity and may represent the formation of a small planet."

* * *

An hour after Becky had received her copy of the Poliahu data, a copy of it was on an officer's desk at Air Force Space Command, located at Peterson Air Force Base in Colorado Springs. Lieutenant Charles M. Perry hovered over his copy of the imagery and paged through the data along with the asteroid's all-important telemetry.

"Darn it all, Becky Hildebrand! You cooked this one real good," he murmured to himself in admiration.

"I count eight objects all clustered together. What a nightmare to track!"

But unlike Becky, whose career Charlie had followed over the years, the Air Force officer found the telemetry data of more immediate interest, especially the part about the severe radar scattering quality of the asteroid. But with its imagery, even that now made good sense. The radar returns also confirmed the earlier USAF assessment of asteroid's homogeneity and probable stony-iron composition. Even its course had remained steady for a near-Earth passing still sometime in September 2012, just as Toutatis was in the neighborhood. But what really opened the lieutenant's eyes were the asteroid's acceleration and velocity.

"What's this? Negative acceleration and declining velocity curves? It's slowing down? How could that be?"

So Charlie pulled out the Poliahu file and in particular wanted to review the results of the AFSC's previous five-point scan on that heavenly body. There was something different between then and now and it nagged at him. Three minutes later, he had the answer – mass.

"So," he said to himself, "five satellites then, eight now. But with more mass you should be speeding up, not slowing down."

Sitting back in his gray-colored government-issued office chair, he considered if that was even possible. While his cognitive side said, "Those facts make no sense given the laws of physics." His intuition said, "Man, this is really getting strange – no, weird. How can an asteroid cluster slow itself down?"

* * *

At about the same time that Charlie Perry was scratching his head over Poliahu's telemetry data, Becky Hildebrand was doing the very same thing. But unlike Charlie, who had the classified AFSC data before him for comparison, Becky did not, so her train of thought was running off into completely other quadrants.

"Could a gravity well be affecting it? A small black hole in the neighborhood that we don't know about? No, that couldn't be," she argued with herself. "Its course has remained within parameters. A gravity well would have deflected its current course. *Darn! Just what's going on out there?"*

And then her office phone rang. Picking it up, she curtly answered, "Hildebrand here."

The sharp answer momentarily stunned the caller before he managed to recover. "Ah, is this Dr. Rebecca Hildebrand?"

"Yes, it is. Who's this?"

"Well. Dr. Hildebrand, that is a very difficult question for me to answer, but are you as puzzled as I am about your asteroid's telemetry data?"

Stunned absolutely silent, Becky unconsciously put her hand over the phone's receiver and looked around her office for any evidence of a bug or camera. Seeing none, she finally answered, "Ah, yes. I find it most interesting. Why do you ask?"

"Because, Dr. Hildebrand, I would really like to know why Poliahu is slowing down."

Oh my God! Screamed Beck's mind.

"So, does that mean that you know why Poliahu is slowing down?"

"No, I do not, Dr. Hildebrand. But what I can tell you is that three years ago Poliahu only had five satellites. Now it has, by my count, eight, and the basic laws of physics are not taking effect, Dr. Hildebrand. Poliahu is decelerating."

Still quite shaken by the anonymous caller's intimate knowledge about her asteroid, in addition to details about it that she did not possess, she finally found her tongue.

"I see. So you say three years ago Poliahu had five satellites and now it has eight, yet it still has negative telemetry."

"That is precisely correct, Dr. Hildebrand."

"Do you have a name?"

Pause.

"Ah, Charlie will do for the moment."

"And Charlie, do you have a last name?"

"Dr. Hildebrand. Let's just say that I have been a fan of your research for quite some time. My job – I've a doctorate in astronomy – is very much related to NEA tracking and their assessment. That's about all I can say."

"Then that makes you either government or military."

The accusative way Becky spit out that sentence made Charlie wince so hard that he almost hung up.

Silence.

"Okay 'Charlie,' or whoever you are, why did you call me?"

"Professional courtesy, Dr. Hildebrand, professional courtesy. I had data that I knew you needed. I had data I knew would assist you with your analysis of Poliahu. Otherwise, hell, I can just imagine what you were going through. Mysterious gravitational anomalies – gravity wells, black holes. Heck, who knows what you may have considered. But Poliahu remains curious, Dr. Hildebrand. You and I both know that it should be accelerating instead of decelerating with all of that additional mass."

Now with a considerably less aggressive voice that verged on gratitude, Becky said, "Thank you, Charlie. I can now see that what you have just shared with me is probably classified. Is there some way we can perhaps meet to talk about this?"

"To your first question, yes, my superiors would not at be pleased. But to your second question, are you going to be attending the annual convention in San Diego this year?"

"Why, yes, I am," she said brightly. "In fact, I'm giving a paper."

"Fine. I'll be there. Goodbye, Dr. Hildebrand."

And the phone went dead.

Sitting there, staring at the receiver, Becky felt for perhaps the first time in her life that someone understood her.

Jesus! She thought. *He even knew what I was thinking might have affected the telemetry!*

But as for "Charlie," the astronomer figured his reference to "my superiors" that he was military. If he was military, then he was probably Air Force. And if he was Air Force that meant the Space Command in Colorado Springs. *After all,* Becky concluded, *who else would be so patched into Arecibo? The Air Force built it in the first place!*

CHAPTER XXVIII

Amsterdam Again

Through bleary eyes Professor Dr. Willem van der Boek scanned through all the e-mails that had amassed since he last looked in his university mailbox two weeks ago. The continuous grading of exams will do that to you. Forty-seven in all, most from his students that represented late submissions of their final examinations, four interdepartmental announcements – one for the always boisterous New Year's Eve Party – six that were pure spam, three from his wife, and one from Dr. Sharil Moussa of the Cairo National Museum. Now what did she want? And then there was this mysterious one from a certain jwrichards@nei.edu. As he read the e-mail from Moussa and then reread it again, tears of relief filled his bloodshot eyes, and his heart seemed to want to explode in joyous exaltation that befitted the nearing Yuletide season.

> Dear Professor Dr. van der Boek:
>
> Please allow me to be the first to inform you of some wonderful news. I have just received word from the Head of the Egyptian Antiquities Organization that an executive decision has been made to release for publication the tomb clearance and vast majority of your research concerned with the Meryptah cache.
>
> The only item that is to remain embargoed is the forensic description of Meryptah's mummy. It has been decided that this scientific data will be co-published at a later date under your name and that of the museum's own Department of Restoration.
>
> Additionally, a source for the funding of the publication costs has been secured.
>
> Expect shortly an official letter from the Egyptian Antiquities Organization regarding this long overdue decision and further

specifics on the specific materials to be released.

Again I wish to congratulate you on this long awaited news and wish to personally thank you for your patience concerning this matter.

My father sends his best regards.

Sincerely yours,

Dr. S. Moussa
Director, The National Museum of Cairo

As van der Boek sat before his monitor in shock, he printed a copy of the Moussa e-mail more out of disbelief than anything else. Somehow as he reread it in his shaking hands the hard copy message seemed more real, more tangible, and even more unbelievable.

Well, he thought. *I'm going to have to edit the tomb's manuscript and make it as a separate fascicle to the site's excavation publication. But that should not be so bad. In all, maybe just a couple of days' work. The photography, however, will take some time, but again not that much. Regardless, it will be good to put that project finally to rest.*

Now, what's this other e-mail about anyway?

Dear Professor Dr. van der Boek:

Allow me to introduce myself. I am an associate professor in Egyptian philology at the Near Eastern Institute in Chicago, Illinois.

At the suggestion of the Head of the Egyptian Antiquities Organization and Dr. Sharil Moussa, I have been asked to approach you about an archaeological project - a project that they have already tentatively approved dependent upon you and your team's participation.

I assure you that funding for what I am about to describe has been guaranteed for a period of not less than ten years, contingent of course upon the results of a preliminary topographical survey.

Frankly, Professor Dr. van der Boek, I am a philologist. I am not a trained archaeologist, much less one with your considerable experience and credentials. Nonetheless, I propose that we work together to first locate what I believe to be the treasury of Amen Re. To date, my philological research has narrowed its location down to ancient Thebes, the Karnak temple complex, and the Fourth Pylon of Thutmose I in particular. Only a proper topographical survey will pinpoint its exact location.

Naturally, I fully understand that you probably think that this e-mail is either a) from a crackpot, or b) a really cruel joke from a malicious colleague. But as you can see from the addresses appended above, I can assure you that I am neither a crackpot nor a joker.

Actually, I am seriously seeking to join up with a seasoned archaeological team. When I first approached the Egyptian Antiquities Organization seeking a topographical permit, I requested their recommendation and they unanimously suggested you.

Hence this e-mail.

While I realize that as the end of this year is fast approaching, I would nonetheless like to begin the survey in late January or early February to coincide with our academic break. I have secured a private source of non-matched funding for three seasons of survey work. If we locate the treasury, as I believe we will, then full funding for its exploration, clearing, publication, etc., will be authorized.

I look forward to hearing from you soon.

Best regards,

J.W. Richards

Now sitting back in his office chair, van der Boek printed out a hard copy of this e-mail as well and the archaeologist found himself drifting in thought, and the deeper he got, the wilder his speculations grew.

Now just what the hell is going on in Egypt? First the vast majority of the Meryptah cache has suddenly been released from its embargo. And now I read that the Egyptian Antiquities Organization has recommended me and my team for a topographical survey within the Karnak complex? Just what is going on? To be sure, as soon as we show up, the French will be as mad as hornets! While I would most heartily enjoy that to no end, I just don't know if I am up to all the grief! But it's about high time that someone began to intrude on what they consider their own private archaeological preserve. If I was a young man, I would not dare such an intrusion. But as I am fast approaching my pension, their institutional pressure I could almost ignore. How delicious . . . he thought with a chuckle.

While the hour was late, almost ten o'clock, van der Boek decided nonetheless to brew another pot of coffee in his Krupp machine. And while it chugged along and released its pleasant-smelling vapors, he returned to his monitor, clicked on the Reply icon, and began to type.

Dear Dr. Richards:

I am flattered by your invitation to collaborate on a topographical survey within the Karnak complex next spring, and yes, I and several of my graduate students could be made available during the early portion of February. However, if we wish to indeed move quickly on the logistics of this matter, then may I suggest that you call me at the following telephone number at your earliest convenience?

Cheers,

Professor Dr. W. van der Boek

* * *

It was nearly midnight before van der Boek fumbled his house key into its lock. Nearing retirement and at the age of sixty, the archaeologist ruminated on his current flood of good fortune and the near-tidal ebb and flow that his academic career had taken.

"It's either feast or famine," he murmured.

Too tired to bother to wash his face and brush his teeth, he left his clothes in a pile at the foot of the bed. Quietly slipping in next to his sleeping wife, Ingrid, he finally let out a satisfied breath.

"Well, Willy, how did the grading go this time?" So did his wife whisper to him in Dutch.

"Ah, you're awake. Very well, my love, very well."

"Den why are you home zo late?"

"I received some very good news and so I had to immediately respond by e-mail."

Now sitting up next to her prone husband, Ingrid gave him a peck on his cheek and said, "Now dearest, go to sleep und just remember to tell me all about it in the morning."

CHAPTER XXIX

Spring Break

Professor Dr. Willem van der Boek was beginning to feel a bit ludicrous as he and his survey team of three graduate students stood waiting with all of their gear in a pile near the curb outside the First Pylon of the Karnak Temple complex. At first light, the natives of the sleepy town of Luxor still were asleep, while a seemingly endless stream of tourists disgorged from their fashionable and air-conditioned hotels into massive air-conditioned tour buses.

Expecting at least several of them to stop at the temple, van der Boek was surprised when none did. Instead they all motored on by the quartet leaving bluish clouds of diesel exhaust in their wake. Removing his worn floppy canvas hat from his head and scratching his now mostly bald head in thought, the aging Dutch Egyptologist was next startled by a hearty greeting of "good morning" from off to his left. Turning to see just who could be so cheerful so early in the morning, van der Boek saw two figures approaching from the tourist entrance of the temple complex. One was clearly, or nearly, his contemporary, the other an extremely fit young man who wore a broad grin.

Murmuring, van der Boek commiserated, "Vell, dhat youngster must be Richards."

Now quickly stealing a glance at his wristwatch.

"Vell, at least he's on time. But who is dhat mit him? Somehow he looks very, very familiar."

"You must be Professor Dr. van der Boek!"

Richards stated with hopeful excitement.

"Ja, I am." answered the slightly pleased Egyptologist at the American's acknowledgement of his full academic title, just as any European scholar would.

"Und dhat makes you Dr. Richards, I presume. Eh?"

"Correct, sir. And may I introduce to you my colleague, John Milson, Professor Emeritus of Egyptology."

Then the dawn broke for van der Boek.

Vhy, of course! Richards must be Milson's protégé.

But vhy is John Milson, the foremost living Egyptologist in the United States, here on a topographical survey of the most picked over property in all of Egypt?

"Vhy, Professor Dr. Milson," van der Boek intoned as he extended his hand. "It is my distinct pleasure to meet you, sir. I must admit that I am surprised to see you here, but am pleased nonetheless."

Noting the intrigued expressions from his graduate students, van der Boek caught himself.

"Und, gentlemen, may I introduce to you my topographical survey team, who just so happen to be my best archaeological students as well? Here ist Horst Willing, a topographical surveyor und genius mit die laser theodolite. Here ist Brigitte Claus, my most promising epigrapher. Und finally here ist Claude Assmann, an absolute artist mit der digital camera."

At these words of praise from their mentor, blushes broke out and shuffling feet pawed the earth as each was introduced. Then there occurred that awkward moment that always occurs whenever two groups are first introduced, where neither wishes to appear either too eager or verbose. But Milson, immediately seeing the dilemma, stepped forth to fill the gap.

"Folks, if you do not mind my directness, we have a lot of work to do, and we have to do it in a brief span of time. As you all already know, the Egyptian Antiquities Organization has granted us just two weeks to complete our preliminary survey for this season, that being, the survey of the area encompassed by the Fourth Pylon. As you all well know, this is a large and ruinous area that was the architectural contribution of the Pharaoh Thutmose I to the Karnak complex. During these two weeks, we will have the total run of the Karnak Temple to ourselves."

Milson then chose to add for emphasis, "Yes, you did hear me correctly. I said only us. All tourists and even the French Epigraphical Survey will be excluded from the site while we'll be working here."

The shock on the Dutch team's faces was complete. Van der Boek's mind was rapidly reevaluating the situation, the financial implications on local tourism, and just how much clout it must have taken to actually kick the French off of the site, a site that they had been working on for, well, for ages.

Van der Boek then bluntly stated, “Professor Milson, just vhat are we doing here?”

Quite frankly, sir, Joseph and I are just philologists. When I asked the director of the EAO for his best recommendation of whom he would team up with to take on such a formidable task, he named you. And so here we are.”

“May I ask, Professor Milson, just vhat sort of evidence led you and Dr. Richards to the conclusion that a treasury even exists, much less within the Fourth Pylon?” queried van der Boek.

“A fair question,” Milson began. “In the main, practically all of the pylons at Karnak have been found to be constructed as hollow structures, which were later filled with the rubble of reused materials. For some reason the Fourth Pylon was not. That suggested to us that the pylon was off-limits for such activity and that makes it a good candidate for a hollow core.

But besides that possibility, we are of the belief that if a hidden subterranean treasury of the Great God and its priesthood had indeed been established, then it had to be done early on during the renovation and development of the Karnak temple complex. This we know occurred during the reign of the Pharaoh Thutmose I, when he made Thebes Egypt’s capital and Amen Re the principal god of the Two Lands. Moreover, the Fourth Pylon once had a twin-leaved door of beaten Asiatic copper inlaid with gold. The French Egyptologist Georges Legrain once estimated its size as ten meters high by six wide. And by the way, an inscription refers to that portal as ‘Amen mighty in wealth.’

Finally, this pylon has two suspiciously placed side chambers, chambers that could have offered access to the core of the pylon itself by way of a hidden entrance.”

Milson then prodded, “Consequently, I and Dr. Richards believe that the most fruitful area to begin the survey will be with the Fourth Pylon, and from there extend the work inwards toward the earlier constructed Fifth Pylon, if necessary.”

With a grunt of enlightened understanding that still did not dispel his natural skepticism, van der Boek then asked, “Do you have a plan that you wish to go by? Something dhat ve can use as a baseline?”

"Yes, indeed, Professor van der Boek," answered an eager Richards. "In fact, I have several blown-up copies of Gun Björkman's fine plan that I made from his *Kings of Karnak* publication. Here they are."

"Björkman!" van der Boek exclaimed.

"Gun and I studied together for a time with Säve-Söderbergh! That was, of course, before he completed his doctorate at Uppsala. At the time, he vas in continuous correspondence and on good terms with the French archaeological mission here. Vell, fine choice, Dr. Richards. You could not have chosen a better baseline for us to begin with."

After several minutes of scrutiny and discussion of the baseline, it was decided not to split up the group into two teams, but rather stick together and try as best as possible not to get into each other's way. Richards, being both junior and not an archaeologist, was saddled with the maintenance of the field log, while van der Boek and Milson made the decision to first survey the southern of the two chambers of the Fourth Pylon, as it was the largest with two niches and that there was once an adjacent stairway next to it.

After an initial photographic log of the area was made by Assmann, climbing over and around the remains of the pylon's foundation at its southern end proved early on to be a frustrating exercise. There was so much heavy rubble and debris. Finally, it was the surveyor Willing who first spoke his mind.

"Herr Professor, just vhat am I looking vor?"

Smiling, the Dutch archaeologist answered, "Vell, Horst, a good start would be locating a cutting in the chapel's floor pavement vor a passage, or better, a door pivot. I would imagine that such a ding vould be required for a hidden doorway of some kind."

"Ja," Willing mused. "Dhat vould be logical. Look vor door pivots."

Fortunately, by the end of that first sweaty day, no one had sustained any serious injuries, either moving or working around the pylon's blocks and rubble. That is not to say that there was not the occasional surprise discovery of a scorpion or two and the usual blisters, scrapes, abrasions, pinched and bloodied fingers that all come with the territory.

Unfortunately, after looking around and under many blocks of limestone, or at least those they could move, no cuttings or pivots had been located within the southern chapel of the Fourth Pylon. Calling it a day, the team agreed to resume their search at the northern chapel the following day.

* * *

They began again at the crack of dawn. This time, however, the team was a bit stiffer in the joints, with aspirin taken for some muscle aches and with some bandages applied to fingers. The foundation blocks that circumscribed the northern chapel of the Fourth Pylon outlined a long and narrow room complete with a single statue niche at its farthest end. While smaller in total square footage than its twin to the south, the line of common limestone casing blocks that fronted the pylon's core was actually a bit longer. While the Dutch graduate students and Richards focused on those, van der Boek and Milson had wandered out of earshot to have a frank discussion. Richards, who had seen this development, had purposely buried his nose in his field log, dutifully noting down all the preinvestigation photo shots that had been taken by Claude, describing their orientation, f-stops, and number. Richards knew that Milson could hold his own with the Dutch archaeologist and he reasoned it was now just a matter of time before all hell would shortly break loose.

With Horst's measurements of the chapel completed and logged to a new precision down to one tenth of a meter, Richards joined his two colleagues, while they methodically worked their way in from the two extremes. For Richards, the excitement was just too much. He could not just show them where the pivot block was. They had to find it themselves. The real question was just who would be the lucky one and how soon. In fact, Milson and he had built a pool around just those two questions. Both thought that the pivot would be found before noon for sure, but while Milson favored Brigitte as the discoverer, Richards had pinned his hopes on Claude. At stake for these two high rollers was a cold case of Coors longnecks.

But as things turned out, neither American won this wager as the heavy foot of Horst's six-two frame had by accident fractionally dislodged the critical pivot block from its position. While Richards watched with his thudding heart threatening to fill his throat, Horst himself did not recognize his discovery as he was probing amid the rubble behind the block. It was only when the surveyor had lifted away one of Richards carefully replaced camouflaged blocks that he saw the arced grooves of the pivot block, which were etched into the core's floor surface. Then he noted the odd shaping of the left-hand inner corner of the block – it was not squared but rather had a piece trimmed off of it at a forty-five degree angle. Stopping and cocking his head in Teutonic disbelief at what his eyes were seeing, Horst bent over and began to carefully brush away all the sand and stone chips that Richards had strewn about, and in the process, started removing and stacking several blocks out of the way. Now with the rear of the big casing block clear of all rubble and sand, the big German squatted down and, with a low grunt, pushed with both of his hands at the block, which immediately grated and gave way, while pivoting around its left end!

"Mein Gott!" he exclaimed. "Herr Professor van der Boek," he shouted loudly. "Ich habe es gefunden!"

At Horst's first shout, Brigitte and Claude had come leaping to his side. Richards, trying to play dumb, simply said, "What's up!"

Moments later, van der Boek and Milson had both joined them, a bit breathless at their hurried arrival.

Horst, now standing proud and tall above his discovery, pointed it out to the eager eyes.

"Look, vill you! Look at dhose marks! I dink dhat if I move dhat block. I vill find a pivot beneath its left corner!"

But van der Boek, ever the archaeologist, said, "No, not yet, Horst. But gut job nonetheless! Damn gut job. Claude! Quickly take a series of photographs. And don't forget to include a scale! We must record this event for posterity. Und now I must make a call to Cairo as well!"

* * *

Needless to say, the rest of the day seemed to fly by for the survey team as their collective morale soared. Indeed, Horst had been correct. The stone bulge of a pivot was found when the block was picked up and dutifully photographed, measured, and recorded. Careful clearing and sweeping of the area behind the pivot block further revealed extensive grooving to the flooring of the pylon's core, which confirmed that the original passageway was probably about four to five feet wide. By day's end, it became abundantly clear to all that they next must begin clearing away a mound of rubble down to this level if they had any hopes of finding any subsequent passageway that might lead to the treasury. And to do that meant heavy lifting machinery.

The following day, Milson inquired with the Egyptian Antiquities Organization and found out that a light crane mounted on the back of a small pickup truck just happened to be indeed available. As luck would have it, it was the same dilapidated truck that Richards recognized as the one favored by Major Tuna Cartwright and his team. With the assistance of the EAO, an area outside of the temple complex proper was designated as the location to inventory all the blocks and rubble that were to be removed from the area. Once photographed and numbered *in situ* by Claude, each would be removed and deposited there, where each and every block would be logged by Brigitte and inspected for any possible epigraphical details.

By late Thursday, a neat swath of some twenty-three feet of debris had been cleared and swept from beyond the threshold of the door pivot. In the process Brigitte had discovered and logged about a half-dozen painted hieratic graffiti that appeared to be architectural construction labels. But to the great disappointment of this hardworking team, nothing more had yet to be found. By Richards' own private estimate, evidence for the first step of the descending ramp was still a good five to ten feet distant, which unfortunately still lay under a considerable pile of fallen stone.

As the exhaustion of the day finally took its toll, the Director of the Egyptian Antiquities Organization arrived on the scene. Amid the many introductions and congratulatory shaking of hands at their progress, the director beamed with enthusiasm and invited the entire crew out to a celebratory, but early evening dinner.

As the dinner wound down and the team's eyes began to glaze over due to the fine meal, the director, out of deference, looked over to van der Boek and asked, "Willy, just what does your team need? Looking around at them now, tired as they are. What's missing?"

"Vell," answered the Egyptologist, "really ve are moving at a good pace right now, but ve could use two men to help with the moving of the stone. Would that be at all possible?"

The director nodded at the reasonable request and said nothing. Then looking to Milson, he asked, "And what about you, John? Is there anything that you or young Richards here need?"

"Not a darn thing," stated Milson flatly. "Joseph and I are learning how hard archaeology really is and we're learning from the best of the best. So, to your question, no, not a darn thing, but thanks just the same for asking."

* * *

The next day, Friday, the Muslim day of rest, the team took the day off to write letters, do laundry, go sightseeing, and just loaf. That afternoon, van der Boek and his students took a tour over to Western Thebes and luxuriated within an air-conditioned bus that took them on a whirlwind visit of all that was deemed important, which of course included several stops at locations where authentic antiquities could be acquired. To van der Boek, it was as much a diversion for his students as it was a banal tribute to his profession.

As for Milson and Richards, their afternoon was spent within the Karnak complex itself, while Richards took the part of a rather special tour guide for his academic mentor. As they slowly strolled about in the bright sunlight, Richards regaled Milson with his precise memories of what it all had really looked and even smelled like. What was where and what wasn't. For Milson, it was such a revelation to hear an eyewitness account of such a famous place at the highs and lows of its existence. For Richards, it was nothing less than a rare and precious gift freely given to a dear friend.

* * *

By Saturday morning, all were rejuvenated, well-rested, and raring to go, and to van der Boek's surprise, two powerfully built men joined up with them as well. When asked what their backgrounds were, both responded that they were civil engineers in the Egyptian military. The effect of these two newcomers to the team was incredible. With ready broad smiles and eyes that glittered with mirth and curiosity, Labib and Naguib soon proved their worth with their sure mastery in the movement of stone, the use of clever tricks of leverage, their ingenuity with the crane, and sheer muscle power. By day's end a full five feet of rubble had been cleared. By Richards' best recollection and with the brawny pair's steady aid, Sunday would surely be the day. Trying as best he could, Richards found he could not sleep that night. The sheer excitement and anticipation of the coming moment was too great.

* * *

Whenever faced with a truly momentous day, there are points during it which seem to drag on without end and others that seemed to smear into an almost incomprehensible blur. Professional athletes experience this phenomenon before every play-off game. Young children do the same while they are in rapt anticipation of Christmas morning. Lucky mortals in love experience it during their wedding celebrations.

* * *

For Richards, who manned the field log, his role was to record as accurately as possible the day's events. Given Doc Allen's memory enhancement sessions, none was better qualified to do so.

So, on Sunday morning at 8:43 a.m., Richards logged the word, "Bingo!"

After LB 83 (limestone block number 83) had been removed, a portion of a descending cut step had been revealed in the pylon's stone flooring. All work stopped and Brigitte was immediately fetched to view the find. The euphoria was so electric that it actually brought tears to van der Boek's disbelieving eyes. Milson simply beamed and then had his back slapped by van der Boek in congratulatory victory. Forty minutes later, the entire width of the descending passage with its broad central ramp and flanking stone steps was exposed, recorded by Claude's cameras, and precisely measured at 2.625 meters in breadth that calculated precisely as five Egyptian royal cubits. Horst then added the feature to his excavation plan. Brigitte said that she had never seen such beautifully cut limestone steps. For all, it had been truly a Kodak moment.

At dinner that night the students' speculations abounded. As for van der Boek, he was overjoyed with the results thus far and clearly was shell-shocked at the near machine-gun rapidity of all the successes, something that never happened in archaeology.

"Do you realize, John," the Dutchman excitedly spoke, while he unconsciously rubbed his hands together, "just how significant the vidth of dhat passage truly is? It means dhat die old royal cubit of the New Kingdom vas used instead of the longer cubit of the Twenty-Sixth Dynasty! It means dhat the passage vas most likely cut during the New Kingdom und maybe even during the reign of Thutmose I! Just as your philological analysis suggests! Und, I almost forgot with all of the excitement, ve must inform Cairo of this."

The next several days of excavation passed in an almost anticlimactic fashion. One cleared step led to two, to three, to four, and by Wednesday afternoon, step number sixteen, and there was no indication of any end in sight. What had become apparent, however, was that the slope of the descending steps went in a gradual four to one ratio, which made eminent sense to van der Boek, given the central ramp by which heavy objects would have been dragged up or down.

Another development was that the passage's sides were discovered to be smoothly formed, unadorned, white-washed walls. As yet, at the sixteenth step, they had yet to encounter a roof. The only heartening tendency from the encountered fill was that it had become more and more manageable to remove, to the point that the traditional tried-and-true tire buckets were used more and more to quickly haul out the material. This loose fill then had to be sieved by Brigitte out at the inventory quarry, and quite soon she had taken on the pallor of a dusty ghost. Van der Boek clearly did not want to miss any clues or be accused of shoddy methodology.

As their last day arrived, fully eighteen steps had been cleared and still they had not found whether the passage had a roof nor could they provide any evidence that it had just collapsed. It seemed as if they were confronted with an endless mountain of packed debris and rock, the stuff that nightmares are made of, pressured further by the fact that they had come so far, but were now nearly out of time. At the noon break, van der Boek, just as crestfallen as any of them, finally had to deliver to his hardworking team the bad news – here we stop until next season. All knew the reality of the announcement. None were surprised by it. But none wished to accept it.

So they stopped that season at the eighteenth step. Unknown to them, they were just eight steps short of the start of the passage's ceiling and twelve steps before the first evidence would appear of a possible breakthrough. Bitterly, van der Boek had been here before, had remembered how he had to wait it out until the following season before he could open Meryptah's tomb, and what that event had meant to his winding down, but glorious career.

Spreading out a thick plastic tarp across the untouched wall of rubble and firmly staking it in, several truckloads of Brigitte's carefully sifted sand and small rubble arrived and were unceremoniously dumped and shoveled into their carefully excavated trench. Now with it filled in and smoothed to the pylon's inner pavement flooring, it had looked as if their past week's labors had never occurred, as if the excavation had never taken place, and that was just how van der Boek wanted it. Truly the only evidence of their presence was the partial and neat clearance of the pylon's core and about one hundred or so numbered blocks lined up neatly in the vast inventory quarry located to the south of the temple complex.

CHAPTER XXX

The Recruit

"As surely as I live and breathe this woman will be a real challenge for Joseph," Milson sighed to himself as he reread yet again the classified dossier of the candidate his Russian colleagues had sent him.

Regardless, the emeritus Egyptologist was inwardly pleased with their choice. They had taken the hint, made their choice, and then sponsored her in the hopes that the Philology Annex would reject her. And if we do, what would that devious nation of chess players be ready to counter with? No doubt they have that figured out as well with a scenario to cover each and every one of our possible moves and countermoves.

Looking down at the open file before him and fingering the border of that sober, yet striking black-and-white glossy of Vesna Gregorieva, he sighed. For the photo was subtle in its own right as her listed dark green eyes were not in evidence. All of this Milson considered and weighed.

What was that clever quote that Sir Winston Churchill had said of Russia? "A riddle wrapped in a mystery inside an enigma?" Yes, indeed.

But here, what is there to be suspicious of, much less reject? All I see is an accomplished linguistic specialist with a master's degree from the University of St. Petersburg. Her diminutive size and black hair present no problem for fitting into the general population of the period. Those eyes might be a liability or a plus. On that there's no knowing. Given her dancer's training and the lithe, taut muscles that result, balance, dropping, and landing should not present any difficulties. In fact, she might not even need the jump school curriculum. Check that. She's going anyway, if only for the self-defense training.

The offspring of a Russian and Yugoslav: he a degreed mechanical engineer schooled at the University of Moscow. She an embassy official from Tito's regime. Well, that makes Vesna's mother probably more a field operative for the former Yugoslav intelligence community. I just wonder.

Then a correlating notion came to mind and the scholar again paged through the documents and upon finding what he was looking for, he smiled a dark and cagey smile.

Ah, ha! He thought. *I knew it! Gregorieva, just like Piankoff, has all the earmarks of being a prize agent of Karlov Drazinzka, the Director of the Special Projects Directorate, which provide internal security for the Russian Academy of Science. Oh, how intriguing. Oh, how impressively intriguing.*

Now, I just wonder whether Gregorieva and Piankoff knew one another. Or instead, had they been carefully compartmentalized?

* * *

"Vesna," her linguistics trainer said. "Let us begin again with the fifth lesson in Egyptian that Major General Piankoff prepared for us. There are some nuances contained within it that I believe you will find most helpful with your future assignment."

"Future assignment!" started the suddenly alert woman.

"Why, yes. It seems that Director Drazinzka received word yesterday of the Americans' interest in you as Major General Piankoff's replacement. In fact, within a month's time I would expect you will undergo your initial battery of tests in Chicago. And if you pass them, which I do not doubt you will, then it would be logical that the next steps in your recruitment would be further training, and then an orientation visit at their Horizon Pass facility."

"My recruitment?"

"Why, yes," stated her trainer. "I found that a rather quaint word choice myself. But the Americans are after all – Americans. But what that should mean to you is that you will be probed, observed, prodded, poked, and psychoanalyzed at every opportunity. Just because they look friendly and even inept, don't believe it for a moment! They cultivate the appearance of intellectual dullness whenever they can. Just look at their intelligence agencies! They alone have brilliantly achieved the single most negative marketing campaign imaginable. To the media and their public, no one believes them to be operationally effective or their sources credible. What remarkable camouflage! What a magnificent tactic! And while everyone is laughing at them, they are operating full tilt and in the open, protected by their carefully nurtured image of mediocrity."

But all during this canned analysis of American guile, Gregorieva was not listening. Instead, her mind was in a whirl of concealed excitement.

Imagine! Me! Following in the footsteps of Major General Piankoff! A simply brilliant linguist. A demanding and experienced instructor of field craft. A superb physical specimen.

"Vesna Gregorieva!" snapped her instructor when he saw that distant look of distraction.

"Have you heard a single word that I have been saying?"

"Why, yes, Colonel, every single syllable."

In fact, she thought, far too many syllables as this pompous ass just loves to lecture on and on.

Blind to the utter disdain that her intelligent eyes this time managed to conceal, her trainer continued with a certain cruel enjoyment.

"As I was saying, while at the Horizon Pass facility, you will undergo a technical orientation followed by a full body shave, head to toe, then . . ."

"What!"

* * *

Milson had been dead on. Not only was Gregorieva a handful, but Richards was absolutely livid that he had not been included in her selection. Yes, he was busy with his classes, but what about an e-mail? What about a phone call? Never before had the retired Egyptologist witnessed such a volcanic reaction from his protégé. But after two days of simmer, Richards finally had gotten used to the idea that his new field assistant might be Gregorieva.

After all, Richards reasoned, she still had to pass muster and that meant conquering a long laundry list of tests, tasks, and simulations – not to mention jump school.

But deep down, something else was troubling the young Egyptologist. No one could replace Piankoff, and given his absence, he was now the veteran. Now every move he made would be scrutinized and appraised by a stranger that he had to depend upon utterly. Grudgingly, Richards began to appreciate just what Piankoff had gone through with his training of him. The proof of the pudding would be the creation of a training plan of his making. Instinctively, Richards knew that he could not craft such a curriculum on his own. While his first impulse was to discuss the matter with Milson, his intellect quickly nixed that idea and voted instead for the sage wisdom of Doc Allen. And so he called him up to discuss his predicament, and after a few moments the secure connection between Chicago and New Mexico was completed.

"Joey, my boy, how are you!" the folksy Oklahoma voice said as the physician began already to suspect why it was made as he glanced over at his copy of the Gregorieva file resting on his desk.

"Just great, Doc. But truth be told, I am sorely in need of some advice. I need to jaw some."

I thought so, smiled the physician at Horizon Pass to himself. *Joey is such a straight arrow. So refreshingly direct.*

"So, son, just what's the itch that you wanna' scratch?"

"Doc, I need to build a training curriculum for my possible new assistant, and frankly, I need the wisdom of someone far more experienced in these sorts of things than I."

And brutally honest about himself and his limitations to boot!

"Wow," he began. "That's a tall order for a phone call. Any chance that you can get your butt down here for the weekend? That way, I can do some preliminary thinking and you can too. And then we can chew on it all. How's that sound?"

"Sounds like a plan.

"See you late Friday afternoon."

* * *

Vesna Gregorieva's instructions when she arrived at O'Hare International Terminal were as explicit as they were succinct: be patient, proceed through customs, and secure your baggage. They will meet you beyond the security checkpoint.

For Gregorieva, this was her first time on American soil. While she had been briefed on the culture and spoke the language well, albeit with a British accent, she really did not know what to expect at a personal level. Since the Aeroflot flight plan took them the polar route from Moscow that then descended over the vast virgin expanses of Canada, Gregorieva had not been prepared for her first sight of Chicago's clustered nighttime skyline. Its orange-colored grid of streetlights seemed to stretch off in three directions beyond the horizon. Its downtown area looked like a mad collection of crystal spires.

With her nose pressed against her airline seat's window, she gaped in amazement.

So this is Chicago – the Second City! It's not even as big as their New York or Los Angeles! But it's so huge! And that skyline is just breathtaking!

The plane landed with an authoritative bang that suggested the aircraft's pilot might have once landed on aircraft carriers. After a brisk taxi, Vesna now saw the gracefully curving stainless steel roof of the international terminal and the motorized approach of the M17 gate bridge. Exiting the plane, Gregorieva's first smell of America came from the rubberized and knobbed Pirelli nonslip flooring of the gateway that was soon followed by a tallish, colorful, well-lit, and airy interior of corridor passages that seemed to lead on forever. While the signage made it abundantly clear that this was indeed the way to "Customs" and "Welcome to Chicago," the field operative saw many security cameras along the way. She also noted all the blacked out surfaces that bespoke of the airport's extraordinary security measures.

While the ritual at customs seemed ridiculously brief and perfunctory by Russian standards, the eyes of the young male customs agent were anything but dull and lifeless. Adjectives like cool, appraising, and analytical were far closer to the mark. And even though she had purposely adjusted the blouse beneath her lone string of pearls and gray two-piece business suit to her best advantage, Gregorieva was shocked to note that the customs agent's eyes had never wavered from hers. So she registered another adjective: chilling. No, these Americans are not soft. That indeed is part of their clever defense, just as my language officer said.

The wait at the baggage carousel had been brief and she found her luggage intact and undamaged – yet two other signs of difference with her homeland. Pulling on the handle of her lone Samsonite wheelie, Gregorieva walked to the final customs agent, presented a claims form that was unremarkable, and was waved through – although that time her blouse was indeed noticed and with an appreciative set of eyes.

At her nearing approach, the broad twin tinted glass doors marked "Exit" automatically slid aside, opening to a sea of expectant faces, many carrying flowers of welcome and small sleeping children on their shoulders as the local hour was late. Many wore tired smiles and clutched at handkerchiefs ready to daub their already moist eyes filled with excited anticipation. Still moving, but not knowing where to go, the young business woman decided to slow, scan the crowd, and find a gap to exploit.

After having successfully negotiated her way through this first phalanx of "meeters and greeters," Gregorieva saw several men dressed in black suits, who held up small placards before them. One, a young and nicely built man with a short cropped haircut, held one that announced "Ms. Gregorieva" in largish block letters with "Philology Annex" printed neatly below.

Walking directly up to him chin high, she figured the man for military by his posture and announced in her clipped British-schooled English, "I am Gregorieva."

An appraising set of eyes smiled back and the man said, "Ms. Gregorieva, may I please see some form of identification?"

Producing her passport from her outside right suit jacket pocket, the driver carefully examined it, its date of issue, and her face. Satisfied, he again smiled, returned it to her, and said, "Ms. Gregorieva, welcome to Chicago. My name is Joey. May I take your bag?"

Surprised and taken aback by both the casual introduction and the offer of assistance, the Russian at first balked and then gave in with a suddenly self-important smile that one would reserve for a servant.

"Why, yes. Please do, Joey."

The ride from the airport to the south side of Chicago where the Philology Annex was located took about fifty-five minutes by the Russian's American-made Timex watch. While she had caught the driver watching her occasionally from the rearview mirror through the glass of the privacy partition, it was not because of her, but because she had failed to put on her seat belt. This she was firmly told to do, and she quickly complied once she had figured out which buckle went where.

How strange these Americans are! She thought. *The police will actually initiate a traffic investigation if a seat belt is not fastened!*

Then a quick calculation took place in Gregorieva's mind where either the Americans have one policeman per citizen or that the police do not have much, if anything, to do. Both notions brought an unconscious smile to her face – one that the observant driver saw.

But despite her driver's gruff request to "buckle up," she was impressed with how Joey deftly maneuvered the big black Buick away from the airport and through the broad lanes of high speed traffic. Alone in the gray leather backseat and looking out of its heavily tinted windows, the Russian found herself feasting upon all of the foreign sights around her. It was all so new, so very different from her homeland, and for that matter, Europe as well.

Imagine, four broad lanes of autobahn in each direction? Imagine, traffic that actually uses turn signals? And look at all the cars with just one passenger in them? Practically all of them!

At that point a fire-engine red sports car briefly pulled up beside Gregorieva's window, snarled its motor, and then just as suddenly moved off. Forgetting herself, the Russian tapped on the privacy window, which immediately lowered.

"Yes, Ms. Gregorieva?"

"Joey. What kind of car was the little red one that just passed us?"

"Why, that was a Chevy Corvette. I think it was a Z06. Why do you ask?"

"Oh, it's just that I have never seen one before. It's so low and small. And it sounded so powerful. Do many people in the United States own such a powerful sports car?"

"Plenty, Ms. Gregorieva. Plenty. There are even organized clubs of Corvette owners."

To that response came a stunned and neutral "Thank you, Joey." And Joey got the hint and raised the screen.

For the rest of the trip to the Annex, Gregorieva observed all that she could from her limo's fishbowl perspective. Upon turning off the toll way, where citizens paid to enjoy its convenience, her driver drove east, following the course of a numbered orange city street sign. Along this stretch the Russian could clearly see signs of deterioration in the building fronts and older automobiles, not to mention the listless stagger of some of its inhabitants. Her driver now turned this way and that through narrow treed streets, and the neighborhood changed to a better and tidier one with neatly trimmed hedges.

Stopping before a handsome three-story brownstone on a corner, Joey announced that they had arrived.

Getting out, the driver fetched her wheelie from the "trunk," not the "boot," and walked her to the building's front door.

Putting on his best smile, the driver extended his hand and said, "Ms. Gregorieva, welcome to the Philology Annex and have a pleasant stay."

He then waited a beat, watching for the Russian's reaction. Seeing the blank expression that he had half expected, the driver just smiled again, and left with a half over the shoulder wave.

Left standing on the stoop, Vesna Gregorieva just stared as the beautifully polished black limo pulled away.

How strange, she thought. *Was I supposed to shake his hand and thank him for what was clearly his duty? Or was I to give him a tip?*

She then shook her head in dismissal.

Americans!

As Associate Professor Joseph Richards drove down the block, he was shaking his head as well.

Boy, will she be a handful!

* * *

Vesna Gregorieva's first night at the Annex amounted to a jet-lagger's hell. While the local time was past midnight, her circadian cycle was still broad daylight. Then there was the issue of the mattress. It was too soft. Vesna thought that she was either falling through it or being enveloped by it. She wasn't sure which. Getting up for the second time and looking out the third floor window of the brownstone didn't help much either, as there was precious little to see. What she did know was that she was inside a university community, or campus, as they call it. The signs were everywhere and her limo driver, Joey, had pointed them out as if he were a proud member of it: the student union, the coffee house, here's the main library, over there's a really good steak house, and that's the football stadium. With her athletic body screaming at her after the long flight, the Russian decided to go out for a cleansing run. Then, perhaps after a hot shower, she'd stretch and maybe be able to catch some sleep, but not right now, no way.

* * *

"Dr. Richards?"

A sleepy "yes" answered the phone.

"Our guest, sir, is about to go out for some air, perhaps even a jog or run from the look of it. What do you want us to do about it, sir?"

"Oh, hell. Let her go. Dollars to donuts, she's all jet-lagged out. Just put a couple of tails on her so she doesn't get herself into any sort of trouble. This is, after all, the South Side, for Christ's sake."

"Roger, sir, will do. I'll task two minnows from my school. Sorry for bothering you, Doc."

"Not a problem, Tuna. Thanks for looking out for our guest."

As Major Tuna Cartwright put down the phone, he just had to smile.

Doc is probably right on. That Russian is probably all screwed up and is just trying to shake loose some of her cobwebs.

Picking up the phone again, he dialed four numbers that connected him to his school's "reef." At the second ring, it was briskly answered. The order was given, and three minutes later two guardian joggers were deployed to protect one valuable and attractive asset.

* * *

Dressed in a clinging dark blue Nike nylon jogging suit to protect her against the cool spring air, it did not take Gregorieva long to realize that she was being followed. Or at least, she thought that she was. For early on during her run two lean joggers, who were talking incessantly, had fallen in behind her at a reasonable distance. At every turn she would sneak a peek back at them, noting their consistent distance and babble and what they wore – baseball caps, sneakers, light-colored shorts, and gray T-shirts. By the look of them and the broad spreading stains of perspiration across their chests, she figured that they would soon be stopping for a breather, but to her surprise, they didn't. They just kept plodding along, gabbing and waving their arms and hands this way and that. In the end, Vesna decided to relax, ignore the noisy pair, and enjoy her run.

* * *

"Major,"

Callahan, the taller of the pair of shadows, called in over his small stem mike.

"Our subject is jogging toward no-man's-land. What are your orders, sir?"

"Initiate friendly relations. Keep her out of there, Callahan, or I will have your ass in a wringer. Got that?"

"Roger, sir, commencing friendly relations."

Callahan and Sanchez just looked at one another as they broke into dead runs, while reaching up to conceal their mike and ear pieces under their ball caps.

* * *

Gregorieva, much to her surprise, suddenly found herself flanked on each side by the two joggers, who had appeared as if from nowhere. She certainly hadn't heard their approach and that troubled her.

"Miss," the taller of the two with black curly hair said. "You must be new in town, because you are heading toward a very dangerous area. You just might want to stop, get your bearings, and turn around."

Now slowing to a halt, Gregorieva found that her alarm bells were ringing off the hook. That complex statement had just been made without so much of a gasp for air. In fact, looking from the taller to the smaller one, neither was even breathing heavily. They were sweating to be sure, but they were hardly winded.

The taller one, seeing her appraising look, then broke the ice.

"Miss, my name is Callahan and this is Sanchez. We're members of the Crimson's football team."

Now indicating with his thumb.

"Sancho here is our star wide receiver. I'm the team's tight end. If you're lost, we would be more than happy to walk you back to your dorm. It's kinda' late, and animals, of the two-legged variety, if you know what I mean, have been known to prowl these streets at this hour."

Finally finding her tongue, Gregorieva said with her British lilt, "So you're footballers?" and then pointing to Callahan's shirt, "And you're number forty, is that right?"

Sanchez was the first to start laughing. Callahan, who never liked being the brunt of any joke, looked confused. Then his teammate helped him out.

"Hey, Calli-baby, look at your T-shirt. She read its size, XL, for your number. That's forty in Roman numerals."

At this point Sanchez was near hysteria with laughter. Callahan and his very Irish temper were about to explode, but the British-sounding accent reined him in.

"Missy, despite your joke that Sancho is so enjoying, I think it best that we get you to your dorm. It's late. How about it?"

Throughout this entire exchange Gregorieva did not and could not decide what was what. Clearly the smaller one named Sanchez or Sancho was thoroughly enjoying himself at the taller one's expense. But the taller one's concern for where she was appeared to be genuine. Their offer to take her "to her dorm" seemed oddly sincere and so she said, "All right. I suppose that I can have two handsome footballers escort me home, but I will race you there!"

And off she bolted in the general direction of the brownstone's sanctuary.

"Ah, shit!" whispered Sanchez between his teeth as the pair took off in pursuit.

For Gregorieva, it had been far, far too long since she had actually raced against anyone, much less two American footballers. Glancing over her shoulder, she could see them and they appeared to be just pacing her, as if she were the prey and they the predators. It seemed that no matter how hard she would run, the gap between remained always the same. Seeing the looming brownstone on the corner from a half block away, Gregorieva stole one last glance over her shoulder and with disappointment discovered that she was again alone.

"Shit!" was all she could say.

*   *   *

"Major. We have successfully herded the subject back to the nest."

"Well done, Callahan. "Any issues?"

"None that a really good cold shower wouldn't cure."

"That good-looking?"

"Awesome, sir. A real looker and as fast as a gazelle. Doc Richards will have his hands full training that one."

"Roger that. Well done, gentlemen!

"Out."

*   *   *

Following the printed schedule found on her nightstand, Gregorieva prepared herself for breakfast and then took the elevator to Sublevel 2. Upon entering the sparsely populated cafeteria, delicious smells assaulted her, and her stomach responded as if on cue. Confronted by such a variety of unfamiliar and exotic-looking foods, the Russian opted for items that she could at least identify – black coffee, dark bread and butter, two bananas, and a bowl of hot onion soup. Pausing before the juice dispenser, she tried a glass of orange and found it to be fresh, complete with pulp. Downing the glass where she stood, Vesna dispensed another and drank it down too. Picking up her now full tray, she started to walk over to an unoccupied table in the corner but was waved over to another where a kindly looking man sat with a newspaper and a half-finished cup of coffee.

As the Russian approached the table, she smiled and offered a cheery British "good morning" to the now standing male.

Seating herself, she continued, "My name is Vesna Gregorieva. And yours might be?"

Offering his huge mitt of a hand in greeting, the Russian took it. The grip was firm, warm, and sincere. She liked that. Ruddy and freckled, balding with a peace wreath of reddish hair, the Russian unconsciously guessed him to be of either Irish or Viking heritage.

"Dr. James H. Allen at your service. People around here call me Doc Allen or even just Doc. Anyways, welcome to the Annex."

Seating himself after she did, which she noticed, he continued, "I guess you could sort of say that I'm the house physician. I handle everything from headaches to good advice. So, how was your flight from Moscow?"

Gregorieva briefly felt a naked chill at the physician's forwardness, but then tempered that with the fact the Annex's community was probably a small one and the appearance of any new face would be well announced in advance.

"The flight was uneventful. Thank you for asking."

"Any trouble sleeping? Any jet lag issues?"

"I did have some trouble getting to sleep, but I managed."

"Okay, fine. But if you need anything in the future, just call my office." He said while he groped and then found his card in the oversize breast pocket of his white lab coat.

"So, Vesna, please dig in. You're probably starved to death! And don't mind me, I haven't finished the sports page yet. Besides, I'm trying to catch up on how the Crimson's football team is doing."

And eat she did, rising twice to get more orange juice. Noting this, Doc Allen piped up from behind the pages that he was buried behind.

"Myself, I hate to fly. I get so dehydrated from all that filtered air. Like the orange juice?"

The Russian answered in almost mid-gulp, "It is very good."

"Indeed it is. When I retire, I intend to plant several fruit trees on my land, a couple of orange, one grapefruit, a lemon, and maybe even a key lime. Together they mix real nice into a refreshing and tart summer drink. They're even better with a bit of vodka," he added with a wink over his half-moon reading glasses as he returned to his reading.

Fascinating was the only word that Gregorieva could conjure. *So much personal information offered. Why do they do that? And then it hit her right between the eyes.*

They're trying to break down my barriers! Attempting to gain an edge. This kindly physician. The athletic footballers. Even the polite driver. They all are most likely the Annex's agents!

All the while Gregorieva was digesting this revelation, Doc Allen was peeking over his glasses, observing her. Reading her like a book, the countrified physician decided to really jar her with a question pitched to her in his best fatherly voice. Neatly folding up his paper before him, he began, "You know, Vesna, we all have the highest hopes for your success during your stay with us. However, I must be blunt with you. There are several among us who do not relish your presence here. That, frankly, is their problem and not yours. So for the meantime, please think of me as your personally appointed welcoming committee. I'm not much to look at, but then again that is not my function. I am a doctor and a good one."

Stopping to take a sip of his coffee, Doc Allen continued on in his matter-of-fact, clinical tone.

"But as for you, Vesna, your sole job is to do the very best that you can. And of that I have no doubt. However, on the other hand, you have some unlearning to do. To date, you have been trained to trust no one. That is understandable given the culture that you were raised in. However, if you aspire to replace Major General Piankoff, you will have to learn to trust, because in our business, trust is really all that we have.

"Have I made myself clear?"

"Quite, Dr. Allen. I am quite accustomed with dealing with the irrationality of male chauvinism."

Then with a sad smile, Doc Allen said, "Vesna, I am happy to say that male chauvinism has nothing to do with it at all, and positively nothing whatsoever to do with you. In point of fact, it was we who requested a female candidate of your caliber from your people. And I can assure you that your superiors were not pleased with that request. Nonetheless, here you are. Now, as for my colleagues, their issue about you was one of choice and selection. They were left out of the process entirely, they positively threw a fit, and now they have to grow up and live with it. Win those folks over, Vesna, and you will be home free."

As Doc Allen spoke, he noted that Vesna only occasionally looked up at him, preferring instead to study her carefully folded hands.

Well. That's not good. She's listening, but how hard?

Pause.

Let's find out.

"One last thing, Vesna, how comfortable are you with your body?"

Now sitting up erectly in her chair, Gregorieva demanded with a soft but firm voice, "Now, doctor. What precisely do you mean by that?"

Ah-ha! She was listening.

"Well, what I mean 'precisely' by that question is the following. Clearly you care for your body. You are in top flight physical condition and this morning's adventure was only proof positive of that."

Pause.

Right now, given the flush of her face, I'm willing to bet that her pulse is close to pushing 160!

"In fact, Vesna, what you choose to wear and how you wear it is quite revealing in itself of your attitude toward your body. My point is this. You have been taught to use clothing to your advantage. To be alluring in an almost theatrical sense. Is that not so?"

Pause. Cool silence and slightly narrowing eyes.

Vesna! I am waiting for an answer. Speak you bullheaded sphinx! Allen practically screamed in his mind behind his placid exterior.

"Y-yes. You are correct, doctor. I have been trained to use clothing to my best advantage. But every woman knows such things!" she added with a rush and a dismissing flick of her left hand.

Pause.

And now in a very calming voice, Doc Allen continued, "Yes, Vesna. You are correct. Every 'modern' woman does know. But how confidently would you carry yourself if you were culturally required to bare your chest?"

"What? What sort of questioning is this! This is insane, or, or you are some sort of sex pervert, yes? Yes! That is it. You wish to use me for some sick and perverted purpose. Well, my dear doctor, as you Americans like to say, go bugger yourself!"

And with that said Gregorieva gracefully stood, slid her chair precisely back into its place, performed a perfect runway pivot, and returned to her quarters.

Sighing inwardly, Doc Allen concluded, *Well, at least I tried. Now it's all up to Joey. Hope that he has better luck penetrating that stubborn ego.*

Looking up toward the ceiling, the physician said, "Well, I hope that you got all that. I would venture that she has some personal issues. I didn't even have the opportunity to tell her that she'll have to shave her head. Jesus! What a firecracker!"

* * *

On the basis of Doc Allen's assessment of Gregorieva, it was decided that she and Richards would not formally meet until the Russian passed the multiple physical workups, laboratory tests, psychological profile, and an advanced linguistic acuity battery. In all, these trials took a grueling eight days, at the end of which Gregorieva literally and figuratively was shot and in need of a break.

On her "day off," she was escorted by Milson, who took her on a tour of the nearby Near Eastern Institute's museum and its collection. Thereafter, they lunched at the University Faculty Club and after that took a cab to the Field Museum to take in its impressive Egyptian collection. At four o'clock, the pair then went to a quiet bar, Milson's favorite, which was buried deep within the bowels of the city near its historic water tower. Sitting in luxuriously deep and soft leather winged chairs, they sipped at their drinks as their feet recovered from all the walking. Only halfway through his glass of sherry, Milson confided, "You know, Ms. Gregorieva, all this entertaining will put me in an early grave. Right now I feel exhausted, just like I used to feel after having wooed a faculty candidate for four days straight! I'm tired, and this drink is just what the doctor ordered!"

"Dr. Milson, I am sorry that I have been such a burden to you," the Russian soberly stated, while looking over her frosty double vodka martini with anchovy olives.

"Vesna. That was an old man talking. It is not often that I have had the pleasure of being a tour guide for such a fascinating human being."

Sigh.

"By the way, I think that you should know that you passed all your tests with flying colors. Not that I had any doubt you would," he said with a congratulatory raising toast of his glass, while reaching over to clink his with hers. He then continued, "Your oral mastery of the ancient Egyptian language is, by the way, extraordinary. I suspect that the late Piankoff had a hand in that. Am I correct?"

"Yes, Dr. Milson, you are correct. In fact, Major General Piankoff actually trained me before he went West," the Russian answered, mixing English with an Egyptian idiom for death.

"I don't doubt it. After all, the exercises that he constructed for us had to have come from somewhere. They were all so well organized, overlapping, and organic in their structure. He possessed a fine mind. He would have been a phenomenal teacher."

Pause.

"It was such a pity . . . Excuse me, Vesna. I am beginning to babble. It's just that I admired and envied that man. I wish that I could have known him better. That's all," he concluded, looking thoughtfully down into the empty glass that he now held in his two hands.

"You know, Dr. Milson, I too miss Alexander, perhaps too much. He was a brilliant linguist, a superior instructor, and a fine man. I frankly worshipped him."

As a misty look began to fill her green eyes.

"I truly wish I had known him better as well."

That sole admission told Milson volumes, but he logged it away under the rubric of "Vesna, a human being, Evidence of."

Tilting his head to one side, the aging Egyptologist decided to ask, "My friend, what about today's adventures didn't you like?"

A knowing smile answered.

"So, Dr. Milson, I didn't know that you were a psychologist too!" she said playfully.

"What I didn't like about today was that I was denied a good long run, a steaming hot shower, and a massage. But what I did cherish about today was that I got to know you. In many ways, John, you are much like Alexander. Both of you know how to be considerate, caring, and almost intimate, but at a comfortable distance. Both of you are consumed by things Egyptian – you by trade, Alexander by an unrequited love. Both of you selflessly share this passion freely and without reservation. For both of you, Egypt is a joy. And I thank you for so freely sharing your first love with me."

All that Milson could do in response was smile and slowly shake his head in acceptance.

"You know, Vesna, Alexander was a powerful teacher. You have said as much. We teachers are like spiders. All we can do is spin our silk and release it to the four winds in the hopes that maybe one or two students will catch a few of those fragile threads. It is clear you were Alexander's prize student, just as Joseph was for me."

Now cocking her head to one side, Gregorieva asked, "Joseph who?"

"Why, Professor Joseph Richards."

Now with a sly smile and slitted eyes she probed, "And does this Professor Richards ever go by the nickname of Joey?"

Putting his head back against the chair's headrest and smiling to the ceiling, Milson said with a devilishly evil chuckle, "You know, Vesna. I am going to warn you. Joey can be a real handful."

"Why, that bloody bastard!"

"The very same!"

CHAPTER XXXI

The San Diego Conference

Academic conferences are unique social events, be they of either a scientific or humanistic bent, for nowhere else can so much be made of so little. A harsh indictment perhaps, but it is one that contains more than a dram of truth.

Consider for the moment the conference's attendees themselves. Let's begin with the officers and hangers-on of the various and allied learned societies. They are easily identifiable by their lavish conference badges that are often augmented with brightly colored ribbons and the like. Then there are the select editors and salespeople from the various distinguished publishing houses that sell the books appropriate to the disciplines represented. These types are also easy to spot because as genuine business people, they wear fine and well-tailored clothing current with the times. Look especially for crisp and silky wools in muted colors. Then there are the distinguished scholars, who are there to present seminal papers that might change the course of a field's scholarly future. Expect wild shocks of white, gray, and salt-and-pepper hair that are *de rigueur* for these confident and eccentric types, whether male or female. A comfortable and rumpled look in out-of-date clothing is another sure giveaway. Lesser scholars and faculty of every rank are there as well to read their research papers, make an impression with their perceived betters, and link up with kindred spirits. These have typically youngish faces and you can spot them in their poorly fitting clothing, with quick gaits or important-looking frowns eternally etched into their brows. Graduate students and freshly hooded PhDs are there as well, who follow their dissertation directors around like so many sheep following their protective shepherd, in the hope of a strategic introduction here, a kind word dropped there. These same listen intently to their mentor's profound moments of wisdom, provide laughter at appropriate times, but at all times feed their master's or mistress' overblown ego. Just look for any slowly moving crowd. Then there are the officious and sometimes even disgruntled faculty, who are present only because it is their august duty to judge this prospective job candidate against that, all for the greater good of their department's sole open position. These are only seen when they are either at lunch or out to a four-martini dinner. Spotting one can be difficult, because they don't want to be identified by any candidate that applied to their department to whom they didn't deem worthy the grant of an interview. And finally, the bulk in attendance represented the great unwashed, hungry, and desperate PhDs without positions, but who are in search of one. Sadly, in most cases, any *bona fide* position where they can hang their hat will do. Among this crowd, almost anything goes: ties and sweaters, corduroy suits, bow ties, even sports jackets with blue jeans and sneakers.

* * *

As for Becky Hildebrand, she had a lot going for her. She was young, single, and had as solid a research position as you can get outside the government and private sectors. Add to that Becky could be quite pretty when she put her mind to it. Such is the case with natural beauty.

But she was in San Diego for several distinct reasons. On account of her paper, she applied for and got her airfare to the mainland and lodging covered, along with even a reasonable per diem. As much as she loved the Big Island, its cultural isolation drove Becky simply batty at times. Conferences like these were places where like minds gathered and professional contacts were made. While her colleagues at Keck were the best, she needed more and so here she was. Then there was that mysterious Charlie fellow. She really hoped to run into him and even pitched her paper his way on the basis of what he had told her over the phone. While she knew that she was going out on a limb, Becky knew that her theoretical discussion of asteroidal acquisition of mass and how to detect it would attract the crowd that she wanted. If worse came to worse, the entire junket would become just another line on her already impressive *curriculum vitae*.

* * *

The delivery of her paper and the question and answer session that followed had gone extremely well. Almost too well, she cautioned herself. But nonetheless, she had now in her possession five personal cards from fellow researchers. One, who much like her, was a research fellow at the Green Bank Telescope. Another was a member of NASA's Near-Earth Object Program, and a third from NASA's Ames Research Center.

It never hurts to have contacts within NASA. You never know.

She smiled to herself as she quickly went through the cards once again before she left the large conference room. But on her way out she caught the eye of a rather tall, rugged-looking man with blondish hair. He was wearing a very finely cut business suit that aced him out as an academic. Acknowledging her contact, he casually smiled a genuine smile and fractionally tipped his head in approval toward her.

Intrigued, and a bit hopeful as well, Becky approached him and took note his conference badge that said:

LT. CHARLES M. PERRY, PHD
USAF SPACE COMMAND
PETERSON AIR FORCE BASE
COLORADO SPRINGS, CO

Smiling up at him, Becky asked, "So, Charlie, what's the 'M' stand for?"

"Martin, Dr. Hildebrand," he said, extending his hand and receiving a firm handshake.

"I enjoyed your theoretical discussion and would very much like to talk to you about it. Are you free?"

Looking around and then shrugging her shoulders, Becky said, "Sure, looks so. How about a beer? I'm really thirsty after all those questions."

"That sure works for me, and oh, yes, Dr. Hildebrand, I'm Charlie," he said with a wicked smile and eyes that twinkled.

"Well, Charlie. Pleased to meet you. I'm Becky," she said as they shook hands again.

* * *

That beer lasted until dinner, which lasted to almost midnight mainland time. They talked about everything: shop, sports, childhood, their families, food, politics, their jobs, and then shop some more.

As midnight approached, Charlie found himself intellectually drained. His head felt like a freshly squeezed lemon. In sum, he was dead-dog tired and sorely needed to crash. But for Becky, it was only eight o'clock, but she could tell that Charlie was really hurting and she finally said so. While it was an awkward thing to say, Charlie thanked her for acknowledging it, generously paid the bill, thanked her again for the great time "catching up," as he put it, shook her hand, and left the restaurant.

As Becky was getting herself organized to leave, a very strange thought hit her squarely between the eyes.

Okay, Becky, just how are you going to get in touch with Charlie again? How, girl, did you just let that intelligent hunk of a man just slip through your fingers?

Then the magic words came to her: *Lt. Charles Martin Perry, Space Command, Colorado Springs, Colorado.*

* * *

The Air Force officer had a usually immaculate desk, but today it was a wasteland of receipts and travel documents that he was assembling into his expense report. As he added all the totals to his spreadsheet, one slip of paper he thought about more than the others. It wasn't the total that bothered him. It was all of those wonderful memories that were attached to a long evening of dinner and shop talk. Smiling at what could have . . . should have been, he taped the chit to his document and moved on.

"Lt. Perry," the base operator said over his telephone's intercom speaker. "Incoming call on line 1."

"Thanks, Sally."

Punching the appropriate phone button.

"Hello. Perry here."

"Is this Lt. Charles Martin Perry, PhD?" a woman's voice said.

"Ah, yes. With whom do I have the pleasure of speaking?"

"Why, Charlie, clearly with the person with whom you are speaking."

Now answering with a bit of terse shortness.

"Yeah. Okay. I'll buy that. Now, what can I do for you?"

“Ah, now that’s a really good question. How about a beer? After that long flight, I’m really thirsty,” the woman said playfully.

Now smiling into the receiver, Perry gambled.

“Ah, now I remember. You’re the one with the crazy hypothesis about asteroidal mass accumulation.”

And that answer contained its own reward.

CHAPTER XXXII

Horizon Pass

As the Paschal Season neared, the campus' student population began to thin, some by plane, others by train, but most by car. The reason cited was because airport security had just become such a hassle. Not so for Richards, for his out-of-town plans had been scheduled way in advance by his colleagues at the Annex. His vacation would be "work oriented" in preparation for an excursion to take place during the summer recess. A key part of those preparations, not to mention a tweaking of his physical conditioning, were to be several deep hypnotic sessions with Doc Allen at Horizon Pass, which were meant to further buttress his already formidable mental shielding. The why of it Milson had explained to him as a simple precaution.

"Joseph, my boy, let's face it. You have become a valuable asset. With Piankoff's unfortunate passing, you are the world's only operational temporal field agent and the only experienced one at that. So guess what? We're walking on eggshells every time you deploy. So guess what? We've got to get Gregorieva ready, like pronto! I know that she's got the right stuff, and you know it just as well."

Milson then raised his hands as if in surrender.

"Granted, there are some kinks to work out. But that's all they are, kinks, not show stoppers. So we must look ahead. We must prepare the two of you as best we can for any eventuality.

"And one of those unfortunate eventualities just might be an encounter with one, or worse, both of Akhenaten's sons. On the basis of your own report, you said that Meryptah had characterized them as already 'playing dangerous games.'

"So, we want you and Vesna prepared. Prepared far better than even Piankoff had been against any attempt of psychic rape. So, that is why the two of you've been scheduled to have Doc Allen do some more work on that thick skull of yours, and Gregorieva's as well," he concluded with a lopsided grin.

* * *

Richards' previous trips to the secret facility of Horizon Pass, hidden right out in the open within the southwestern Sun State of New Mexico, all began at the heavily secured military side of O'Hare International Airport. For Gregorieva, this heightened level of security was not new. In fact she had expected it. Since the retirement of Philology Annex's own Hercules C-130J to the Air National Guard unit in Minneapolis at the commencement of the Iraq War, their new lift was a drab, and at first glance unremarkable, Gulf Stream V.

Because of Richards' Air Force brat upbringing, he knew the craft was far more than it seemed. More to the point, he was positive it was military owned and maintained, but by whom remained the question. And Richards' instincts were right on, for the Gulf Stream represented a special order by the government to a rather famous West Coast aircraft engineering firm known for its ingenuity, the very same group who had in the past done spectacular work for the CIA and U.S. Air Force. That this aeronautical firm was the only one authorized to submit a bid was a fact that was as secret as the plane itself – much less its special specifications. Nonetheless, scuttlebutt had it that after the aircraft's trials had been completed the plane's owners had leaked to several other entities just what it had done. As a result of this insider chatter, other agencies including several foreign governments were invited to test the plane. The consequence of this show-and-tell was predictable. If Johnny has a shiny new red wagon, ergo, so must I. As the many buyers lined up for their very own and specially outfitted business-like conveyance, the engineering firm benefited as did one black unit of the U.S. Army, for they had been reimbursed in full for their marketing efforts.

The airframe was not that of a commercial Gulf Stream V on account of the exotic materials used. Its cabin had a passenger capacity of sixteen, which made it perfect for Major Tuna Cartwright's school of twelve highly trained security "specialists," known internally as Tuna's "school," who were tasked to the Philology Annex and protected the portable Soap Bubble during deployment. With its tall T-shaped tail, dual engine pods attached at the rear of the fuselage, and its swept wings ending in graceful canards, the aircraft looked like it was doing its civilian-rated top-end of .87 Mach sitting on the tarmac. With an advertised maximum commercial range of six thousand five hundred nautical miles, transatlantic travel between the States and the Continent became a nonstop affair.

Richards' sharp eye could tell the plane had been tweaked, and the hints were there out in the open for anyone to see. The telltale signatures of two hard points located near the plane's wing roots just outside the landing gear bays were the perhaps the most obvious. These were added to allow for external fuel tanks, but tanks that were deemed unnecessary for flights within the forty-eight states. Also apparent was the aircraft's extended tail section. Its now pointed profile reached out by some four addition feet. Another detail was the slightly enlarged engine housings and flares that concealed the plane's special Pratt & Whitney F119 engines and their directable thrust-vectoring nozzles. Fitted with these powerful engines, the Gulf Stream's top-end doubled to 1.6 Mach, and its ability to turn and maneuver rose to eight gees – hence the need for its special airframe. Perhaps most obvious to the casual observer was the bulging of the fuselage that began its swell just aft of the nose landing gear compartment. Although sculpted nicely into the plane's overall lines, this bulge nonetheless made the craft look like a slightly pregnant porpoise. Because of this ventral swelling, the plane's landing gear had to be extended a full two feet to provide for proper clearance, while its cargo-carrying capacity had effectively tripled. But at its thickest point, the bulge's skin had three parallel seams that betrayed the presence of doors to a depressurized bay, which could accommodate a variety of nifty items that ranged from a photo reconnaissance and ground-mapping radar suite to a rotary missile launcher.

But far less obvious were the Plexiglas sunroof added to the cockpit's overhead escape hatch, the roof mounted, flush-fitting trapdoor that led to an aerial refueling receptacle positioned just aft and starboard of the cockpit's cabin, six circular chaff and antimissile flare ports in the extended tail section, and two shrouded fiberglass gun ports in the nose. Of vital importance, but seldom appreciated by the general public, was the outfitting of the plane's head with a pressurized and vacuum-sealed toilet seat. While flimflam politicians have often railed for decades on the supposedly wasteful spending of the military on such items as $250 toilet seats, the simple fact of the matter is, "Do you want your aircraft's honey pot emptying while you're flying inverted?"

One detail that was not at all obvious to a casual eye was the plane's paint and registration markings. After the flight crew learned of Richards' zoomie upbringing, and prompted by his pointed questions regarding their instrumentation, they proudly demonstrated something quite remarkable. Once airborne, the copilot could trickle with a flip of a switch a low voltage charge throughout the plane's outer skin that allowed the surface to subtly change color and shadings in order to mimic its immediate surroundings. While in flight, the plane's surface was said to shimmer or ripple as it passed by and through clouds, all the while its surface coating automatically adjusted itself. Similarly, the copilot could at will alter the lettering of the craft's registration markings, clearly going one step further than the rotating license plate brackets of James Bond's Aston Martin DB-5. Such aerial camouflage and bureaucratic tomfoolery were considered necessary for the plane's survival. Although hardly a fighter jet, by virtue of its heavily modified and beefed up airframe, the aircraft was the closest thing to it in terms of speed, maneuverability, ceiling, and range. All of these additions, at least in the crew's mind, were advantages that might even up the long odds on their survival. After all, who would expect to encounter a self-camouflaging commercial business jet that was more maneuverable than most governments' military aircraft? Not to mention, a civilian-looking plane that packed air-to-air missiles and a pair of M-61A1 20 mm multi-barrel cannons? The simple logic was: if one 20 mm cannon was good enough for an F-16, then two were better for the Gulf Stream.

For Gregorieva, these minutiae remained utterly transparent, for she did not possess any frame of reference as to what a normal business jet even looked like. But once she entered the fuselage, the reality of the situation became imminently clear, for the usual commercial interior airplane panels, baffles, and partitions were all missing. The immediate visual effect was an opening up of the plane's light tan interior, and it looked as spacious as it was. Seating was pure military transport – comfortable but ugly, quick-release aluminum frames entwined with olive green webbing, massive but comfortable head and neck padding, five-point harnesses, all arranged in two staggered rows with a wide common central aisle. General interior lighting was battle-station red with convenient reading lights mounted on the hull next to grounded, twelve-volt outlets and an adjustable ventilation port. Additional storage was provided next to each seat with more olive green webbing in addition to generous tie-down opportunities in the form of hull-mounted rings, hooks and Velcro strapping. At a glance, Gregorieva knew that this was a military aircraft, but one that sure did not look like one on the outside, and that fact kick-started her mind into a sort of recording mode.

After all, she reasoned, *if the Americans went to such lengths to gut and modify this interior for a specific purpose, what else might be so very different about this supposedly normal-looking commuter jet?*

Richards, noting that Gregorieva momentarily frozen stare at the plane's entrance, was followed by her darting eyes glazed over in thoughtful recognition. He did his best not to smile, for it was natural. He had had the same reaction as well upon seeing the jet's interior for the first time. And so he decided to soften the blow.

"Welcome, Ms. Gregorieva, to the U.S. Army's very best accommodations in commercial aircraft. Allow me to help you stow your gear. We can leave nothing loose, as loose stuff tends to be dangerous while flying upside down."

"What!?"

"Indeed. In fact, I suspect that the flight crew just might want to show off for you as you are the new greenie aboard."

"Greenie?"

"Ah, yes. First-timer. Novice. Newcomer."

"Oh."

But despite Richards' warning, the flight to remote Holloman Air Force Base went uneventfully – much to his disappointment. For this same crew had really put him through his paces on his maiden flight. The airbase, located about ten miles as the crow flies sort of west of the backwater New Mexican border town of Alamogordo, was located in no-where's-ville. Nearby White Sands had been officially closed down lock, stock, and barrel. These facts, however, hardly could refute that a low profile, high-security installation did still exist somewhere in the region. But where, nobody knew. And frankly, nobody cared to mess with the feds, much less the military, to find out.

While the Gulf Stream landed, topped off its fuel, and returned to its Chicago-based maintenance hangar, its two passengers did not.

Nor did they dawdle at the base. Instead, they boarded an awaiting Sikorsky H-60 Black Hawk helicopter that took off heading into setting sun, the deep desert, and its backlit mountain range. If a flight record would have been filed, landmarks such as the White Sands Missile Range, Lumley Lake, and Strawberry Peak would have been mentioned. But since one had not, they were not.

As the helicopter flew along its westward trending flight path, Richards soaked in the familiar desert terrain, which rapidly gave way to foothills and eroded mountains. He marveled, yet again, at how mesmerizing the beauty and colorfulness of this swiftly passing desert was. As the chopper skimmed along just south of Strawberry Peak, it rose and fell as it followed the hills and contours of Parson Canyon. Then, as the canyon opened up at Sulphur Pass, Richards espied their distant goal: a curious sort of lone, split-fingered rock outcropping.

When the helicopter neared that feature, Richards turned to Gregorieva to get her reaction to the raw natural beauty that was playing out before them. What he saw surprised him. With eyes tightly shut, mouth clamped, and her face a ghastly white, Gregorieva was clearly in serious trouble.

Jesus, he thought. *She's air sick and trying hard not to barf up her guts! Best not trouble her now!*

Then the chopper, still flying hell-bent for election, slowed with a lurch, flared, and descended over a dimly lit cement helicopter pad that had seemed to magically appear out of the shadows of one of the nearby outcroppings. With a mild bump they were on the ground. Glancing at his watch as a dodge, Richards pretended not to notice that Gregorieva, now wide-eyed at the landing, was still rigidly clenching her jaw as a result of the breathtaking fourteen-minute roller-coaster ride.

Jumping down from the unmarked and flat dark gray Sikorsky, the two passengers, with their gear in hand, bent over and ran out from under the still twirling blades as the pilot throttled his collector, began his ascent, and returned to base.

As the dust cleared and the sound of the chopper blades' muted whoop-whooping faded away into the distance, Richards became aware of several things: the distinctively delicious smell of desert sage brush, the crystal clear air of the 5200-foot-plus elevation, and the sound of Gregorieva heaving her guts into a nearby bush, while an elderly white-haired gentleman in a bright red Nike jogging suit stood by supporting her in her efforts.

"There, there, Vesna. Get it all up. Don't hold back! Good girl. Good girl." He soothed, "Now here, rinse your mouth out with this bottle of water."

Looking up from his recovering patient, Dr. Peter Borov smiled warmly at Richards.

"Joey! How are you doing, son? Give me a hand with Vesna here. She's in quite a pickle. Those bastard helicopter jockeys just shook her loose all the way to Sunday!"

Now reaching into his pocket and offering his personal handkerchief to the Russian, Borov continued, "Hell of a welcome to Horizon Pass, wasn't that!"

When he turned to Richards, he found himself enveloped in a bear hug.

"Peter! It's great to be back, even if it is for just a long weekend. How are your old bones doing?"

"Old bones! Heck! Be careful or I'll race you back to the shed. Besides, that reminds me, let's get Vesna here inside and out of the evening's chill. Let's move!"

At Borov's pronouncement, the elderly man then turned and broke into a loping jog, leading away from the camouflaged concrete helipad. Richards, now unconsciously leading a rapidly recovering Gregorieva by the hand, could only smile and hope that he would be in such shape at that man's age.

* * *

Horizon Pass, as with many secret government facilities located in the American southwest, was a subterranean complex that takes good advantage of the local native rock formations. Its camouflaged entrance was comprised of a rickety lean-to shack of weathered silver pine that backed up against a sheer two-hundred-foot rock face overhang. Once inside the shack, a gray, featureless, and hardened steel door greets the visitor. The shack itself, really a sophisticated x-ray booth, scans all who stand before the steel door. Borov just waved at the entrance and it opened broadly to accept his passage. Then Richards stepped forward and waved in imitation and the heavy steel opened for him as well. But the Egyptologist could not stop himself from smiling, when remembering his first time before the door. Gregorieva, however, noting this strange behavior before the heavy door, chose not to approach it, but instead had stopped short of it and then she too waved. Suddenly, the earth before her disappeared and the Russian found herself teetering at the forward edge of a gapping eight-foot-deep security pit bedded with pea gravel. Wavering, but not falling in, Gregorieva quickly recovered herself due to her superb dancer's sense of balance. Standing before the pit in a rage with her fists tightly clenched against her sides, the Russian then challenged the door at the top of her lungs.

"Nice try, you American bastards! Now what's next? Collapsing walls with spikes?"

From the other side, Borov looked up into Richards' eyes and quietly murmured, "I think that we're going to have our hands full with this one."

* * *

At the Russian's shrill insistence, and only when Borov himself stood atop the restored entranceway's trapdoor, did Gregorieva move an inch forward. Still quite hot, but now under control, the Russian stiffly entered the facility under the alert gaze of two fully attentive armed guards. Borov, feeling somewhat responsible for the entire flap, personally escorted the silent and indignant Gregorieva all the way through a warren of passages to her private quarters. Stopping before its closed door, the old scientist turned to the young woman and addressed her in their common mother tongue.

"Ms. Gregorieva," he began in a coolly formal manner that could barely conceal his elevated temper.

"Please accept my apologies for the rough helicopter ride. I can assure you that it was not intentional. In fact, we have all had to deal with its discomfort from time to time. However, as you will soon see, the entrance pit does serve a purpose and provides a test of sorts – a very important one. For that I will not apologize.

"But as for your behavior, I suggest that you take a very cold shower and reflect. I know for a fact that Alexander would not have approved of that childish outburst before the security pit. On the other hand, he would have very much approved of your remarkable sense of balance."

Pausing for a moment, he then continued with a softer tone.

"Now Vesna, we will not speak of this again. Sleep well. Tomorrow we will begin early and work late. Good evening," he stated with a mildly courtly bow, after which he turned on his heel and jogged off, sneakers squeaking down the highly polished flooring of the passageway.

Watching the elderly scientist smoothly loping motion, Vesna could feel the blush of embarrassment reddening her cheeks, could sense the certain knowledge that Borov had been absolutely correct. Her Alexander would have not approved at all.

* * *

Meanwhile, for Richards, every visit to Horizon Pass reminded him of some villain's underground lair out of a James Bond movie. The impression was inescapable. Its rough concrete walls painted bright reflective white, the exposed piping and tubes of all kinds, shapes, and colors along the ceiling and walls of every corridor and tunnel, the emergency phones and lighting fixtures, fire extinguishers every fifty feet, the omnipresent overhead fluorescent lighting, the bright yellow painted stripes running down the center of the twenty-foot-wide corridors and connecting tunnels, and last but not least, all the convex traffic mirrors at every intersection.

"After you settle in," Borov had said, "shower and grab some grub. Make a point to get over to Tombstone early tomorrow morning. I want to show you something."

True to form, Richards, at the mere suggestion of a hot shower and meal suddenly became very weary from the bone-jarring trip, and dutifully followed his security escort to his assigned private quarters.

Time to fuel up and crash.

* * *

Navigating around Horizon Pass would have been very confusing if it were not for the fact that each corridor, intersection, and tunnel was named in large stenciled letters on the floor. As with so many things, Borov's humor was everywhere: Yellow Brick Road, Penny Lane, Trafalgar Square, Times Square, Appian Way, and the like.

These accesses interconnected the dormitory area that was named "The Swamp" in honor of the *M.A.S.H.* television series – a particular favorite of Borov's. The mess hall, bakery, and kitchen was Betty Crocker's, the gym Venice Beach, the main lab complex was Frankenstein's Castle, but over time it was shortened to just Frank's.

The high security area devoted to the testing and storage of the Soap Bubble itself was a far more serious place, and its name reflected that fact. Richards eventually found himself before that sealed, circular double door that looked like the entrance to a bank vault. The black stenciled letters on the floor before him solemnly announced – Tombstone. When the Egyptologist stood before the vault's entrance, four security cameras trained on him recorded his every move.

Guard One: "Well, well, here comes that Richards fellow again. The log says that he was here three weeks ago. Bet ya' some sort of op must be in the works," he concluded.

Guard Two: "Yep. Sure looks like it."

Guard One: "Check out his heat signature, very dense. He seems to have lost some mass since the last reading. There's not an ounce of fat on him."

Guard Two: "Yeah. You're right. One friggin' tough cookie. I heard that even Tuna's men prefer to keep him at arm's length. Most definitely not one to screw with."

Guard One: "Yeah, no doubt."

Checking to make sure the "Drop Security Lockdown" indicator was negative, the guard thumbed the rocker switch that engaged the opening mechanism. As a result of that simple two-step action, the double door to Tombstone began to vertically split open and extend out into the corridor, gradually driving Richards back several feet.

Richards always held in awe what lurked beyond those massive steel doors. Stepping through, he found himself on a steel grated landing that stood about fifty feet above floor level. Always impressed by the sheer volume of the area, he leaned over the railing and took in the view. What once had been a fair-sized cavern was transformed into a massive engineering bay with a workshop, a climate-controlled computer room, and a generator area. In the dead center of it all the latest and greatest version of the Soap Bubble stood. It represented a revolutionary series of machines that proudly proved their theoretical basis, justified the purpose of cutting-edge engineering, advanced materials research, and provided the very essence of wonder itself.

Walking down a long curving ramp to the Tombstone's floor level, Richards got a revolving look at that most strange and marvelous creation of man. Four black rectangular pylons, each about six feet tall, arranged symmetrically like the cardinal points of a compass outlined a circle about twenty feet in diameter. Each pylon had its own thick power cable and attached at their tops were short, horn-like devices that were oriented inward, also with their own power cables. In the center of this circle of pylons and horns, a thick, white, Hula-Hoop-like object about four feet in diameter floated horizontally and still about five feet off the ground.

Reaching the bottom of the ramp, he found Borov and Gregorieva with their heads together, deep in conversation. Not wishing to crash their moment, the Egyptologist slowed his approach to hang back and listen in for a convenient entrée. But Borov somehow sensed him and called out, "Joey, my boy! Good morning! What took you so long? You're late."

"Several wrong turns, Doc. Sorry. Won't happen again."

"Boy do I have a surprise for you! I was just explaining it all to Vesna."

Clasping his hands together in anticipation, the scientist briskly walked over toward the center of the chamber and its Stonehenge-like cluster of equipment. Stopping about four feet from the nearest black pylon, he spun on his heel to face the pair.

"Vesna, Joey," he stated, bowing slightly to each at the pronunciation of their given names, he nodded in introduction to the arrayed technology before them, "meet the new Mark VII, the latest tweak in temporal exploration."

Leaping ahead as if he were a mind reader, Borov went on, "Now, Joey, I know that you have many questions, but before you begin pelting me with them, what do you remember about our past discussion of quantum mechanics and particle physics? It turns out that Vesna minored in physics! Can you believe it!"

Caught dumbfounded by the exuberance of the aging scientist, the revelation of Gregorieva's background, the subject and directness of the question, Richards gave a sheepish shrug and said, "Some, Doc, but I know not enough."

"Well, brace yourself again, my boy, for what I am about to tell you just might freak you out. The Mark VII here has a tighter calibration. We can now place you within three seconds of reality. New software computing upgrades make that possible, and we have new operating software that does all the load-balancing far more efficiently."

Now with his arms crossed across his chest, the scientist stood back, beaming a beatific smile to his wide-eyed audience.

"And with that upgrade, Joey, my life's work has now been made complete.

"My point behind all of this, folks, is this. The Soap Bubble's technology, as far as I'm concerned, is stable and established. All those drops through the ring that you and Colonel Piankoff made, have helped to make that happen.

"You still have to climb a tower, fall or jump through the drop ring, and for an infinitesimally brief moment in time, be in two places at once. Your physiology will continue to react to that brief temporal event. Remember, our bodies are nothing more than sensitive biochemical electrical engines. Doc Allen's has warned you Joey that your physiology may change over time. In fact, Doc Allen already suspects that your physiology has been subtly affected by those earlier jumps in the earlier versions of the Soap Bubble. Joey, I mention this because I know that you already have had two visits with Doc Allen about the lengthening of your post-drop recovery."

A worried face and affirmative nod confirmed what Borov had stated. Gregorieva, noting this as well, reacted with a furrowed brow of her own.

"Vesna, to date, we have no idea whether a female physiology will be affected by dropping. You are the first." Admitted Borov.

* * *

The pair's next stop of the day was Doc Allen's office. Arriving at the appointed time, Richards found himself knocking on the now familiar doorframe of the infirmary. Nurse Stewart, the pleasant Minnesotan looked up and smiled with her usual folksy warmth. Then she briefly started when she caught sight of Gregorieva, and unconsciously, a wave of jealousy passed over her.

"Well, Dr. Richards, it's good to see you again! And let's see here, you must be Ms. Gregorieva. Is that correct?"

"Yes, it is."

"Well," the nurse began as she sized up her competition, "I'm Nurse Stewart, pleased to meet you."

"Why, thank you," the Russian replied already sensing in the air the electricity that is primordial feminine competition.

"Well, you two go right on in. Doc Allen is waiting for you in Room No. Two."

Thanking the nurse, a warm smile was returned that promised much, but was directed at only one of them. While Richards missed this silent communication, Gregorieva had not. So they walked over to Room No. Two's door and knocked. Next was heard the deep, throaty voice of Dr. Allen, beckoning them in. Upon entering, they were welcomed with the traditional ham-fisted greeting of Dr. Allen, who by Richards' reckoning now must have weighed in around a buck eighty on his five-eight frame.

He's lost some serious weight!

Ruddy-faced, balding, freckled, and calling Oklahoma his home, Doc Allen, silently pointed Gregorieva over to the large examination table and simply said, "Sit."

After the usual pulse and blood pressure check, Doc Allen decreed that Gregorieva had the readings of a vampire. He then noted in her chart the remarkable readings and asked, "When did you have your last menses?"

Then after about a half dozen more such personal questions, the doc turned to Richards.

"Okay, you muscle-bound brute, now it's your turn.

"One hundred and ninety-four pounds, that's better. The last time I saw you, you were way too developed and cut. Much, much better. Now remove your shirt. I need to see some skin. Yes. Better, better Joey. But I still think that you need to ease up a bit on the upper body lifting. More light reps, less weight," he concluded.

Then Allen turned to the Russian in explanation.

"You see, Vesna. Joey here broke a cardinal rule about time travel. He had gotten a bit overzealous, you might say, with his workouts and got too big, muscle-wise. The problem was that the natives noticed it. Joey forgot that he was to blend in, not stick out. That is why I had to ask you all those personal questions."

"Oh," was Gregorieva's only reply to the explanation that had opened her eyes as much as it took her breath away.

No, she decided. *These Americans are not amateurs at this game. Not at all!*

But jarring her out of this momentary revelation was Doc Allen's voice.

"Okay, Vesna, let's get to work."

"Ah, I'm sorry. I missed what you just said."

Smiling, Doc Allen again pointed Vesna over to the large Lazy Boy recliner and said, "Please make yourself comfortable."

Obeying the directive, the Russian stretched out and found herself sinking deeply into the soft and form-fitting padding. Meanwhile, Doc Allen shooed Richards out the door, gently closing it, and dimmed the room lights to a twilight setting. Now alone with the Russian, the doc began.

"Okay, Vesna. This is what we are going to try to do. I suspect that your people have already briefed you on what you may be up against, and what you may have to do. Is that correct?"

"Yes, doctor. They have. But I am concerned about what they said Alexander went through. Then what I heard from Doctor Borov about the variable physiological reactions to the temporal drops has me wondering whether I have made a terrible mistake."

Inwardly pleased that the woman was frank enough to voice her fears, the doctor said, "You know, Vesna, what you just said makes perfect sense. Ever since the dawn of human cognition, fear of the unknown has been with us. We can't shake it. And we won't ever. It is a thing that must be confronted, recognized, and overcome. From where I'm sitting, you have recognized the issue. Just how you confront it, you have to decide. Just whether you can overcome it is your decision as well. But let me be clear. What you have just expressed is normal. But what you need to tell me now is, do you wish to continue? You have already gone through a lot of examinations, laboratory work, testing, and whatnot. So it's decision time, Vesna. Do you have the courage to continue?"

Pause.

"Yes, Dr. Allen, I do. Just let me say that it is not patriotism, nor ego, that drives me to such a conclusion. I am curious, fiercely curious. I want to know why Alexander was so impassioned about Egypt."

Pause.

"I want this. I really want this."

"Well, Vesna, that's good enough for me. So let's begin.

"What I first need from you is an image. That image must symbolize in your mind the most invincible, impregnable thing that you can imagine. It must be a thing that can stop anything that could harm you."

After several seconds, the Russian smiled and answered, "Dr. Allen, I have that image."

"Good. Here we go.

"Now what I am going to do first is place several deep suggestions in your mind to begin the process of implanting your cover. Once that is complete, I am going to ask you to think of your image as a self-activating defensive mechanism that will be your block. I want you to be able to turn on and off that defensive mind block at will. And hopefully you will be able to do it without invoking an adrenaline hangover. Once we are finished for today, we'll meet again tomorrow for reinforcement. I will also give you some exercises and drills. The brain's just a muscle after all. It needs its exercise too.

"But for now, I just want you to sit back, relax, and close your eyes. Good. Now, I want you to imagine that your extremities are slowly sinking deeper and deeper into the chair."

Gregorieva readily complied and felt herself relaxing, sinking, and beginning even to almost to drift off.

Hearing the physician turning in his chair, Vesna next felt a warm glow caress her forehead. Allen had turned on a tightly focused halogen spotlight.

"Vesna," he said in a comforting and subdued voice, "can you see the light through your eyelids?"

"Yes."

"Good. Is the light too bright?"

"No, not at all."

"All right then. I want you to continue to relax and just sort of unconsciously focus on the light. Everything's okay?"

"Yes."

Thirty seconds passed.

"Okay, Vesna, now I am going to slowly count down from ten. As I do, I want you to imagine that you are sinking deeper and deeper into the chair so that by the time I reach one, you are almost asleep. Okay?"

"Yes."

"All right, here goes.

"Ten."

Pause.

"Nine."

Pause.

"Eight."

What Gregorieva was not aware of prior to the countdown was that the chair in which she was sitting was actually a highly sensitive cardiac and cephalic recording device. On the computer screen that was embedded in Doc Allen's desktop, the physician was simultaneously observing her pulse, heart rate, and several brain wave patterns as he counted. Given the Russian dancer's marvelous physical condition, Allen was not at all amazed how quickly the young woman had settled herself out. This was all the more remarkable given her present level of uncertainty within an alien culture, not to mention her frankly expressed fears. Allen then noted how quickly her brain patterns had fallen in line and had begun to settle out as well.

"Seven."

Pause.

"Six."

Pause.

"Five."

Pause.

"Four."

Pause.

"Three."

Pause.

"Two."

Pause.

"One."

Now Allen paused for a full ten seconds.

"Can you still hear me, Vesna?"

"Daaaah."

"Good. Just relax and focus your mind on my voice. We are about to go on an interesting journey."

CHAPTER XXXIII

Summer Break

After some frenetic grading, some last-minute student appeals for generosity and mercy, having finally addressed the ever-multiplying mound of clothing in the laundry hamper, and enjoying another memorable dinner with Ms. Kelly, Richards was off to the Annex to drop off the keys to his flat. That brief errand earned him a surprise kiss from its secretary.

"Why did you do that?"

"For luck, and, as chum."

"Chum?"

"Yes," she said with breathy emphasis. "I intend to extensively debrief you on your return."

Now with slightly rubbery knees, Richards caught his ride that took him to the military side of O'Hare Airport, where again his other "lift" was patiently waiting. As this was a recon mission, Gregorieva would not be accompanying him. At the last minute, it was decided that she wasn't ready for the trip, much to her great disappointment, and secretly, Richards' delight.

While riding in the backseat of the smallish four-door, Richards reckoned himself lucky that he had survived his first academic year and listed in his head all the things that he had accomplished, all the people that he had one way or another touched. On the other hand, several coeds had had him in their crosshairs, or so they thought. As it was, he had just managed to escape several difficult and sticky social situations.

Then just about a month and a half ago, sometime shortly after midterms, Richards had received his marching orders to get tan in preparation for his next deployment. The mission would be a challenge. Look for Akhenaten's aerial craft, that shining disk, that damnable machine with its laser light show that had first scared the stuffing out of him, when he had first seen it over the main Aten Temple at Akhetaten. But how would he find it? He would need help, but from whom? The venerable Meryptah was dead. Wily Piankoff was dead. He may have to recruit someone, but who?

But Richards already had an inkling as to where the Aten might be kept. It was a hunch based on an attractive observation made by a British architect familiar with the modern archaeological site of Amarna, ancient Akhetaten. The theory was presented on the web in the form of a carefully constructed speculation about the orientation of the boundary stelae that delimited the ancient city and the temple architecture within of the city of Akhetaten itself. What the Brit had noted was that all of these monuments seemed to be oriented toward a cleft in the eastern mountains that overlooked and surrounded that ancient urban settlement. Through that cleft the sun rose and spread its life-giving rays across the city, and located at about that position, but deeper within those mountains, the heretic Pharaoh Akhenaten had built his royal tomb. Where else, the Egyptologist therefore reasoned, would there be a better place to store and conceal his shining flying disk, his Aten, than either at or near Akhenaten's tomb?

While the particulars of Akhenaten's royal tomb, its multi-chambered layout and decoration, were well-known in modern times. But finding it, getting near it in antiquity, could prove to be a very hazardous undertaking. Frankly, Richards expected to find the area under considerable security after the king's mysterious disappearance due to his and Piankoff's murderous assistance. For sure, a necropolis police force patrolled the area, at the very least surely a dedicated branch of the Aten priesthood. While bribery was always a possibility, but as with anyone susceptible to such larcenous behavior, treachery was sure to soon follow.

The young Egyptologist well knew what the minimum penalty was if captured while skulking around the necropolis. The judicial papyri recorded the loss of one's nose followed by banishment into the desert. However, being caught *in flagrante delicto* while defiling a tomb meant a swift death at best, at worst, the removal of the nose, extensive torture, and then death. Somehow, someway, he had to get into that wadi of the Eastern Mountains, get past any guards, and find the Aten's hideout. Perhaps the Lady of the Two Lands, Nefertiti, could suggest a name or two?

Richards lift to Luxor was again the drab, but hardly unremarkable Gulf Stream V that had ferried him and Gregorieva in and out of New Mexico. But since this flight was an international one, two teardrop-shaped external fuel tanks had been attached to the hard points near the wing roots. Far less obvious to Richards was the military payload of one thousand rounds in the plane's nose and what lurked in the depressurized bay. There resided a rotary launcher with four air-to-air, fire-and-forget Griffin Talon missiles, each with a thirty-five mile range, each armed with thirty-five pound thermium nitrate warheads.

Since Richards' flight originated from the military side of the airport, a flight plan was not required, but a brief fuel stop at Gander International had been planned to top off the tanks and change crews. From Newfoundland, the final leg would cross the Atlantic, bifurcate the Straits of Gibraltar, and overfly the length of the Mediterranean. Then the onboard flight plan called for a turn south just west of Cairo International Airport's airspace that continued on in a southerly direction enroute to Luxor. In all, Richards roughly figured on some eleven and a half hours of flight time that spanned some 110 degrees of the Earth's latitude and crossed eight time zones.

Settling in with his laptop, a new spy thriller, and a pair of Bose headphones, Richards girded himself for the long haul.

This is truly the lap of luxury in comparison to that deafening C-130J!

* * *

Upon his arrival at Luxor, the young Egyptologist was greeted by a now familiar pair of tail lamps attached to a dilapidated half-ton pickup truck. Its swinging Arabic license plate remained affixed with only two uneven lengths of wire. With its brakes squeaking to a halt about thirty paces from the newly arrived aircraft, a jaunty figure in freshly pressed desert chocolate-chip cammies and cap emerged from the driver's cab and strode forward.

Stopping before the grinning academic, the driver snapped a smart salute and exclaimed with a smile, "Welcome back to Luxor, sir. Now stow your gear aboard. Your limo's meter is running."

* * *

As soon as Richards had slammed the truck's tailgate shut with a crash and jumped into the cab, its ever-efficient driver, Major Tuna

Cartwright, fired up its motor with a belch of smoke and jammed the truck into gear with a wincing metallic crunch. With a lurch from the clutch, the pair took off. Waved through the airport's security checkpoints, Cartwright expertly maneuvered west and through the outer urban sprawl of a third world provincial town. Driving through newly tarred streets and around mud-brick hovels, the truck vaulted over the high mound of a railroad track and then made a sharp right turn onto a rutted dirt road. The short fifteen-minute drive from the Luxor airport to the archaeological preserve known as the Karnak complex went uneventfully.

They were greeted by an Egyptian Antiquities guard in a tan uniform, who had stepped forward from the tiny open-aired guard shack that was behind the fenced in area.

"Welcome, Dr. Richards," the guard said in Arabic with a slight nod of the head. "It is truly good to see you again. May Allah bless you on your journey."

Richards, surprised by the greeting, furrowed his brow and snapped a look at the major for an explanation.

"Damnation," murmured the major under his breath. "I just have no operational security around this place anymore."

Richards then said to the guard in Arabic, "May blessings fall like heaven's own rain upon your household as well!"

Pleased, the guard smiled with a truly broad grin.

As the pair walked into the archaeological preserve, they walked through the ruined brown mud-brick walls of the temple's outer enclosure wall that once divided the profane from the sacred. The men saw before them the ruined expanse of a vast, monumental architectural wonder beyond imagination. Indeed, the Karnak Temple represented a single, rambling complex of limestone buildings that first began as a single core structure, then was added on to over the millennia. The grand First Pylon, or entrance to the Great Temple, was just short of a quarter of a mile distant, straight ahead. Richards and Tuna Cartwright were in essence heading for the temple's back door and its womb-like holy of holies.

As they skirted around the ruins of the many monumental limestone columns, pylons, and walls of the precinct, they finally arrived at a long, narrow room with rose granite walls – the innermost sanctuary, the holy of holies of the great god Amen Re himself. Here, in the midst of floor-to-ceiling hieroglyphic texts carved into the granite walls, stood the four pylons of the temporal device in the middle of that most sacred of ancient chambers. Incongruously, a crude wooden scaffolding of rough-hewn and lopsided beams tied together with hemp rope had been erected over the high-tech equipment. Attached to one of the overhanging beams was an equally ancient-looking wooden pulley and rope with a noose tied to one end. At a glance, it resembled more a poor attempt at a hangman's scaffold than a temporal drop off and retrieval point.

Beneath the wooden framework, sat the Soap Bubble Mark V-A. Powering the American temporal device was the small field generator sitting nearby on the floor with the usual number of four connecting cables to each of the pylons and their emitters. What was slightly amusing about the power source was that it was attached to what looked like a typical backpacker's frame.

Following his eyes, Cartwright chimed in, "That is just one of Doc Borov's latest tweaks. The portable unit is now good for about seventy-five minutes of uninterrupted, surge-free run time. Previously, as you might recall, we had a forty-minute maximum. The increase in run time, I'm told, is due to some improvements in the superconducting materials and the software."

"Boy," whispered Richards, "Piankoff would have been impressed."

"No shit," stated the major with a face as serious as a heart attack. "And to think that I saw him drop a total of four times with that old gurney-carried power pack with less than fourteen minutes of run time. Now that took some serious brass."

"The drop ring is still three and a half feet in diameter, is still fragile as hell. The ferric and ceramic coating remains quite brittle. So I suppose that you don't have to go on a crash diet to drop through it," the soldier said with a grin as he eyed the Egyptologist's compact and well-muscled profile with a tinge of professional envy.

"The thing that I'm impressed with is that Doc Borov and his gang of lunatic crazies managed to somehow squeeze more horsepower out of the Little Beast mini-computer. It's still constructed with ultra-fast molecular wafer circuitry, but its MOSFETs – metal oxide semiconductor field-effect transistors – possess even shorter gate lengths that are far more efficient than before. Its layered, parallel processors can now tune the Soap

Bubble's field and ion flow to a temporal horizon within any three second period, of any day, within any target calendrical year."

* * *

Via an encrypted satellite phone, Richards, per the book, double-checked with Dr. Borov that the temporal insertion data of September 23rd, 1359 BC at 2:12 a.m. had been the correct one entered into the Little Beast. Confirming that all was right with the world, the Egyptologist, once again soon-to-be temporal field agent, then reiterated the obvious.

"Yes, Peter, I will be careful. And yes, I promise that I will not touch any suspect well water either! By the way, is John there?"

After a brief pause, John Milson's soft and fatherly voice answered, "Yes, Joseph, I'm here. What's on your mind?"

"Well, I just wanted to confirm with you the names of the four individuals that we discussed in Chicago."

"Shoot."

"First, the High Priest of the Aten was a man with the unlikely name of Meryre, 'beloved of Re,' who carried the title of 'Greatest of Seers of the Aten in the House of Re.'"

"Correct."

"Second, a foreigner, perhaps of Syrian origin, named Tutu. He was the First Prophet of the Divine King and supposed 'Mouth of the Whole Land.' Hermann Kees thought ill of him, if I recall. He said that the man 'exercised apparently a pernicious influence over the king,' meaning Akhenaten. Given what we know, I still find that odd. Perhaps the opposite was more the case."

"Not at all, Joseph. While we know that Akhenaten really was a powerful line of sight telepathic and telekinetic alien, Tutu surely wasn't. If I had to guess, Akhenaten probably played his every action like a puppeteer and used him as his surrogate mouthpiece, hence his claim of being the 'Mouth of the Whole Land.' Why now all the concern?"

"I really don't know. It's just a hunch really, but I think that if I run into him, he could be real trouble."

"Agreed," answered Milson. "Avoid him like the plague, no pun intended."

"None taken John.

"Third, as for Smenkhkare, we agreed that Horemheb will have him removed from the picture. Given that he's a first generation line of sight telekinetic telepath, are we committed to the hunting trip?"

"I would expect so. Just make sure that it looks like a fine, visceral hunting accident with lots of excitement. That should cover any anxieties that Horemheb or his men may be suffering from."

"Consider it done.

"And now, the big enchilada, Paneshy, the First Servant of the Aten in the Domain of the Aten in Akhetaten. This guy I just have to meet. With a title like that, he could well be caring for the Aten himself."

"Again, I have to agree, but as ever, be very, very careful."

* * *

With a shaved and well-tanned head, applied eye paint, even body tan, reed sandals, and wearing a fresh white linen kilt, Richards sat poised on a timber above the drop ring with a small neck pouch filled with precious stones and golden rings. As Tuna Cartwright supervised the scene, one of his school manned the controls of the Little Beast computer, turned the twin keys and began the powering up cycle. As the electromagnetic field began to build, Richards could felt the static charge engulf him. Then the drop ring raised to its full operational height of five feet, Richards paused for it to stabilize with a silvery smooth sheen. With the ring floating at its operational height, Tuna signaled to another of his men. He was equipped with a plastic fish-eye lens probe connected to a fiber-optic cable, which was attached to the soldier's Darth Vadar helmet visor screen. Often used in dangerous surveillance work for peeking around corners or under doors undetected, this time the soldier carefully dipped the probe into the silvery field at first only a couple of inches, and then a couple of inches more. He gently twisted the cable between his fingers, rotating the lens several times. Satisfied, he announced that he was removing the probe, at which time the other soldier at the Little Beast reversed the ion emitters. At getting the high sign, out came the probe.

"Major Cartwright," Corporal Callahan reported, "the sanctuary is clear of any personnel. The statue is back in place along with a bunch of lighted oil lamps."

"Thank you, Corporal."

"Okay, Dr. Richards. It looks like you can drop. Just remember what you learned in jump school, and God willing, in ten days your time, I should be retrieving your sorry ass.

"Break a leg!"

"Gee thanks, sir."

And with that Richards dropped his neck pouch through the temporal field. And, ever the smart ass, snapped a salute in the major's direction, and dropped through into *somewhen*.

* * *

It was the same, but somehow different. Dropping through the ring seemed sticky and humid, but wasn't. Having landed bent-legged and with his ankles together, his drop recovery within the innermost chamber of Amen Re was a textbook-perfect side body roll. And there he lay, disoriented and nauseous, gasping before the near-life-sized image of the Great God, looking as if gripped in some sort of religious rapture. This time it took a good two minutes for the reaction to clear, something that Richards would discuss yet again with Doc Allen, for his recovery times were indeed lengthening with each drop.

Lightly dozing in a scribal pose before the massive twin cedar wood doors that opened to the most holy of holy places within the Great God's house sat a *sem*-priest, a Second Servant of Amen Re, a soul named Simut.

At first, this priest, who had been ordered by Prince Horemheb to assure that the prayers of the Noble Mayneken go undisturbed, believed that such a guardian vigil as a task more worthy of a mere acolyte. He had seen that noble priest enter the sacred chamber of the Great God just two hours ago after having returned from overseeing the burial of the Osiris Meryptah, a most worthy and pious duty for an adopted son. But then Simut understood why he had been asked to perform this mundane task, for only moments after the heavy doors of the sanctuary had been closed behind Mayneken, a bright white light seemed to illuminate the entire chamber. Simut had reasoned thus, since a brief and very uncommon glare had streamed out from beneath the doors and at the central vertical join of its leaves. Then nothing. Then after the passage of some time, again moments ago or so it seemed, the brightness momentarily reappeared only to quickly vanish yet again. Now fully alert, his ears were the first to perceive a muffled rustling from within the chamber that was shortly followed by someone opening the massive doors. It was of course Mayneken, but the man that left that most sacred of realms for all appearances now seemed to be ill.

Out of a reflexive concern, the priest quickly asked, “Most noble one, do you need assistance?”

Mayneken, who caught himself leaning heavily against one of the open leaves, merely whispered, “No, no that will not be needed. But what I need is rest. If anyone comes searching for me, tell them that I will be resting within my father’s house.”

Bowing to his expressed wishes, Simut began to lead the noble out of the temple, but found that he had not been followed, for Mayneken had turned left and was making way for a seldom-used doorway through the structure’s southern wall that was hidden by the shadow of a black granite statue of the goddess Sekhmet.

Smiling to himself, the second servant of the Great God Amen Re noted that Mayneken knew his way around the temple quite well enough and surely did not need him as a guide.

Finally, he thought with considerable approval, *my bed and wife await!*

* * *

Richards arose at dawn refreshed, invigorated, and above all, hungry. After completing his morning toilet of a bath and head shave, he fortunately found some overly ripe fruit and a bit of moldy cheese in Meryptah’s kitchen. The bread, however, was a total loss being rock-hard stale, but perfect for making beer. Smiling to himself at that idea, Mayneken then gorged himself on what he did find, all the while vowing to go back to the temple and have a couple *wab*-priests tidy and stock up the former high priest’s quarters in anticipation of its occupation by his replacement, a priest named Harkhuf.

It’s the least that I can do, he thought.

Meryptah’s successor must take over the reins of this institution as soon as possible to ensure the recovery of the priesthood and the greatness of Thebes. Then I am going to pay a visit to the household of Horemheb. Hopefully the prince is there, for we have much to discuss – the reestablishment of the Amen Re priesthood, the revival of Thebes, preparations for the moving of the royal family back to Thebes, and of course, there is that minor matter of Smenkhkare. But before all of that, I must secure a boat for my journey north this evening to Akhetaten, pay a visit to Queen Nefertiti, and begin my true mission – the location of the Aten craft. And in that endeavor, a certain Paneshy just might be of considerable assistance.

* * *

As soon as the stonemason from Abydos had heard the news of the founding of a new city, he moved his entire family lock, stock, and barrel to the site of that barren and undeveloped waste. While the first months living out of several tent frames had been a true adventure for his still young family, the wages were very good, supplemented with daily food rations and sweetened with the promise of permanent housing complete with a private well and toilet. Such were the advantages of signing on early to the Akhetaten construction project for skilled workers and laborers. What was more remarkable were that all the promises had been kept as the architects drew their lines in the sand, the laborers dug the foundation trenches, and the bricklayers began building row after row, street after street of a well-planned, spacious, and hygienically progressive housing community.

In many respects, this building of a city *de novo* was a daring act that broke with tradition. But for the stonemason Paneshy, it had been a godsend for this impoverished tradesman. While a capable stonemason, Paneshy was not a master craftsman. The calculations needed to grid out a work in cubits confounded him. For him, he could better eyeball the needed proportions of the Egyptian Canon of Art than know precisely where to snap the caulk-dusted string. As a result, sometimes his commissions were even and balanced, sometimes not. So when the Akhetaten project took off at its breakneck pace, Paneshy's mason's eye did well in an artistic environment that had abandoned the traditional Canon of Art for a more free-flowing naturalism. In short, he was in his element and naturally excelled, so much so that the Great Lord himself had singled him out from the masonry corps to instruct him in what the Great One, Akhenaten, had in mind for a series of boundary stelae.

The royal commission of these massive markers, some fourteen in all, were to delimit the extent of the city of Akhetaten and to proclaim to all the greatness of the Great One himself and of his god, the Aten. In addition, each stela was to have a specific orientation that the chief architect himself would provide, an orientation that would relate to the city's divinely inspired plan. What Paneshy marveled at was the absolute clarity of vision that he had received from the Great One as to how he wanted the boundary markers to appear, what they were to contain, and how they were to be adorned with the royal images of the king and queen beneath the life-giving rays of the Aten itself. The warm confidence that he had felt emanating from the Great One in his personal ability to complete such a magnificent commission had filled Paneshy's heart with overflowing joy and zeal. While it was currently the eighth month of Year Four of the Great One's reign, all must be completed by the same month of Year Five. Despite the brief time frame, Paneshy knew that he could do it and began planning his work and enlisting those whom he trusted in this great artistic endeavor.

For the next year, Paneshy's forearms and upper body bled freely from the flying stone chips. His arms, shoulders, and torso became hard like beaten bronze. His artistic eye and intuitive knack for proportion became better and better and much progress was made. The Great One often made visits to his work sites, located as they were sometimes quite distant from the main urban construction. At first, his presence had caused quite a commotion among Paneshy's work gangs, but over time they had become expected, even welcomed by the workers. Such royal interest in their work only seemed to spur them on to greater and greater feats of labor, creativity, and production.

On the occasion of one such royal visit, at a location some five kilometers south of modern Tuna el Gebel and the ancient burial ground of Hermopolis on the western bank of the Nile, the king found Paneshy toiling alone over a massive stela some 4.3 meters tall by 2.3 meters wide that faced the northern end of Akhetaten on the opposite side of the river. Most pleased with what he saw, the king rewarded the head stonemason with a smile and a slight bow of his head. The impact of that simple royal acknowledgment threw the man into a near spasm of joy and elation, for never before had the king "spoken" to him with such praise.

The point of relating this event was that nothing had been physically said, for the king had spoken to him directly and most intimately, without words, with only his thoughts. For Paneshy, such telepathic contact was not comprehended as such. Rather that it even occurred was proof positive of that divine kingly attribute known as the *sia*, loosely translated by modern Egyptian philologists as divine understanding and perception. But for Paneshy, this tangible exercise of the *sia*, as he had just experienced it, was something far more substantial. In truth, the stonemason found himself conflicted between an immense sense of humility, precious intimacy, and an intellectual sharing that staggered him. All the more so, as this exchange had occurred directly between he and his Living God.

As the final month appeared on the stonemason's calendar, so did the completion of the last boundary marker. His industry, artistic sense, and organization of the worker gangs had greatly pleased the pharaoh, who in turn raised the humble station of the former stonemason to that of the First Servant of the Aten within the domain of Akhetaten. Paneshy, once an obscure stonecutter, had earned both the vocal adulation of his god-king and another intimate, although brief, telepathic smile from the Great One that warmed his soul. His housing was upgraded to the posh side of town in the artisans' quarter. Three household servants were now his to command. He and his wife now enjoyed a place within the royal court. Never again would he have to heft the wooden mallet and bronze chisel. Henceforth, Paneshy was to see to the care of the Aten itself!

That was then and here is now.

Now the middle-aged Egyptian, with shoulders and arms grown soft and hands no longer callused, grumbled and growled in an ever-growing cycle of frustration that fed his anger and built on his worst fears. His frustration was firmly focused upon the Aten itself. Since the Great One's sudden and mysterious disappearance, since before the most recent Inundation, the Aten disk had refused to stir, much less fly, and bless the gathered populace at the main Aten Temple with its life-giving rays at Re's first appearance. All told, counting today, neither the Great One nor the Aten had made their appearance for over some sixty days. So he found himself asking a very seminal question.

"How can I fulfill my Lord's wishes as First Servant of the Aten?"

The Egyptian's anger stemmed from the fact that he had cared for the Aten disk, just as the Great One had instructed him, and still it would not move from its secret chamber in the Eastern Mountains. He had polished its surface with pure beeswax until it seemed to glow a bright and lustrous electrum color. He had carefully fed the Aten all that it had required according to the Great One's careful admonitions – daily sixteen measures of the purest water. Yet, since the Great One's absence, the Aten had not moved. The Aten did not exert itself. The passive Aten did not require feeding as its stomach had remained satisfied.

But it was the ever-growing sense of fear during these past sixty days that troubled the man. The Great One had not returned from wherever he had so suddenly gone. The people were growing ever more restive and aggressive day by day. While the sacrifices to the Aten and food distribution to the people continued under that mad demon Smenkhkare, it was clear to all that Smenkhkare was not favored by the Aten disk, for it had never responded to his prayers, petitions, summons, or even heated threats. While the people yearned for the curative sensations that came from the Aten's life-giving rays, Smenkhkare could not call the Aten. If he could not summon the Aten, then perhaps the Aten chose not to do so. Anyone within the mob with half a mind could see that the Aten was displeased with Smenkhkare's prayers and sacrifices. Anyone could see that the Great One was absent. The mob's train of logic continued that if the Great One has fled us, then has not the Aten and its life-giving rays as well? If this is indeed so, then to whom should we turn to for divine protection? Who will represent us before the gods? Who will protect us from the dark powers of chaos?

To Paneshy, all was clear. Divine abandonment meant the end of the city of Akhetaten, to its temples and priesthoods, its entire purpose for existing, and in particular, the cessation of his personal gravy train of power, influence, and material well-being. To Paneshy, formerly a mere stonemason until discovered by the Great One and made First Servant of the Aten, new alliances clearly were required and quickly, if he and his household were to survive until the next Inundation.

* * *

Refreshed and fed, the *sem*-priest Mayneken departed the cool shade of his adopted father's house and strode purposefully into the daylight glare and mounting heat. His immediate task was to visit the docks and arrange for his transport north to that "other" city. But even as he passed through the open threshold of Meryptah's property and began to head through the streets of priestly housing, temple granaries, workshops, and scribal schools that made up that section of the Amen Re temple complex, Mayneken felt the hair on the back of his neck tingle with the feeling that he was being watched.

His movements were hardly anonymous, and eyes were recording his every move. His peripheral vision began to catch stray movements within a shadowed window here or doorway there. Any people encountered moved deferentially aside at his passing with their heads bowed in quiet respect. Here and there, a priest stopped whatever task he was doing just to watch him walk by. At seeing their sometimes open-mouthed stare, Mayneken would silently nod and smile in their direction, which was always returned with a surprised, and smiling nod as well.

Damnation, Richards thought, *it seems that I have become some sort of celebrity! And back home I just wish that my peers would show me some reasonable level of respect! If they only knew.*

Then a second thought occurred to him.

Maybe the news of Meryptah's burial and my role in it has become common knowledge. And who ever said that gossip and rumor do not swiftly travel!

Once having passed through the massive outer brick wall of the temple complex proper, the fawning attention abruptly stopped and none too soon, much to the priest's relief. As always, the marketplace was a beehive of commerce and the delicious smells of freshly baked sweetbreads and honey set his flat stomach a-rumbling. Ignoring that vocal organ, Richards reached the docks and began to inspect what there was to be had in the way of river transport. After a quick inspection of a likely craft, an agreement was reached with little haggling. The clout of the massive ambassadorial ring of the Lady of the Two Lands, Queen Nefertiti, had once again worked its wonders.

That errand accomplished, Richards next goal was a visit to the extensive noble properties of the hereditary prince Horemheb that was located a brisk twenty minute walk south beyond what we moderns call the Luxor Temple. With powerful strides, the priest headed off in that direction, first following the course of the river and then moving inland along the long avenue of sphinxes that connected the Karnak and Luxor temple complexes.

Along the way, Richards noted everywhere the neglect of the past years during the Amarna Revolution. The Temple of Karnak had become a stone shell looted and stripped of its precious inlays, copper cladding, wooden doors and frames, anything that was removable. Overzealous followers of the Aten had cruelly defaced with their blasphemous chisels the sacred name of the Great God wherever it had been found. The many gardens of flowers and stands of fragrant trees had withered and disappeared, leaving behind barren areas and dried stumps. Where reflecting ponds choked with fragrant and flowering lotus once reflected the cloudless blue sky, now only muddy stagnant pools remained that provided a troublesome breeding ground for flies and mosquitoes. Upon reaching the Luxor Temple, the same abuse and careless neglect that plagued its twin temple to the north was obvious to anyone who cared to notice.

"This has got to change," he whispered to himself.

"No, this will change," he vowed.

Now south of Luxor, Richards began to weave his way through the narrow alley-like streets of the living quarters of the local inhabitants. Here he found himself struck again by the delicious aromas of cooking fires, the early morning serenade of cooing doves and quail, and the nose-wrinkling smells of rank open latrines. Passing by a public well, the young Egyptologist peered in and was appalled at its condition, and what was coming out of it.

This has got to change and change quickly, he again vowed.

Reaching Horemheb's estate, Richards once again noted how truly modest the high priest Meryptah's dwelling had been in comparison. For Horemheb's household was fully four, if not five times, larger in total area, with a grand colonnaded entrance, massive multi-roomed household, two separate annexes, whose functions he knew to be dedicated to beer brewing, winemaking, and the grinding of grain. If that were not sufficient, four private, freshly whitewashed, conical granary magazines stood all neatly arranged in a row along the eastern side of the plot. And Richards reminded himself that this was only the southern residence of this prince of Egypt. God only knows how extensive his holdings were in cultivated lands that supported this dwelling and its northern twin in Memphis, not to mention all of its inhabitants.

Standing at the complex's threshold, the gatekeeper, an elderly man leaning on a stout staff, greeted him, who in turn called to a younger helper to announce Mayneken's presence. The head housekeeper appeared and offered Mayneken the opportunity of dusting his feet after his long walk, an offer Richards gratefully accepted.

* * *

"So, my elder brother, I see that you have grown!" the prince exclaimed in greeting as he gripped Richards by the shoulders.

"And stronger too, I notice," Horemheb thought to add.

Then with his ever-appraising eye, "What is in your heart, dear brother?" As the prince steered his houseguest into the coolness of the dining room where they both sat down on gaily colored cushions filled with duck feathers.

"I wish to let you know that this evening, I will be journeying north to visit with the Lady of the Two Lands, Nefertiti. I thought it wise to let you know of this, just in case you wish me to carry a letter."

"Ah, most kind. But noble brother, I know you very well. Just what do you want me to write in this letter?"

Richards, smiling broadly, let out a chuckle, and said, "Am I that obvious?"

* * *

"Without question, my prince, much needs to be done before the royal court can return to sacred Thebes, as stripped and neglected as it currently is. The water wells must be attended to and the sewer trenches made clear so they may properly flow. Then the temples need to be restored, their grounds replanted with fragrant trees and flowers, their pools cleaned, refilled, and stocked with fish."

And as Richards stopped to take a breath, Horemheb raised his hand to halt his litany.

"My dear brother, how am I to accomplish all of these needful works so quickly?"

"Put to work those who are idle. On my journey to your household just today, I counted over fifty strong backs that are so available. Not only that," and Richards then inwardly cringed at what he was about to say, "idle hands are the fertile fields of Set. Have you not noticed any rise in lawlessness?"

"As always, my brother you always have such a poetic way of expressing yourself on common affairs. Nonetheless, you are correct. There has been a spate of stealing within the marketplace, even my granaries have been broken into by the hungry. So what you propose is that I put these men to work?"

"Why not? They will bless you for it."

"Why not indeed! What else is in your heart, my brother?"

"Smenkhkare."

"Smenkhkare! That young whelp! What of him?"

"He must be sent West before the royal court returns to Thebes. You will not be an able elder brother to Tutankhaten until the evil influence of his brother is permanently removed. His seed must be no more."

"Ah. Finally we have arrived to a topic that is far weightier and more appropriate to the concerns of my brother, the warrior-priest," Horemheb stated as he studied his hands.

"What you ask is difficult. I have heard ghastly rumors of what that monster can do with a mere glance from his foul, evil eyes. It is even said that he killed a foreign ambassador just so right before the entire royal court!

"Mayneken, such a thing is no easy task!"

"True," Richards began with care. "But one man's concentration can be distracted by lively and exciting events, such as a royal lion hunt. Could it not be arranged that the monster would not return from such a desert adventure?"

"Mayneken, your crafty and cunning solutions to problems sometimes frighten me. But what you say makes sense. I now believe that I know what I should write in my letter to the Lady of the Two Lands. But I must first think on it for a time, as only I, and not my household scribe, must compose this letter."

Then shifting topics, the prince added, "As for the needed preparations in anticipation of the return of the royal court to Thebes, I will tell the queen of these as well. These preparations may take some time. So, my elder brother, before you leave this evening, I will place in your care a letter to deliver."

* * *

The day and a half river journey north to Akhetaten went uneventfully. While the boat's provisions were meager –bread, cheese, warm beer, and a handful of dates – its lack of fleas and lice was most welcome. Alternately sailing and drifting north with the Nile's current and the prevailing breezes, Richards arrived at Egypt's new capital just past dawn's first light. Painted against the clear sky he saw the wafting plumes of the first meal's cooking fires, and the activity along the quays jammed with grain transports, river traffic, foreign merchant traders, and passenger boats just like his.

Rubbing his chin, Richards thought of other concerns – the itch of his quickly deteriorating grooming for one. While in Thebes, he had been shaved last at his adopted brother's house. Then his stomach grumbled mightily. Yes, he would have to see to that as well upon landing, perhaps two small loaves of honeyed sweetbread, some dates, and fresh cheese.

As the starboard side of the craft made its berth, mooring ropes flew to two dockhands, and the passengers prepared themselves to depart. Without any baggage or wares, Richards was the first to use the boarding plank.

Richards lost himself within the crowds of the quay and the many stalls of the daily market. Having silenced his stomach, he moved on to find a barber. After having himself groomed to his satisfaction, he then moved on to seek out the Lady of the Two Lands, for he had another papyrus scroll to deliver.

After winding his way through the marketplace, Richards began to work his way over toward what he recognized as the central section of the city. Getting there was not a problem, for the main north-south thoroughfare of the new capital, the Royal Road, led passed the royal apartments to the west and the royal palace to the east. At the moment, neither of these interested the Egyptologist as he continuing on along the Royal Road, heading in a northerly direction. As he passed through the central portion of the town, he entered a domestic neighborhood and beyond that appeared several structures on the left, which was his goal.

The northern portion of the city, and its so-called Northern Palace, was where the Chief Wife, the Lady of the Two Lands, Queen Nefertiti, had been sequestered since the Year Fourteen of Akhenaten's reign. Now with his passing, she was free, but still stubbornly chose to remain within the protection of her gilded cage.

Walking boldly, the ambassador and priest stepped unopposed through the palace's main entrance that led directly to a broad courtyard with a small shrine on the left. This time Richards pointedly ignored the shrine, crossed the courtyard, and approached the stairs of the entrance porch to the Northern Palace itself. While climbing the porch's stone steps, Richards heard a rustling of movement above. Two Nubian Medjay now stood just inside the shadows of the porch's entrance. The sheer breadth of their massive shoulders blocked all access.

Stepping forward with authority, Richards stopped atop the last step and announced with a strong voice, "Noble Medjay, announce to Neferneferu Nefertiti that her ambassador and *sem*-priest, Mayneken, has arrived true and faithful to her command!"

* * *

After about a quarter of an hour wait within the relative coolness of the official "waiting place for those who wish audience," Richards was led to the formal reception chamber. As he passed through the small forest of brightly painted lotus-bundled columns, Richards was pleasantly surprised at seeing a clear change in the Lady of the Two Lands.

She sat before him on a raised three-step dais in the stiff formal poise of an Egyptian monarch. With her hands lying flat upon her thighs and her eyes focused straight ahead into infinity, she looked whole again, serene, once again truly the Lady of the Two Lands. Behind her sitting figure stood, to her right and left, massive and towering Nubian Medjay with their dangerous weaponry drawn, and in the open for all to see. Also standing near her, Richards recognized Nefertiti's personal servant and second nurse, Kia, who stood proudly on the right with her chin high. And rightly so, for the loyal and patient Kia had literally nursed the queen back following Akhenaten's brutal rape of her mind. Also in the royal presence was an adolescent noble or prince by the look of his slight pot belly and lack of manly definition. He too stood proud and erect with his hands behind his back to the queen's left.

Christ! That has to be young Tutankhaten, Richards realized, while blocking his mind in the next instant.

Oops!

Now I just wonder how much I allowed slip, while gazing at the queen before I slammed the door in his face?

* * *

Perhaps the Scottish poet Robert Burns said it best in his quaint poem, *To a Louse.*

O' would some Power the gift give us,
To see ourselves as others see us!

For at the very moment when Richards firmly "slammed the door," Tutankhaten had visibly winced.

Up until that point, the curious young prince had been fully taking in this mysterious visitor named Mayneken, royal ambassador and *sem*-priest, with all of his six senses. But it was with his sixth, his *sia* or "perception," that the young man "felt" the most impact. As the powerfully built priest strode into the reception chamber, it was as if a great wind or flood had suddenly appeared.

Tutankhaten, impressed and a bit unsettled by the ambassador's entrance, unconsciously began to gently read Mayneken's mind.

A powerful mind.

Supremely confident.

And one put out and frustrated at being forced to wait for this audience with the Lady of the Two . . . No! Wait. His Nefer. His beloved Nefer, the private name that she had asked him to use.

Surprised by the revelation, he immediately realized that this was his stepmother's lover!

And then there was also the obvious warmth radiating from the queen at his presence!

Despite her formal posture, she was almost nearing orgasm in sheer anticipation of being held again in his powerful arms, of feeling him deep within, of final release.

As the young royal returned his focus back to the visitor, he caught Mayneken's eye, his spark of recognition, of just who he was.

But I have never met this man before? How could he know who I am? And what is a "Christ"?

And then, much to Tutankhaten's total astonishment, it was as if he became a blind man. Not blindness in the visual sense, but suddenly the mind of the ambassador who stood before him, not twenty feet away, had gone blank, as dark as an empty tomb's entrance.

Confused, the young royal looked back again at Nefertiti, who simply glowed an enveloping warmth of happiness and pleasure at the sight of the man standing before her.

Turning again back and focusing on Mayneken, all that the young man could sense was a cool darkness, and then the image of a massive, two leaved, copper-clad cedar wood doorway inlaid with golden hieroglyphics that read, "He who breaches this entranceway will suffer the utter wrath of Amen Re by the hand of his loyal servant Mayneken!"

At the shock of that message and its implied challenge, Tutankhaten stopped his intrusive mind reading and turned contemplative.

Do all sem-priests have such power? My father never before had spoken of such barriers. I have never before encountered such a gateway, much less one that threatened the wrath of a god if I did! And it was he, Amen Re, who warned me off!

* * *

Richards saw out of the corner of his eye, with both relief and satisfaction Tutankhaten's initial wince, vacant stare, and then blink of confusion.

God bless Doc Allen and his hypnosis sessions! The block is up, running, and holding!

The Egyptologist also detected the surprise on the lad's face when he looked at the queen.

Wow! I'll just bet the farm that Nefer must be really broadcasting big time to earn such a look and a reaction like that!

Upon reaching the customary approach distance of foreign dignitaries and ambassadors, Mayneken put down the papyrus that he was carrying on the floor and prostrated himself before the queen with the back of his neck exposed. At lowering himself to the floor, Richards performed a sort of negative push-up that fully displayed his back's muscular development – not to mention its impressive scars. None of this was missed by the queen or, for that matter, the young prince.

He then announced to the polished limestone flooring, "I offer myself as a sacrifice before the Lady of the Two Lands."

"What do you, a mere insignificant mortal, wish to say to Us?" Nefertiti ritualistically intoned.

"I, your humble ambassador, wish to deliver a communication from the Hereditary Prince Horemheb, who currently resides in most sacred Thebes."

"We are pleased," the queen neutrally stated.

"Kia! Fetch that papyrus and bring it to me.

"And as for you, noble Mayneken, my ambassador," words now spoken with remarkable softness, "you may dust your feet within my household after your long journey. Kia will see to this as well. As the day is almost past, you will dine with Us. You may now go and attend to yourself."

As Richards carefully got up, he noted that he did indeed need to dust his feet as the muscles of his arms, chest, and thighs were coated with a fine layer of white limestone from the audience chamber's pavement. Resisting the impulse to brush it off, he instead bowed, stole a peek up at the queen, momentarily caught her eye, roguishly winked, and respectfully backed out of her royal presence with a bowed head. For her part, only a faint smile creased her otherwise stoic composure.

When Richards was finally out of sight and earshot, Tutankhaten, fairly bursting at the seams, turned to his stepmother and said with a sly smile, "Well, I did not know that my father's chief wife had befriended such an interesting priest. Just who is he, this noble Mayneken?"

Slowly turning her head to face his question, Nefertiti first smiled and then said coolly to her youngest stepson, "Take care,

Tutankhaten. He once was the assistant of the magician and seer-priest Piankhotep. He is also my personal ambassador and as such is under my protection. I can assure you that he is not one to trifle with."

Although the queen succeeded in hiding most of her thoughts, Tutankhaten could tell that the queen had witnessed this Mayneken kill, and kill with the swiftness of a lion.

Mayneken, "young lion" indeed!

As for the mention of Piankhotep, his name had already become legend within the royal court and harem as the kindly priest with the magically healed foot. And this Mayneken was his former assistant.

Most powerful Aten protect me!

* * *

Following a warm bath and an invigorating massage of fragrant cedar oil by two attentive servant girls, Richards found himself lounging on a guest room bed frame, blissfully enjoying a gentle breeze, just on the edge of dozing, when his stomach growled so loudly that he opened his eyes to a surprise.

"Well, my Yo-ee," the queen exclaimed using his private name. "I hear yet again that your stomach is in need!" She smiled with mirth.

Now wide-eyed, Richards gasped out, "My Lady, just how long have you been watching me?"

"Long enough to feast my eyes several times on your magnificent form, my Yo-ee. But clearly, I first must feed you, before you me," she said with a wickedly private smile of anticipation.

Richards rose from the bed frame, wrapped his freshly washed kilt about his waist, and hand-in-hand allowed his Nefer to lead him to their evening meal.

As before, the private dining area, two stories up, was open on two sides, affording a breathtaking view of much of the Nile's northerly course and surrounding agricultural fields.

They sat on low, couch-like padded furniture without any backs to lean back on. Made of fragrant, imported cedar wood and inlaid with costly ebony from Central Africa and carved ivory inlays from Syria, one was expected to either sit or recline while dining.

The table before them, raised to the height of the couches, was crafted of cedar and decorated with ivory, ebony, gold foils, faience inlays, and semiprecious stones. This unique *object d'art* was literally covered from edge to edge with floral arrangements, and a quantity and variety of foods that staggered the imagination. Roasted quail, pigeon, and duck, cooked and smoked perch, sweetbreads, cheeses, jars of honeys, spicy concoctions and sauces, dried dates, grapes, and raisins. As for the liquid refreshments, Nefertiti's household offered three different types of wine and four of beer.

The queen began the evening meal with a toast with her favorite cup made of beaten silver. With an erect back and proud voice, she said, "The gods have again smiled upon Egypt. The temples of the Great God Amen Re will again be restored. Sacred Thebes, in all of its aspects, will again be restored. May all trace of the name of He-who-is-in-his-grimness be struck from all memory, all monuments. May his many temples and constructions crumble and blow away like the sand from which they were built. May those of his seed live no more."

After the toast, the queen drained her goblet dry. In response, Richards did likewise and added, "I see that you have read Horemheb's letter."

"Indeed I have, my ambassador. Several times. And I have composed one of my own for you to deliver to him, whenever it pleases you."

Again smiling that quietly wicked smile, she then continued, "Horemheb has much to accomplish before the royal court can return. He may be in need of your wisdom. Give it freely."

Breaking her natural train of thought, Richards intruded.

"My Lady," he began, but her look stopped him.

"Allow me to begin again. Nefer," which rewarded him with that smile yet again, "do you know of a man named Paneshy?"

"Why, yes. He was a stonemason, a trusted one of He-who-is-in-his-grimness. Why do you ask?"

"I wish to meet him. Perhaps speak with him about the Aten."

"Such a curious priestly request from one usually so serious of purpose. But as for this Paneshy, I can arrange an introduction with him, whenever it pleases you."

Spoken again with that smile and the pair continued with their meal, sharing several goblets of wine. When both had eaten their fill, it was the queen who continued the conversation.

"My ambassador," the queen clearly shifting from the trivial to the weighty, "your suggested plan for the murder of that brat Smenkhkare, while logical, cannot and will not succeed, for I have already sacrificed four of my most trusted Medjay on just such a mission."

Richards' shock told the queen that she should continue.

"Allow me to tell you what happened as Tutankhaten was witness to the deed. What he told me so disgusted him that he came directly to me, almost as a young child, in tears out of pity for those sacrificed and out of fear for his own life. For while he and his elder brother, Smenkhkare, were in the Western Desert in search of lions, my four guards attacked. It wasn't a fair fight. All four fell to their knees while holding their heads in extreme agony. This continued until all four were balled up in a pain so excruciating that they moaned and drooled as if they were infants.

"You see, my ambassador, Smenkhkare simultaneously violated all of their minds, much the same way mine was by done by He-who-is-in-his-grimness, but to a far more deadly effect. The prince is an unstoppable monster, noble one. If you encounter him, beware and carefully guard your strong thoughts with innocent ones."

"And what of Tutankhaten? He is also such a monster?"

"Potentially, but no, he has not the stomach for it. The touch of his *sia* is soft, gentle, and subtle. He intrudes constantly, perhaps even unconsciously, but a murdering monster," the queen shook her head, "Tutankhaten is not. He is just vexing and meddlesome. An itch that one cannot reach to scratch."

"My Lady," he stated this time with emphasis despite her frown while he held her shoulders, "you must recognize that the royal court cannot return to sacred Thebes with Smenkhkare among them. He must go West, even if I have to perform this awful deed myself."

Clasping a hand over her mouth, tears began to burst forth, and as she buried her head into his chest, a whimpering sound emerged from her throat.

"Must you, my Yo-ee?"

"Indeed, my queen, I must," he gently murmured into her left ear. "For Egypt must be restored. Thebes must be restored. The gods must be restored."

Now gently turning her face toward him between his strong hands. "After all, what truly is the cost of one man's life when balanced against such needful things?" he concluded showing her a soft smile before he continued.

"Besides, my lovely Nefer, the monster Smenkhkare is in for a surprise. I am prepared for his tricks and devilry. My master, Piankhotep, taught me well. And do not forget that all of the ancient gods are behind me in their manifest support, above all, Maat herself.

"Trust me, my queen. His seed will be no more before the beginning of the next cycle of the moon."

CHAPTER XXXIV

Nearing the Fringe

As the recovery trio of scout surveyors began to near the neighborhood of Earth's solar system, they had long become accustomed to the incessant chatter that seemed to endlessly and mindlessly radiate out from that world's audio and video spectra. The three could not believe the planet's inhabitants were so unaware of the magnitude of their exposure, the cumulative impact of their transmissions, and how much they unconsciously told about themselves. So, with their sensors queued to recognize certain genres, the recovery team sifted through the vast majority of the detritus and easily harvested that of substance.

To date, what they had gathered and took special note of was that the planet had survived several near planet-wide conflicts and dozens of other localized ones. This proved to the three scout surveyors that the dominant species had remained proficient at self-annihilation and were perfecting the genre. While a nascent form of global representation had been established, the species did not possess either the want or will to adopt a common language, preferring instead to accept the inevitability of linguistic ambiguity and its oftentimes dire results.

Scientifically, they had explored their nearest satellite, sent probes to neighboring planets and beyond, dabbled in fission and fusion, completed their genetic mapping, had become ecologically aware, and mastered coherent light. Yet, they remained saddled with a remarkable capacity to believe pure gibberish: warp drive, racial superiority, crop signs, and the Big Bang Theory – not to mention their own divinely granted uniqueness among the universe. Yet this species showed promise, for the SETI Project – the Search for Extraterrestrial Intelligence, directly mimicked one of the basic mission parameters of the Survey Institute community, which in many respects engendered the entire point behind sending out the scout surveyors, to venture forth and investigate for such sources.

Regarding the planet's capacity for outright aggression, the trio's sense of astonishment had long ago ceased to provide any meaning. Despite all the thorax thumping and scientific and technological advances, nonspecific genocide of the species still occurred with a frightening regularity and with increasingly frightful efficiency.

On the subject of space beyond their satellite, powerful search radars and lasers had regularly been detected several light-years ago, which fostered much discussion as to their detection and logically their own security. Whether a planetary defense system had been established was unknown, but was highly doubtful given their bellicose proclivities. While the news of several cycles did indeed refer to the establishment of a "Star Wars Initiative," the planet's sheer divisiveness, the three concluded, could not build one.

So on the basis of The Survey Institute's established forty-eight universal parameters that measure the relative development of a given species, this planet's development was calculated at level eleven, mainly because their planet-wide survival remained at issue. To initiate direct contact at this level of development was not a recommended option. Given this species' capacity for agitation and paranoia, the uproar caused by any off-world contact would only hamper its natural development.

Earth, in other words, was a dangerous place. Time was needed to allow for its natural incubation, which had to occur before there could be any hope for direct contact, much less a sincere cultural exchange. With that shared conclusion in mind, the trio put their collective minds to work on what had to be a covert recovery plan.

* * *

While the crew of The Redemption contemplated their recovery of the Hope, a select handful on Earth were eagerly watching their blistering inbound progress, furiously calculating potential trajectories, orbital crossings, and any gravitational influences that might ricochet the path of this newcomer. Without question Poliahu was an NEA. Without question, its September passage would be spectacular, but how spectacular was the issue that remained the troubling. As for the slower moving Toutatis, also inbound, betting pools were placing odds that the two would practically arrive in system at the same time. None contemplated, much less could calculate, that the two heavenly bodies would precipitate a spectacular collision.

CHAPTER XXXV

The Conversion of Paneshy

Paneshy's head was in a spin, for never before had he been summoned to the Northern Palace by the Lady of the Two Lands. On the one hand, the former stonemason was curious, especially given all the courtly gossip about the Chief Wife's absence from the royal suites years ago, her banishment to the Northern Palace, and then the frightening rumors of her survival from a mysterious ailment. On the other, given that the Great One had recently disappeared, another sort of opportunity came to mind as well, perhaps even something regarding Smenkhkare. Nonetheless, The Most Beautiful One was not to be kept waiting. Clearly from the impatient look of her two Medjay standing before him, he was more than willing to oblige.

* * *

"Rise, Paneshy," a soft feminine voice commanded.

As the man levered himself up off of the audience hall's limestone pavement, the First Servant of the Aten dared to directly gaze upon his interlocutor. What he saw was a woman of unsurpassed beauty, a woman that he had only seen before from afar. But sitting in the rigid and formal pose of a royal monarch with her blue crown, crook and flail crossed over her chest, she was truly formidable. But the figure that stood at her right side frightened the former stonecutter even more. For there was a man, a tall and very powerfully built priest, one whose confident presence went far beyond that of royalty. The immediate sense was of spear-won respect. In fact, the musculature of this priest's upper body reminded the bureaucrat uncomfortably of himself, but at a time before he had become so soft. Unconsciously, perhaps a bit nervously, he lowered his eyes in a quiet personal shame only to behold a washboard stomach of rippling muscles and two powerfully built legs set wide apart in an open statement of outright challenge and protection.

By all the gods, he mentally gasped, *just who is this priest? A guardian perhaps?*

Again came that voice, which jarred him from his thoughts.

"Paneshy, We have need of your wisdom."

She spoke with a soft command that breached no quarter.

"My ambassador and *sem*-priest of Ptah, Mayneken, also has need of your wisdom."

A sem-priest of Ptah!

With a still bowed head, his reply emerged haltingly. "What wisdom do You wish of me, Most Beautiful One?"

"The Aten, Paneshy. You are its First Servant. Where does it reside?"

Initially struck with a bolt of surprise and confusion, then fear washed over the First Servant of the Aten, for he had sworn himself to absolute secrecy as to the location where the Aten slept.

My oath to the Great One! But where is he? Where has he gone? Oh, how I need his guidance, his protection, he silently prayed.

While standing before the Lady of the Two Lands and her ambassador, a sheen of sweat appeared followed by rivulets that began to run down the sides of his freshly shaved head.

"Noble Paneshy, your continued silence tells Us several things, some most noble, some most stubborn.

"We suspect that you have bound yourself to an oath, an oath that my former husband, He-who-is-in-his-grimness, no doubt forced upon you. Your faithfulness to this oath is most noble. We now relieve you of this burden and obligation. However, if you continue to remain silent, We will have you examined most closely. After a time, your tongue will most surely wag like a jackal's tail. The choice is yours to make. But take heed, and be mindful of your family's welfare as well."

At the mention of his family, anger flared deep within the First Servant of the Aten, causing him to blurt out, "How dare you threaten my family! They are my life. The Aten is my life. The Great One is my life!"

With a slight leftward tilt of her head and squinting of her eyes, the queen coolly replied, "Indeed, noble Paneshy. You cherish your family as I once did mine. But be aware. My family is all but dead. As for He-who-is-in-his-grimness, he has already gone West. His seed is no more."

While the queen waited a beat for the full import of her words to break upon Paneshy's conscious like great rolling whitecaps, she continued, "Now, noble one, share with Us your wisdom."

With haunted eyes, a quivering chin, and a suddenly dry mouth, the First Servant of the Aten indeed spoke as commanded.

"You are wise, Most Beautiful One. The sacred residence of the Aten is to the East toward the rising of his first appearance."

"This fact," the queen hissed, "We already know. But the direction of the Aten's residence is not what We seek, but rather its exact whereabouts."

Then smiling with her mouth only, she shifted to a different topic.

"Noble Paneshy, what do you know of Our affliction? Surely it was well known throughout the many warrens and precincts of the royal court and harem."

"None, absolutely nothing, oh, Most Beautiful One!"

"We think not. But just in case you are speaking the truth out of ignorance or politeness, allow Us to tell you. My former husband, He-who-is-in-his-grimness, invaded first Our body and then Our very being. As a result, We were again rendered as if a newborn. Without speech, without bodily control, unable to even feed Ourselves. It was horrible, maddening, shameful. Do you understand Our words regarding this matter?"

The obvious shudder was proof enough.

"Yes, Most Beautiful One. I do indeed understand, for I have seen with my own eyes Smenkhkare reduce a Syrian ambassador into a drooling, babbling idiot."

Then hesitatingly, "And . . . and that was done, such a violation to you, Most Beautiful One?"

While the curt nod received from the noble one was good enough for Paneshy, it was her haunted and anguished eyes that definitely confirmed the magnitude of the injury. Having seen those eyes, his decision became easier.

"Most Beautiful One, whatever Your desire is, will be my duty to grant."

* * *

The ride east from the Northern Palace across the open desert toward the towering cliffs of the Eastern Mountains was rough, but not quite as bone-jarring as Richards had imagined. Nonetheless, he had to consciously relax his jaw muscles so as not to accidentally chip a tooth or bite his tongue. Even though the pair was supported by the leather mesh flooring that dampened out some of the shock from the chariot's wooden axle, it was not enough. One had to loosely flex one's knees as well to soak up the jarring. Then there was the dust, grit, and rock that were kicked up by the horse team's hooves.

The Egyptologist unconsciously yearned for the relative safety of a visor and motocross helmet as he squinted his eyes and hung on for dear life to the chariot's fragile wicker framework. Catching a glance over at the chariot's driver, Paneshy eyes were mere focused slits, his forearms rigid bands that deftly controlled the dual reins, while the rest of his body seemed to naturally rock, sway, and bob with the many undulations. Richards could not help but admire the man's style. He also had to admit this ride was a dream come true.

After all, how many of his esteemed colleagues could ever hope to top this and, in the process, risk taking a flying rock in the teeth? *Not many*, he concluded.

What was once a distant vertical crease in the near continuous wall of rock and cliff was rapidly becoming an impressive gap known today as the Royal Wadi. Carved into the northern side of its entrance was a spectacular monumental inscription that included free-standing statuary of Akhenaten and Nefertiti along with several of their daughters as well. This particular inscription, today referred to by Egyptologists as Boundary Stela U, was only one of a total of fourteen such stelae that delimited the area of Akhetaten along both sides of the Nile's course. Standing almost twenty-six feet tall, the boundary stone was topped with a semicircular upper field decorated with an arched sky-sign above the dominant symbol of the radiant Aten sun-disk. Its brightly painted hieroglyphs were written in both vertical columns and horizontal lines. First inscribed in the Year 6, it was later updated with a postscript of sorts in the Year 8 of Akhenaten's reign.

As the chariot neared the boundary stela at the wadi's opening, Paneshy slowed the freely sweating and panting horses to a gentle canter. With bits of froth dropping from their mouths, the heaving of their barrels slowly began to subside as the pair slowed to a walk.

The small stone guard hut before them, built against the side of the wadi's northern rock face, was their goal.

In Richards' mind, this was another priceless opportunity as they slowly passed by a monument that was cut only eleven years ago. As Doc Allen had instructed him, he slowly scanned the scene, memorizing as he went, the many details – the statues so riotously colored, the extreme sharpness of the carvings, the entire tableau from top to bottom. This the Egyptologist did four times and all within about twenty seconds.

Paneshy, noting Richards' attentive stare, narrated with a master stonecutter's pride.

"Yes, noble Mayneken, this was my best creation for the former Great One. The earlier ones contained small and minor imperfections in their design that I later improved upon with each subsequent effort. But the limestone at this location was simply superb to work with. It was as soft as alabaster and without flaw. Its color and grain were consistent. Even the text is slightly different from the others, especially since it guarded the way to the Residence of the Aten."

Upon hearing this and looking now at the man with renewed respect at his achievement, Richards could not help but ask, "How so, noble Paneshy? What do you mean that this stone's text is 'slightly different' from the others?"

Pulling the horses to a final halt before the guard hut, Paneshy carefully wrapped the reins in a convenient slipknot along the upper handhold of the chariot's wicker frame. Stepping down, he simply said, "Come."

Taken by the command and pride of the man, Richards docilely followed along in his dusty footsteps, leaving the two Egyptian guards standing before the cooling horses. Both carried full body shields of stretched and lacquered oxhide and short thrusting spears. Both knew Paneshy quite well and both equally despised his rather cavalier attitude toward them. In fact, both ruefully shook their heads as the two men walked over to the boundary stela.

"Look how that old fart Paneshy is leading that priest by the nose. He must be giving another one of his art tours!" one murmured, finishing with a snort.

To which the other replied, "Perhaps so, but look how big that priest is! And look at those scars! I do not relish crossing spears with that one!"

Now standing before the massive epigraphical work, Paneshy pointed to a vertical column of hieroglyphs and began to read aloud, adding emphasis as appropriate.

> His Majesty mounted a great chariot of electrum, just like the *Aten when He rises on the horizon from His residence* and fills the land with His love, and *took this goodly road from Akhetaten, to the place of residence which His servant had created for the Aten that it might be happy therein.* For it was His son Waenre who had founded it for Him as His abode when the Aten had commanded him to make it.

"So," Richards concluded aloud. "We essentially took the 'goodly road from Akhetaten' to this spot. Is that correct?"

"Indeed, Mayneken."

"Since the residence of the Aten is near where the Aten 'rises on the horizon,' then that must mean that we must enter this opening in the mountains."

"Again correct, Mayneken," the man said with an appreciative smile.

"But will the guards over there allow us to pass?"

"They had better. I know both of their fathers. They were once stonecutters. They too worked with care on this inscription and are now influential men of the royal court much like me."

* * *

By Richards' estimate, once they had left the guard hut behind and had traveled along at a leisurely gait for about twenty or so minutes, they arrived at the left-hand entrance of what we moderns call the Northern Wadi. The entrance here too was fortified with its own stone guard hut and a low fortification wall meant to block all access. Within this wadi is where the royal burial of Akhenaten and his family had been secreted deep within the rock. But Paneshy passed right by it without remark, instead choosing to continue on deeper and deeper into the mountains, ever heading toward the eastern horizon.

At a point about five minutes later and as the gorge began to noticeably narrow, casting long cooling shadows down its right-hand side, Paneshy at last halted the chariot, again tied up the reins, and led the team over into a convenient shadow to rest. Patting their noses and assuring them that he would be back soon, and with some water for them, the Egyptian then turned to Richards and flatly stated, "Noble Mayneken, up to this moment, I have been faithful to my oath with the Great One. The Most Beautiful One has released me from that fearsome oath, but I must be sure of one thing. Has indeed the Great One gone West?"

Richards, a bit taken aback, looked straight into the man's eyes and simply replied, "Paneshy, you have my word as a *sem*-priest of the Great White Wall that this is indeed so. In fact, I was witness to it. "

With their eyes locked on one another, Richards could easily see the conflict, the emotion, the doubt, and finally the sadness that plagued the man. Then, he arrived at a sort of resolution that softened the Egyptian's initial hard look of disbelief and mistrust. Quickly looking down at his feet, he abruptly made up his mind and said hoarsely, "Follow me."

Briskly moving off to the right, Paneshy strode with purpose into the shaded portion of the gorge and toward what looked like a sheer rock face. From Richards' point of view from near the center of the gorge, the Egyptian then abruptly turned to his right and appeared to magically ascend the rock. But when he himself arrived at that same point, it became clear that a cunningly concealed footpath had been cut into the face. Narrow and climbing quickly with sharply cut switchback turns, the American had to hurry in order to keep pace with the Egyptian, who at this point Richards thought must have been part mountain goat. With sweat from exertion and the fear of falling streaming down his face, neck, and shoulders, the Egyptologist focused his eyes down upon the serpentine path to ensure a stable purchase for his papyrus sandals. As the path rose in altitude, Richards began to unconsciously lean into the rock in search of some sort of purchase. When the path suddenly widened into what looked like almost a natural ledge, Richards found Paneshy with his hands on his knees, gasping for breath.

"You know, Mayneken. When I was a younger man, I could have made that climb without shedding one precious drop of water! But look at me now! I am heaving like a wounded cow! Old age is so cruel!"

As both men caught their breath, Richards peeked down over the edge and could only softly whistle. Turning around, Paneshy wore a wry smile and said, "Noble Mayneken, please do not take offense, but you are a very strange priest. I could have easily pushed you over the edge right then, and the secret of the Great One would have been preserved. But by the look of those scars on your back, I can see that you have already survived many great trials, which suggests to me you would make a better friend than enemy. Is that not so?"

Gulping and blanching at his rank stupidity, Richards could only acknowledge the rebuke with a nod. Finally finding his tongue, he said, "Trust, Paneshy, is sometimes given, but most times earned. You now have mine."

Surprised by the priest's answer, Paneshy then pointed out, "Please notice that the path continues beyond this point and leads farther above. But for our purposes, we have arrived at the entranceway to the residence of the Aten. But let me be clear, Mayneken, for what I am about to show you no one else knows, only I."

Then with a heavy sadness in his eyes and voice, the Egyptian continued, "You see, noble Mayneken, many good men, many friends and kinsmen, died in the construction of the Aten's residence. Not that many died because of carelessness or accident, which is so oftentimes the case, but rather because the Great One had searched each of their hearts. If he found that their hearts were not pure, then he had them executed. I alone remain. Now I alone will break my oath."

And with those words, the Egyptian turned, faced the rock's face, pushed with a considerable grunt, and a portion of the rock moved inward. After another heaving grunt, the rock moved again, but this time leaving sufficient room that a crouching man might pass, which Paneshy did, disappearing into the darkness beyond.

With eyes bugging out, Richards first thought was, *My God! Not another hidden passageway!*

And with that image still in his mind, the intrepid American then stepped forward into the dark void and the entrance closed behind him.

* * *

It seemed like an eternity before his eyes began to adjust to the dim light of a single candle's flame. After having become accustomed to the full brunt of the wadi's limestone glare, Richards' eyes ached from the rude transition.

Recognizing his plight, Paneshy kindly suggested, "Close your eyes, Mayneken. Allow them to rest from the brightness outside. Wait until you can see the candle's flame through your eyelids."

Heeding his guide's words, Richards agreed and stood quietly while his pupils began to expand, and then said, "Thank you, Paneshy. My eyes are now much better. But how is it that you can see in such darkness having come in from Re's full illumination?"

"Ah, Mayneken, that is an easy thing. I kept one eye closed for several minutes before I entered the passage, then opened it once I was safely within the darkness. But enough of such tricks. Follow me and follow until your eyes are fully opened."

And as the stonemason turned, the light of the candle spread accordingly before him to reveal a stout wooden lever that had closed the hidden entrance, followed by a well-formed stone tunnel that measured about the height of a man and about twice as wide. Another short wooden beam lay on the floor before them as did a passage with smooth undecorated walls that gradually sloped upwards into darkness. To Richards, who had to slightly bend over to prevent skinning the top of his head against its roof, the passage vaguely reminded him of the ramp beneath Karnak. The biggest difference, however, besides the lack of the two flanking sets of steps, was the freshness of the air. Clearly, he reasoned, this passageway did not lead to a sealed environment.

Their climb lasted about fifty paces, by Richards' best estimate, at which time he sensed that they had entered a large enclosure whose extent could not be seen as it was beyond the candlelight's reach.

"Wait here, Mayneken, while I brighten the Aten's residence, and, as before, mind your eyes."

Again following his guide's advice, Richards closed one eye and waited. And it was well that he had, for soon a glow began to emanate from a location off to his left that reminded the American of the ignition of a halogen streetlamp – slow at first and then suddenly a reeling gush of blinding artificial light. Now, with both eyes closed tight, the glow through Richards' eyelids remained staggering, but as his pupils again began to adjust, he was able to sneak a peek through his now slitted eyes. And what his eyes beheld was almost beyond wonder, much less description, and so the young Egyptologist went into was what he considered his "record mode."

First, he thought, this is clearly a large natural cavern or hollow in the rock that extends some one hundred feet in either direction. But upon closer examination, he noted that the walls were too regular, their surfaces too even, to allow for that possibility. In fact, in the light's glare, the faint shadows of chisel work were everywhere apparent. No, this was not a natural feature, but instead one created by sheer manpower.

As he slowly turned on his heel, scanning with his eyes as he went, Richards realized he was in a roughly rectangular bay or hanger-like facility. Why that particular image came to him, he did not know. Perhaps it was the brightly glowing disk-shaped craft resting on the stone support in the enclosure's center. Or then again, maybe it was that he had seen the Aten airborne several times. But whatever it was, there was something more, something distinctive in the air, something that Richards could not identify. Something remembered from his childhood. Something remembered from one of his father's military bases. Just what was it? His olfactory senses were alive with a message that he couldn't grasp.

As he stepped forward toward the massive black granite landing cradle that easily measured twenty feet on a side, Richards caught sight of Paneshy hefting a large and heavy amphora of something from a wooden storage rack off to his right. Staggering slightly under its weight, the Egyptian, gripping the burden by its two side handles, waddled the storage jar up a mildly graded ramp that was incorporated into one of the sides of the stone cradle.

Resting directly upon this igneous pedestal was the Aten itself, a shiny, glowing, bright, silvery disk devoid of any feature. About forty feet in diameter and about a third as thick toward its center, it reminded Richards most of a discus. Stopping about two-thirds the way up and below the overhanging curve of the Aten's smooth and shiny fuselage, Paneshy then surprised Richards as he spoke directly to the craft, which in turn answered by quietly opening and dropping a ramp before him. Lugging his burden up and into the Aten, Richards then heard the Egyptian swear an oath, which was shortly followed by his return, still struggling with his amphora. Upon exiting the Aten, the ramp and entrance silently retracted and sealed without a trace.

With the storage jar returned to its racking, the heavily sweating Egyptian turned to Richards and said between gasps for breath, "Mayneken. I am fed up. Ever since the Great One left us, the Aten will not stir. It will not eat. As often as I try to feed it. As often as I care for its surface with expensive bees wax. Just as the Great One had instructed me. The Aten refuses to move. I am at wits' end! I can no longer care for the Aten as the Aten no longer needs me. It refuses all my attempts."

Then Paneshy got down to the real point of it all.

"Mayneken. I am the First Servant of a god, who has turned his back on me! What shall I do?"

Fortunately, Richards' curiosity provided a foil to the Egyptian's frustration.

"Tell me, Paneshy, you said that the Aten no longer seems to require sustenance. What did the Great One instruct you to feed the Aten in the first place?"

The question caused at first a blank stare with a slightly tilted head of reflection. After a protracted pause, the following carefully phrased and enunciated answer came forth.

"Well, noble Mayneken, are you asking me what is fed to the Aten, or whether my stewardship of the Aten is in question?"

"Just what is fed to the Aten. Your loyal stewardship is a thing beyond question."

Unconsciously breathing a sigh of relief, Paneshy freely offered, "Well, what the Aten requires on a daily basis is really quite easy to supply, for over there is an entrance to a tunnel and a deep water well of the purest waters. From it, I gather water and feed the Aten, who up until the Great One's disappearance, drank deeply from my jars. Sometimes as much as three jars at a time! But now, and ever since the Great One's absence, the Aten does not take to the sky. The Aten does not visit the great temple nor spread the gift of its healing warmth upon us. Now, the Aten remains still, unmoving, not taking to the winds and not healing us. It is as if the Aten has become a mute man, who formerly had been a great and beloved singer of songs."

"Paneshy, you have several times made mention of the healing light of the Aten. I have not, unfortunately, experienced this miracle. Have you?"

Answering with wide unblinking eyes, the stonemason said. "Why Mayneken, I have myriads of times, as has my family. In fact, during the great plague that afflicted the whole of the holy city, the Aten, and the many precautions of the Great One, prevented that horrific calamity from spreading throughout the land. Even so, many perished, even those of the royal family before the curative light of the Aten and measures of the Great One took full effect."

"Forgive me, Paneshy, but what healing light and how did the Great One prevent the spread of this awful plague of which you speak?"

"Mayneken," the Egyptian chided. "Surely you have heard of the plague's passing during the year 16! As for the Aten's warm light, I myself have seen its touch cure the sick and those near death. As for the Great One's precautions, each and every one of our homes, no matter how modest, was provided with its own source of pure water, its latrine connected to a common drain. Never before had such been done. While the plague ravaged the city, the Great One told us to remain in our homes while he cleansed the city. Those afflicted, he commanded to be brought to the great temple so that the Aten would heal them. And this was done before my very eyes."

As this urban disaster was narrated, Richards had become reflective. This reaction that Paneshy misinterpreted as thoughtful and respectful listening was in fact the American beginning to have some doubt as to what he and Piankoff had done. Richards was wondered whether their assassination of the Great One had been the correct response to his introduction of alien DNA into the human gene pool. After all, Richards reasoned, these details had not been known, much less made part of the equation, when making the decision to eradicate the entire royal family and its alien progenitor.

Then that faint smell again tickled the American's nose just enough to get him to shift gears.

Richards now sensed and began to make a connection between what his nose had earlier caught a whiff of, and what he now began to suspect. He then pressed the dejected Egyptian for further details.

"So, you say that the Aten no longer feeds. Is that not so? Perhaps I could better understand that fact if you showed me how this thing is done. Are you willing to do so? And as my share of the bargain, I will carry the heavy jar for you."

First nodding, and then smiling at the offer of lugging the heavy amphora, Paneshy readily agreed.

"Why certainly, Mayneken, it is not a difficult thing, but it is one that must be attempted on a daily basis, or at least so it was in the past. So, bring that jar over to the ramp and I will instruct you as the Great One had instructed me."

Nearly jumping at the opportunity, Richards went to the rack, grunted up the jar that Paneshy had just put back, and did his version of the waddle as he made his way over to the Egyptian. Clearly pleased at Richards' enthusiasm, Paneshy, with his hands on his hips, could only grin with approval as the formidably muscled *sem*-priest so willingly did his bidding.

With the pair now standing beneath the curvature of the Aten's outer fuselage, the former stonemason turned, squared his shoulders, and faced a seemingly blank portion of the craft's shiny silver skin. He then ritualistically intoned, "I am Paneshy. Your First Servant. Open to me!"

With the voicing of the last word, Richards noted a subtle shimmer, an opening appeared, and then a short ramp descended. But as soon as the portal opened, a gentle exhalation wafted forth that almost knocked the American over, while he simultaneously fought down his gag reflex.

My God! He thought. *Something is rotting in there! And it reeks just like a spill from a honey-pot truck on dad's airbase!*

Noting Richards' reaction, Paneshy thought to add before entering the scout craft, "Yes, Mayneken, the Aten does indeed smell of death itself. And it has been getting progressively worse ever since the Great One disappeared. In fact, I believe that the Aten has not stirred, has not required sustenance, because it too has gone West. This notion is not without its own logic, for the Aten and the Great One were inseparable. I know this because the Great One told me of this intimate relationship, of how he and the Aten were one. How he and the Aten could converse without speech. The Great One told me because I had once inquired as to how he called the Aten to appear above the great temple.

"Now come. Breathe through your mouth to lessen the smell, and I will now show you how to feed the Aten."

* * *

All during the chariot ride back to Akhetaten with Paneshy again at the reins, Richards still could not believe what he had just witnessed. During his trip back upriver to sacred Thebes and even right up to his scheduled early morning retrieval, he still shook his head in near disbelief. His debriefings would be a bitch. That was for certain. He knew that what he had seen would be questioned, doubted, and in some cases written off as the babbling of an insane man. His only saving trump card would be if the Residence of the Aten could be located in his own era, and the craft recovered to prove his sanity.

CHAPTER XXXVI

Another Teleconference

"Gentlemen," Milson began as he addressed the video feed to his Russian colleagues half a world away. "Regarding the Aten report of Dr. Richards before you. Now that you have had sufficient time to read it, no doubt several times, do you have any questions?"

So began what would be one of the most momentous scientific negotiations of modern history. Completing the American panel in Chicago on the secure satellite uplink were to Milson's right the sober image of Dr. Paul Young and to his left one sneezing physicist, Professor Ernest Jung. While Young sat quietly in his usual pose with hands folded as if in prayer, Jung was fully engrossed with his box of nose tissues sneezing, wiping his nose, and tossing the used tissue into an off-camera wastepaper basket – all performed seemingly in one continuous motion. The Russian observers found it a fascinating exercise, illustrating the conservation of motor energy.

As for Milson, who called this meeting, his yellow legal pad before him was covered with neatly written notes jotted down in several colors. Richards' field report, already with its bottom right corners bent and well-worn from many reads and rereads, betrayed similarly colored marginalia that were marked with encircled capital letters – letters that matched those on the first page of Milson's legal pad.

As for the three Russians joining in – Rosovec, Ostrogorsky, and Drazinzka – only the young Rosovec, himself the Director of the Advanced and Theoretical Technological Research Institute, seemed responsive to Milson's opening gambit, while the two older poker players of this powerful trio sat back deeply in their heavily padded chairs, pretending mild disinterest.

Rosovec, with a black curl of hair rakishly hanging down over his forehead, speaking for his panel, stated openly and forthrightly, "Indeed we do, Dr. Milson. In fact, we congratulate Dr. Richards on his report. His level of detail was found to be quite exacting. His descriptions clear. But his interpretations, well, we thought quite frankly that they represented extraordinary leaps of intuition for an Egyptian philologist.

"Specifically, his notion that the Aten was powered by some sort of hydrogen propulsion system is quite possible, especially given the quantities of water loaded aboard it on a nearly daily basis. But one might conclude that the organic systems aboard the craft also needed the water.

"Also his thesis that at least a portion of the Aten was composed of organic technology, on the basis of the reeking smell he had encountered, we are, at least in principle, sympathetic to and in agreement with.

"However, where we most strongly differ with Dr. Richards' assessment is with what he described as the so-called pilot of the craft. The bloated and decomposing pile of seemingly disorganized optical sensors, limbs, vascular bodies, and other similar appendages appeared to have been incorporated directly into the craft's structure. We prefer to understand this organic material as the Aten's organic technology itself and do not interpret them as the rotting remains of a pilot per se.

"Finally, Dr. Richards' outlandish suggestion, albeit based on what he had heard from contemporaries on the scene, that somehow the target Akhenaten and this so-called pilot were linked in some sort of telepathic union, we find far-fetched. While we recognize that the target Akhenaten was indeed a powerful inline telepath – as were his offspring – we have no evidence whatsoever that would suggest such a linkage between the target and the Aten craft. To us, it would be far more reasonable to assume that the target controlled the Aten craft via some sort of sophisticated mechanical means."

All during this read oration on the part of the Russians, Milson and Jung had been taking furious notes. The latter having plugged both of his nostrils with tissue in order to prevent their dripping upon his yellow pad.

After several moments of silence following the delivery of Rosovec's prepared remarks, Milson looked up, smiled, turned to his left, and nodded to Jung, who cleared his throat.

"Academicians Ostrogorsky, Drazinzka, and Rosovec. We thank you for your reasoned comments regarding Dr. Richards' field report. In many ways, we too share your concerns."

Given the solicitous tone of Jung's preamble, all three Russians' attention were piqued to hear the implied "but" that was about to arrive. And they were not disappointed, for Jung immediately cut to the chase.

"However, given the level of alien technology that has been superficially described, and given our total lack of understanding regarding organic systems, we think it best to first cast our net quite wide. And when it comes to the purported telepathic linkage between the target Akhetaten and the Aten craft, the same applies."

Pause for a sneeze.

"Especially given the well-known and documented Russian experiments in parapsychology, telekinesis, remote scanning, and telepathy, I find it remarkable that you now consider it fanciful for a being on the ground to telepathically communicate with an airborne aircraft. So, given this turnabout, would you be so kind and enlighten us as to why you support this negative position?"

While Jung's pointed question still hung in the air, an uncomfortable stirring broke out among the Russians as they looked meaningfully at one another. One way or another, the subject clearly was an awkward one that the Russians preferred to avoid. But nonetheless, they knew that they had to answer. Give some reason. Silence would not do.

Finally, Ostrogorsky cleared his throat, sat forward, leaning his arms heavily on the conference table before him, and then stated flatly, "Gentlemen, I regret that we are not prepared at this time to discuss this still-classified topic. However, I do promise to answer Professor Jung's query in full. May we table this for another time?"

The Americans were taken aback by Ostrogorsky's deference, and only two silently nodded their heads in unison, but all with eyes slightly slitted in wariness. Collectively, they all thought, *Yep! We know all about you. Now, why are you suddenly being so tight-lipped?*

Jung, undeterred and without batting an eye, continued, "Well. Does that mean your side is not interested in the take if we are lucky enough to recover of this craft?"

To which Rosovec quickly replied, "Just what are you referring to, Professor Jung, as 'the take,' as you so poetically put it?"

"By 'the take,' Academician Rosovec, we specifically mean the technological windfall that the successful recovery of the Aten craft and its subsequent study may represent."

"Well, sir," coolly answered Rosovec, "that was surely never implied. Furthermore, we consider ourselves full partners in this endeavor and have already paid our 'down payment,' as it were, with the service of Alexander Piankoff. Now, where is this conversation going?"

The Russian concluded with considerable steel in his voice, but with a maddeningly polite smile.

"Oh, nothing much." Jung shrugged as he absentmindedly wiped his dripping nose. "I was curious as to your level of commitment, sharing of information, especially given your country's research in parapsychology. As for us, we believe in full disclosure. We also believe that such disclosure is tantamount to the future formation of a very valuable commodity – trust."

Ostrogorsky allowed, "Trust is a thing earned. Not a thing given freely."

"Agreed, Academician Ostrogorsky, but when do we collectively begin that process?" Jung returned while purposely using the word "collective."

He knew that it had confounded the USAF's translation software as the Russians had "collectively" winced at its use. As with so many things, context is king.

"Then I suggest," Drazinzka began, "that we begin trusting one another now. As of this moment, not to would be folly. Now, that said, Professor Jung, what precisely do you want to discuss regarding our *former* parapsychological program?"

"I do not wish to churn through its entirety, Academician Drazinzka, but I am quite sure that we would like to hear why your panel believes that it is unlikely or impossible for an individual to be in remote telepathic communication with a craft like the Aten?"

Again after several shared looks among the Russians, Rosovec began, "Professor Jung, in reply to your question we believe it to be highly unlikely that an individual can remotely fly a craft, like the Aten, using telepathy alone. We have already tried, and we have failed miserably. The individual in question, frankly, became highly unstable as a result."

Following about ten seconds of silent staring, Young broke the deadlock with the following suggestion.

"Well, Academician Rosovec, thank you for your frank answer. And thank you, Professor Jung, for your contributions as well. Now, shall we move on?

"We still have to approve the assassination of the target Smenkhkare by Dr. Richards and Ms. Gregorieva. To date, she has done very well. Has accepted the deep hypnotic implantations. Consequently, we believe that she and Dr. Richards will make a good team. Are there any qualms from your side on either the constitution of this dual deployment or its intended agenda?"

Team constitution? Intended agenda? Drazinzka thought. *What oddly neutral and antiseptic ways to describe an assassination team and its target. Only that bloodless Brit could have enunciated it in such a cool manner. As for Vesna Gregorieva's fitness for such an arduous task, I have absolutely no doubt. She is an absolute lioness. But whether she would make a dependable teammate? Now that I would like to see!*

During the time that Drazinzka was musing on the above, the Russians all glanced around, exchanging unreadable looks that the Americans could not decipher. Then, finally, apparently by previous assent, Rosovec spoke for them all.

"We do not have an issue with either the deployment of this assassination team nor its intended target. We only wish for its success."

Now it was the Americans turn to gape in dismay at the Russian's blunt use of language. Gulping unconsciously, Young almost answered, but somehow was beaten to the punch by Milson.

"Academician Rosovec, thank you for so clearly reminding us of the true purpose of our precious, joint assets on this critical temporal mission. We too wish for their success, but also for their safe return. In fact, during several training sessions, Ms. Gregorieva has proved to be a quite formidable and resilient presence. She is highly motivated. But of these things, you no doubt already know. But what you probably do not know is the source of her true motivation. That which drives her so. Surprisingly, it is the blessed memory of Alexander Piankoff himself, her self-proclaimed hero, beloved mentor, and we also suspect secret crush."

During the delivery of this measured discourse by Milson, all three Russians became exceptionally attentive. Drazinzka, smiling inwardly, again rued the day that Milson was not a member of his own security department. Ostrogorsky winced at the accuracy of the Egyptologist's remarks. As for Rosovec, much of this information about Gregorieva was real news. By the silent and downcast eyes of his so-called colleagues, they were more than well aware of it. More evidence, Rosovec had to conclude, that his colleagues had again purposely compartmentalized his knowledge base. For what purpose he did not know, but the fact that they had deeply troubled him. And for perhaps the first time, Rosovec began to consider why he was sitting here? What was his purpose? So this proud man made perhaps the most important decision of his life.

I must contact the Americans directly and very quietly. Then perhaps I will finally get some straight answers. And who knows? Perhaps some personal alliances can be made. Regardless, I must meet with this Milson. What a brilliant mind!

Milson continued, "Consequently, Alexander is Vesna's goad and also her source for revenge. It is this desire for revenge, which she has managed to tightly focus, that will no doubt sustain her on this mission. Sadly, at least in Vesna's mind, she has no real choice but to confront those who so tortured her teacher. And then there remains the issue of Dr. Richards and Ms. Gregorieva," slowly shaking his head of snowy white hair side to side.

"Their ability to form into a cohesive team, well, let us just say that is a work still in process."

Drazinzka actually smiled at that statement.

That's my lioness!

CHAPTER XXXVII

Team Building

Richards bent over, panting and dripping wet from his own sweat. Never before had he run for so long or so hard at the elevated altitudes of pristine New Mexico. As his still-burning lungs struggled to enrich his starved blood with the available oxygen, he looked down and saw his calf muscles visibly twitching on the verge of failure. Never before had college football ever done that to him! Now looking up and over to his colleague nearby, he grimaced slightly as Gregorieva was stretching out her right hamstring with her heel elevated high on a rock, while she touched the forehead of her darkly tanned and shaved head to her knee.

Ouch! That hurts just watching her do that. Even her naked diaphragm barely seems to heave after that grueling run. Damn dancer!

Noting his appraising gaze, Gregorieva smiled back pleasantly and sweetly challenged, “Want to race again?”

Richards’ jock-self briefly considered taking up that minx’s dare, but then sanity quickly kicked in when he reconsidered what an unnecessary injury would mean. So he just shook his shaved head in quiet negation.

Grinning with victorious glee and punching the blue sky with two extended fists, she simply exclaimed, “Yes!”

Richards, now recovered and standing erect with his hands on his hips, added, “Time to go home.”

“I’ll race you back!”

“No you won’t,” he flatly stated. “It’s time to recover, shower, eat, and meet with Doc Allen for our final tune-ups. Let’s go.”

“Joseph!” she scolded while waving her arms above her head in mock frustration.

“You’re no fun! You’re always so by the book! You never take chances!”

Spinning on her in a flash that took her breath away, Gregorieva suddenly found herself enveloped in a powerful bear hug.

Now nose to nose, Richards whispered with a growing rage and sneer on his face, “Well, my dear colleague. Doing things by the book means survival. Taking unnecessary chances is pure stupidity.

And in case you haven't noticed, all of this is not some sort of athletic event put on for your benefit, some sort of conveniently orchestrated pissing match to stroke your fucking ego! What this is all about is the brutal assassination of a madman telepath. Or have you somehow forgotten all that? And oh, by the way, I need you. You need me. Are you now ready to get serious? Or do you want me to conveniently wash you out based on irreconcilable differences?"

With eyes locked, she purred, "So you really are all business, aren't you?"

"Absolutely, totally, and without question."

"So you prefer buggering young boys?"

Immediately releasing her as if Gregorieva were dangerously radioactive and stepping back, Richards first sighed deeply for control and then replied with a frostiness that chilled the air between them, "Careful. Be most careful, Ms. Gregorieva. For if you are not, at my first opportunity, I will personally feed you to the crocodiles – alive."

* * *

"Doc, Lord knows I have tried, but Gregorieva is impossible. She is so unpredictable, so quirky, I just cannot depend on her to do anything that she's told to do."

Doc Allen, listening to the young Egyptologist, opined with a straight face, "So, to generalize, what you are telling me is that Gregorieva possesses an independently minded spirit, is imaginative, and can think and make decisions on her own. So, where's the downside?"

"Careful, Doctor," Richards nearly growled.

"And in addition, you seem really tense, if not openly hostile. Joey, when was the last time you got laid? Would you like me to prescribe something? In fact, there's a certain somebody right here at Horizon Pass that, and I quote, 'would love to jump your bones and get tangled in the sheets with you.'"

"Doc, that's not professional and you know it."

"I know I'm treading in a gray area. But that's nonetheless precisely what you need. Think about it. Here you are trying real hard to be professional while you are training and working out with an erotic goddess that is practically buck-naked. Tell me, my friend, and tell me true. You have to admit that she is, at the very least, attractive."

Doc Allen's question was met with silence and a clenching and unclenching jaw.

After a full thirty seconds of an eyeball-to-eyeball staring match, Doc Allen continued, and as he made his points, he counted them off on the fingers of one hand.

"Well, one thing's for sure, you're just as stubborn and bullheaded as her. Match. You're both alpha-types, perhaps even super-alphas. Another match. Then there is the narcissism that you both share with your rightful pride of your bodies. Yet another match. You both worship the memory of Alexander. Match. You, because he was your mentor and shield against the unknown. You, because you enjoyed the comfort of following in his formidable shadow. You, because the two of you, but only after considerable initial conflict, finally bonded as warriors do the world over.

"But for Gregorieva, Alexander was the ultimate super-male. Bright, experienced, authoritative, a beautiful physical specimen, yet coolly distant and professional. But that cool distance that Alexander so carefully maintained really bugged Vesna at her core fantasy level, because she had a near-fatal crush on the man. Basically, she wanted him and not just as an esteemed mentor and father-figure. If you don't believe me, Joey, then listen to this. Vesna's defensive blocking image is not your slamming copper-clad gateway of Amen Re, but the very image of Alexander himself as Piankhotep! Resplendent in a diaphanous and suggestively billowing priestly kilt of virgin white with his arms crossed upon his chest. Need I say more?"

At this bit of trivia, Richards' demeanor softened and eyes took on an almost dreamy aspect.

"Doc, I get your point. So, how are we to bond? It seems to me that once I cold cocked Piankoff outside of my flat, it was then, and only then, that he began to respect me, began to accept me as at least capable."

"Well, Joey, my boy, it seems to me that you have about a week to figure that one out, but from my vantage point you're already real close. Now, before I cut you loose, about that other matter, the one that you consider unprofessional, do you want me to hook you up for some R & R or not?"

"Well, Doc, just who do you have in mind?"

"Nurse Stewart."

"You mean our Nurse Stewart? The redhead right outside!"

"The very same."

"Wow."

"And by the way, her first name's Margie."

"Didn't know."

"She's been fantasizing about you for a good year now. The best part of the situation is that she is utterly professional, so things won't get messy."

"So, Doc, why are you telling me all this?"

"Consider it a professional courtesy. Besides, I am responsible for the well-being of everyone in this facility, both mental and physical. I consider it just doing my job."

* * *

We all have personal preferences that some would even call biases. This is especially true in our choice in mates. We can't help it. Some like bookish types, others flashy and loud types, still others outright jocks.

* * *

Margie Stewart always had a big weakness for the latter ever since junior high, when she fell head over heels for – of all things – a hockey goalie. She rationalized later in life that it was the responsibility of the position, the one place on the ice where the puck finally stopped. The pressure, the limelight, all really turned her on. In fact, try as she might, she could not remember either his name or face, but good old 78 stuck in her mind and took her virginity as well.

Then there was college, more jocks, and then the discovery of a nursing career in the military, where this nurse could nurse to health lots and lots of jocks. Not that Margie Stewart was a woman of easy virtue. It was just that she was highly selective in which steed she chose to ride.

After two re-ups with the U.S. Army, during which Margie ran into Doc Allen, it became inevitable that he and Horizon Pass would steal her away. The facility provided her quadruple the former salary and exclusivity. Because of the remoteness of Horizon Pass, trips to the nearby boomtowns of Truth or Consequences and Alamogordo got real old real quick. So to preserve her sanity, Margie began working online on a master's degree in business administration through the local state university. To preserve her God-given natural beauty and help cool her internal fires, she worked out a lot and became a hard body.

When Horizon Pass went operational several years back, security tightened and those day trips vanished. While weekend junkets to Las Vegas were always available free of charge for the staff, after the first couple visits, even that got stale. And that was the entire point. Margie was getting stale and she knew it. On the verge of completing her degree, this good-looking and fit redhead with freckles had a serious career decision to make. The fact that her biological clock was ticking away only made matters worse. She knew that she had to get out, get back to her northern Minnesota roots, and settle down. But after all that she had seen, done, and accomplished, even that prospect she found seriously lacking, if not stifling.

As her good friend and colleague Doc Allen had so aptly put it, "Well, Marge, it's either put up or shut up time."

So she stayed put, completed the MBA, and began another – this time in law. Then Piankoff arrived, he represented the most intriguing, yet socially cool personality that she had ever met. But when young Richards made his appearance before her desk, old, deep, and primal alarm bells, long silent, had gone off. Prone to blushing, she knew that she had – deeply. Fortunately for her, Richards had not seemed to notice the vascular reaction, but Doc Allen's sharp eyes had, and had even informally mentioned the fact during her last fitness evaluation.

"Marge, you and I know that we're only human. Besides, Joey Richards is as healthy as a horse and is all dosed up with Ephiphedrin-5. I say that's a green light, if, of course, that's what's on your mind."

Remembering her pretended outrage at Doc Allen's randy suggestion, Margie nonetheless felt a thrill run right through her that warmed her in all the right places. And now here he was again, standing before her desk. Looking up with her best winning smile,

Richards smiled back with that goofy boyish grin of his that stretched from ear to ear.

"Why, Dr. Richards, it's so good to see you again at Horizon Pass. What can I do for you?"

"Well, Doc Allen told me to stop by and set up some appointments for Gregorieva and I. Something about 'final tune-ups' or something."

At the mere mention of Gregorieva's name, Margie was more than shocked at her instantaneous competitive reaction, but managed to seamlessly toggle to the appointment schedule, efficiently found two time slots, entered the names, and printed out the individual schedules.

While Nurse Stewart was busy, so were Richards eyes as he surveyed the nearby terrain with considerable interest.

Man, is she pretty and well put together, he concluded, *for a woman of her age.* Then he chided himself, *but then again so is Jenny Kelly. In fact, come to think of it, they could almost be sisters!*

Finished printing, Nurse Stewart took the two printed schedules from the output tray, turned, and handing them to Richards, looked up into his face, and what she saw were two extremely dilated pupils.

Forgetting herself as her nursing instincts kicked into high gear, she reached out, grabbed his wrist for a pulse, and exclaimed, "Dr. Richards! Are you okay?"

Smiling back, the Egyptologist softly said, "I am now, Marge. By the way, has anyone told you how incredibly pretty you are?"

* * *

"Vesna," Richards asked quietly between mouthfuls of a once enormous, but now half-eaten breakfast, "would you be willing to show me some of those dancer stretches of yours? I find your flexibility remarkable, and I think that they may help me some. Whadda' ya' say?"

It was a crude attempt at peacemaking. But it was a beginning, and Vesna saw the opportunity for what it was – the discovery of a middle ground between two strong-willed individuals. So with a sly smile, she responded, "Deal. But we'll have to start slowly. After all," she continued, now with her wicked grin on full display, "we cannot jeopardize the mission by taking any unnecessary chances."

* * *

Doc Allen could not have been more pleased. Before him sat Gregorieva and Richards. Their collective body language portrayed complete inclusion – their shoulders slightly turned and legs crossed toward each other. But what the good country doctor's antennas really noted was the absence of friction, electricity, and competitiveness. Somehow, someway, they had found a way. The how of it tickled at his curiosity. He dearly wanted to ask, but couldn't. He instead would just have to slowly piece it all together. He began, "So, have you two decided on a name and figured out what your relationship is?"

"Why, yes, we have," Gregorieva volunteered. "My Egyptian name will be Maatkare."

"Well," the physician allowed, "it sure has a pretty sound to it. Does it have a meaning?"

"Yes, it surely does, Doc." stated Richards. "In fact, it's a fitting name for one so hell bent on destructive revenge and the constructive desire to restore the divine order of things."

"Oh, you don't say," was all that Doc Allen could barely choke out. "And of your relationship?"

"Elder brother and younger sister," the Russian supplied. "And I am following in Mayneken's footsteps as his assistant."

"Oh, good," replied the wide-eyed doctor, but he remained as game as ever, and so he next asked, "So, how is your mat training and coordinated attack drills going?"

To his surprise, Richards looked over to Gregorieva, who then took the cue.

"Very, very, well, Doctor Allen. But all of our training may be for nothing if we cannot manufacture several distractions for the target to focus upon. We may have only one opportunity in which to act. But before we can, we must first get close enough. In short, as with Akhenaten before, we need distractions."

"And to add to that, Doc," Richards piped in, "Smenkhkare has already proven his ability to brutally subdue several assailants simultaneously. So he has become a naturally cautious, if not paranoid, being experienced with personal attack. Put simply, our collective blocks must not fail."

"Agreed," stated Doc Allen with certainty. "Now why have the two of you requested a follow-up on your blocking hypnosis?"

Gregorieva smiling mischievously.

"Dr. Allen, we believe that we have come up with a way to produce the ultimate distraction for the target, but we first need your help to implant it."

"Ah, good, at last, I'm happy to be of some help to you two."

CHAPTER XXXVIII

His Seed is No More

As the pair sat together, straddling the wooden crossbeam above the powered up drop ring, the static charge of the ring began to move several of the outer braids of Gregorieva's natural hair wig. Covering her mouth with a free hand and stifling a giggle, the Van der Graff effect began to extend her wig's braids outward in a vague imitation of a sea urchin's spines. One of Tuna Cartwright's men inserted the cobra-headed optical probe into the stabilized field. Bobbing his head toward the power pack's operator to reverse the ion flow, the probe was extracted and an all clear declared.

Satisfied, Tuna then roared, "Okay, you two half-naked hippies, you're free to drop! Break a leg!"

Looking into each other's eyes, both of the droppers simultaneously murmured, "Knees bent, ankles together, and gently roll clear."

Gregorieva was the first to drop. Ten seconds later, Richards pitched in his neck pouch of goodies, and then disappeared as well.

"Damnation!" Tuna exclaimed rather loudly. "That is one bitchin' gorgeous, young morsel!"

Callahan, who was manning the Mark V-A's power pack, then loudly queried his commander so that all could hear.

"Colonel, how do you suppose Doc Richards keeps control of himself around that honey bun?"

"Simple, Corporal," Tuna replied even louder. "He's a professional. And, unlike you and me, Corporal, he knows which heads rules!"

* * *

What a deliciously sensuous feeling that was! Like slithering through a thin massage oil, Gregorieva thought as she smoothly landed and seamlessly rolled to her left.

Landing: piece of cake!

And before she could fully clear her slightly blurred senses, she heard the impact of Richards' money pouch, and thereafter the heavy thud of his landing. Looking over, Richards slowed and groggy movements soon told her that his transit had disoriented him, something that he had warned her about and to watch out for. Lying on his back in the dim light of low-burning oil lamps and the incense-filled atmosphere of the holy of holies of the Great God Amen Re, the Egyptologist murmured quietly in ancient Egyptian, "I am upside down."

Blessedly, however, the American's reaction to the drop passed within fifteen seconds by Gregorieva's best estimate – a far shorter period than he had said he had experienced his last drop.

Sitting up and shaking his head, Richards announced, "I am in good health. We must go."

At Richards' command, Gregorieva, for the first time, looked around to orient herself. That is the massive two-leaved cedar wood entranceway off to my right and so that means to my left…gasp! The Russian was not at all prepared for the golden statue of Amen Re, for its dominant presence and sublime beauty quite literally took her breath away.

Unconsciously, she thought, *Now I understand what Alexander was trying to tell me that day. The sheer wonder of it all!*

Then an intrusive, but gentle, tug on her forearm broke that cherished thought. She turned to see her partner on one knee, motioning her toward the cultic chamber's only exit.

* * *

Upon exiting the holy of holies by squeezing themselves between the barely opened door leaves, they passed by the black granite statue of Sekhmet, whose shadow had cleverly obscured the little-used side passage that Alexander had so long favored. Now free of the temple, they decided to see if the house of the high priest Meryptah was occupied as yet by his chosen successor. But as they did so, Richards stopped Gregorieva en route and simply said in Egyptian, "Look up," as he pointed heavenward. As she did, wonder filled her eyes at the clarity and brightness of the Milky Way as it displayed its flowing tresses.

"I could almost read by such light! And the sky is so clear, so breathtaking."

"Indeed," stated her partner.

"Is it any wonder that the inhabitants of Kemet included in their religious beliefs such stars?"

Then finally breaking the fragile moment.

"We must go to my father's house."

Finding that its new occupant had yet to move in, the pair entered the venerable old man's former bed chamber and made themselves comfortable. As the excitement and tension of the drop began to bleed off, the coolness of the night air beckoned them to slumber, but not before Gregorieva surprised Richards with an entwining and affectionate embrace that told him of her hungry need. After that need had been satisfied at long last, Richards privately concluded before he dozed off that perhaps he wouldn't feed her to any crocodiles after all.

The following morning at daybreak, each having first attended to their personal needs, Richards discovered to his pleasure that the house had indeed been cleaned up and stocked with beer and wine. But since it was not occupied, the household still lacked any fresh cheeses, dried fish, breads, or fruit. Noting this, the pair decided to visit the marketplace for breakfast and thereafter arrange for their passage north to Akhetaten and their target.

About halfway to the marketplace, Richards reviewed in his mind the early morning tryst and tried to understand why his partner had initiated it. The more he thought about it, the more confused he got. Granted, as a team they had come a long way, but had that act of sudden union helped or hindered them? He didn't know and certainly wouldn't ask. Nonetheless, the introduction of this variable troubled him. Finally, in quiet resignation, the Egyptologist decided that time would tell.

As for Gregorieva, she knew why she had initiated the passion. She wanted to know firsthand whether the American was a real man. Now Vesna knew. Besides, she shamelessly admitted to herself, she was more than just curious. She just hadn't expected Richards to so promptly return the favor, so well, and for so long.

* * *

Having left Thebes that mid-day on a swift river craft that Richards had pointedly inspected for lice and the like, he and Gregorieva a day and a half later arrived at the heretic's capital of Akhetaten. As before, Richards marveled at the dockside activity and the broad mixture of cultures that flocked to it. In a low voice, he described to Gregorieva just what she was seeing and from where these merchants and their wares had come from: coastal Syria, the island of Crete, mainland Greece, and the island of Cyprus as well. Lost in his narrative, the Russian grabbed the American's forearm in unconscious excitement, then catching herself, she scolded herself for the unnecessary but supportive contact. Deep down, Gregorieva was beginning to trust the American, was beginning to enjoy his easy personality, his knowledgeable presence, his strength.

Disembarking as the boat's hull brushed up against the dock, the pair made their way for the marketplace for a late lunch, but Richards was positively insistent on getting groomed first. Recognizing what all that entailed, the American enjoyed quite a chuckle as the Russian negotiated a bath and grooming herself. But once all these personal items had been straightened away, their joint hunger pains again announced themselves without deception. Leading the way, Richards pointed out to Gregorieva his favorites, some she tried, and some she passed on. So it went. One leading and the other acting upon impulse. Despite all the intriguing sights, sounds, and smells that assaulted her senses, Gregorieva began to notice the American's subtle respect – no, deference, that he showed to all that he spoke with.

"Which of these fine fish would you give to your own sister to eat?"

"Of these fine sweetbreads, which would you select for your own mother?" Hearing these diplomatically pitched words emanating from a priest, and seeing their impact upon a commoner's ears, told Gregorieva volumes. With the old woman that sold sweetbreads, the one with a nearly toothless but ready smile, Richards' proffered payment was gently brushed aside.

"Dear kindly priest," she quietly said. "Pray for my *ka*'s survival, for I know you will. Your eyes are clear and guileless, unlike the others."

Thanking the woman with a respectful nod, Richards' then surprised the woman by taking her hand, kissing it, and simultaneously slipping a small gold ring unto one of her heavily callused fingers. Gasping in disbelief and wonder, she clutched her finger tightly with the other hand as if the finger were seriously injured. Looking up, Richards only smiled.

"Old, venerable mother, let it be known that He of the Great White Wall will care for you in the West as you have cared for one of his lowly priests among the living."

With heartfelt tears streaming down her wizened visage, Richards turned to leave and heard as he did so yet another gasp.

"By the gods! It is he! He's the one that I saw entering the Queen's own household! Those magnificent scars prove it!"

For Gregorieva, Richards' approach in the marketplace told her of an inner strength and generosity of spirit that she had not before detected in her partner. Nonetheless, the revelation warmed her heart and made her smile.

Imagine, she thought. *A Christian within a pre-Christian context. What a revolution that would be!*

Having fully eaten their fill, the pair finally stopped at a public well that the Egyptologist deemed very drinkable, if not delicious. There they both filled their bellies until they were distended. Now, fully fortified, their mission's goal became their sole focus.

* * *

Knowing where the royal palace was did not present a problem, for all knew where the edifice was located. Frankly, one could not miss it. The palace's sheer mass and its centralized location made it the natural nexus of the town. But such centrality also meant getting past a veritable gauntlet of courtly bureaucrats in order to attend the daily royal audience. That would present a challenge.

However, one's presence and attitude can go quite far when confronted with such challenges and the *sem*-priest Mayneken and his lovely assistant, Maatkare, possessed these qualities in abundance. An ambassadorial ring from the royal household also has its own unique privileges. Sheer, brazen moxie too had its place.

Mayneken, freshly groomed, bare-chested, and striding forth powerfully in his white linen kilt, walked directly to and confronted both of the tall blue-black Nubian Medjay palace guards at the appropriate side entrance. That the American's unarmed approach had been effective was subtly evidenced by the guards hands, which unconsciously slipped to the pommels of their vicious-looking chariot scythes that hung heavily from leather straps supported by their broadly muscled shoulders.

Stopping before them with a smile, the *sem*-priest addressed them, all the while looking directly into the eyes of the bigger of these formidable twins.

"Worthy guardians of the royal palace. I, Mayneken, ambassador of Queen Nefertiti, and my sister, Maatkare, wish entrance to the royal palace."

A bit taken aback at the acknowledgement of their "worthiness," two backs straightened slightly and two chests swelled as well. The taller of the two, now with his eyes slitted in his best look of interrogation, spoke, "What is your business, ambassador?"

Continuing to smile up at the towering man, Richards fenced back.

"That, my powerful friend, is the concern of the Great One within. May we now pass?"

Smiling back down at an ambassador that could well be a most formidable peer, the guard allowed, "You both may pass."

As they did, the gaze of the guards' eyes naturally followed and once out of earshot they made their assessments as do all such guards, regardless of culture or time period.

"Keke! Did you see the scars across his back! Such marks of honor! Indeed, he is what his name proclaimed, 'young lion'!"

"And, Beketka, did you see his sister? What a truly fine form she has! I nearly swelled at her approach."

"And when you swell, Keke, can you then actually find it?" the taller of the pair crudely guffawed at his subordinate's expense.

The side entrance of the palace led to a long and narrow passage that eventually emptied into a rectangular receiving chamber of sorts. Along the base of its long walls were low masonry benches, known as *mastabas* in the modern Egyptian tongue, and every square inch was already occupied with petitioners. Stopping in the center of the room, Mayneken slowly surveyed the scene and finally found just who he was looking for – the major domo, who guarded the doorway opposite.

Turning around to Maatkare, Mayneken smiled and stated, "This beautifully colored waterfowl is all yours."

Smiling back with a mischievous grin, she answered, "Watch me pluck him bare and steal his eggs!"

Standing boldly in the center of the room as they were, the pair had already made their presence known to all within for the gentle purring of conversation had dwindled to silence. A quick glance around at this audience revealed a good many petitioners from all parts of Egypt: traders, businessmen, and some foreign merchants as well. But clearly none of them represented anyone of any significant domestic or foreign stature. So the pair recognized that this chamber was only the second vetting process. And so Maatkare smoothly glided toward her target with movements that reminded Richards of a stalking cobra.

This guy's gonna' be dead meat, he smiled to himself.

The palace bureaucrat in question, officiously titled The Royal Fan Bearer, was a soft middle-aged male, whose fingers held far too many rings and whose layered neck was far too burdened with a heavy pectoral necklace of lapis lazuli, carnelian, faience, and gold. He wore lotus hemp sandals decorated in gold leaf and a short white linen kilt decorated with a leopard skin girdle that supported his extended stomach. Annoyingly, this palace official flicked his ivory pommeled horsetail flyswatter this way and that, more out of officious emphasis than anything else. At Maatkare's sultry approach, he watched with interest from his place at the exit of the receiving chamber.

Finely formed and beautiful, he daydreamed, as the black-wigged vision approached him in commoner's sandals and wrapped in a white, single-shouldered, and near diaphanous linen with her left breast fully exposed.

As Maatkare reached the proper distance of address for such an official, she stopped, bowed low toward the man's kilt, and noted a growing bulge.

Ah, she thought. *I see that I do indeed have his full attention.*

Rising from her bow, Maatkare stood erect and proudly before the official with her left nipple now fully extended.

"Most noble one," she purred. "I am Maatkare, sister of Mayneken, personal ambassador of Queen Nefertiti."

Pause.

"We wish audience this very day with the Great One, the Son of the Aten."

As calculated, the heady mixture of visual stimuli, lust, pheromones, and the introduction of the "personal ambassador of

Queen Nefertiti," all caused this usually insufferable and imperious official to stop his affected and incessant flicking. After a few seconds of stunned silence, while he blatantly feasted his eyes on Maatkare, he finally blurted out a bit too gruffly and loudly, "Where is this personal ambassador to the exiled queen?"

Striding forward in a full flex of his upper body, Mayneken soon stood behind and to the left of his partner, forcing the man to somehow look beyond Maatkare's graceful shoulder and bared breast.

"Here, noble one, I am Mayneken, and here is my signet ring of ambassadorial authority."

As Richards slowly and theatrically extended his powerfully sculpted arm forward with a fist to better display the symbol of the Queen's authority, he then continued, "But regarding the current position of the 'true' Lady of the Two Lands, I seriously doubt that she considers herself in such a plight. In fact, such news would amuse her. Would you like me to share with her your ill-advised indiscretion?"

Now wide-eyed and in full spiritual retreat, the official stuttered out that that was not ever his intention, that he was ignorant of the queen's true situation, and that she had at her disposal such ambassador-at-large. Amid many hidden snickers, The Royal Fan Bearer allowed the pair to pass on.

The hall of royal audience was actually a quite small, intimate chamber. Also rectangular in form, paved in smoothed limestone, and having six brightly colored papyriform columns supporting its high cedar wood ceiling, only one piece of furniture adorned it – a camp chair-like wooden throne atop a low, three-stepped stone platform. Crammed into this enclosure were no fewer than six Medjay guards who stood framed within the columns and sixteen important personages of various high stations, nationalities, and cultures. Some were engaged in idle conversation. All, excepting the Medjay who watched them on each side, faced toward the raised throne in anticipation of the Great One's arrival. None noted the arrival of a lone priest and his womanly companion, none except the Medjay.

Looking to one another and now finally within striking distance, this assassination squad from the future had to wait. With their palms moist with nervous sweat, each automatically began to inventory their surroundings. Noting the armament of the Medjay, for each had a dagger scabbard in addition to a vicious chariot sickle slung over their massive shoulders, the pair observed who else was with them in this most inner of royal audience chambers.

After a good twenty minutes, the sounds of scraping sandal bottoms could be heard from a small doorway located to the left of the raised throne. Through it, an ancient man who was the royal herald emerged, and once standing before the first step, he turned to the silenced gathering before him and barked out, "Abase yourselves immediately before the brilliant and magnificent presence of the Son of the Aten!"

As commanded, all fell to the floor facedown, with the backs of their necks ritualistically exposed in an act of total submission. As seen from the perspective of the throne, the floor had been instantly transformed into a sea of colors, textures, human heads, and necks all directed forward.

Several minutes would pass before again the sounds of scraping sandal bottoms were heard, but this time the solitary pair of feet that entered the chamber briefly stopped to survey the groveling multitude, and when satisfied, only then ascended the divine throne of Isis.

The voice of a young man was next heard, who dully stated, "Arise. We wish to see your faces."

All did rise, some levering themselves up with considerable difficulty, some rising quickly, but the two last guests to this gathering rose very slowly and remained hidden in part behind the others. These last two also had separated to the opposite sides of the chamber, lest they be perceived too quickly by the young Pharaoh Smenkhkare. As surmised, the young pharaoh did indeed perform a cursory scan of his gathered flock and in the process actually managed to miss the two of them, for they had totally blacked out their personality signatures. They just as well might have been incorporeal entities, excepting of course that two physical forms remained behind. But within such a packed gathering and since both were partially, if not wholly, hidden by those who so dearly wished to be recognized and noticed, their initial concealment from the young pharaoh's sixth sense was total.

Sitting stiffly upon his royal throne with his hands pressed flat against the tops of his thighs, the pharaoh chose to wear this day the blue military crown as it was lighter and less awkward than the formal red-and-white crown of Upper and Lower Egypt. Literally at his feet and sitting cross-legged on the first step was the king's first scribe, who would dutifully record the day's proceedings. To his right stood proudly his royal herald, leaning heavily upon his stout wooden *w3s*-staff of authority.

Now looking straight ahead and fixing his eyes on a point above everyone's head, the king then intoned, "Read to Us the first petition."

So the audience began with the royal scribe reading a legalistic plea from three foreign dignitaries from the Levantine area, who begged for Egyptian troops and financial aid as their cities were in danger of invasion from a northern military power called the Mitanni. To this plea, the king listened, considered for a moment, and then sent the trio on their way with a talent of gold, but no troops.

"Read to Us the next petition."

Four members of the audience moved forward as the scribe began to read. At issue were the boundaries of four administrative districts, or *sepats*, which required the king's wisdom as to how to resurvey lands changed by the recent inundation of the Nile. The lands in question were prime agricultural plots that had been lost to one nome and claimed by the other three. To this petition, the king again listened, thought for a moment, and declared that which the river god Hapi had deemed worthy of moving should remain in the hands of those so fortunate to receive them. Clearly, reasoned the pharaoh, the lands must have been misused by their former owner.

"Read Us the next petition."

Two merchants stepped forward upon hearing their issue read aloud. At this point, both Mayneken and Maatkare were out in the open and without cover. A quick glance from one to the another signaled that the time had arrived, and Maatkare, the designated "batter" in this instance, moved forward five full steps, which placed her next to the nearest Medjay guard to the king's left. At this distance, less than twenty paces from the king, he was already a dead man. To the Nubian guard, she was not seen as a threat, but rather as a sweetly smelling morsel of overly ripe fruit ready for picking. In fact, the guard was totally distracted by her presence and was getting a bit flustered as well.

While the king did not see this movement, he nonetheless felt its effect from his guard, and it felt strange as there was no personality signature associated with that movement. Curious, he looked up in Maatkare's direction and almost started as this was the first time that he had beheld this most beautiful creature.

Now where did she come from? He silently asked himself. And when he looked again with his *sia*, or sixth telepathic sense, he almost started again as there was nothing there!

It is as if she were but a living body without a ka!

As this little vignette was being played out, Mayneken chose to move as well toward the king, some six paces this time, stopping and turning his head as if he were either hard of hearing or particularly interested in the reading of the petition's substance. While the nearest guard on the king's right noted this movement, he ignored it, as he too just then saw Maatkare's beautiful form.

Nonetheless, and despite his perception of a living void before him, Smenkhkare did both see and feel Mayneken's approach. Now scanning him with his *sia*, his blood went cold as he too was a living body without a *ka*!

How can this be? His mind screamed.

Just then, the first scribe finished his reading of the trade dispute and the two petitioners moved forward, so did Maatkare and Mayneken, two steps each. Now both were within sure kill range, for all six guards were behind them. Only two petitioners were before them, a sitting scribe who was busy recording oral arguments and remarks, and one very old herald with his heavy forked *w3s*-staff.

Instantly, all of Smenkhkare's alarm bells went off, with *ka*-less ones to his right and left! His escape to his right was blocked by the muscular one, any escape ahead by the woman. He quickly calculated. *My guards are totally unaware and out of position to act on my behalf.*

JUST WHO ARE YOU! He pulsed out with a devastating mental power that slightly staggered the two assassins. Then he saw who they were, for in Maatkare's mind stood her beloved brother, Mayneken, with his powerful arms crossed across his chest, glaring back and daring any passage past him whatsoever. Shocked, he looked to Mayneken, and the image revealed there was of Maatkare, holding a golden royal cobra entwined on each arm and out of her mouth a forked tongue extended, sexually licking in his direction.

Then the pair moved.

Instantly recognizing the encircling movement, a telepathic shriek of "***NO!***" was projected and the rightly panicked pharaoh next pulsed out a generalized and devastating shotgun-like death wish to all assembled in the chamber. While the assassins were somewhat slowed by that authoritative command projected by the young pharaoh's highly developed *sia*, the others had already become lobotomized cretins with blood flowing freely out of their ears, noses, eyes, and mouths. Their collective eyes rolled and glazed over at the onslaught of the sudden telekinetic death shriek. Moments later, they began to dumbly drop to the floor as lost cerebral function and gravity took their normal course. Thudding to the ground right and left like so many sacks of potatoes, Maatkare, as rehearsed, reached Smenkhkare first and delivered the first telling deathblow as she expertly rammed the palm of her left hand up into the king's delicate nose, sending splinters of bone and cartilage into his fore brain, in effect, physically lobotomizing him. Now stunned and with his eyes wide open, the king next saw the floor rush up to his face as Mayneken had just decapitated him with one of his own guard's chariot sickles.

Kicking his head so that Mayneken could speak directly into the face of the fallen one, the American said simply, "Your seed is no more."

Then all sensation left the young pharaoh as his skull was crushed in with the heavy back end of the weapon, in effect, instantly evacuating the blood supply from the king's brain.

"Why did you do that?" Maatkare asked in shock.

"Habit," Mayneken simply replied.

All silent except for their heavy panting of effort, the pair began to stagger their way toward the exit of the audience chamber, a chamber that had already begun to fill with the heavy aromas and foul, putrefying smells of a battlefield. Maatkare, removing an unsoiled bit of cloth from a fallen body, quickly wiped clean the majority of the young king's imparted blood splatter from Mayneken's legs, arms, and chest.

While so doing, she whispered to him, "Noble Mayneken, you did well this day. Our Piankhotep would have been most proud of you."

Noting her care and foresightedness, Richards answered, "And as for you, most beguiling Maatkare, you kill indeed with the speed of a cobra. Piankhotep too would have been most pleased at your vengeance."

Then he concluded, "It is best that we leave this place."

CHAPTER XXXIX

Return to Thebes

Ahmose was really confused. True to his boatman's word, he had indeed kept his craft at the ready for the return of the queen's ambassador and his lovely sister, Maatkare.

What a beauty she was!

But it was such a curious arrangement. Paid to do nothing and paid to wait. From his point of view, who in their right mind would undertake the long journey all the way from Thebes, only to arrive that mid-morning at their destination and then to return on that afternoon of the same day!

As for the ambassador Mayneken, he did not begin to relax until the sight of the city of Akhetaten had disappeared in their wake. At the same time, he had to smile at the sheer moxie of his assistant, who, at every turn during their daring escape, had seemed to brush aside with a confident and commanding wave of her hand all peril. *Imagine walking serenely away from such carnage!* And they had effectively accomplished just that.

At precisely that same moment, the ambassador's assistant and sister, Maatkare, was reviewing in her mind the very same events, but with a distinctly different point of view. She rightly concluded that fate had kindly allowed their survival. Only the pharaoh's silent scream, which had instantly killed the entire room full of dignitaries, courtiers, *and* guards had saved them. She rightly doubted they would have survived the furor of six palace guards, much less their calls for assistance. Rage also began to build within the woman, as she now realized that they were not meant to survive this mission.

That the mission was an elaborate setup of some kind. A mission without an escape route. An assassination that took place within the royal palace itself.

Madness, utter madness! But for what purpose?

She, Vesna well understood, was an expendable asset, a pawn on Drazinzka's already much-bloodied chess board. But what would her devious countrymen gain at the loss of the American Richards?

Much she concluded, very much, as they could then groom another from their own as Annex's primary field operative.

Now smiling.

Yet we have successfully accomplished this dark deed and have walked away from it. And, as of this very moment, are still alive to tell of it.

Richards, noting Gregorieva's dark and distant smile, misunderstood it for his own.

"My sister, you did very well today, and I am in your debt."

"Nonsense, my brother, we both did very well today. Clearly the gods have chosen to protect us both. I just wish that his boat could move faster."

Noting that concern, Richards' mind began to churn, and relieved to focus upon something else, got an idea.

"Just watch, my sister."

Rising and going to the stern where the boatman was idly minding the tiller, the American inquired, "Ahmose, do you have a spare sail aboard your fine boat?"

Surprised by the question, the ambassador was given a positive response.

"And Ahmose, would that mean that you also have spare rigging aboard as well?"

"Well, noble one, some, but surely not enough for a full rigging. Just enough for a quick repair. Why do you ask me such questions?"

"Because, Ahmose, I have an idea and I need your assistance," waving Maatkare over. "Would you be offended if my sister steered your fine boat while we try something?"

"Not at all," then thinking quickly. "Would I have to pay for her assistance?"

To this question, the American barked out a laugh that almost brought tears to his eyes. Finally catching his breath.

"No, my dear Ahmose, her assistance will not cost you a thing!"

So with the tiller so ably manned by the Russian, Ahmose and Richards began rummaging about the boat's various cubbyholes. Various lengths of rigging were located, which the Egyptologist assessed as sufficient. Then, from beneath the planking, the two grunted up a very damp and folded rectangular sail that matched the one currently flying. With the planking replaced, Richards folded the sail diagonally in half, in essence forming a crude triangle. Then he said to the boatman, "Which corner is which?"

"Well," Ahmose began, scratching his head. "This one would be the lower left and that one would go to the upper spar. That means this one is the lower right."

"Are you sure?"

With a shrug, "Reasonably so."

"Okay, then," the American began to explain. "Here's what we're going to do."

From Gregorieva's point of view at the stern, it looked as if Ahmose and Richards were first tearing apart the boat's hull and then building it back together. Then the two of them, sometimes laughing, sometimes cursing, began to struggle with what looked like several unequal lengths of rope and a huge wet tarp. Then Ahmose practically threw a fit when the American wanted him to drop his filled mainsail, which after a mixture of encouragement, the frustrated boatman finally did. Now as the boat slowed against the current, stalled, and eventually began to slowly slip downstream from where they came, Gregorieva began to worry.

Just what is this American up to anyways? We're trying to make our escape and here he's dropped our sail!

"Mayneken, my brother? Just what are you two up to?"

"Patience, my sister. Ahmose thinks me already a madman. Just a few more minutes. That is all I ask."

Having successfully secured another length of rigging to the main sailing ring and having already tied off another to a tie-down on the boat's portside gunwale, the two men together began to raise the rigging, and as they did, the extra sail rose as well. Once the mainsail was up, the wind immediately caught it and it blossomed as before, halting the boat's drift and righting the craft into the river's gentle current.

"Alright. Fine. So we have now partially raised my spare sail. So, ambassador, for what purpose? To dry it out?"

Ahmose, now sweating heavily, stated with unveiled sarcasm.

Now smiling that smile that Gregorieva had long learned to rue ever seeing, Richards, also sweating heavily, said, "Just watch my friend."

Taking the loose starboard rigging, the American began to flap the wet triangular sail free of its fully extended twin, and when doing so, the wet sail, now transformed into a foresail, caught the wind as well. Quickly looping several coils of rigging on a starboard tie-down, the crude spinnaker filled, much to the amazement of Ahmose and triumphant pleasure of the ambassador.

"How can this be?" exclaimed the boatman.

"How can the wind find a sail in front of another one? And yet I see it with my own eyes! I still don't believe it!"

From Gregorieva position at the stern, the addition of the crude spinnaker had improved the boat's progress quite a bit. Just looking down at the stern's white water wake was sufficient enough proof for her.

Now just imagine how fast we could go once Richards properly trimmed that forward sail!

Meanwhile, Richards was doing just that as he began slowly playing out the starboard rigging, expanding the spinnaker's bloom ever farther. Then, once satisfied, he firmly tied off the rigging with a quick-release knot. This entire display of seamanship left Ahmose slack-jawed. When he finally found his tongue, he asked with considerable respect in his voice, "Ambassador, what is this kind of sail called?"

"Ahmose, I do not know. I just saw this sail used once during a contest of boats."

"A contest of boats?"

"Yes, boats from several cities and towns once gathered in the Great Green in a contest to see who would win the honor of a great silver goblet."

"Really! You have been in the Great Green!"

"Yes, I have," Richards allowed, referring to the Mediterranean Sea. "And I have sailed upon it to faraway Byblos. Have you heard of that city?"

"Yes, yes, I have," stammered out the boatman excitedly, "but only from merchants from there."

"Well, in that region of the Great Green, seamen from many places compete for a great silver goblet and it was during just such a contest that I first saw this kind of sail."

But Ahmose persisted, "But, ambassador, you do not know what this kind of sail is called?"

"No, I do not. But Ahmose, what does it look like to you?"

"Well, it fills with wind so well. It is so rounded. It almost looks like a woman's belly great with child."

At which point Maatkare cleared her throat very loudly.

"Well," the boatman sheepishly allowed, "perhaps not. But it does fill so well and pulls so strongly."

After a few moments, he then stated with conviction.

"I know what this sail must be called. I will call it an ibis-sail, for it looks like that bird's wing to me."

"Well, then," the ambassador agreed. "Ibis-sail it is."

What Richards did not choose to mention was that the ibis was also a bird sacred to the god Thoth – a divinity known for his wisdom, judgment, and learning, not to mention the patron god of scribes.

* * *

Thanks to the ibis-sail, the return trip to Thebes was fully halved. Ahmose was as incredulous of his boat's newfound speed as he was proud of all the shoreline attention that he received as he sailed by the many waving curiosity-seekers.

Their arrival at Thebes constituted almost a festive occasion, for quite a crowd had amassed itself along the docks as Ahmose proudly coasted in on his ibis-sail alone. Once tied up, the boatman was mobbed with questions and tried answer them as best he could. During this melee, Mayneken and Maatkare made good their escape to the marketplace, where they had themselves appropriately groomed and then greedily shared several deliciously roasted doves and several beers, which left the two of them mildly inebriated.

Given that they had time enough to kill until their extraction during the early morning hours of the next day, Richards decided that a cultural tour of ancient Thebes was in order. Gregorieva thought it a good idea as well, and off they went, brother and sister arm-in-arm, American and Russian, to observe the daily affairs of a former capital city preparing itself for its new beginning.

* * *

At about the time that Richards and Gregorieva nearly staggered away from their meal to "see the sights" as it were, Prince Horemheb was informed of their presence in Thebes by his chief houseman.

"Are you absolutely sure, Ramose, that it was Mayneken you saw at the marketplace?"

"I am quite sure, noble one. I saw him disembarking from a most curiously outfitted riverboat with two sails. There was a most beautiful woman with him that moved most gracefully, and both availed themselves of the marketplace's groomers and then ate a midday meal together. My guess is that they had just arrived from somewhere distant downriver. Perhaps even that dreadful place of the heretic-spawn. My lord, there is no mistaking Mayneken's form, as you yourself well know. I know of no man with such magnificent scars on his back."

Smiling a crafty smile, Horemheb chuckled.

"Well, what do you know?"

Pause.

"Ramose, since it is still only midday, I'll wager that we may well have two dinner guests. And if we do, perhaps we will get to meet this beautiful woman of which you speak. In the meantime, make all the appropriate preparations. I think that I am going to take a walk."

"Do you wish your sedan chair, noble one?"

"No, Ramose. That will not be necessary. I think that I am going to do some quiet inspections of the public works that I commissioned to be done. Then, perhaps, find my adopted elder brother," he finished with a wicked smile.

"Most intriguing, noble one. Your father would have approved!"

"Yes. I think that he would have as well."

* * *

Horemheb's unannounced tour of the various public works projects reaped several surprising and not so surprising results. The first that he encountered was the clearing of a local well that had gone into disrepair. While the dredging out of fallen debris had been quickly accomplished, the shoring up and replacement of its masonry was another matter. But despite these challenges, Horemheb's workmen were succeeding because of two factors that he could identify from his unseen vantage point. Kawab, a one-time vagrant, appeared to be a natural leader and clearly had the rest of the men well in hand, organized, and busy. The other factor was the local neighborhood people themselves, who pitched in and helped the work gang. It was a pleasant surprise for the prince to see the two working together as one. Smiling with genuine pleasure, the hereditary prince of Egypt quietly moved away, repeating Kawab's name so that he would not forget it.

Walking farther on toward the sacred precincts of the Harem of Amen, what we now know today as the Luxor Temple, two gangs were busying themselves with the restoration of a large pool. One group was sweating heavily while they attempted to clear away a decade's worth of windblown sand and accumulated garbage that the locals had unceremoniously dumped into the all too convenient depression. Again choosing to observe from a distance, Horemheb noted the sluggishness and mindless quality of those who worked, while the others just sat and watched. He also saw that neither gang possessed a leader, nor was the neighborhood seeing to their needs for water or encouragement.

Like a clap of thunder, Horemheb at that moment in time realized an important analogy to his own land's serious situation. If Kemet were to be left to its own devices, then it would be as this pitiful scene before him – going either too slowly or going nowhere at all! But if Kemet was led, and led well, then with the assistance of the common people, virtually any challenge, no matter how big, had a better than equal chance for success.

Turning away from the chaotic scene before him and deep in thought, Horemheb ran directly into Mayneken, who had been observing him observing the two comical work crews. Startled and then happy to see his adopted elder brother, Horemheb unabashedly hugged the American in greeting and blurted out, "Mayneken! You would not believe it! But I just now had a vision about how . . ."

What caught the impassioned prince's speech in middle sentence was what he saw standing behind his brother, an incredibly beautiful woman, the most incredibly beautiful woman that he had ever seen.

Noting Horemheb's momentary tongue-tied situation, the Egyptologist quickly interrupted the prince's thought and said, "My brother, this is my sister, Maatkare. She is also my assistant as I am teaching her in the ways that Piankhotep had taught me."

Turning now to the slightly amused look of Gregorieva, who had her hands on her hips and head cocked over to the left at the still-embracing males.

"My sister, I present to you the hereditary prince Horemheb, who has adopted me into his household as his eldest brother. It was he who instituted the public work projects that we have been visiting. It was he who looked after the venerable high priest of Amen Re, the Osiris Meryptah. It was he who buried the Osiris Meryptah . . ."

This time is was Horemheb's turn to interrupt.

"Excuse me, my eldest brother, but please do not continue to embarrass me before your most beautiful sister."

Then, looking pointedly at their feet, the prince proclaimed in no uncertain terms, "Well. I see that the two of you have been on a long journey, no doubt from parts north. And perhaps are even thirsty. Well, I propose that we cease our inspections for the day and retire to my household where we can dust our feet and refresh ourselves. Follow me."

Turning on his heel, the prince led, while his eldest brother and newfound half-sister dutifully followed in apparent silence. However, Maatkare was able to quietly ask her partner three questions. The first was, "How did he know we were at Akhetaten?" The second was, "What is meant by 'to dust one's feet'?" And as for the third, "Is he *that* Horemheb, as in 'the pharaoh of all Egypt'?" To the first question Richards frowned and concluded that the prince had many eyes in many places. To the second, he just chuckled and said, "Enjoy." And to the third, he gave the Russian a very serious and meaningful nod.

* * *

Ever true to his word, Horemheb's evening meal was as sumptuous as it was refreshing and in many ways was a tribute to his marvelous household staff, which seemed to delight in throwing such instant bashes for their young prince. The fact that this same young prince cared for each of his staff as family certainly played a large role. But as the head houseman had once obliquely mentioned to Mayneken, Horemheb always expected their respect of him, and so he always extended his trust in them.

As was custom in his household, the long and low table was covered with every sort of food that was readily available: roasted quail, duck, and dove, baked fish, vegetables, cheeses, breads, fruits, and sauces. In short, it was a feast both for the eyes and the stomach. And despite their earlier snack, Mayneken's stomach growled loudly as soon as he sat down, which caused a merry chuckle from Horemheb.

"My brother," he smiled. "Some things never change and one is the timing of your stomach's needs. I will again commend the cooks as they will be pleased as well!"

Once all three were made comfortable, sitting as they were on pillow-like pads on the floor, the hereditary prince of Egypt offered the following toast to his guests.

"I wish a hearty welcome back to my household of my elder brother, Mayneken. May his stomach be forever silenced! I wish warm greetings to his sister, Maatkare. May she be satisfied as well in equal measure as much as her beautiful form graces this table. And to sacred and beloved Thebes, may it arise again to its former glory."

Draining in one long pull from his priceless goblet made of beaten foreign silver, the prince simply beamed at the pair.

"You know my brother, my new half-sister, you do seem to appear at the most interesting of times. For I have just received word this very afternoon from that godless place to the north. It seems that the eldest son of the former heretic, the vicious man-child named Smenkhkare, has gone West."

Indicating to one of the hovering house servants that the pitcher of cool beer should be left at the table, the prince then kindly dismissed the ever-helpful pair for the rest of the evening. Now safely alone and out of earshot of any innocents, the prince continued, "How is it, my brother, that whenever you appear at my household, momentous events seem to occur?"

Richards, noting fully the tone of serious accusation in the prince's question, answered him directly, and as the Egyptians are so fond of saying, from the heart.

"Brother, what you say contains much truth. At the same time, the return of the royal court to Thebes and your mentorship of young Tutankhaten could not happen without the death of that jackal. As you probably well know yourself, he reduced four Medjay guards of Nefertiti's into near infants and then left them in the desert for the vultures to feed upon – alive. Now the royal court can return to Thebes when Thebes is ready for them. In the meantime, and until that reality is realized, several others must lead our land until its true master is ready to grasp firmly the reins of state."

Horemheb, listening carefully to all that his elder brother had said, then asked, "Mayneken, what you have just told me I know to be true. But as so many times in the past, you have left so many details out, or, perhaps better said, to be inferred. I harbor no doubt whatsoever that Smenkhkare's blood is on your hands."

For the first time addressing Maatkare, "And perhaps also on yours as well most beautiful one."

A thought that he completed with a slight shiver.

"But this reference to 'others who must lead our land until its true master is prepared,' while I can grasp the concept, I do not fully understand."

"My prince," Mayneken began, "on your inspections of the public work projects today, what did you learn?"

Without skipping a beat, Horemheb responded, "That strong backs need leadership and motivation to be successful."

"Precisely, my brother, and if the true master is to lead Egypt out of its current plight, patience, care, and support will be required from those currently in power. And in this instance, your greatest ally is the Lady of the Two Lands, Nefertiti. She will know the way of it."

Having absorbed those words, Horemheb changed the topic.

"Mayneken, are you truly a seer-priest as your master Piankhotep? And for that matter, what evil has befallen him?"

"Why do you say that, my brother?"

"Because he is not at my table, because you are grooming your sister as your assistant. It is obvious."

"My master, Piankhotep, has indeed gone West. He contracted an illness that his stout heart could not overcome. In a land to the north, beyond the land of the contrary rivers, he is properly entombed. I, myself, as with Meryptah, performed the sacred ritual for the freeing of his *ba*. All is in order."

During all of this, Mayneken's eyes had filled unbidden, tears had briefly streamed down his cheeks, and his voice had twice cracked. This Horemheb duly noted, as did Maatkare.

"The passing of Piankhotep to the West," the prince quietly said, "is a loss for our land. But his mentorship of you, my brother, was his most excellent gift."

At the voicing of this softly spoken tribute, Maatkare began to quietly sob.

"So," continued the prince, "you also knew of this Piankhotep."

A nod was his answer.

"While I suspect far more, I will not intrude upon your private grief."

Then shifting topics yet again, Horemheb directly asked of Mayneken, "So, my farsighted brother, just who are these others who will lead our land before the true master is ready?"

"My prince, I can only speculate."

"True, but your speculations are far better than other's facts. Please, speak with your heart."

Shrugging, Mayneken spoke with his heart as commanded by his princely brother.

"My suspicions are that royal blood must rule the Two Lands for a time, perhaps a young man such as Tutankhaten. Thereafter a man from the military will briefly succeed him. This military man will have to be an experienced member of the royal courts at Akhetaten and Thebes. He will need troops to take control and calm the people."

"Ay!" exclaimed the prince. "He's currently the Master of the Horse. It has to be him!"

Sighing in relief that Horemheb had indeed realized the situation, Mayneken then continued, "Consequently, the true master of our land must replace this man's former position in the military. To do so, he will need the assistance of the Lady of the Two Lands, Nefertiti. Then, when the time is right, the true master can replace this usurper and restore Thebes to her former glory."

Energized, the prince quickly concluded, "I must craft a letter that you will this very night deliver to the Lady of the Two Lands!"

"I cannot," was Mayneken's instant reply.

"Why not!" was the prince's startled reply.

"Because my brother, my face and that of my sister are too well known in that accursed place. In fact, the safest places in all of our land are here, in your household and within the temple of the Great God himself."

Sitting back in confirmation and looking at them both, the prince smiled, "So, you two did make a royal nuisance of yourselves."

"Indeed."

"And I suppose that you two will spend some time within the sacred precincts of the Great God?"

"Yes, my brother. That is, of course, if you intend us to visit your household in the future. In fact, Maatkare and I are going to be making ourselves, how can I say, unseen for a time until the transition of power completes itself and our faces are long forgotten."

"Most wisely stated," the prince said approvingly. "Well, enough of such weighty matters. Let us now satisfy our stomachs! Here, have some more beer!"

And the feasting and drinking began and continued into the night with much laughter and lightheartedness. But finally, as with all such events, the host eventually begged off, and in this case to his library, to write a letter to a certain lady of power, to be delivered by a member of his household.

As for the two temporal agents, they, both near staggering, paid their respects to their generous host and made their way to the great temple to await their scheduled retrieval.

CHAPTER XL

Recovery of the Aten

Any attempted recovery of the Aten craft would have to be during the hottest time of the year. In other words, the hunt would take place sometime during the months of August and September, when strict water discipline was an absolute must for survival. While that notion might seem perverse in the extreme, especially given the 120 degree noontime temperatures of Middle Egypt, operational security required it. Logically, the chance presence of tourists and locals too would be at a minimum, but not necessarily that of local bandits, politico-religious dissidents, or outright terrorists. Any other chance encounters with either mad dogs or Englishmen would be deftly handled by Tuna Cartwright's much-augmented school. Nor could such an undertaking be even imaginable without the full knowledge and cooperation of at least one Egyptian government official. So the Director of the Egyptian Antiquities Service and his daughter were brought aboard.

Logistically speaking, the exercise was guaranteed to be a nightmare. Based on Richards' field report on the location of the hidden underground hanger, heavy machinery could well be deemed a necessity and their transport alone, much less maintenance, in such a remote location presented serious challenges. But despite all the armchair hand-wringing and Monday morning quarterbacking, no one once doubted that such a task could not be accomplished, for the value of the prize was just that great.

* * *

Dead tired, thirsty despite the liter of water that he just got through chugging, dusty, dirty, and in need of a shower, the nearly shivering soldier in the rapidly cooling night air nonetheless bowed over his laptop as he composed his final e-mail of the day to his superiors.

```
Mission log: 19th August, 2011, 23:30 Lima.
Location: El Amarna, Egypt.
```

```
Midday temperature: 117 degrees, in the
shade!
Evening temperature: 59 degrees.
Current humidity: 4 %.
Wind: Southerly, 8-10 mph.
Visibility: Unlimited.
Cloud cover: None.

Immediate Situation:
Team arrival - 05:00 hours Lima.
Secured/established perimeter of Royal Wadi
- 12:00 hours Lima.
Recon uncovered no bad guys, but plenty of
scorpions and snakes.
Prepared for expert examination of area.

Immediate Assessment:
Uninhabitable area; the dark side of the
moon; place really sucks.

Immediate Needs:
10 cases, bottled drinking water.
4 cases of MREs.
12 IR motion detectors.
4 2-seater, Honda ATV 4-wheelers.

Major Charles Abraham Cartwright
Special Command Detachment
USARMY
```

Hitting the SEND key, Tuna's day was finally over as he disassembled his mini satellite dish, stowed it and his laptop into his military issue computer bag. It, like the rest of his clothing and gear, was appropriately colored a tawny light brown with small brownish flecks or blobs decoratively scattered about. Lately, like for the last five years since the Annex went live, Tuna seemed to live in his chocolate-chip desert cammies. It wasn't that he didn't like the color scheme, it was just that because of them he was beginning to think and act more and more like a desert lizard.

* * *

On the other side of the world, in another desert area known as New Mexico, Dr. Peter Borov chuckled as he read his crack security chief's e-mail.

"Place really sucks."

"Boy that's an understatement!" he commented under his breath. "I must inform Joey that all is ready for their inspection."

* * *

Richards rose early that day in Masr el Gedida, the modern name for the ancient city of Heliopolis. Enjoying the American hotel's hot shower, he shaved directly in its soothing spray. Toweling off his smoothly shaved head still sporting an even dark tan, he turned on his laptop and continued dressing for breakfast. Once on the Internet, he found that he had six new e-mails, but the one from "PB" – Dr. Peter Borov – was one that commanded his attention.

Smiling to himself as he read the good doctor's go-ahead green light authorizing the recon of the Royal Wadi, he then found himself chuckling at the attached operational transmission from Tuna Cartwright.

"Place really sucks."

"Well, no shit, Tuna! I've been there!"

* * *

Having informed Dr. Sharil Moussa of the situation, who was also conveniently located in Heliopolis, Richards next called up a certain unlisted number on his cell phone and requested that a shuttle be prepared for two passengers. After several moments, a second voice got on the line, which requested two very specific instructions to be read to him. Richards, tearing open one of four dated manila envelopes for just this purpose, began to read aloud a rather long series of numbers and letters, at the end of which he was almost dizzy with all the "Alphas," "Echoes," and "Tangos." But once authenticated by the disembodied voice, specific instructions were given to the Egyptologist as to what they were to bring, when, and where they would be picked up. It was all just that simple, and they had three hours to get their act together.

* * *

Shouting over the wind buffeting despite the stalk mikes of their helmets that the airman had provided them, Richards asked Sharil, "What do you think of flying by helicopter?"

"It's all very exciting! I have never seen my country from this perspective before. It's like I am a soaring bird, but much faster."

Fast indeed, for aboard the Sikorsky UH-60 Black Hawk on loan from the Delta Force base near the Giza Plateau, they were very rapidly eating up the 175 or so miles to El Amarna. Streaking south with the chopper's doors wide open in the brilliant late summer daylight, the desert terrain below was a blur, while the emerald green of the agricultural fields that bordered the canals and course of the Nile passed by to their left.

After a little over an hour in the air, the chopper landed smartly in a cloud of dust about two hundred yards from the entrance of the Royal Wadi or Wadi Abu Hasah el Bahri. Waiting in the fuselage for the whirring blades to spin down, Sharil had difficulty imagining how quickly they had arrived, for usually the drive down from Cairo would have taken them a good six to seven hours. It was all just so amazing.

Grabbing their gear – one small rucksack a piece – they were met beyond the reach of the rotor blades by none other than Major Tuna Cartwright, who immediately introduced himself to Dr. Moussa.

He then turned to ask, "Dr. Richards, have you ever ridden on an ATV?

"You mean like the kind with three wheels?

"Well, sir, you at least got that partway right. No, this one much safer. It's got four wheels. Are you game?"

"You bet!"

"Outstanding, sir!"

Then turning to Dr. Moussa, who was totally lost by the previous exchange, the major requested, "Madam, where we're about to go is treacherous even for a Humvee. So we've flown in some two-seat, four-wheeled vehicles that allow us to go quickly from place to place. In the hands of an expert, they're as agile as a mountain goat. If you don't mind, I would prefer that you ride with me, an expert, instead of Dr. Richards here, a rookie."

Smiling back at the big Louisianan's own toothy and ingratiating smile, Sharil readily agreed. Following a brief overview with Richards, the trio was off, with their rucksacks bouncing on their backs. They began by working their way along the base of the steep-sided slopes of the wadi's meandering course. Moments later, they subliminally heard over their loud exhausts the chopper lift off and quickly lost the sound of its blades whooping as it faded off into the distance.

Now within the wadi, with the buzz and popping of their motors echoing off of the surrounding slopes and cliff faces, Richards tried to recognize anything that looked familiar and soon found himself almost in a panic, for absolutely nothing looked right. Worming their way around fallen boulders and skating across vast fans of eroded rock scree, they finally, after about thirty minutes' ride, came to a halt at a branch of the wadi that led north. Incongruously, the route was marked with a windblown sign that said in both Arabic and Latin characters, "This way Royal Tomb." Although there was no evidence of the guard hut or security wall that he remembered blocking the entrance to this side wadi, Richards nonetheless was mightily relieved. For he now knew that the entrance to the Aten hanger, if it could be located at all, lay only some five minutes ahead and to their right at a narrowing of the crevasse.

* * *

Even though it had already been quite a day, Richards was driven nonetheless to at least check out this one rock face that looked so promising. Standing beneath it and upon yet another broad fan of scree, the Egyptologist now had to estimate where the original floor of the wadi had been relative to where he was standing now. He needed some point of reference and some way of measuring and establishing a horizontal line. After some thought, an idea came to him.

Approaching the major, he asked whether any of his men had a laser gun sight and a level. The major, now squinting at the Egyptologist through his dust-laden eyelashes, thought a moment, grunted, and then called out to one of men to get his butt down into the wadi, pronto. Then, reaching into one of his many thigh pockets, the officer pulled out a two-thirds empty plastic bottle of water and said, "Will this do for a level?"

"Should do fine.

"Now what I have in mind," Richards began, "is to approximate a surveyor's laser transit by using this soldier's rifle and gun sight with a bottle of water atop it as a level."

The confused corporal looked to his commander in supplication, but did not get any as Tuna understood exactly where the Egyptologist was going.

"So, Doc, if I get your point, we have to find a point in the wadi that best approximates its floor. Is that there you're going?"

"You got it, Major. Then when we pan over to that big fan of rocky rubble over there, I will be able to estimate roughly where to begin looking for the entrance."

Pleased that he had for once understood an academic's cockamamy idea, Tuna turned to his soldier and said, "Fan out, Fernandez, and find me the lowest point in this general area."

Nodding at a command that he could readily grasp, about two minutes later and about 150 feet away, the major heard from behind him, "Major! This looks to be about as a low point as I can find in the immediate vicinity."

"Fine, Corporal. Now stay there. We'll be right over. Let's go, Doc."

Standing next to the corporal, Richards said, "Okay, now what I want you to do, Corporal, is to sit down and sight your weapon over there at the base of that big rock face. Yeah, just like that. Major, now rest your water bottle on his barrel to level it out. Yeah, that's it. Now, Corporal, hold that position while I run over and find your laser dot. Okay? Here I go."

And off Richards ran, looking like a giant bunny rabbit, bobbing and weaving through the rocks toward where he thought the marksman had his weapon trained.

Finally stopping, the Egyptologist called back, "Am I close?"

After a brief conference at the other end, the major bellowed back, "No. Go about twenty feet farther!"

Richards complied, then turned around to face them. As he looked down, he saw in the fading light a little red dot wiggling slightly above his left kneecap. *Ah-ha! There it is.* Then stepping aside and lowering his head to the appropriate level, he again found the spot on the rocky scree itself. Scrambling over, he placed the corporal's hat on the exact spot and turned around. Seeing that the major was now flashing a thumbs-up sign, Richards waved the two over.

When they arrived, the Egyptologist returned the corporal's hat and then pumped the arm of the corporal for his help, which for his part was the first time that he had ever sighted on some rock and had been so congratulated for it.

Now turning to Tuna, Richards said, "You know, boss, we just might be in luck. But that will have to wait until tomorrow. The light is really failing quickly in this gorge."

With that, Richards got down on his hands and knees and began building a small rock cairn to definitively mark where Corporal Fernandez's sniper rifle had been trained.

After having spent the cold night in a sleeping bag atop the unforgiving face of an elevated boulder, Richards had to admire the others around him, who had not spent the night so comfortably. The lone command tent had been turned over to Dr. Moussa as it was screened in and floored.

As the major so aptly put it, "I will not have one hair on Dr. Moussa's pretty head ruffled by some scorpion or adventuresome snake. Trust me, Joey. There are plenty of them about. Already two of my school have had close encounters. And since you are such a tenderfoot in the ways of the desert, I'm putting you in the penthouse. That is, atop that big isolated rock over there. You'll be plenty exposed to the wind, my boy, but pretty free of creepy crawlies."

Curiously, what Richards remembered most about that practical sermon on desert survival was the phase "pretty free," and that first night's sleep was "pretty fitful."

Following a breakfast of delicious MREs, or Meals Ready to Eat, the major stood and watched as each and every one of his charges, both military and civilian, drank an entire liter of water. With that ceremony concluded, the soldiers disappeared into their surveillance positions, while the major and civilians returned to the position of the rock cairn.

"Folks," Richards began, "as best as I can remember, this is the rock that I ascended with Paneshy, the First Servant of the Aten."

The major interrupted, "What do you mean by First Servant?"

"Well, strictly speaking, a First Servant is the high priest of a god. But in Paneshy's case, his god was the Aten itself. He had been trained to maintain the Aten craft. Polish it. Load it up with fresh water on a daily basis, that sort of thing. Beyond that, I do not know. Just that this Egyptian came here every day to be the maintenance mechanic for the aircraft that I hope we'll find."

"Thanks for the info, Doc. Please continue."

"Well, since this marker approximates where the ancient floor of the wadi was, then, let's see now, I remember making five switchbacks on a crudely cut footpath before reaching a level and wide landing of sorts. I also remember looking over the edge of that landing to see how high up I was. It looked like a good four stories high. So if I'm correct, then we should start clearing rock about forty feet above this marker."

Now turning to Sharil, who had just joined them.

"Doctor Moussa. Please remain standing here. I will need you for a reference."

Then facing the major, he simply said, "Let's go."

Up the pair began scrambling atop the long fan of rocky debris that had calved off and eroded down the rocky mass before them. After going only about fifty paces, it became very apparent that they were practically treading in place as the weight of their steps dislodged the fine gravels beneath their feet. In some ways, it was almost comical. In others, the situation was quite frustrating, but the pair persisted and was rewarded when they reached material that was packed more firmly.

Perspiring now quite freely, the men stopped to catch their breath and orient themselves to where Dr. Moussa still stood. Perversely, their altitude in relation to her did not seem to change much, although it clearly had, but how much they didn't have a clue.

Richards muttered, "Oh, my kingdom for a theodolite!"

To which Tuna retorted, "Hell, a simple surveyor's transit would do."

Then it was as if a light bulb had comically appeared over the major.

"You know, Doc, I just got an idea. I'm pretty good with navigation, and navigation has a lot of geometry and trigonometry in it. I'll just bet that we'll be able to sight forty feet of elevation from that rock pile down there. I'll even be able to use the calculator function on my laptop to calculate it right quick. Whaddya' say that we mark where we are now and try?"

Smiling a broad grin, the Egyptologist beamed, "Major! I'll make an archaeologist out of you yet!"

* * *

With the aid of Tuna's laptop, Corporal Fernandez's rifle, and the stone cairn, the forty-foot elevation had been sighted and range noted. The entire calculation and fidgeting with the rifle sighting had taken eighteen minutes flat. The funniest part, however, was that the marker that Tuna and Richards had erected up on the slope was only five paces low. Go figure!

With three soldiers who were volunteered by Tuna as helpers, in practically no time, eight stone markers were erected along the roughly calculated forty-foot elevation.

Now it was time for the really dirty work to begin, and Richards, with a broad grin on his face and a ton of hope in his heart, took with him upslope one of the soldier's collapsible trenching tools. Finally reaching the forty-foot elevation, the Egyptologist looked up into the rocky mass above him, recalling with his photographic memory what he had seen above him and remembering Paneshy's remark that the trail continued on above as a ruse. Then looking side to side, he tried to gauge just where the entrance had been and he began to shuffle first this way and then that, all in an attempt to get his bearings.

To Sheril below, *It's almost looks like Joseph is a hunting dog trying to catch a scent. No. It's as if he were some sort of radio receiver trying to catch an elusive radio signal.*

Her analogy was not far off, for that was precisely what the man was doing. Finally settling on a position, Richards looked up once again and then realized that he had a good five feet of scree above him, five feet of material that could potentially slide into and fill each and every shovel load that he removed. With a rueful smile and resigned to his task, he deeply planted his first shovelful, feeling much as the toiling tragic figure Sisyphus when he began pushing his first boulder uphill.

He adjusted the trenching tool to a ninety-degree angle and started removing the rocky material doggy style – between his legs.

Much to his surprise, he found the motion relatively easy and quickly found a comfortable rhythm that conserved his strength. After a sensible period, he rested and was rewarded with a slight dish-like depression forming in the side of the slope, while an ever-widening spoil fan formed down slope.

He concluded. *This is doable.*

A full hour later, the once dish-like depression had become a sizable gap in the slope, but one that threatened to eventually collapse. Richards continued on. Well into his second hour, the point of the trenching tool reached the rock face itself. Now clearing away the material more carefully, the American began to work sideways. Stepping to the side and stopping for a breather and a long drink of water, the slope at that moment decided to slip, effectively filling in all of his labors. But in the gap created above, Richards saw something very encouraging – a small line and an exposure of the rock face itself! Quickly scrambling up to check, he quickly ascertained that the line continued to the right and left.

Yes! He thought. *I was digging almost directly beneath the entrance itself! The collapse just exposed the upper portion of the entranceway!*

For the next several moments, the slopes and cliffs of the wadi became the echo chamber of one very deliriously gleeful man. Meanwhile, several bets were being paid off among Tuna's school.

* * *

After all the racket that he had made at his discovery, it was a matter of moments before Tuna had four members of his team clearing away the rest of the material deposited around the suspicious portion of rock face. To Richards' immense satisfaction, when the soldiers had completed their clearing, a narrow portion of the cliffside pathway had been preserved as well. Shaking his head in near disbelief, he thought, *God bless Doc Allen for all of those photographic memory exercises!*

With Sharil now at his side, the pair began to meticulously trace and clean the entire outline of the entranceway, blowing and brushing away any and all of the remaining fine debris, sand, and dust. Satisfied that everything that could be removed had been, all that was left to do was see if the rock pivot of the passageway still functioned.

Admittedly, this final moment of truth was one that was quite surreal. So, surrounded by Sharil, Tuna, and four soldiers, Richards put his hands against the rock and pushed, and then pushed again, and then just pushed even harder again. Nothing moved.

Glaring at the rock and now dripping in sweat, Tuna suggested, "Dr. Richards. Allow my men a try."

Nodding his head in defeat, the Egyptologist stepped aside, while first two and then three of Tuna's men put their collective shoulders into the task.

On the fourth attempt, a distinct grinding noise was clearly heard, to which Richards clearly exclaimed, "Holy shit! That's it!"

In his next breath, Richards profusely apologized to Sharil for what he had said.

Then Tuna boomed, "WELL, MEN. ARE YOU GONNA LET A LITTLE ROCK GET IN YOUR WAY? NO FRICKIN' WAY!"

Then he thoughtfully amended, "Sorry, madam, my apologies. I just let myself get a little too caught up in all this."

So, somehow, all four soldiers got into the act and pushed yet again, and this time a five-inch gap formed. So encouraged by their success, the four continued to pound, push, and lever their way against the rock until a man could just barely press himself into the opening. But even that space was not really necessary as Dr. Sharil Moussa was only a size four.

* * *

Armed with their hand torches, Richards and Sharil could stand up fully once beyond the entrance's blocking stone. Shining their beams around, they quickly found the wooden lever that Paneshy had used to close the stone plug. From all appearances the passage looked just as Richards had remembered it, and in fact better, as the illumination of their flashlights proved to be far better than Paneshy's lone candle stub, which they found.

Moving slowly forward, the upward sloping passage was encountered. It too seemed intact as there was no evidence of any cave-in debris on its floor whatsoever. Hopeful and looking at each other meaningfully, they began to ascend the passage, purposely shining their lights on the floor before them. As they again continued, Richards counted his footsteps, and as he reached forty-two, their collective beams of light disappeared before them as they were swallowed up whole in the vast gloom of a chamber that they had just entered. Stopping at the threshold, they both noted that the air was fresh. Slowly shining their beams around and above revealed nothing. Just that they were inside a very large chamber.

"Well," Richards said quietly, as if he were in church. "Let's move forward until we run into something. Whaddya' say, Sharil?"

"Makes sense to me, Joseph. Let's go."

* * *

When the pair finally emerged from the hidden entranceway to the Aten's hanger, some two hours later, it was already mid-afternoon, and Tuna was fit to be tied out of worry.

"Major Cartwright. I understand your concern," Dr. Moussa soothed. "However, while archaeology is indeed a dirty business, it is anything but quick. In fact, tomorrow we'll be more than happy to show you, and with your approval of course, any of your men, just what you have been guarding. Please let me assure you, Major. You and your fine men are indeed guarding something beyond price. Now if you will excuse us, we have to make several calls."

Now fully mollified by the Egyptian's reasonable explanation of the situation, the major took a deep breath and smiled.

We just might be able to pull off this wild goose chase after all!

* * *

Following a spirited twenty-minute conversation in Arabic between Sharil and her father, the Director of the Egyptian Antiquities Service, it was Richards' turn at the satellite phone. With the assistance of one of Cartwright's men, Richards dialed up Dr. Borov's office using a special one-time cipher. At the other end, the phone rang twice before it was answered.

"Peter. This is Joey. How are you, Doc?"

"Fine, Joey, now cut to the chase. How are you doing?"

"Well, frankly, unbelievably well. Is John there?"

After a momentary hiss and change in volume, Borov placed the call on conference mode and John Milson piped up, “You bet! Now what do you have?”

“Well, guys, in short, the whole enchilada.”

“That is positively wonderful!” Then Milson thought to add, “Are there any technical hurdles to overcome?”

“Yeah, I suspect so. Sharil and I could not find the hanger doors, much less how to operate them. Yet, the entire chamber is continuously flooded with fresh air. So, I suspect that tomorrow we’ll go in with several of Tuna’s men and start rootin’ around. Maybe we’ll find something, maybe not. But at this point, I just don’t know. But I can say this for sure. We’ll need technical support just to maneuver the craft off of its granite cradle. So send ’em on in. But then again, we might get real lucky, for if the hanger doors open directly above the Aten, then we still might get away with using a Jolly Green Giant to hoist it out lock, stock, and barrel.”

“Joseph,” Milson stated with mock sternness in his voice. “You’ve been hanging around that Major Cartwright too much. Now, just what the hell is a Jolly Green Giant?”

“Well, John, it’s one, big, whoop-ass helicopter.”

* * *

As it turned out, Richards’ surmise that the doors of the Aten’s hanger were directly above the craft’s cradle turned out to be dead on. However, the triggering of them to open, which they remarkably did after remaining dormant for over three and a quarter millennia, proved to be no more a stunning achievement than the craft within the hanger itself. But just as important was the discovery that the Aten’s hanger contained much, much more than just the scout craft itself.

The mechanism that tripped the massive and split overhead hanger doors to open proved to be a simple communication’s squawk at the 1000 FM radio frequency. The discovery was accidentally stumbled upon by Tuna’s radioman, Staff Sergeant Jeremy Brown, who on sheer intuition slowly and patiently clicked his way through the channel dial of the team’s radio. The hanger door mechanism’s response to the appropriate frequency squawk had been so instantaneous, so noisy, and such a surprise, that all of

Tuna's men who were within the hanger at the time were convinced they had been caught in the middle of an earthquake. At first, there was the deafening and slow grinding of rock on rock, followed by a brief cascade of falling sand, light rubble, and pebbles. Then the slow formation of a huge slit above them that continued to widen well beyond the width and size of the Aten craft. Then all was silence and bright sunshine.

After that event, many had admitted that they had thought about their life insurance policies more than once. Those who were not in the vast chamber, but were still at their security posts, witnessed the disconcerting horizontal sliding aside of most of the rocky top where they had been stationed for the past days. In the process, two positions had to be abandoned as soldiers scurried this way and that to get clear of harm's way. Once the movement had ceased, Tuna's men gazed at one another in total awe and amazement. Some from above looked down into the newly formed gap in the mountain, while their mates looked up and into brilliant sunshine. No one spoke as the words just would not come.

When asked afterward just what the radioman had had in mind, Brown shrugged his shoulders and gave the following explanation.

"Hell, the only thing that made sense to me was that the hanger doors worked on some sort of remote garage door principle. Ya' know, the kind with a clicker that you would have in your car. So that meant that there had to be a transmitter in the flying saucer and a receiver of some sort in the hanger itself. Well, I knew that there was some sort of black box up there. Rudy had told me that he found it and had traced its wiring over to the gearing. It all just made sense to me at the time. That's all."

As to what Corporal Rudy "Spiderman" Weiss was doing along the upper reaches and roofline of the hanger, are best appreciated from this point of view. Each special operations team possessed members with odd talents and abilities.

Rudy Weiss, a wiry kid from the Bronx, was a really big Spiderman fan. He read all the comics and watched all the cartoons. But when the first Spiderman television shows came out, Rudy became a man obsessed with heights, climbing fearlessly, and barehanded without tethers or ropes. The fact was that his sense of balance was extraordinary, and that ice flowed in his veins. Rudy was a natural cat burglar. When the law caught up to him, he was given a choice and so Rudy joined up. From his very first run through the obstacle course, his master sergeant knew that this kid was a cat and his personnel jacket only proved it. Used to scaling yards of cyclone fencing, quickly picking his way through razor wire, pulling himself up fire escapes, climbing downspouts, and walking the edges of rooflines, the camp's wooden walls, teeter logs, rope nets, and his favorite, the rope swing across the moat, were all a cakewalk for Rudy.

Then the Army taught Rudy what a piton was, how ropes could be used like a spider's silk, and above all, how to repel. He found himself in hog heaven and fast becoming one of the most skilled second-story men in the business. When the Spiderman movie came out, Rudy's upside-down kisses became the bomb with all the girls.

So here he was in Egypt, with the best of the best and on Tuna's crack team. He was inside this huge natural hanger and his commander presented him with a challenge like no other. First, take a look and see if the ceiling could move. Second, if so, crawl around and find out how. Well, it took Rudy a good forty-five minutes to figure out where the first grooving or track of the ceiling mechanism was located. After another twenty, he spotted its parallel twin on the other side of the chamber. What had given their presence away was the telltale trail of finely powdered rock dust that had been deposited with every passing of the hanger door's heavy bronze wheels. Continuing to sniff about like a hound on a hot scent, Rudy then found, after squeezing himself through a narrow access passage cut into the surrounding rock, the gearing that made it all happen. There he found a "black box" and some stuff that he guessed was wiring of some kind. That was when some spooky tech-heads took over.

But along the way, Rudy also found no fewer than ten air shafts that had been cunningly placed in such a way that the air within the hanger remained fresh as a spring day. When he told the tech-heads that he had found these as well, the experts began wondering about why that was, and in particular, what was it about the Aten craft's propulsion system that might require such ventilation.

While Dr. Richards had reported that the Egyptian caretaker of the craft, Paneshy, had "fed" the craft jars of water on a daily basis, the question remained as to where this water source was located that Richards had alluded to. Once found, the next step was to determine through chemical analysis whether there was anything particularly special about that water source.

But before Brown's solution to the opening of the hanger doors had been found, Weiss was doing his Spiderman thing totally in the dark. Meanwhile, the recon team of Corporals Tony "Sancho" Sanchez and Pat "Calli" Callahan were tasked to find that well and, if at all possible, to collect several samples from it. The pair decided to make for the nearest wall, split up, and follow the hanger's perimeter with the idea of eventually meeting up. A truly logical and sensible plan, even for these two recon pukes, but neither of them had any inkling of the things that they would find along the way.

Calli had gone right with his flashlight leading the way, while Sancho had gone left. After some minutes, Calli literally ran into a wooden racking that supported five large earthenware jars. Given that they stood some three feet high, Calli guessed at their volume as being around seven to ten gallons. As they were unsealed, the five amphorae were all bone dry, but their presence alone was encouraging nonetheless and confirmed that Richards' report, at least in this aspect, was accurate. Having recorded everything he found on his issued camcorder complete with narrative, the Irishman eagerly moved on in the hopes of beating his partner to the well.

Having gone left, Sancho worked his way along while panning his two flashlights, one in each hand, side to side in an overlapping pattern. All he noted at first was that the near vertical walls of the hanger were not naturally formed, but had been made so by using hand chisels. The shadowing of the chisel marks were caught in his flashlight beams and those signatures clearly showed where one workman had ended and the next began. Some stonecutters, Sancho noted, worked their chisels flat and others on more of an edge. The soldier also began to realize that the stone was worked from the top down in a sort of waterfall pattern first from right to left and then, probably as their arms got tired, switched hands and continued in sweeping downward curves from left to right. With the passing of every yard, Sancho's respect for those long-dead craftsmen grew.

Freaking unbelievable, he thought. *They must have been really cut to do such work hour after hour, day in and day out!*

This daydreaming by Sancho was broken when he found a series of six rectangular, door-like cuts in the hanger's wall that were about the width and height of a man. Each of the six was evenly spaced about six feet apart. Shining his flashlights' beams into each of the six, each appeared to be about eight feet deep with regular sides, ceiling, and floor cut flush with that of the hanger's. Their purpose was a mystery, until Sancho decided to backtrack and enter the first that he had encountered. What he discovered was that the niche was not a dead end, but opened to a short corridor to his right, and that all six passages connected. Flashing his two beams around, he quickly noted two items. This side corridor from floor to ceiling on its right side was fully inscribed in Egyptian hieroglyphics all arranged in neat vertical columns about three feet across. These the soldier made a careful video recording of. Along the smooth walls of the corridor's left side was another passage opening, one that was offset in such a way as to hide its presence from the hanger area itself. To Sancho, the entire arrangement of these passages reminded him of an exaggerated letter "E" tipped over on its side. Standing before the new passage and shining his beams deep within it, the soldier saw, besides a continuation of the smoothly chiseled surfaces, a brief landing and then a descending stair-stepped passage. Intrigued, he moved forward, sniffed the air, and smiled. And although his flashlight beams could not reach the stair's bottom far below, he knew.

Water! I can smell it!

While Sanchez was gloating over finding the well that Dr. Richards had reported, Callahan had discovered a broad inscribed archway that led to a side annex. Carved out of the living rock as well, this side chamber had a much lower ceiling in comparison with that of the main hanger area, which was decorated in skinny, yellow painted five-pointed stars against a dark blue field. The space itself was a small forest of square pillars, eleven in all, each of which was decorated with columns of brightly painted Egyptian hieroglyphs against a white-washed background. They were like ten white shafts of light shooting up into a starry heaven. In the exact center of the room, which Calli now suspected was a perfect square, stood a solitary short square column about three feet high. Painted white like its neighbors, it too was covered on all of its sides with painted hieroglyphs. But resting atop the diminutive pillar was an elegant cedar wood box. It was carved to look like the exterior of an Egyptian shrine with gently sloped sides and a flat-roofed cornice that served as its lid. Curious beyond words, Calli dared to lift the lid to peek inside the box and saw that it contained a single roll of papyrus that was bound at its center and its two ends with what looked like a heavy cotton yarn. The yarn tied in the center was dyed a deep reddish color, while the other two were yellow. As for the roll itself, it looked to the soldier like a thick daily newspaper all rolled up. To his everlasting credit, Calli had the good sense to leave the papyrus roll be and just let his camcorder do all the talking. For Callahan, he had never before seen anything like this in his life. For that matter, no modern Egyptologist had either. But he had his orders, so he continued to just slowly pan his camcorder across the historic find.

* * *

With the Aten's sanctuary now open to the elements, the craft's recovery was indeed performed by helicopter, but not a Jolly Green Giant. Instead, a dual rotor Chinook CH-47D was requisitioned. With its thirteen-ton lifting capacity, it easily and neatly snatched the Aten craft off of its granite cradle and into the air. That's not to say that there weren't some nervous moments, for the engineers didn't have a clue as to the weight of the Aten, much less whether the cargo netting that they used to lift the craft would have been sufficient for the job. As it turned out, however, the Aten's mass was no more than that of two fully loaded Cadillacs, or around eight and a half thousand pounds.

Once out of its hanger for the first time in millennia, the Chinook flew it due west from El Amarna into the Western Desert and then continued north on a beeline to the Delta Force's airbase. This entire sortie was accomplished on a moonless night and over the desert in order to avoid waking up anyone with the fly over, while minimizing any notice by the local inhabitants.

Once at the airbase, the Aten was stored in its own hanger and was placed under heavy guard by Tuna's own second team, which really miffed the military police on the base. Now bedded down, safe and sound, the next leg of the Aten's transport to Wright-Patterson AFB outside of Dayton, Ohio, would be accomplished atop NASA's own specially modified Boeing 747 that ferried space shuttles.

But that ride would have to wait a month and a half as a team of aeronautical engineers cooked up a custom attachment system, so that the Aten could ride atop the aircraft's ventral fuselage. With the docking mechanism in place, those same ever-clever aeronautical comedians, in order to complete the charade, painted two parallel white stripes across the Aten's featureless hull in imitation of a revolving radar dome, making the NASA 747 look like a huge telemetry platform. But that fancy paint job turned out to be quite a task, as it was quickly discovered that the Aten craft had a layer of beeswax protecting its outer skin.

With the loaded 747 flying east bound and only in darkness, it enjoyed an escort of four F-16s armed to the teeth. Several midair refueling missions were flown over the Atlantic in support of this formidable quintet. The 747 completed the first leg of its homeward progress when it landed at Gander, Newfoundland. After a change of crews, the final leg left Gander, again at night, and flew directly to Wright-Patterson AFB.

This historic ferrying operation of an extraterrestrial craft aboard a terrestrial one took place during the last week of October. When once safely ensconced within its very own security building, all further internal military references to the "package" referenced it as only a spare electronics parts inventory, in part to camouflage reality, in part to continue a long tradition that began with the so-called UFO crash that occurred at Roswell, New Mexico, in 1947.

* * *

While all the logistics behind the recovery of the Aten craft were in preparation, two teams of experts descended upon the hanger facility. One was led by Major Tuna Cartwright, whose first team remained on as the site's security unit. Augmenting these, two military engineers and two high-tech types were flown in from Wright-Patterson Air Force Base to first investigate and hopefully remove for further study the remarkable overhead hanger door opening mechanism. Cartwright identified Corporal Rudy "Spiderman" Weiss as a key player in that effort. What became obvious, however, was that where Weiss could climb and squirm with effortlessness to reach the mechanism, only one of the four specialists could match.

Fortunately, Technical Sergeant First Class Mike Brown, often referred to as "Runt" by some of his colleagues, was physically small enough and sufficiently fit to follow, although with some difficulty, Weiss' precarious high wire act. Nonetheless, this wiry twenty-four-year-old from Nashville, Tennessee, and former high school point guard managed to overcome his fear of falling because of his fierce curiosity.

"Hell! Here I am in Egypt of all places, the Land of the Pharaohs. We've a job to do. If I have to climb up some rope and crawl along some narrow ledge to do it, then I'll do it! Besides, I am not going to let some Army-type Spiderman embarrass me. No, sir!"

So up went Sergeant Brown, all gussied up in a repelling harness tied to a safety tether that Weiss had rigged for the purpose. So secured, the airman quickly crawled up the hanger's wall. And in no time, he got his feet down on the narrow western ledge. Once steadied, Weiss showed the man the fine dust layer that coated the ledge.

"Sergeant," the soldier said as he casually swiped a trail with his finger across the ledge's smooth surface. "My guess is that the massive metal wheels that I'm about to show you created all of this dust."

"Wheels?"

"Yeah. Up ahead. The biggest metal wagon wheels that you'll ever see. We'll even have to crawl over them to get to the black box and its wiring. You ready, Sergeant?"

"Yep, lead on, Mac Duff."

Off the pair went, bent over and working slowly along the narrow ledge that ran horizontally and just below the hanger's roofline. As they neared about a third of the way to the corner, they disappeared from sight as they began squeezing their bodies over a series of five massive and broad metal wheels that apparently supported that particular section of the hanger's doors. With his flashlight on, Weiss was the first over the wheels and into the relatively open space beyond them. Brown, murmured in wonder about the width and massiveness of the wheels, finally caught up to Weiss.

"Corporal, those wheels are really big! They're almost three feet across by four high!"

"No shit! Now take a look at this."

There behind the carriage of five wheels was the black box that Weiss had first reported, complete with what looked like two cables or leads that appeared to be connected to the wheels behind them. Fascinated, Brown squatted down, looking at the featureless rectangular apparatus. He shone his flashlight's beam between it and the wheels behind him several time while tracing the path of two cables. Then Brown had an idea.

"Corporal, have you checked out the other three corners of his hanger?"

"Yep."

"And I'll bet that you found exactly the same setup at each corner didn't you."

"Yep again."

"Damn," the airman concluded. "Probably four synchronized electric motors. Very, very cool. But where's the power source?"

"Who knows?" Weiss stated. "Do you think that the power source might be in that black box?"

"I'd be really surprised if it was. What we're talking about here, Corporal, is moving tons of rock, and its wheeled framework. What we're talking about is real power, lots of power, and unbelievable torque.

"Okay, Corporal. Now, lead the way to those other corners, I want to check 'em all out."

"You got it, Sergeant!"

While those two were crawling around, the other three airmen, Second Lieutenant Doug Brisby, Technical Sergeant Bob Royal, and Corporal Robby Griss were busying themselves with the operation of the hidden entrance that Tuna's men had forced open. The trio quickly surmised that the entranceway worked on a pivot and counterweight arrangement that allowed the massive rock to move with relative ease, if one knew just where to push. But given its present state, it was clear that the doorway's counterweight had shifted over the millennia. So the three shoved, pushed, and levered with two borrowed trenching tools the counterweight back into place. Fortunately, Royal and Brisby were game for such heavy work given their massive frames, while Griss placed the blades of the trenching tools into the seams that the other two grunted open. In all, it took them about an hour of work and the counterweight was back to where it originally was. But did the mechanism still work?

After removing some sand and small debris from the doorway's track, Griss pulled down on the doorway's lever and the rock slid effortlessly back into place with a satisfying thump. Then, pushing up on the beam, the entranceway cracked open. It was then the trio figured out the purpose for lone short section of wooden beam. Royal was the first to wonder what the purpose was for the carved notch in the doorway's wall. Reopening the entranceway to its fullest extent, Brisby then saw a matching notch-like groove on the doorway's exterior surface. Logic then demanded that Royal would position the beam against the interior wall, while Griss pushed at the beam to close the entrance. Royal knew that he had only one chance, so he made sure that the free end of the blocking beam lodged securely against the closing doorway. And the beam held!

Then stepping fully outside, Royal yelled, "Get clear!"

Then he kicked in the beam with all of his might, stepped back, and the hidden entranceway closed behind him, and for all purposes, perfectly disappeared from sight, and he was only standing three feet away from it!

Meanwhile, Weiss and Brown had completed their tour of the hanger door mechanism. Indeed, all four sets of wheels and black boxes were identical, and as hard as Brown had tried, he could find no evidence of any physical connection between them. That only meant that their synchronization had to be something akin to a simple radio control relay. But the real question still had to be answered. If Cartwright's radioman again squawked 1000 FM, would they close? That experiment, Brown concluded, would have to wait until they had evacuated the site.

* * *

The other team that was working within the Aten's hanger, once the Aten had been removed, was led by Dr. Sharil Moussa, who personally represented the authority of the Egyptian Antiquities Service on behalf of her father. Her handpicked team comprised a very select group who literally set up camp within the hanger's open bay. Her team included an Egyptian philologist, an architect, a sketch artist, and a field photographer. Their formidable task was to as expeditiously as possible record all the hieroglyphic inscriptions that Corporals Sanchez and Callahan had found and plot out the hidden installation's physical details before it would again be sealed.

But Sharil Moussa's absolute first priority was the isolation and transfer to the Cairo National Museum's Department of Restoration the cedar box and its precious beyond words contents. In fact, Dr. Ahmed Rashid himself, the museum's Chief Curator, drove down to El Amarna to properly prepare these artifacts for transport, accompanied them back to his own laboratory, and then unpacked them, placing them in a controlled environment.

While the exquisite cedar box required precious little in the way of environmental stabilization, the papyrus roll, if it ever was to be read, had to be unrolled. Consequently, the delicate papyrus had to be very slowly rehydrated within a neutral and sterile environment that was constantly filtered in order to either remove or prevent any spores of mold to develop. This process would take time and exercise the team's patience, but this was how it was done.

Prior to the start of the rehydration process, however, the vital statistics of both artifacts were recorded, and to Rashid's surprise, the papyrus roll itself weighed in at a hefty 1.1 kilos. Then the appropriate photographic records were made. And just prior to placing the roll within its hydration incubator, Rashid himself carefully severed all three of its yarn ties, placing each with his tweezers into their own sterilized test tubes for further study.

Relieved in the knowledge that the cedar artifact and its contents were safely secure and in the care of Dr. Rashid and his department's staff, Sharil focused her considerable energies on recording the many columns of inscriptions. As one might expect, here too a proven process for such a task was considered *de rigueur*.

Known the world over as The Chicago Method, this painstaking process ensures the highest degree of accuracy in the recording of epigraphical monuments via a series of tried and true steps that include photography, sketching, reading, rereading, and then the double-checking of past steps. But with the advent of computers and digital photography, the duration of this once lengthy process was greatly accelerated, while still retaining its extraordinary accuracy.

To assist Sharil, who herself was a gifted philologist and experienced field archaeologist, she chose John Milson, who agreed, but only as a virtual philological colleague, as his doctors temporarily forbade the aged emeritus professor from going into the field. Besides, his tools, other than his legendary memory, were located within the Near Eastern Institute's formidable library.

Next, her choice for a sketch artist was an old friend from her Cambridge days, Marie Danton, whose distant relative had been none other than Ms. Georges Jacques Danton – a member of the Committee of Public Safety during the French Revolution. Sharil knew that she could depend on Marie's sharp eye to recover any missing details that were so critical to the restoration process.

For her field photographer, Sharil trusted in the kind recommendation of her colleague Dr. Rashid, who said that Louis Bando was nothing short of a digital wizard. Bando, a native Jamaican with an infectious smile, had provided Rashid with a three-dimensional digital archive of the museum's Predynastic flint tool collection.

Finally, her choice for an architect again came from her own field experience. Fortunately for her, the Englishman John Pendergast was more than willing and able to assist as he was between excavation seasons, working in the urban quarter of ancient Ephesus.

One week after the Aten craft had been moved to the safety of the Delta Force's airbase, the team gathered within the hanger's vast space. Acquiring the chemical toilets, portable showers, tents, sleeping gear, and cases of MREs thoughtfully airlifted in and left behind courtesy of the U.S. Army, the team immediately got to work. None had been told what had been removed from the main chamber and its annex, nor anything about the gap above them. Consequently, Pendergast's first architectural impressions of the place were that of a smallish open-air American basketball arena. For Bando, it all reminded him of something out of the American Southwest, something almost like an Anasazi cliff-dwelling chamber. While Danton, standing atop the granite cradle with her hands on her hips, merely stated, "Sharil, something really big is missing from here. Just look at the relationship between this pedestal and that hole in the roof. What just flew out?"

* * *

After their first week of furious survey investigation, recording, measuring, photographing, sketching, and generally nosing about, the preliminary verdict came in. This was one weird place.

Item: the overall layout and relationships of the main chamber to the well and annex were "quite symmetrical."

Item: the central or main chamber was laid out as a regular-sided, equilateral pentagram with its fifty-two meter long sides accurate in length to within two centimeters. In short, from above it looked much like the home plate of any American baseball diamond. The estimated height of the vault above was reckoned at fifty-two meters as well. This pentagonal arrangement was quite unique for an ancient construction, much less one of this magnitude.

Item: the central granite pedestal, which measured six and a half meters across by four high, had a concave or dished upper surface that suggested to the architect that it might have been a giant water basin of some kind. But Pendergast was quick to point out that if so, then the filling and draining of it would have been "quite a job." As for the associated ramp that ascended the pedestal and faced the wooden racking of amphorae, the architect reported that it was constructed in a precise ratio of one unit of rise to five of run that produced a very manageable approach grade of about twelve degrees. This caused Pendergast to reconsider and scratch at his curly head.

"Well, maybe they could fill up the pedestal relatively easily."

Item: the side chamber's entrance was found to be centered on the base side of the pentagonal floor plan directly opposite the exit of the entrance shaft in the main chamber's flooring. The central pedestal was located directly between the two. As for the side chamber itself, its floor plan was perfectly square and its eleven columns perfectly spaced and aligned. Pendergast too had his suspicions about the purpose of the small central column. It was clearly the focus of the room, but he didn't have a clue what that focus or something was until the associated hieroglyphic inscriptions on all the columns were translated for him.

Item: the six side entrances to the well passage. Again, why there were six passages instead of one remained unknown. Nonetheless, while their alignment was precise, the meaning of that alignment escaped him. He noted that there were eighty-four steps that led down to the well itself, with a landing occurring at every twenty-eighth step. The last five steps were now totally submerged due to the water table rise as a result of the construction of the Aswan High Dam. Offhand, however, he couldn't think of any significance of their number, and neither could anyone else. Once again, Pendergast said that he would have to wait for a translation of the associated glyphs before he could go any further with his assessment.

Item: Bando reported that he had been able to complete the digital photography of the well's corridor inscriptions as well as those of the side chamber's eleven columns. All were then immediately transmitted to Milson for his review. What really challenged the Jamaican was how to digitally capture in a meaningful way the sheer size of the main chamber and its central pedestal. Regardless, he would have the time to contemplate this, for that series of shots could only be taken once all of the team's paraphernalia had been airlifted out.

Item: to Danton's surprise, she nowhere noted any unfinished inscriptions, erasures, or evidence of salt damage that would require restoration. She also noted that the pigments used were still exceptionally bright and that they should technically reproduce very well in Bando's digital recordings.

Item: while Danton had not as yet examined the inscriptions of the side chamber, she nonetheless had more than enough ammunition, so she unloaded. Given her more than passing acquaintance with Egyptian hieroglyphs, having sketched them and restored their incomplete or damaged parts, the French artist pointed out on the basis of artistic style and vocabulary used, that the inscriptions of the well's corridor were without question late Eighteenth Dynasty. Given that the archaeological site of El Amarna was located nearby, she did not find that surprising, but what Danton did find very interesting, if not unique, were all the repeated references to the Aten disk itself. So she enumerated them on her fingers. A curious phase that referred to this place as "the House of the Aten," not to mention other strange references that alluded to the "feeding of the Aten," the "bathing of the Aten," the "polishing of the Aten's skin so that it may remain as brilliant as Re-Herakhte" – an Egyptian divine euphemism for the sun itself.

Item: Danton noted as well that the leading edges of the pedestal's rim had undergone considerable abrasion, as if something very heavy had rested upon it or twisted atop it much like a millstone, something she again rather pointedly asked her old friend Sharil about.

"Okay, my dear. Now tell us all, just what have you removed from the pedestal of this chamber?"

* * *

In the end, Brown finally got his big chance to test his theory. With all the "cultural" investigators and their gear airlifted out and with the hidden entranceway sealed, the hanger was again restored to its pristine condition – minus several items. Brown, now sitting cross-legged atop and near an edge of one of the hanger doors, turned on the portable radio backpack unit of Tuna's radioman, checked for the one hundredth time that it was indeed set to FM 1000, and keyed the mike. After a very brief moment of anxiety, Brown first felt the rumbling of the hanger doors' massive wheels through his bottom before he sensed their closing movement. And moments later, the Residence of the Aten was again sealed from the elements. The only hint at the presence of the hanger doors was a long, remarkably narrow, and straight crack across a portion of the massif's summit. Given time, that crack would quickly fill with windblown dust and sand and disappear entirely.

Just what kind of Eveready batteries do those black boxes have anyways!

CHAPTER XLI

Of Inscriptions and Papyri

As soon as Milson received the first series of e-mails from Louis Bando, each with their massively packed zip files of digital imagery from the Aten's hanger, his heart skipped a beat. He was a city kid again, exploring the woods on his Uncle Bill's Georgia farm in search of high adventure, largemouth bass from the hidden pond, and all creatures big and small.

The first batch contained the inscriptions of what came to be known as the Well Corridor that Corporal Sanchez had first filmed with his excited, herky-jerky, and breathless video, filled with all of the soldier's unconscious expressions of "Wow," "Cool," and "Check it out!" A careful examination of that film alone had given the Egyptologist a fair guess at what Bando's imagery might offer. Now it was all before him.

First downloading all of the attachments into his laptop's internal drive, he next copied all seventy-three MG into his memory stick. Checking carefully that the stick had indeed loaded correctly, Milson removed it from the USB port of his laptop and then deleted the heavily encrypted e-mails one by one. Now satisfied that his memory stick was his backup source, he then removed the stick and put it into a small security safe in the bottom right-hand drawer of his desk.

Returning to his laptop, he began the tedious process of unzipping all of the files, examining each exposure, and then printing out the best ones in order to make a representative mosaic of the five vertical panels that comprised the entire hieroglyphic text. After a little over two hours of careful work, Milson had before him the five panels, each composed of six taped eight and a half by eleven sheets of paper printed in color in landscape mode. By observing the direction that the individual hieroglyphs faced, Milson quickly knew that the inscription began in upper right corner of panel E, according to Bando's own numbering system. That issue resolved, the careful philologist then marked all the remaining paper panels D through A and folded up each and placed them in their own individually marked file folders. That accomplished, his yellow legal pad appeared from his center top drawer, along with several freshly sharpened, yellow No. 2 pencils. Dividing the pad into three columns, Milson finally got down to work by first reproducing each character or character cluster in his own freehand style in the first column, transliterating it into Latin characters in the second, while reserving the third for the eventual translation.

Painstakingly, he worked at Panel E's first and second columns until six sheets of his legal pad had been filled with his precise and careful handwriting. Sitting back with a crick in his back, he stretched, was rewarded with the usual several crunches from his vertebrae, and then to his horror noted that it was already past 8:30 p.m.

John! He thought. *You've gotta' get outta' here. Get some supper and grab some sleep, so that you can be back tomorrow, bright-eyed and bushy-tailed!*

* * *

Returning to his office the next day, Milson, after first checking his e-mails for anything interesting, dove into his roughing out of the Well Corridor inscription. By noon, his insistent stomach told him in no uncertain terms to go to the nearby University Faculty Club for some lunch. That uneventful task done, the Egyptologist returned to his office and renewed his intellectual siege, for he was beginning to understand the basic gist of what the inscription was all about. By three that afternoon, he had completed the two columns for Panels E, D, C, B, and A. As for Panel A, it turned out to be mostly a repetitious rehash of E.

Now came what Milson often referred to as "magic time." This was that precious moment, while all the details are still fresh in your innocent and unfettered mind, where true insight and inspired intuition take over. While for some, this was "crunch time," to Milson it had always been the magic moment when the papyrus, inscription, or graffito seemed to speak to him directly, informally, through the words of the original composer. Sitting back and closing his eyes, he began to play back the words, the phrasing, all the while opening up his mind's boundaries so that it might play. And then it all came to him.

This is neither a medical treatise nor cookbook, but rather a serious and potentially frightening instruction on the care and feeding of the Aten craft! In fact, if I were to publish this highly classified document, then that would indeed make a quite excellent title.

Now settled on the inscription's main theme and context, he then began to break it down into its constituent parts.

Let's see now, he began.

Panel E, praise and attribution to Akhenaten, a vicious and hideously described curse to warn off those not appropriate to continue with the inscription, ending with a curious incantation or spell that authorized the opening of the Aten.

Panel D, is a rather surprising and clinical discussion of the Aten's need for water, what kind, what level of purity, where to obtain this water, how to gauge how much to deliver, and where to put it.

Panel C, again a rather specific instruction as to how to care for the skin of the Aten: how to correctly wax it, what kind of wax to use, how to correctly polish it to a bright shine, what to use for this task.

Panel B, the most curious panel of all, tells in rather metaphorical, but specific and detailed terms, how to care for the well-being of the Aten's own sheut, *or double.*

And finally Panel A, a stern reiteration of the terrible curse of Panel E for all those deemed inappropriate, but who have nonetheless read the inscription.

While the old philologist knew that there would be several further translation issues, he knew that in the main he had the inscription's general thrust. But Panel B's content again returned to him like a greasy slider. The key to understanding and translating this panel hinged on the interpretation of what was meant by the Aten's *sheut*, or double. Milson's encyclopedic knowledge and intuition told him that this was truly virgin territory, for nowhere in the literature was there a hint of such an Egyptian religious concept that a divinity could even have a *sheut*. Only humans have a *sheut*, as one aspect of their souls. Then it struck him between the eyes like a bolt of lightning. Furiously scrambling to retrieve his transcription of Panel B, it did not take long to realize that all those curious details made a hell of a lot better sense if the Aten's caretaker was taking care of both the Aten craft and its pilot as well.

Jesus, Mary, and Joseph!

The old Egyptologist gasped as his hands quavered.

This is bona fide written evidence of at least two sentient extraterrestrials on our planet! After all, the sheut *is the "double" of an individual, like a shadow, or even a statue. And in this case, the term* sheut *means "the twin," or perhaps better, "the teammate" of Akhenaten!*

* * *

Meanwhile, a half a world away at the Cairo National Museum, another surprise was about to unfold. For in the laboratory next to Dr. Rashid's office, where a certain papyrus roll last week had begun its slow process of hydration, a coworker happened to notice that almost the entire incubation cabinet was filled with a lengthy papyrus that had entirely unrolled. Surprised by the sight, the same coworker later related his observation to Dr. Rashid during that afternoon's tea. With the head curator's eyes widening as his colleague mentioned seeing this magnificent example of hydration, Rashid, interrupting the man in midsentence, quickly excused himself, and ran toward the laboratory in question. Upon opening the door, Rashid's heart sank through the floor in worry that he had somehow set up the incubator incorrectly – in essence being guilty of over-hydrating the precious artifact too quickly and in effect transforming it into near mush. But the machine's settings were indeed correct in all respects. In fact, they were still his, set on the conservative side. Upon opening the incubator, Rashid was greeted with a gush of fragrant air that reminded him of freshly cut grass, the kind that he remembered smelling during his university days in England. Daring to gently touch the outermost arc of what looked like a very long and continuous papyrus scroll, he found it to be of a firm and pliant texture and not at all in danger of falling apart into its constituent sheets or even worse.

Carefully closing the cabinet and sitting down on a nearby stool to collect himself, Rashid realized that this roll was ready to begin the unrolling and drying process. The only fly in the ointment was that the maximum length that the museum could currently accommodate was twenty-four English feet. If a papyrus was any longer, traditional practice dictated that it should be trimmed in two, at a convenient point, again stretched out, and if necessary, trimmed again. Since long rolls of papyri were extremely rare, if ever encountered, Rashid found himself in unknown territory. What should he do? Imitate traditional methods and then hide behind them? Or can he instead do better and find some alternative?

Then a thought occurred to him. He peeked through the end glass of the incubator to see whether the papyrus had been written in columns, and, Allah be praised, it was. At least he could, as a last resort, make a series of trimming cuts if need be.

Now with the scientist's mind at ease, he began thinking about his papyrus, and for some odd reason, the long red entranceway carpet of the nearby Nile Hilton Hotel came to mind.

* * *

"Mr. Robertson! Thank you so much for finding some time for me in your busy schedule," Dr. Rashid said, while reaching across the desk and shaking the conservatively dressed, middle-aged man's hand.

"It was the very least that I could do, Dr. Rashid. After all, it is not often that a museum official asks to speak to me about our hotel. Instead it is our guests who visit your fine museum. But, sir, what was it that my secretary said, something about our carpeting?"

"No, Mr. Robertson," Rashid began. "I was just curious to know where you send your carpeting to be professionally cleaned. And in particular, to whom do you send your long red entrance carpet?"

Surprised by such an operational question that he did not have an answer for, the hotel manager reached for his telephone, punched in some numbers, briefly waited, and started asking questions. Listening to the person on the other end of the line, he began writing down an address on the notepad before him. Finishing the conversation with a grunt of thanks, he then turned to the museum curator.

"Well, sir. You're in luck. The firm that we retain for such maintenance is located here in Cairo. Here is its address," The man said as he tore off and extended the sheet of paper. "May I ask, sir, why are you interested in such a subject?"

"Mr. Robertson, I have always admired your hotel's appearance. It is just that our museum's carpets are sorely in need of some care. Thank you again, sir, for your time and kind assistance."

* * *

Rashid was not at all surprised at the carpet cleaning firm's Khan al-Khahlili address nor its location deep within that famous and frenetic marketing district. Famously known for its factories and shops of authentically reproduced ancient artifacts, jewelry, automotive parts, perfumeries, plumbing supplies, bedding, and mothballs, everything that one could imagine could be found there. Sometimes just finding an address within that bazaar presented a challenge, even for those who were born and raised in the city. But find it Rashid did along a narrow side street located near the Mosque of el-Mutahhar. Upon entering, the Egyptian was overwhelmed with the smell of cleaning chemicals and damp moisture as he was confronted with a veritable forest of hanging and drying carpets of every color, design, and description.

Then, as if out of nowhere, the owner appeared, and noting Rashid's coat and tie, bowed solicitously and said, "Good morning, sir, I am at your service. How might I help you?"

"I am Dr. Rashid," the curator began. "I am the Chief Curator of the Cairo National Museum. I have just left the Nile Hilton Hotel, where I spoke with its manager, who told me that your firm cleans its long red entrance carpet. Is that so?"

Brimming with pride, the proprietor replied, "Oh, yes, Doctor. It is. The Nile Hilton Hotel is one of our very best and most satisfied customers."

"Well then, I am curious, just how can you clean such a long and beautiful carpet so evenly and well?"

"Why we employ hard workers, and in the case of the Nile Hilton's carpet, we use a particular method that assures only the best quality of cleaning."

"The carpets of our museum too are in need of some care. May I see your process?"

"Why, most certainly, Doctor!" as Egyptian pounds began to swim through the owner's eyes.

* * *

By the time Rashid had completed his tour of the carpet cleaning facility, he had a firm idea on how he would tackle the unrolling and drying of his papyrus roll. Since it measured no more than thirty-five centimeters in width, the racking system that he envisioned would not need to be much over forty-five. Since sheer length was the crux of the issue, he decided to enlist the main internal hallway of the museum's administrative suite as his unrolling and drying area. As access to it was limited to the museum's staff, security should not be an issue. The curator then ran the idea past the museum director for her approval, which he instantly received.

With his laundry list of materials in hand, he next paid a visit to the museum's maintenance manager, a personal friend, informing him of just what sort of mischief he was up to. After a brief discussion, he successfully enlisted his aid and considerable ingenuity. As a result, three days later, Rashid had his unrolling and drying racking in place.

It was a thing of beauty, but only from a certain point of view. First, the maintenance manager had two of his best carpenters fashion eight identical, eight-foot ladder-like frames constructed with rust-proof screws and latching mechanisms so that they all could be easily attached to one another lengthwise and interchangeably. Next, each frame had a fine linen cloth tightly and smoothly stretched across its uppermost side, which was then stapled in place. Rightly proud of their work, the carpenters appeared at first glance to have manufactured eight, narrow, old-fashioned airplane wings.

The next detail to be applied turned out to be the most expensive – the fiberglass screening material. Fortunately, the screening came in one meter wide rolls, so the ever thrifty maintenance manager bought precisely one half of what he required, full knowing that once he was back at the museum, he would have the roll carefully cut lengthwise with centimeters to spare. Then, Rashid showed up on the last day with the last element of his plan – a sack full of wooden clothespins.

The entire idea behind Rashid's racking design was to carefully and evenly dry out the papyrus roll and flatten it at the same time. Working with two of his most experienced assistants, they first pinned down the end of the fiberglass screening to the underside of the first frame and left the remainder of the material rolled. Then Rashid, wearing cotton gloves, came over with the fragile papyrus roll, placed it down at the first frame's end, and gently began to unroll it, which it readily did given its state of hydration. With a good three feet of papyrus so exposed, his assistants then delicately began to roll the screening over it, stopping here and there to gently stretch the flexible material across the still-damp papyrus before they secured the taunt screening down with clothespins to the frame's edge. This process was repeated about every three feet. Eventually, frames number two, three, and four were locked into place, then five and six, and finally number seven. Fortunately, the eighth frame was not needed, although Rashid knew that bets were being placed among the carpenters on any number of possibilities.

By the day's end, the papyrus had quite noticeably relaxed as it dried in place. The osmotic transfer of moisture from the papyrus to the linen backing had worked perfectly. The soft and flexible plastic-coated screening, which provided an even pressure across the entire papyrus surface, did harm or inhibit the drying process. His two assistants, constantly hovered over the forty-two feet of racking like busy bees in search of nectar, fussed over the screening, stretching it here and tightening it down there, administering to any stubborn section of papyrus a squirt of finely misted distilled water. The clear result was that drying and flattening process was proceeding very well and all because of a visit to a carpet cleaning establishment.

In fact, it was all happening so quickly, so efficiently, that Rashid almost had to pinch himself in disbelief. As he slowly strolled along the papyrus' length, he marveled at all of the neat vertical columns, all penned in black ink. He saw no holes, no erasures, nor accidental blobs of ink – all marks of a careless scribe.

No. This is a first-class papyrus. It's in extraordinary condition and I'm going to make sure that it stays that way! He silently vowed.

Now, he continued. *I need that photographer. I want this digitally recorded as soon as possible, while it is still in this pristine and intact state.*

* * *

Having finished a rough draft of his translation of the Well Corridor Inscription, Milson's laptop signaled him. There were another cluster of e-mails from Louis Bando. This time six in all and each jam-packed with a zipped attachment.

His first thought? *Oh my! What have we here?*

Pushing aside the draft translation, Milson again began the task of carefully backing up the data, copying it to his laptop's internal drive, and finally squirreling away a backup on the memory stick that he returned to his personal desk safe.

That administrative task out of the way, he then focused on a printout of Bando's first e-mail that explained the logic behind his mad numbering convention for all the digital imagery of eleven pillars that made up the side chamber's inscriptions. While his system all made sense, it was the Jamaican's last paragraph that really caught Milson's attention.

> Well that's all for now. This afternoon, I'm off to Cairo. Dr. Rashid says that he has the Annex Papyrus, that's what he's named it, ready for shooting. When I'm finished with that, expect another zipped and encrypted data dump from me!
>
> All the best - LB.

"'Ready for shooting,'" he murmured to himself. "How did Rashid unroll that papyrus so fast? That's a slow and nerve-racking process that usually takes months!"

Sighing deeply, the Egyptologist unconsciously scratched his head, thought, considered, rejected, and then finally decided that he would e-mail Rashid.

But on what pretext? Philological? No. Rashid wouldn't be able to field such a question and would become suspicious if I did.

Resigned, the emeritus professor decided not to contact the busy curator. If he needs me, he'll get in touch. Besides, I still have a ton of work before me to deal with before I can look at that papyrus.

Now where was I? Ah, yes, Bando's intricate numbering convention.

* * *

It was difficult to know who was more surprised. Rashid that Bando was so readily available. Or Bando that the Annex Papyrus was ready and all set to go for digital reproduction. Regardless, as soon as Bando was finished recording and transmitting the Annex Inscriptions to Milson, he was on the next train to Cairo. But before he left, he promised Sharil that he would return once he was finished in order to thoroughly shoot the evacuated Aten facility.

A quick glance at Louis Bando's *curriculum vitae* was proof enough that he had digitized many a papyrus. But never before in his entire life had he cast his eyes on one in such a pristine state, so perfect and so long! Without any doubt in his mind, this was going to be his greatest digital production. And with that sole thought in mind, he began planning in his mind how he would set up his gear and under what conditions.

"Dr. Rashid. May I have a few moments of your time?"

"Why certainly, Mr. Bando."

"Several things, first, is it possible for me to work during the evening and early morning hours, when the staff would not be underfoot?"

"Absolutely. In fact, I can arrange for that immediately. I believe that you said, 'several things.' What else do you require?"

"Do you want me to shoot IR shots as well?"

"IR, Mr. Bando?"

"Infrared, Dr. Rashid, in order to reveal whether there were any scrapings, erasures, and the like."

"If you have the capability, then please shoot IR as well."

"One other thing, Dr. Rashid."

"Yes, Mr. Bando."

"I have never seen such a pristine papyrus. In fact, I seriously doubt that the IR shots will reveal anything at all. But I wanted you to know that I consider it an honor to have been asked to record such a magnificent artifact."

"Mr. Bando, it is I who am so honored and relieved as well. You see, Dr. Sharil Moussa thinks so very highly of you. Please understand. I am a mere conservator. Right now, I have a pristine papyrus on my hands that is out of its natural element and will do nothing henceforth but deteriorate. And I am helpless to do anything about it. But your records will preserve that which I and my overworked staff cannot. As far as I see the situation, you, Mr.

Bando, are my savior. And if you need anything whatsoever, please call me. I have written my home phone as well on the back of my card. Here it is."

As the chief curator handed the stunned Jamaican his card, he looked him straight in the eye and added, "Mr. Bando, whatever the hour of the night or day, please use that telephone number."

"Yes, sir," was all that Bando could manage to say.

* * *

After a half day of preliminary setup and two nights of nonstop shooting, Bando had his imagery. It just had been so easy once he and that clever maintenance manager had rigged up that wheeled cart.

With his camera and its attachments in place, hovering over the papyrus at an absolutely optimal distance of ten inches, it was just a matter of numbering the column, center, focus, and click three times to bracket the shot. Roll the equipment over about three inches and number the column, center the next column of text, focus, and click, click, click again. This process was repeated for each of the papyrus' sixty-four columns of text, three times, once each in black-and-white, color, and IR.

In Bando's e-mail transmission of the imagery to Milson, he gave the Egyptologist all the necessary details.

Dear Prof. Milson:

Here is the imagery and particulars regarding the Annex Papyrus.

Overall length: 13.7 meters. Certainly not the 43.2 meter world record, but it's longest that I have ever recorded!

Width: 33 centimeters. Above average in size.

Column width: ca. 12.4 centimeters.

Column length: 12 or 13 lines of text.

Column gap: ca. 7.2 centimeters.

Upper/Lower margins: ca. 6 centimeters.

```
Condition: pristine. No holes or any
evidence of deterioration. An extremely
high quality artifact.

Surface: recto only, very smooth.

Text: 64 total columns. Black ink only.
Florid, but neat hieratic maintained
throughout, clearly produced by only one
very smooth hand. Probably left-handed to
judge from the tilt of some columns.

Given the high quality of this papyrus, I
had seriously doubted that the IR imagery
would reveal anything - and I was correct.
Nonetheless, I have included them for your
review, in case I have missed anything of
importance.

Annex Papyrus imagery numbering convention:
BW1 = black-and-white column 1; C1 = color
column 1; IR1 = infrared column 1, etc.

All the best - LB
```

* * *

Two days later, Milson believed that he had a solid translation of the Well Corridor Inscription, a.k.a. "The Care and Feeding of the Aten." He then sent a digital copy to Dr. Sharil Moussa for her review, promising in his e-mail that his original transcription and notes in hard copy were also en route by snail mail.

Now that his desk was cleared for all of thirty seconds, he bypassed the files of the side chamber's, now referred to as the Annex Inscription, and instead called up the black-and-white file of the Annex Papyrus' first column. Call it intuition, but he suspected that the papyrus' transcription and translation would have to be handled by another expert in the field, one more appropriately acquainted with the cursive form of ancient Egyptian writing, a script known as hieratic. And from what he saw on his laptop, it was definitely hieratic.

Now a far more delicate issue confronted him. Just who should be allowed to work on this papyrus? Surely no one in his department was qualified, much less held a security clearance of any kind, to have access to such a document. If it had been written in Demotic, well, then he could have made a cogent case for several of his own, but such was not the case.

Then Milson began to think outside the box. If I had my druthers from among all the Egyptian hieratic scholars in the world, just who would be the best and most logical choices? Not many, he concluded. There was one at Johns Hopkins, one at Göttingen, one in Tel Aviv, and another in Moscow, or was it St. Petersburg? Now given those four, who could be cleared, much less available?

Sigh.

I'll have to e-mail Sharil with the bad news!

* * *

Regardless of age, whether young or seasoned, scholars hate to turn down projects and hate to admit even more that they are unsuitable for a task. Nonetheless, Milson knew his own limitations well enough to squarely face that intellectually harsh reality. When he begged off the hieratic papyrus, he absolutely threw himself into the transcription and translation of the eleven pillars that made up the so-called Annex Inscription.

Studying the floor plan of the Annex and rereading his hard copy of Bando's imagery naming convention, he found the photographer's logic as a sound as ever. Given that the inscriptions of the entrance archway to the Annex were separately identified and numbered as such, all the sequences within the Annex were identified in a clockwise fashion. So, facing into the Annex from its doorway, the first pillar on the left was Pillar A, the second on the left B, and so on until Pillar J, the first on the right, with Pillar K signifying the shorter, central pillar. The four sides or panels of each pillar were similarly identified in a clockwise rotation, but this time with a number from one to four, with the No. 1 Panel of each pillar being the one facing the central pillar. As for the central pillar itself, its panels began their counting from the one facing the Annex's entrance.

That understood, Milson decided to get his feet wet with Pillar K, the small central pillar, and then work his way around according to Bando's numbering convention, or depending on the logic of the central pillar's inscription, perhaps by some other scheme.

As before with the Well Corridor Inscription, the Egyptologist printed out all the imagery for each of the pillar's four sides, taped them together, and arranged them on his desk before him. Noting that the inscription's flow went from right to left, he soon found its beginning and began to copy and transcribe what was before him. As the entire inscription contained a far shorter message than that of the Well Corridor Inscription, the philologist was ready to draft a rough translation within an hour's time. Sitting back again for his "magic time" moment to again occur, Milson instead found that his usually unfettered and free-form mind was stunned in honest disbelief. Shaking his head as if he were a horse with a pesky fly biting at his ear, he rebooted his brain.

Let's see now, as he began to soberly rehash and reconsider what he had just absorbed. *Did I read that right?*

Dazed by its content, he decided to just write it all out and let the chips fall where they may. After several moments of wordsmithery, he had his first rough draft.

Panel 1

Year 16, The Great One, Akhenaten, commanded me, Paneshy,|

First Servant of the Aten, to cause this to be recorded for all eternity.|

Panel 2

I, Akhenaten, the *sheut* of the Aten [disk] (whose) name is The-Most-Hopeful-One,|

have existed as one for myriads of years. (I, Akhenaten) am the first surveyor (?),|

(who) came before all others (?).|

Panel 3

(I, Akhenaten) am the eyes and ears of my surveyor household (?) [community? family?],|

[for I] am the first one to seek the first fountain (?) [source?] of life.|

That most primal mound from which all myriads of life arose.|

Panel 4

> (I, Akhenaten) out of concern that others are plotting evil (?) [against me?], |
>
> (I) have caused this accounting to be. The words [papyrus] wrapped [encased] in fragrant cedar wood|
>
> are the broken (?) [imperfect?] accountings of my many wanderings among the stars of Nut.|

"Well I'll be," the old Egyptologist murmured to himself.

"Imagine. Here on Earth, sometime either before or during the late Eighteenth Dynasty, a sentient being, and apparently quite an explorer from the look of things, visits us. Then he's thoughtful enough to leave behind his 'memoirs,' so to speak. And why does he? Because he senses that we're hot on his trail, 'that others are plotting evil.'"

After pausing a moment to thoroughly digest this thought, another came unbidden.

I must contact Sharil. That papyrus cannot be worked on by just anyone; its contents are just way to hot!

* * *

Sharil had to smile at the day's second e-mail from Milson and his concern as to who should work on the Annex Papyrus. The list of possible candidates that Milson had shared in his first missive she all knew as academic colleagues, some as friends, and others as anonymous, but well-known names in the academic literature. But the papyrus' security was not a concern to her, as she was working on it already and said as much in her response to Milson's concerns.

How interesting, she mused.

That instructions for "the care and feeding of the Aten," as Milson so aptly encapsulated it, would accompany the Aten's water source, as if it were meant to be knowledge to be passed down generation after generation to the First Servants of the Aten. Then in Year 16, the situation seems to have suddenly changed from a generational focus to one requiring far more immediacy.

With these thoughts in mind, she returned to her examination of Bando's superb digital imagery of the papyrus' first column of text.

Unlike Milson's method, Sharil instead printed out individual columns on oversized photocopy paper, preferring to make her notes directly alongside the digital image.

Quietly nodding her head in agreement with Bando's initial assessments, the author was left-handed, for individual wisps, tailings, and symbol connectors among the cursive characters had given away that detail quite independently of the subtle lean or tilt of the column's dense text. As the papyrus began to "speak" to her, Sharil took note of the style of the author, the sometimes convoluted use of words, where the author had struggled with the ancient vocabulary, and sometimes had failed miserably, the grammatical tendencies, and the inevitable quirks. By her second column, Sharil saw the beginning of an organizational plan, a sort of outline to the papyrus. Going on her intuition, she jumped ahead, quickly scanning first this column, then another, and yet another, finally settling in on the final column.

Yes! She triumphantly screamed with mental victory.

Milson had been right and so have I! This papyrus' organization is based upon an initial introduction, followed by a list of sixty-two interstellar waypoints, with what appears to be coordinates, descriptions, and observations for each. The final column contains a final note on our very own planet!

* * *

Dr. Sharil Moussa's "magic moment" was correct in all respects. However, the final and authoritative edition of this highly classified papyrus and its commentaries: literary, technical, and scientific, required two and a half years for an interdisciplinary staff of scholars and scientists to complete along with over seventy-two hours of computer processing time. Such silicon horsepower was required in order to first decode and then extrapolate upon all the coordinates listed, while simultaneously balancing and juggling the constant movement of the entire galaxy *over time*. The bottom line was the successful plotting of the bread-crumb trail of an interstellar wanderer's journey, whose place of origin was located in a star system near our galaxy's core. As to how long he, she, or it had been on this galactic sojourn, no one could directly calculate. Nor did anyone even bother, for the duration of time was simply, *relatively*, unimaginable by human standards.

* * *

Much to Milson's initial disappointment, the text of Pillars A through J from the Annex appeared to be stock, Atenist prayers offered by the Pharaoh Akhenaten on the behalf of his people. But as the Egyptologist slogged his way through the dense and sometimes repetitive religious text, he noted a certain personal sadness to the words, almost at times verging on a dark melancholy that tickled at the edges of his perception. Finally finished and sitting back in his chair, he thought out loud.

"This reads almost like Christ's plea at the Garden of Gethsemane! The man knew that his time was up and was resigned to it!"

CHAPTER XLII

Another First Semester

As Richards sat in the sanctity of his office, he had to admit that things had really changed over the past year, and for that matter, he himself had changed as well. Somehow that marvelously mellifluous Latin phrase *mutatis mutandis* came to mind, which when roughly translated comes out as "what must be changed has been changed."

Professionally, he had become a published scholar with his textbook on Egyptian philology, *The Scribe's Way*, with its first run of three hundred copies exhausted. Already the university press' chief editor clamored for edits prior to its second printing. Several knowledgeable scholars in the field had reviewed it and most quite favorably. Some had comments and criticisms that in the main were either quite reasonable or just flat wrong. However, one had really stung the young scholar. A French reviewer had simply savaged the work, saying that it was "a thoroughly unsubstantiated attempt to turn the study of the ancient Egyptian language on its head," along with several other generously offered and deconstructive assertions. Openly vexed, Richards had approached Milson about the review, who, to his surprise, had also read it.

With a chuckle, he said, "Joseph. Consider the source! You know, Joseph, not everyone in this world has walked in your shoes. Get used to their innocent ignorance. Build some callus around that sensitive ego of yours. And while you're at it, look up this guy. Check out what he's written and note what his peers are saying about him. I guarantee that the exercise will be most enlightening."

Given such a well-defined course and with more than just casual motivation, Richards found out precisely what his seasoned mentor was getting at. The reviewer in question was an academic hack, whose principal contribution to Egyptian philology was as a compiler of other people's facts, an editor of philological colloquia, and, as rated by his own countrymen, was considered at best a fair philologist. In short, Richards concluded, this poor, sad man had never generated an original thought in his life, but from this revelation came another, one far more meaningful to the young Egyptologist. The notion that one must push against the walls of the establishment in order to discover new limits, and that process is neither easy nor should be taken lightly.

As a result of that semester's first departmental faculty meeting, something else became apparent. Richards was no longer considered Milson's pet PhD candidate, who could not to be trifled with. In fact, Richards got the clear sense that several of his colleagues were jealous of his involvement with van der Boek's topographical work at Karnak, and the project's implied clout within the Egyptian Antiquities Organization in particular. While the derogatory comments were aimed obliquely at no one in particular, they nonetheless centered on "summer jaunts in the field," "shameful what dirt archaeology has come to," and the like. These barbs, while surprising, did not ruffle Richards quite as much as that Frenchman's book review had. Instead, he remembered noting how tanned, clear-eyed, and ripped his body must have seemed to these eternally nocturnal library rats. Then looking closely and recalling just who had said what, he sadly saw how pasty pale the complexion of their middle-aged faces were, the sag of their paunches, and the delicate rice paper-like quality of the skin on their hands. A typical day's archaeological labor would have killed them all. So, quite suddenly, Richards realized that such snide remarks coming from such personalities, he could easily discard. After all, he soberly assessed, had he not during his brief lifetime already killed one in cold blood? Assisted in the assassination of two, collaterally dispatched six Medjay warriors, and outright murdered potentially hundreds as a disease carrier? While unimaginable horrors all, Richards was sure that none of these people could have done what he had if their very lives had depended on it.

And here I patiently sit, he concluded. *A cobra among so many fattened rabbits.*

Finishing that thought, he looked down at his hands beneath the conference table and saw a mild tremor. Balling them into tight fists, he commanded them to stop, and mercifully they did.

Also mentioned at that first departmental meeting was the acknowledged success of his book on philology. While none took any offense that it had been so rapidly written, and then so quickly accepted by their own university's press, none of his colleagues had chosen to adopt it for their classes either. But even this, Richards knew, would change with time. After all, he wisely reasoned, adopting my book, or anyone else's for that matter, would require them to rewrite all of their lecture notes that were already so fragile and yellowed with age as to be considered artifacts themselves, wanting only a museum catalog number.

Then the chair announced the reckoning of last year's class enrollments, followed by the official tabulated results of the campus student reviews. Given that the typical enrollment for an Egyptian Philology 100 course was six to eight individuals, Richards' rather gaudy count of twelve for the first semester and twenty-two in the second were considered as noteworthy as they were commendable by the departmental chair. As in the business world, so also in the academic world, positive cash flow was recognized as a good thing, especially since the rest of the teaching staff pulled in an average head count of only 5.2 heads per lecturer for the two semesters. Richards easily recognized the visual daggers being thrown his way, but chose to remain silently oblivious to them.

But when the student reviews were orally recounted by the departmental chair, that was when Richards became embarrassed, not so much for himself, as for his colleagues, who went on a rant about the rigors of professional teaching standards, class preparation, student favoritism (another veiled but obvious swipe at him), and the posing of the eternal question: what value should a student rating be granted to a degreed professional? Blessedly, the chair had chosen not to read Richards' student review scores. Apparently, even he had the good sense to see that the effort was not worth the potential for further bad blood.

Finally came the doling out of the first semester classroom assignments, not the classes themselves, for all knew well in advance of their loads, just where the classes physically would meet. Since the classrooms on the second floor of the Near Eastern Institute were small, upper division and graduate classes tended to fill them up, while the introductory courses with their larger class sizes naturally required more room. To the absolute glee of his colleagues, Richards had been assigned three classes that semester, two introductory and his first second year philology course. To his colleagues, this was considered a near academic death sentence. To Richards, it represented his best opportunity to form his own following. As for the chair, he just saw dollar signs.

After the meeting, Milson invited his young colleague over to his office for a chat. Richards had long ago learned that "a chat" with his good friend John could just as well mean an old-fashioned verbal horse-whipping. So he entered the professor emeritus' office gingerly. But when Milson closed the door, Richards knew something quite definitely was on the man's mind and that he was about to hear it straight from the horse's mouth.

Sitting himself down and folding his hands in front of him, Milson began, "Joseph. I just want you to know that I was extremely proud of you today. You showed 'em good! Your classes' head count killed the bastards! The chair did not even dare to quote your student review numbers! And they all knew it!"

Then the man shifted gears.

"Now, my friend, you were too silent today. Several shots were fired at you and several hits were made. Right now, the bastards are betting that you'll burn out quickly so they can go back to their old and musty ways of doing things around here. But don't you dare! You continue on doing what you're doing! Be cordial. Be civil with them at all times. But do not, I repeat, do not trust a single one of them and that includes the chair. Now, Joseph. For a man who has done so much, how could you keep your mouth shut in that meeting?"

"Well, John, I thought about that, and as I looked around the room, I made a decision."

"And that decision was?"

"That I am going to outlive them all. That today was a minor skirmish of a greater battle of a far vaster war. That said, I am going to slowly start a revolution in Egyptian philology that neither they nor anyone else can stop."

"Damnation, Joseph! I am so glad to hear you say that."

CHAPTER XLIII

Yet Another Teleconference

It had been a while, and as things would soon develop, far too long since the two respective panels had faced one another eye-to-eye. After all, it was three days past Hollow's Eve, and Richards and Gregorieva had together returned safe and sound in late July. In their defense, the American side had been busy first finding, then extracting, and now starting the analysis of the Aten craft and its associated cultural remains. That the Americans were expecting to find their Russian colleagues had become a bit cool during the interim would have been an understatement. While Dean Young was fully expecting that frigid blast, he could not prepare for the actual arrival of it.

It all began so civilly.

The Americans again expressed their pleasure at having the opportunity to speak with their Russian colleagues. To which the Russians responded with neutrally scripted and diplomatic jargon directed back at their esteemed American partners. Then it fell all apart at the seams as the Americans praised the Russian's choice of Vesna Gregorieva, whose performance in the field in the Westerner's words "clearly exceeded all expectations."

Unbeknownst to Young that with that pregnant statement, he could not have rankled the Russians more, because Gregorieva was not expected to survive, much less succeed, much less return, and that included Richards as well.

Then there was the issue of her having delivered the initial death blow. After all, hadn't those Americans asked for a woman? Well, the Russians gave them one. That she was qualified, there was no doubt.

But there was more. By all accounts, she was a loose cannon, a headstrong woman, a free thinker. On top of that, she had worshipped Piankoff, who incidentally was also the only one who seemed to be able to control her. Apparently, Richards could now as well, and they were stuck with her as their temporal field agent! How could she be their representative of their way of doing things, of their agenda! They did not dare wash her out for any reason, in favor of another, for those Americans would get suspicious.

Behind their carefully neutral visages, Ostrogorsky, Drazinzka, and Rosovec were trapped men all. Men trapped by their own plans within plans. Worst of all, they had to learn to live gracefully with the situation – somehow.

Following this American encomium devoted to their temporal field operative, Rosovec innocently asked when she again might be deployed with Dr. Richards, specifically regarding the whereabouts of the Aten craft itself.

To this question, the most delicate question that the Americans knew would arise, Professor Milson answered directly, "Gentlemen. Regarding the whereabouts of the Aten craft. It has been located. It and several intriguing cultural artifacts have been recovered."

Pause.

Milson did not do so for theatrical effect, but because of what he saw from half a world away. All three Russians had stood as one and glared in total, silent disbelief at what their ears had registered.

Milson continued, "Consequently, we wish to invite multiple representatives from each of your respective departments to our country to assist us in the technical analysis of the Aten. Specifically, a materials scientist, a physicist, an aeronautical engineer . . ."

"You wish to invite us to the United States? To participate in an analysis that has already begun?" Rosovec stated with complete disbelief in his voice.

Ostrogorsky, with his eyes bulging in rage, managed to then squeeze out, "Found, already recovered, and is now under intense study. AND NOT ONE DAMN WORD COMMUNICATED TO US FOR THE LAST, WHAT, HOW MANY MONTHS! YOU AMERICANS ARE NOTHING MORE THAN DISHONEST, UNTRUSTWORTHY GANGSTERS!"

The Russian spat out that proclamation with a level of vitriolic emotion, the proportions of which had not been seen by the West, since perhaps the height of the Cold War with the downing of U2 pilot Gary Powers.

Then, motioning off-camera, the florid Russian made the universal signal of running his forefinger across his throat, and, to no one's surprise, the feed from Moscow ended with a white screen of mild audio static.

Jung quickly asked a technician, "Did they totally cut the transmission or is it on standby?"

After a few moments, the answer came. "Only on standby, sir, but as you can see, the audio and video are trash."

"Good." Said Young. "Let them stew. With luck, we still have some hope that they'll rejoin our conference call."

* * *

"Those bastards, those Goddamn bastards, those Goddamn fucking bastards!" Ostrogorsky stated over and over again like some sort of a therapeutic mantra until his voice began to break and his chest began to heave with exertion.

Then silence, followed by a chuckle that began slowly to erupt from Drazinzka, who up until now, had remained silent.

Needless to say, Ostrogorsky's head snapped quickly in his direction.

"Karlov! Just what's got into you! Don't you realize what the Americans are up to! They're going to, to . . ."

"Yes, Vasily, I believe I do. And now they have serious egg on their face. But, Vasily, listen to me, my old friend. They told us what they did. They 'came clean,' as they like to say. And, my old friend, they now want us to assist them in the analysis. So, Vasily, where's the beef?'"

At first, Ostrogorsky could not believe what he was hearing, but as he considered Karlov's words, he too began to understand.

"So," Ostrogorsky croaked out, "the Americans are embarrassed with their unilateral actions. Or, had a sudden moment of conscience. Or, potentially even more delicious, have run into a snag with their analysis and now have come to us."

"Precisely, my colleague, I could not have summed up the situation any better. And, Vasily, did you see who among them had the guts to tell us? The Egyptologist Milson, he is without doubt a most formidable one."

Throughout this entire exchange, Rosovec had not said a word. He just watched the interaction of these two old farts, took notes, and read lips. But he too had to agree on Drazinzka's assessment of Milson.

I just have to meet that man!

But in the next breath, Rosovec thought it nearly unthinkable that Drazinzka had allowed his ever-emotional colleague to blow up before the Americans in order to gain a position of righteous indignation.

Now looking over to the cameraman, Drazinzka asked, "How long have we been off the air?"

"Approximately four minutes, sir."

"Ah. Good." Now rubbing his hands together.

"Gentlemen, are we ready to make our demands?"

Two nods answered.

"Good. Technician. Turn us back on."

* * *

The sudden and quick return of the Russians clearly startled the Americans, who were quietly talking among themselves. In fact, Ostrogorsky took especial glee in loudly clearing his throat, which brought three very surprised faces to attention.

"Gentlemen," Ostrogorsky began, "we accept your invitation that representatives from our departments come to assist in the analysis of the alien spacecraft. What we will need from you is a list of those specialties that you require. Also, it would be convenient to know your timetable and where we should send our people. After all, America is a very big place."

* * *

"You know, Vasily, you really did overplay that."

"Yes, I know, Karly, but I did so thoroughly enjoy myself. And after all, I did blow up so spectacularly."

"Yes, you indeed did, my old friend. For a moment there, I feared for your health."

As for Rosovec, he could not believe what he had just heard, could not believe the game his colleagues were playing.

Chapter XLIV

Another Spring Break

It was difficult to believe that an entire year had passed. Brigitte, now married to a young broker of the Amsterdam financial district, was nearing the completion of her dissertation on the epigraphical styles of Eighteenth Dynasty private tomb narratives. Claude had successfully landed his first position as an assistant curator at the Royal Ontario Museum in Canada, primarily on the overwhelming strength of his rock solid photographic portfolio. The fact that he was part of van der Boek's topographical survey hadn't hurt him in the least bit either. As for Horst, he too had left van der Boek's nest and had started his own surveying firm in Jena.

Nevertheless, all had returned to Karnak eager and raring to go. Much to van der Boek's pleasure, all had remained mum as to what they were up to. He knew firsthand that the temptations had been great, but also there was a goodly amount of fear that this project could be a total bust. Before returning to the Continent at the end of that first season, the aging Egyptologist had told them about the roller-coaster ride of his academic experiences with such emotion, and now they had three funded seasons of preliminary work before them.

As the Dutchman had put it, "It is really very easy to remain silent in quiet anticipation of wonderful things, but it is really quite hard to say one thing and then have to face the ignominy of having to take it back."

And here I am left standing on the curb again, thought the Dutch Egyptologist. *Now just where are those Americans!*

Glancing down at his watch, van der Boek snapped back its leather covering, and then forced himself to temper his assessment.

Okay. Simmer down. They have eight minutes to get here.

But before he could look up from his watch, an all too familiar and cheerful greeting of "Good Morning, everybody!" filled his ears and brought a smile to his face. *Those Americans! And they're even early! God bless them!*

What van der Boek's trained eye noticed, however, was the clearly fragile state of Milson's approaching gait that evoked a sense of brotherly concern for the venerable Egyptologist. As for Richards, he looked as solid as ever and sported a closely trimmed, almost military-style haircut.

Van der Boek bellowed back, “Okay, Richards. What’s up? You’re early!”

To which peals of good-hearted laughter broke out, hugs of friendship, miles of smiles, well wishes, and the usual questions of “What’s up with you nowadays, huh?”

* * *

Both Milson and van der Boek were pleased to find that the core of the Fourth Pylon had not been disturbed. However, someone, most likely from the French mission, had decided to use the neatly cleared core area as a convenient garbage dump. This assessment was convincingly confirmed by the overwhelming proclivity of trash labeled in that language.

As Claude best put it, “It is to be expected. They have worked on this site for over one hundred years. Therefore, they believe that they have the right to deposit their very own midden layer for future archaeologists to puzzle through.”

By ten that morning, the faces of two familiar military civil engineers, Labib and Naguib, showed up for work driving the same ancient pickup truck, but towing a brand-new crane. When asked just how and where they had come across the nifty and agile-looking lifting device, Naguib deadpanned that he had just found it attached to the pickup. Labib shrugged his shoulders in mock innocence and stated that the Egyptian military had no use for it as it couldn’t lift a tank to repair its treads. This act that these two fun-loving and amiable clowns put on was greeted with gales of good-hearted laughter. And at the sight of the new “toy,” of course Horst wanted to know how everything worked.

Resting in the shade of the Hypostyle Hall’s massive columns during the noon break, the first annual bitch session broke out that discussed in detail the heat, the sweat, the dust, the blisters, and of course, the horse flies. To van der Boek, this was healthy banter and all in good jest, for the team had cleared out all of last season’s backfill, had uncovered the plastic tarp that showed no violation whatsoever, and even had swept clean the exposed eighteen steps.

With that muscle-bound Richards freed up from his logging duties, and that new crane operating, the fill extraction had occurred at a furious rate.

But what surprised van der Boek the most was Richards himself. Working and shoveling like a demon, the philologist's physical development, especially of his back and legs, became very apparent. With his wire-rims off, shirtless and in shorts, dripping wet in sweat, the man seemed to have an inhuman endurance. Then there were those scares across his back. Just how did he get those? And Richards' performance had not been missed by Brigitte's appraising eyes either or by the rest of the crew. As one, you could almost hear them state the question, "Just who is this Egyptian philologist?"

* * *

On Tuesday at 3:38 p.m., with Richards again on his stool in his familiar role as the expedition's scribe, he again recorded in the log the word "Bingo" as the intact edge of the passage's ceiling was encountered at the twenty-sixth step. Horst's measurements stated that the ceiling was precisely 2.625 meters high. Yes, precisely five old Egyptian royal cubits in height, all very much to van der Boek's ever growing glee. Claude did his part with the cameras and van der Boek triumphantly called it a day.

* * *

On Wednesday at 11:04 a.m., Richards again recorded "Bingo" as material began to fall away unsupported from along the ceiling line that left nothing but a black void beyond. Now at the twenty-eighth step, van der Boek called a halt to the progress and stated in an emotional and thickly accented voice, "Ve must now inform Cairo of vhat ve have found before ve can proceed. Dhen, ve vill clear vhat little remains here in preparation vor dher inspection of the passage."

* * *

On Thursday at 9:00 a.m., Richards recorded that he, the director of the EAO, his daughter Sharil, Milson, and van der Boek first entered the unblocked passage that had been cleared the previous day. With all carrying flashlights and Richards taking the lead, which van der Boek thought was more than a bit odd given the circumstances, they began to slowly descend the final steps of the ramp so as not to accidentally trip on any loose debris. With only the sounds of scraping footfalls lightly echoing upon their ears and surrounded by the passage's smoothed walls and ceiling, they began to notice that the air was gradually becoming noticeably more stuffy and stale.

During the near silent descent, each found themselves drifting deeper and deeper into their private thoughts. For van der Boek, who took up the rear, would he live long enough to see this project through to completion and publication? For Milson, who was allowed to proceed before van der Boek out of the Dutchman's European sense of deference, he was just happy to experience it all. As for Sharil, who followed literally in her father's footsteps, her mind was furiously churning.

Where have I seen this practical combination of steps and ramping before? Yes, in the Great Pyramid's Grand Galley, and again before Seti I's mortuary temple at Abydos! I'd wager that this passage can accommodate the dragging of truly heavy objects!

Following directly behind Richards was the massive bent frame of the director, whose back was just killing him. But all of these personal musings were suddenly broken as if they were delicate glass as Richards reached the bottom landing. Then he broke the silence by firmly stating, "I count ninety-five steps."

He then announced with an uncommon authority of command that demanded their attention, "All right, we are now at the entrance to the Treasury of Amen Re. What I want you all to do is stand here and please don't move any farther into this passage, as it's potentially very dangerous and most likely filled with booby traps. What I am going to do is walk to this corridor's end and then turn my flashlight's beam back to give you a sense of what we are up against. Then, I will return to this landing and then, and only then, we will proceed. Remember! Stay put," Richards said with considerable force. "Do not under any circumstances move any farther into this passage until I return to guide you."

With that said, off he went. With his echoing footsteps that slowly faded as he gained in distance, he shifted his flashlight's illumination this way and that for what seemed like forever to the quartet at the treasury's entrance. Finally, a single beam of light shown back and it seemed to be a mere speck, almost a distant star. As Richards began to make his way back to the entrance, tens of niches that led to adjoining rooms and subsidiary passageways began to appear in the shadows of his flashlight to his right and left.

Having returned to his colleagues, Richards huffed and puffed.

"Well, by my count, 373 steps to the opposite end of this central corridor. And the air's really poor. Any extensive investigations may require oxygen tanks, or maybe even really big fans."

That comment brought a broad smile of recognition to van der Boek's face.

"But for us, I just want to show you a couple of representative examples of the richness of the Egyptian nation's cultural heritage. Everybody ready? Okay, just remember to stay squarely in the center of this corridor. Go single file. Do not stray near any side passage. You will see why shortly."

After about forty steps, the train of scholars made their first stop as Richards knelt down on one knee and peered into a gap in the flooring to his left.

"People, this is a mantrap. Perhaps not all of these many side chamber entrances are so guarded. But I'm willing to bet that a good two-thirds of them are protected with a false plaster flooring that easily collapses under a man's weight."

The director then asked the question that had to be asked.

"But, Dr. Richards, what does the false flooring cover?"

"Pit shafts that are probably," now peeking in with his flashlight, "some twenty-five feet deep," replied the kneeling young man.

"Pits cut into the bedrock with smoothed walls. Pits deep enough to trap a man. Pits deep enough to break legs, arms, or worse. In fact, at the bottom of this one is ample evidence of its effectiveness."

Clustering in close, five flashlight beams filled the pit with their harsh glare. At the bottom was a grisly form bent back with two hideously broken legs.

"He was probably left behind by his greedy colleagues," Milson surmised.

Reaching over to an edge of the collapsed flooring, Richards easily broke off a fragment and handed the sample over to the EAO director, who examined it in the palm of his hand, and then crushed it between his thumb and forefinger with the comment, "Most treacherous."

Standing up, Richards unnecessarily stated, "Okay, again single file, stay in the corridor's center, and follow me."

About ninety steps later, the group again came to a halt, but this time before a right-hand chamber. Squatting down and heavily banging the heel of his Maglite flashlight at various points of its threshold to test its soundness, Richards then stepped forward and into the chamber.

Richards waited as they all entered the side chamber and what they all saw in the beams of their flashlights took everyone's breath away. All was silence and wonder for there in the center of the room, lying as if on display, was a light, portable framework of sorts with a narrow and aerodynamic fuselage with the tail of a glider. Off to the side was laid out with care its single, detachable, lifting surface painted as outstretched wings. Off to the other side were arranged a series of leather harnesses and belts and a shockingly authentic green, gold, and black hawk-headed helmet with broad shoulder flarings. While Richards fully understood what he saw, the others clearly did not. In fact, the EAO director demanded an explanation.

"As with so many things, it is really quite simple," Richards began.

"The ancient Egyptians, as you can see, must have mastered glider flight."

While he moved among the precious artifacts, he continued, "Here would be the glider frame that the rider would strap into, using all those leather appliances over there. Over here is the detachable, tear-away wing surface. And here is even the glider pilot's aerodynamic crash helmet."

The director just stood in the middle of the chamber with his hands on his hips and with eyes glazed over in disbelief. The phrase "sensory overload" just about covered it.

As for Sharil, she whispered, "Father, do you remember that second-century wooden glider model of Horus that we used to display in Room 22? Well, this discovery will be much, much more provocative."

Milson, forgetting that van der Boek was present, then directly asked Richards, "Well, did you ever have the opportunity to see whether or not this contraption can really fly?"

"Nope, but I know of at least two generations of priests that did fly such gliders," stated Richards with sureness.

"Und just how do you know dhat?" challenged an incredulous van der Boek, for the first time breaking his silence.

Richards, Milson, Sharil, and her father all visibly paled when they simultaneously realized that a serious breach had just been made.

Milson thought, *Oh, you doddering old fool! Now the shit is really going to hit the fan!*

Richards first thought was a far simpler. *Oops!*

That however was quickly replaced with one of Piankoff's more memorable and colorful lessons of field craft: "When life serves you a full helping of shit, then you had better know how to cook it before you are forced to eat it raw."

So with those tender words of wisdom still freshly in mind, Richards quickly broke the uneasy quiet.

"Well, Professor van der Boek, that's more than fair question. And it is one that I can answer this way. Were you not the excavator of the high priest Meryptah's tomb?"

"Ja," croaked out van der Boek in surprise.

"And is it not true that the autobiographical text from Meryptah's tomb contains some rather curious references to 'falcon fliers,' 'soaring on the winds of Re's warm breath,' and the high priest himself being referred to as a teacher of 'falcon men'?"

Now, with some heat mixed with shock, the Egyptologist replied, looking from the young philologist to the EAO director and back, "Okay, Richards. Just how do you know such dings? Especially since de Meryptah cache publication is still at the publisher and is due for release only next veek?"

"Professor van der Boek, I could lie to you and tell you that I had been granted early access to your research. But that would be a lie and outright insult to the trust that you have placed in the Egyptian Antiquities Organization, their representatives, and in particular, this fine man, its director. On the other hand, I could tell you the truth, and in so doing, I would have to betray the trust of many, but would gladly do so if required. Regardless of which you choose, I must insist on your word that you will never, ever, discuss this matter again outside of this chamber. It is your choice, Professor."

Van der Boek suddenly realized that he was seriously and quite literally out of his depth, deep underground, and although not physically threatened in any way, he had the sense on the basis of that voice of such cool and measured command that his career, if not his very life, might be on the line. But the old archaeologist's curiosity was just too great, for he had to know, come what may.

"Dr. Richards! Or vhomever you say you are. You have my vort as a gentleman that vhatever you tell me now that I vill not speak of ever again."

He then added, nodding in the director's direction, "Und I think dhat the director already knows just how gut my vort ist."

Richards, relaxing fractionally, then smiled.

"From me, Professor van der Boek, you should not be afraid. But from others quite definitely, most certainly, if they ever found out what I am about to share with you. First, Professor van der Boek, I am indeed Dr. Joseph Richards, and I can guarantee you that I am an Egyptian philologist and associate professor at the NEI in Chicago. John here can personally attest to that. What I can also tell you is that the high priest Meryptah was a wonderful man and one whom I knew personally, for in his time I was his adopted son, a man known as Mayneken."

Van der Boek's mouth went slack in initial disbelief, but then his eyes bulged in recognition at the mention of the name, Mayneken.

The young Egyptologist continued, extending his arms wide, "As to your question of 'just how do I know' all of this, for instance that this entire treasury is booby-trapped and that the Egyptians had glider pilots, well, I learned of these things from the aged and venerable Meryptah himself. And it was he who first led me down into this treasury, and who had described to me his very own glider experiences over Western Thebes as a young acolyte, which he described to me in his very own words as 'soaring on the winds as if he were Horus.' So, on the basis of his recollections and given the glider frame before you, I would expect that the ancient Egyptians did have the ability of extended glider flight."

"Ja. So it vould it seem. But how could you . . ."

Richards then uncharacteristically interrupted the archaeologist.

"Sir, I do believe that I have told you sufficiently enough, at least for the moment. Now please do not ask me to further jeopardize my own situation."

Wide-eyed, van der Boek just nodded and mumbled more to himself than anyone else, "Ja, ja. You indeed must be involved in somedhing most very secret."

The EAO director then stepped in and broke the seriousness of the moment.

"Well," rumbled the director. "I do believe that we have an incredible discovery on our hands. One that is both corroborated in a literary text and in artifacts as well. By the look of this so-called glider frame, I am quite sure that if we chose to consult some aerodynamic engineers that they would only confirm what we already know."

Shocking the Dutch archaeologist back into the here and now. "Professor Dr. van der Boek," announced the director. "Again the Egyptian nation has much to thank you for. Imagine finding evidence for the harnessing of manned glider flight during the Eighteenth Dynasty!"

Then turning to Richards. "And by the way, as if this revelation has not been enough for one visit, is there anything else that you wish to show us?"

"Not at this time, sir. However, I'm willing to bet that Dr. Rashid and his department are going to be very busy for the next decade."

"How so?" asked the director.

"Sir," Richards answered, "the full exploration and clearing of this complex by Professor van der Boek and his team could take years. I fully expect the warrens of this treasury to be quite extensive. And—"

The EAO director then interrupted Richards and turned to van der Boek.

"My friend, are you up to such a task?"

A wide-eyed and vigorous nod was his immediate response.

"Good. And I and the Egyptian Antiquities Organization will support your efforts in any way that we can, my old friend. Take my hand again," the director gently said, extending his open hand to the Hollander who took it.

Turning back to Richards, the director nodded to him to continue.

"As I was about to say, in fact, I suspect that you might even want to get in contact with the media. That would go a long way toward launching the basis for the needed funding for such an undertaking."

"Now you know, Dr. Richards," the director lectured with a wagging forefinger. "You think very much like my daughter does. As she has so many times told me that 'cultural preservation requires capital investment.' I find myself convinced much of the time with the logic of the argument."

With this comment by the director, both Sharil and Richards shared a knowing smile.

Now spreading his arms wide as if to encompass the entire treasury, he continued, "However, what we have here is something far greater than the discovery of another aspect of my culture's heritage. We have solid evidence of technological revolution. If we are to reap the rewards of such newfound intellectual capital, then we have to make it public! And the first step in that direction will require Willem here to publish and release to the public the Meryptah cache as soon as possible. And that he has accomplished. Then we let the media in on this, otherwise we leave ourselves open to all the fringe interests and quacks! What this treasury really represents is a puzzle to solve, a Pandora's Box."

Milson then smiled and said, "Yes. What you say is absolutely true. But I ask you, what a marvelously envious position to be in? With the publication of the Meryptah material, you begin the dialogue. With an up-front, negotiated media exclusive, perhaps with a reputable educational organization, your future funding woes will be instantaneously solved. Sharil here will be fighting off offers for other media exclusives, and with those, even more capital will flow into the EAO. My dear friend, this treasury represents a media gold mine. The Egyptian Antiquities Organization and the Cairo National Museum will flourish again, as will the pride of the entire Egyptian nation."

Now coming to his closing statement, the aging Egyptologist flatly challenged, "Sir, I urge you to move quickly and decisively on these matters."

With his arms crossed over his chest, the EAO director looked like a reluctant bear with a furrowed brow and slight frown. Pregnant moments passed as the others waited. Finally, the director cocked his head to his daughter and said, “Well my daughter, I have yet to hear from you. Surely you have an opinion on these weighty matters.”

Lapsing into a soft smile, he then gently pushed his question using an Egyptian idiom.

“Tell me, my daughter, what truly is in your heart.”

Standing erect and tall before her father, Sharil smiled and simply said, “My father. What we should do is inform the world of Egypt’s greatness. What we should do is proceed very carefully and deliberately with the media. What we must do before we leave this very chamber of ancient flight is to decide who history will record as the discoverer of this most remarkable find of finds. That and that alone will guide our course as nothing else will. The media will fixate upon it and all of the aspects leading up to the actual discovery. In short, my father, this is just too big to hide. That said, we must agree on our story and then stick to it.”

“I am sorry, my daughter, but I just cannot in good conscience award the discovery of this treasury to the French! That I just cannot do, no matter how politically convenient that may be. However, I do very much want to reward a certain Dutch archaeologist, who in the past had given me his word that he would remain silent about the Meryptah cache. And given his proven archaeological experience and his first-rate team, I am tempted very much to do so. But others must be included.”

Now looking directly at Richards. “Joseph.”

Milson saw Richards’ shock as this was the first time that the director had ever referred to him by his first name.

“I believe that your soon-to-be-very-close colleague Willem here will soon have great need of your formidable philological assistance. In fact, the more that I consider this, I believe that the two of you should be credited with the discovery. Is that agreeable with you?”

“Actually, sir,” Richards responded, “it would not be, although I would not mind being listed as a contributor to this effort. It has been honor enough to work side by side with such a well-respected Egyptian archaeologist and his team. I have learned a lot, but Professor van der Boek deserves the right, not I.”

"Agreed." The other three automatically answered, with only van der Boek remaining silent.

"Now, Willem," the director queried, "and what is in your heart that you wish to share with us?"

"I am afraid that I am bit confused. Perhaps it is my doddering age. But after all, Dr. Richards here was the one who first approached me with a research proposal based upon your department's recommendation. How can I be credited solely for this discovery?"

With a rueful shake of his head, he continued, "While grateful for the archaeological opportunity, I am not the driving force behind this momentous find. I just provided the means. So I personally would prefer that Dr. Richards was made a co-discoverer. After all, it was his philological evidence that suggested the possibility of such a find, which pointed to a general area of investigation. The fact that he possessed some sort of foreknowledge of this place is not part of this debate. Rather, what is important here is that we together were able to recover whatever was left behind."

"Willem, you are absolutely correct," stated flatly the EAO director, and turning to Richards, he then directly ordered, "Joseph, you too will be a co-discoverer. Any questions?"

"No, sir. In fact, I would be most honored."

Glancing down at his watch, "Well, I am pleased that we are in agreement. As for the rest for us, may I suggest that we exit this treasury, for all of this talk has made me very hungry," the director stated with mock seriousness.

* * *

Later that evening, following the earlier dinner celebration, a respectful knock was heard by van der Boek on his hotel door. Impatiently looking up from Richards' field notes that he reviewed every night, he curtly replied, "Enter."

At the open door stood Richards in a T-shirt and shorts, carrying what looked to be a heavy load. Jumping to his feet, the archaeologist helped him in and quickly discovered that the load that Richards was carrying was a box full of ice – from where he found that precious commodity he did not know – that fully smothered six one-liter bottles of Egyptian beer. Placing the box down with a slight thud in the middle of the floor, the young man looked around, saw another chair, grabbed it, sat down before the box, and declared, "Professor van der Boek. Whether you know it or not, I am here to assist you. Three of these frosty cold bottles of beer are yours and three are mine. I propose that we drink them now, while we still have the ice to cool them, and discuss whatever's on our collective minds. Whaddya' ya' say?"

Stunned and a bit taken aback at the blunt presentation, privately the Hollander had to admit to himself that his throat was a bit parched, that the cold beer did indeed look delicious, and that it had been high time to clear the air and loosen up. So in the moments that he considered these heady thoughts, a smile naturally formed on his lips, his eyes began to twinkle, and finally his vocal cords caught up.

"Ja. I vould like dhat very much."

"Great!" Richards replied as he quickly produced a church key that had been conveniently hanging from a string around his neck.

"I'm thirsty too."

The first beers quickly disappeared and were just as quickly followed up with belches. As the second pair was opened, Richards began to tell van der Boek his life's story. His early years as an itinerant Air Force brat, his natural language skills, his reasons for going to the university that he did, his football glories, and his recruitment by Milson. When the third bottles were opened, Richards continued with his training under Piankoff, and then he related some select travel experiences into the *somewhen*. At a point about halfway through his last bottle, Richards then explained to the Hollander why he was telling him so much.

"Frankly, Willem, I believe you to be a good man, but one suddenly placed in a very difficult situation. I want to help. Also, I believe that trust is formed between men when something precious is shared. I have done so at my peril and with several governments. Besides, you swore in the treasury that you would never speak of what occurred down there. I believe that you will keep your word. But that did not prevent me from telling you all that you needed to know if we were ever to successfully work together. Am I right?"

With moist eyes, the archaeologist replied, "Joseph, you are a true phenomenon. In fact, you Americans are so open, almost at times childlike. Indeed, with your sharing, you have relieved a great burden from my shoulders. I now can say that I trust you as well and look forward to working with you. But I do have just one question.

"How in the world did you scar your back so magnificently?"

CHAPTER XLV

Analysis of the Aten

On that early September day, Dr. Roy Allen Peters, now the Director of the Materials Technology Department and Laboratory at Wright-Patterson AFB, sorely needed some good news. What he needed was a diversion, a for-real project, some real stimulation as his current duties had become in the main purely administrative. Since the completion of the SNOWMAN analysis over a year ago, he had been getting stale and he knew it.

Then he got this weird e-mail from the wrench heads down in the Mechanical Engineering Department inviting him to one of their project meetings. Weirder still, his name was indicated as mandatory on the MS Outlook Calendar invitation and he had only fifty-five minutes to get there from here, way on the other side of the base. While put out, inwardly Roy was pleased that he now had a legitimate excuse to abandon all the paperwork on his usually pristine desk and credenza. Grabbing his windbreaker, Roy decided to walk, and upon leaving his corner office, informed his secretary that he was off to a surprise wrench-head meeting, and no, he didn't know when he would be back. Unknown to Roy, there was a world of truth in that statement.

* * *

To Roy's amazement, the wrench head's meeting turned out to be quite an affair, and their principle conference room was filling in with many familiar, but also many more unfamiliar faces by the minute. In particular, two truly stood out, a beautiful young woman with short cropped hair accompanied by a quite handsome middle-aged male with a full head of curly black hair.

Talk about two roses amid this patch of weeds!

Allowing his eyes to further wander, Roy spotted that even the base commander and his second were in attendance.

Deciding to sit in the back and take it all in, someone sat down next to him, settled himself, and then rather distinctly cleared his throat. Naturally, Roy looked over at the impertinent individual and received the surprise of his life, for grinning ear to ear and sitting less than three feet from him was his old buddy, Professor Jerry Graves. *Recently made a member of the emeritus faculty of MIT*, he thoughtfully added to himself.

"Well, Roy," his former mentor teased him. "Did I catch you daydreaming again?" He extended his tanned and thick Iowa wheat farmer's hand that was still quite firm.

Smiling with genuine pleasure at seeing the man, Roy moved over one seat closer and just drawled out in his best southern Indiana drawl, "Ah, nope. Just a-thinkin' about what next I can get myself in trouble with."

The Iowan's eyes then suddenly twinkled. "Careful, Roy, what you ask for."

Now all serious business, Peters asked, "Doc, now just what are you saying? Did you have something to do with me being here at a wrench-head meeting, of all things?"

"Could have," the Iowan allowed. "By the way, I read your final write-up of the SNOWMAN analysis. First rate, absolutely first rate."

Roy could not remember the last time he had blushed so, and given his fair skin and freckles, it was a reaction that he just could not hide. Looking down at his shoes, he said, "Thank you, Doc. Coming from you, well, it's just special."

"Not a problem. The fact is, Roy, that you are and have always been my very best student. You're sensible too. Now those are curiously frightening qualities to have for the head of a government research department," he said with a knowing wink.

And then the meeting began.

* * *

As the room quieted down, Roy noticed out of the corner of his eye that several security types had taken up positions in the back of the room. He also noted the absence of windows, and come to think of it, this room was located in the building's center. As the lead speaker began, Roy started to sense a feeling of *déjà vu* back to a certain brown-bag luncheon talk that he had attended a long, long time ago.

The British-accented speaker began, "Good afternoon, and thank you for gathering on such short notice. I know several of you literally just flew in and several of you from as far away as Moscow via Chicago."

Well, that explains all the new faces, Roy surmised.

"By way of introduction, my name is Dr. Paul Young. I am the Dean of Humanities at the City University that is located in Chicago. I am also the acting CEO of a research center known as the Philology Annex. Frankly, I need your help. But before I bring up the first digital image, I would like to emphasize that what you are about to see, and what we will no doubt discuss, must not leave this room. Would someone dim the lights?

"Now, for the first image."

Roy noted the slight intake of air from throughout the room.

"What you see before you is precisely what you think it is. It's a UFO."

Total silence.

"However, the ancient Egyptians referred to it as the disk, or more formally, as "The Radiant Aten." An appropriate appellation as it was found recently in the Egyptian desert and will arrive here, at Wright-Patterson, in approximately thirty days' time. Figure on or about Halloween. It is being flown in aboard, or should I say atop, the NASA 747 shuttle ferry."

Somehow the silence had become absolutely thick in the room. One could imagine the collective sound of everyone thinking: *"It's coming here!?!"*

"It would have been here sooner, except that the aeronautical engineers are trying to figure out how to securely mount the craft atop the plane's fuselage. Now to the question, why Wright-Patterson? Well, this craft is coming here in order to undergo its technical analysis. The best individual to head up that effort is in this room, your very own Dr. Roy Peters." The entire room began to crane their necks in search of him. "Who, as you all know, is currently the Director of the Materials Technology Department. As of this moment, Dr. Peters will be this project's Chief Investigator. Dr. Peters. You are here, are you not?"

Standing rather slowly on legs and knees that felt like rubber, Roy then raised his right hand in total shock.

"Well, Dr. Peters. Let me be the first to congratulate you on heading up this project. Your name came very highly recommended. And let me add as well, since you hold the title of Chief Investigator, that means that you are to do just that, investigate, build your team, and not push papers about. In short, we want you to be very hands on. You will be provided with a full administrative staff, a security detachment, and a dedicated budget manager to handle all the mundane day-to-day – stuff." At the word "stuff," Young dismissed it with a flick of his hand.

Immediately cheers and clapping erupted at the word "stuff." This, much to Dr. Young's surprise, took several minutes to quiet down with all the handshaking and backslapping that was going on. But finally, as with any storm, the room eventually quieted down.

"Well, Dr. Peters, you have about thirty days to prepare for the Aten's arrival. In preparation for its advent, here's what we already know about it. The disk-shaped craft weighs approximately eight thousand pounds and measures approximately forty feet in diameter, being about a third as thick in the middle."

As this preliminary data was being recited, Young's ego was pleased by all the bowed heads and plastic quills tapping it all down in their handhelds.

"As for its probable fuel, I am told that it drinks lots of water."

At the mention of "drinks lots of water," all heads rose as one in question, and then bowed down again as if in prayer before their personal devices.

"Well, up to this point, I have been the messenger. Now I think it best that I yield the floor to Dr. Peters. Dr. Peters, I am sure that you would like to share some thoughts with your colleagues, given the current challenge before you."

At this point, Roy's state of mind was still a blur. Finally, it was his beaming neighbor at his right elbow, Doc Graves, who nudged him back to the here and now, saying, "Well, Roy, my boy, the gang's all here and waiting on you. Now make me proud!"

* * *

By the time Roy Peters reached the front of the conference room, having found his wits, he smiled out to his audience, and said, "Okay, now. Let's see a show of hands for volunteers."

So it all began with a rapid fire of questions to his distinguished audience. They in turn responded to Peter's questions and challenges with their in-house jargon of quick and truncated scientific and engineering terms that left Young, the Oxford economist, befuddled. At which point, realizing that he was now totally extraneous, Young quietly took a seat. Also during this organizational and brainstorming session, Roy noted that five folks toward the back of the room were listening intently to the discussion, briefly huddling their heads, and then coming back up for air. Curious to find out just who they were, Roy halted this natural flow of the discussions in order to satisfy his curiosity and perhaps make these guests feel more a part of the meeting.

"Excuse me, for just one moment. I see that we have some guests sitting over to my right that I think none of us know. However, I suspect that they too might want to contribute to this harebrained free-for-all of a discussion. Just who are you folks, anyway?"

Several of five huddled Russians looked like they wanted to bolt as the entire room quieted down and turned to look at them. Finally, the tall and really good-looking one with the roguish black curly hair rose, smiled to all, and announced in English with a clearly British edge, "Why, thank you, Dr. Peters, for including us in your most interested discussion. I am Academician Stefan Rosovec, Director of Advanced and Theoretical Technological Research, a branch of the Russian Academy of Science. To my right," he indicated with a mildly theatrical wave of his right hand, "may I present Dr. Petr Dvorak, our group's astrophysicist, Dr. Iosef Stanislov, our distinguished thermodynamicist, Dr. Lubomyr Klibanov, our most daring theoretical engineer, and to my immediate left, Vesna Gregorieva, a member of the Special Projects Directorate of the Russian Academy of Science. Dr. Peters, you are correct. We are not here just to listen and scoot. Drs. Dvorak, Stanislov, and Klibanov are as of this moment on loan to you from the Russian Academy to assist your teams in any way possible. It is, of course, hoped that this gesture will be of assistance to you, given the formidable task at hand."

Silence.

"Well, Academician Rosovec," Roy answered. "That is a very generous offer and one that is much appreciated. Consider yourselves all permanent team members." Looking around the room, Roy then asked his audience, "So, okay. Where are all the stargazers in this room?"

One group of three raised their hands.

"Okay, Academician Rosovec, please send your astrophysicist over to them."

"Next, where are the wrench heads, as if I have to ask?"

This time, a tight group of six hands so indicated their location. "Academician, oh hell, Stefan, please send your wrench head over there."

"Wrench head?" Rosovec queried.

"Sorry, sir, your theoretical engineer."

"Ah, yes. Now I understand, I think," as some good-hearted laughter broke out. "Klibanov, please. Join those people over there."

"All right, now where are the atom crackers?"

And shortly, Stanislov found his proper place.

"Now," Roy continued, "I didn't catch what you two do."

"For now, Dr. Peters, we're just here to observe. Please proceed."

And proceed they indeed did, while the three Russian scientists on loan each received a crash course in American hospitality and the lively art of free-form discussion.

* * *

On the short flight back to Chicago from Dayton following the meeting, Rosovec and Gregorieva had a lot to discuss on the plane.

"I am jealous of them," Rosovec gloomily stated.

"Why is that?"

"Because those three have been thrust into perhaps the most exciting and exhilarating project of their lives, tasked to explore the unknown in an atmosphere of extraordinary candor. What is it with these Americans? Such a meeting anywhere else would have been just cause for murder and mayhem! Imagine, Gregorieva! Being invited to such a meeting and then being told that you are in total, autocratic control! Simply unimaginable!"

"Academician Rosovec," Gregorieva confided. "Trust me, if you can. But trust me the Americans are just as human as we are. They breathe air, need to eat, and require sleep. However, as Professor Milson explained to me one day over an abominable cocktail called a B52, we Russians have been either fighting for or defending our land for almost our entire existence. Furthermore, he says, that we, unlike the West, have never experienced an age of chivalry."

Thoughtful silence.

"Now, Stefan. Imagine hearing such an off-the-cuff historical analysis of our Slavic past from an Egyptologist. And you still wonder why the Americans are so unpredictably and surprisingly American? And by the time your three people are ready to return, they might not come back."

"I know, Gregorieva. I know. I have already made arrangements for their families to join them."

"You have!"

"Yes. And that, my dear colleague, is for your ears only. And that is the true reason that I am so jealous of them!"

After the passing of several minutes, Gregorieva finally dared to ask, "Stefan. Why did you tell me that?"

"Because I thought that you should know."

"But for what purpose?"

"So that someone should know that I am not a man without a soul. Which reminds me, my dear Vesna, it would not be wise to place too much trust in either Ostrogorsky or Drazinzka."

"This I already know. Alexander had warned me about them."

"A wise and insightful man he was," Rosovec stated with a quiet certainty. "And just how wise and insightful are you, Ms. Gregorieva?"

Looking now into her colleague's eyes with a questioning look, "And just what are you fishing for?"

"I am thinking ahead. Both of my colleagues are fast nearing their retirement. I will surely survive them both. As the most technically oriented of our cozy little group, don't you find it curious that you report to Drazinzka and not to me?"

Then abruptly changing the subject, he said wistfully, "A fine man Alexander Piankoff was. I just wish that I had had the opportunity to meet him."

"You just might."

"How so?"

"Are we not having dinner with Professor Milson tonight?"

"Ah, yes. You are right! I had forgotten! He too is a very interesting man and one that I have wanted to meet since I first heard of him. Although neither one has said a word, both of my esteemed colleagues consider Milson to be quite a formidable force."

"John is."

"John?"

"Why, yes. That is his first name."

"On a first name basis, are you?"

"When in America, be American. And, oh, by the way, I wouldn't mind becoming more technically minded either."

"You don't say."

* * *

The restaurant in question was an old and venerable Loop steak house with a history steeped in Chicago politics, where legendary deals had been cut and history made. It was the kind of place where if the walls could speak, they would fill volumes. While Milson was very aware of this seamy heritage, he seriously doubted that his two Russian guests would. But what Gregorieva and Rosovec didn't know, Milson was sure that they would subliminally feel it, and that was important. It was just that kind of place with just that kind of atmosphere. And to ensure a further sense of intimacy, he had arranged for a table located in clear sight of the roaring fireplace, but off to one side in a quiet niche. The niche itself was draped with dark curtains that could be drawn if needed. Set for three, the heavily starched table linens and gleaming formal silverware were perfectly set out. The glassware simply sparkled in the candlelight. In short, Milson had set the stage. Now it was up to his guests to show.

By his watch, the pair, and they made a stunning and handsome pair indeed, arrived three minutes early.

Smiled. *I just love it! No jockeying for position here. While such a direct and refreshing approach I would expect from Gregorieva, I find it even more interesting to see Rosovec following her lead. Or is Rosovec also one not to pussyfoot around? Well, Johnny boy. Only time will tell.*

At their approach, Milson stood and buttoned his suit coat. After the initial pleasantries were expressed, Gregorieva allowed Milson to seat her. Once everyone was settled in, Milson then smiled his very best smile, suggested that he order for them, and they assented. But before he could do that he had to know whether garlic appealed to them, whether they preferred their meat bloody, warm, mildly cooked, or burnt. Did they prefer soups or salads? And after that personal information had been imparted, the Egyptologist waved over the waiter, told the man of their individual needs, and ordered a robust bottle of red wine – a vintage Argentinean Malbeck.

That task done, Milson asked the pair how the meeting in Dayton had gone and sat back to listen. Rosovec used this opening to begin a long narrative description of his first impressions of America. While Milson sat listening to this powerful foreigner's impressions of his native land, he also noted that Gregorieva was listening closely.

Clearly, he concluded, *she is taking his pulse as well.*

Then the wine arrived and as the conversion continued to build in momentum and spontaneity, a second arrived in due time, followed by freshly baked breads and three steaming bowls of a thick potato soup that included three individual shots of sherry on the side. When the main course arrived, it was promptly devoured with the Russians complimenting Milson on his choices for them. All was going so rosy that Milson decided to spring on his guests a very pregnant question that had been on his mind for some time.

"Academician Rosovec," he began as he pushed his clean plate aside. "As you can see, I am an old man. By virtue of my life experiences, I have naturally developed along certain lines, have certain tastes. And as an old man, I have my own opinions, goals, biases, and of course, prejudices. But in many respects, my perspective on the world today has been greatly shaken up by a colleague of mine, Dr. Joseph Richards. Clearly, there is between us a gap of several generations. Hell, there's a technological gap as well. And yet, despite my age, I have managed to learn quite a bit from him.

"And so here is a question that has been nagging at me for some time, a question that truly can only be asked face-to-face and under the right conditions. You see, Dr. Rosovec, at least from my point of view, I see that your colleagues are easily as old as I am – perhaps even older. And so I have to believe that a generation gap probably exists between you and your colleagues in much the same way it does between Richards and me. So my friend, my question to you is simply this: have you ever discussed with your colleagues what their agendas, prejudices, biases, and goals are? And by the same token, have they ever asked you for yours?"

Surprised by Milson's candor, the Russian nonetheless responded with equal frankness.

"Dr. Milson," Rosovec answered while glancing significantly toward his colleague Gregorieva, "it seems that today is indeed one filled with frank talk. And no, to your question, those topics, such a sharing, has yet to occur between Ostrogorsky, Drazinzka, and me. Yet, I also dream of a day that may redefine old lines of thinking. Perhaps one day that may engender a warming of relations, the start of a renaissance of sorts where men of like mind can come together and speak freely. John, allow me be frank, that very possibility is one that I embrace. It is one that I can foster. However, such a spirit of openness is not one that my colleagues would readily agree with. As you yourself have suggested, a generation gap does indeed exist between us. I am clearly the youngest of this litter. And as you would expect, I am often the last to know what my esteemed colleagues are up to. Consequently, the establishment of such a utopian atmosphere will take time. But regardless, we must start somewhere. Yes? So why don't we begin the process this evening?"

Milson, feeling the moment for what it truly was – potentially epoch-making – mentally pinched himself before he replied to this Russian's surprisingly refreshing and farsighted stance.

"Time," Milson declared. "What a marvelous concept it is! In fact, it is also quite ironic, especially given the current business that both of our scientific communities are engaged in. We have a saying here that time can heal all wounds. I pray that that is so."

Then waving for the waiter, a moment later he appeared with a frosted bottle of vodka in an ice bucket and three small glasses.

Milson grinned ear to ear at the arrival, thanked the waiter, and then dismissed him. Cracking open the bottle's seal himself with a quick twist, the Egyptologist poured and said, "You know folks, and I hope that you do not mind, I chose this brand myself just in case a moment like this might present itself."

Now raising his glass to the two Russians in benediction, he warmly stated, "To friendship."

Rosovec then added, "And to progress as well."

* * *

By mid-October, Roy's Raiders, as his handpicked team rapidly had come to be known, had secured their own remote hanger on the base to initially accommodate "the package," as the Aten craft had quickly come to be called. Formerly used exclusively for the clandestine use of aircraft of foreign dignitaries who occasionally dropped by during the Cold War, Roy's Raiders transformed the mothballed facility into an efficiently organized and technologically upgraded research facility. Needed office furniture was purloined out of storage. Network hookups were installed. A huge plastic isolation cell was fabricated to eventually contain and hermetically seal the package. Suspended by nylon tethers scrounged from several suddenly discovered out-of-spec parachutes, the big bubble was designed to act much like an airtight hospital incubation tent complete with several airlocks, a filtered ventilation system, and its very own internal fire control. The bubble's purpose was clear: contain any sort of biological contamination that may exist. All the containment gear was subsequently labeled "DANGER: HAZMAT CONTROL" as a further security feature, just in case someone happened to blunder into the area.

In order to more easily maneuver the package about, Roy's Raiders made another acquisition: a gutted Abrams A1A tank chassis, complete with a fully functional gas turbine engine. Once in the hands of Roy's wrench heads, a specially fabricated cradle called the MPC, for "mobile package cradle," was quickly cobbled together with conveniently available materials from the base. The plan called for the hoisting of the Aten craft into the air. Then the MPC would maneuver itself below it. The package would then be gently lowered to the MPC's cradle that was mounted where the tank's turret assembly once resided.

Needless to say, with all of these goings on, the base commander should have been fit to be tied. But he wasn't, for Roy Peters was not only the King of the Hill on this project, he was also the base commander's best friend and partner-in-crime. In fact, Rebecca, the base commander's wife, even designed the much coveted "Roy's Raiders" patch: two big red and slightly overlapping capital r's – much like the Rolls Royce logo – stitched on a flat black and shield-shaped field with a glossy black border. Even a handy Velcro patch was affixed on the back. Needless to say, when Roy personally handed these out to each and every member of the team, all of these handsome insignia were affixed on jackets, coats, and windbreakers before day's end. Only one was not so personally delivered. It instead was express mailed to a farm address in central Iowa with a note.

```
Thanks.

And oh, by the way, no slacking!

Remember: you're a member of this team too!

R.P.
```

* * *

On October 30th at 02:35 in the morning, the package arrived from Gander, Newfoundland. As the big dark shape of the lumbering NASA 747 ferry finally broke through the low overcast on its final approach, Roy, straining through his binoculars, tried mightily to get an early glimpse of his new arrival. And there it was.

Dang! He thought. *It looks just like some huge radar platform!*

Flaring near stall as all big jets do on landing, only the outer edges of the saucer could be seen head on. On touchdown, multiple puffs of tire smoke briefly dotted the runway in the heavy atmosphere. The beast had safely landed. Then, and only then, did Roy begin to breathe normally, for he had been unconsciously holding his breath the entire time. Having been diverted over to what had come to be designated as Hanger P, the 747 taxied over smartly and stopped precisely where the ground control personnel with their orange popsicles had waved them.

That plane is big! The farmer from southern Indiana allowed. *But the package actually looks almost in proportion to it.*

Then he noted the package had been camouflaged as well with two broad white parallel strips across its otherwise flawlessly smooth surface – traditionally signifying as revolving radar dome markings.

Those clever aeronautical engineers, Roy smiled. *Probably all of them went to Cal Tech!*

Then, almost as if by magic, two scissor lifts with extending bridges appeared on both sides of the aircraft's fuselage and below its external cargo. Once locked in position, their air wrenches starting making their familiar high-speed zip-zipping sounds as they loosened, but did not remove, the package's many tethering bolts. Then the coughing start-up of two massive helicopter engines was heard as the base's own Chinook began its warm-up and its crew went through their checklists. At the same time, the specially fitted cargo net that had first extracted the package from its ancient hanger bay was unloaded from the aircraft and then loaded aboard a three-quarter ton truck, which was carried over to the slowly rotating Chinook. There, four airmen wrestled the net free, opened it up, and spread it out on the tarmac, while attaching it to the chopper's central lift point. Receiving a thumbs-up, the chopper's twin motors began to slowly spin, while the crouching airmen spread out and secured the cargo net against the deck and the formidable rotor wash. Lifting slowly, the airmen expertly played out the netting, which once airborne, looked like a limp, trolling dishrag.

Moments later, hovering directly above the package, the chopper pilot deftly lowered the rigging atop the saucer shape and even managed to spread most of it out on the first attempt. Quickly grabbing for the netting's interlocking straps, the package quickly looked as if it were hopelessly entangled in a spider's webbing. After all double-checks were completed, an airman on the ground radioed the pilot for some lift. As the slack slowly was taken out of the cargo netting, the air wrenches again began their furious buzzing with nuts, washers, bolts falling freely. Below, ten volunteers collected these potentially dangerous foreign objects, or FOBs, as they fell, eventually accounting for every last one of them. With the package now free of its mother ship, the Chinook rose to clear the 747, gracefully side-slipped over to the idling MPC, and gently deposited its precious cargo.

In all, from touchdown, to the securing of the package on the MPC, then on to its parking within Hanger P, the entire process had taken only twenty-two minutes time by Roy's watch. As his chest filled with a mixture of pride and relief, the base commander firmly shook his hand and said, "Well, Roy. We successfully delivered your package and in record time. Now do us proud!"

"Thank you, Commander! Be sure to give all your people a really big atta-boy!"

* * *

On the second day of investigation and with the package fully shrouded in its milky white plastic cocoon, Roy Peters and his crew were having some difficulty finding any seams, access ports, much less a crew hatch. They did, however, manage to grind off a sample of the craft's surface for analysis, which Peters had requested, based on sheer intuition, to be cross-checked with that of SNOWMAN's.

Over the weekend, a certain Dr. Joseph Richards flew in from Chicago to help out Peters' team in locating the crew hatch. To Roy, this Dr. Richards looked more like a bodybuilder than an academic, but what did he know? He just wanted in and he didn't really care what it took. But before Richards had indeed opened up the package, he was more than a bit skeptical.

Shaking hands with the young man and being on the receiving end of a firm grip that made for a good first impression, his confidence began to slip as Richards explained to him just what he had to do.

"Well, Dr. Peters, it's like this. The Aten craft's entrance and internal ramp are voice-activated and the individual voicing the command has to be standing before the hatchway. The problem here, as you can probably tell, is we don't know where the hatchway is. So, I will have to slowly work my way around the ship, stopping every few feet, face its hull, and repeat the voice command."

"Well, why didn't you just tell me that on the phone, and I could have had several of my technicians find it?"

Smiling, Richards then let him in on a little secret.

"Most logical, Dr. Peters, but do any of your technicians speak ancient Egyptian?"

"What! You got to be pulling my leg! You mean to tell me that this thing is voice keyed to an ancient language?"

"Yep."

"Well, at least I know why you insisted on coming on down here personally. At first, well, I just thought that you wanted an excuse to sneak a peek at the package. Now I know why."

"Perfectly understandable, Dr. Peters, and by the way, I was the one who found the Aten and led its recovery. I am very familiar with how it looks, and smells."

"What do you mean by smell?"

"Because, Dr. Peters, I suspect that a good part of the ship's components are organic, hence one of the reasons for fueling it with water. But I also suspect that at least one of its engines might be hydrogen fusion based."

"In a hull that small?"

"It's extraterrestrial. Why not at least consider the possibility?"

"Yeah, right, you make a valid point, Dr. Richards."

Pause.

"And by the way, what's your doctorate in? Physics? Aeronautics? Engineering?"

"No, Dr. Peters, I'm an Egyptian philologist."

Pause.

"A language expert. Okay. Makes sense, especially considering that voice-activated hatch mechanism."

"Yep, and a very specialized one too."

"I see, well, so do you need anything special? Any tools?"

"Nope, and I have my roll of masking tape right here. That's all I'll need."

"Masking tape?"

"To mark off the hatch once I find it."

"Oh, yeah. Good thinking!"

Pause.

"And by the way, Dr. Richards."

"Yes?"

"If you're going to help us with pack . . . ah, the Aten as you call it, then you have to wear this patch."

"Cool! But what do the red 'RRs' stand for?"

"Roy's Raiders."

"Does this mean that I'm an honorary member of your team?"

"Nope, only full members get a patch."

"Awesome, Doc! Thanks!"

"You're very welcome, Dr. Richards. Now just open up that dang Aten for me!"

"Yes, sir!"

* * *

As Richards proceeded to work his way around the Aten craft, a curious crowd naturally formed following his progress. One of them thought that it was a rather spooky-looking cultic ritual that was suspiciously like an exorcism. Another compared Richards' solemn demeanor and intoning of strange words to a Jew praying before the Wailing Wall. But about halfway around, the Egyptologist was indeed rewarded with the appearance of a flickering ovoid border in the hull that was soon followed by a hiss of a colorless, rancid-smelling gas and a steep and smooth ramp that extended itself all the way to the floor. As the gagging organic gas was released, all those assembled quickly donned their gas masks that were always worn at the hip. Richards just made it and got his mask on and sealed. Another didn't and decorated his mask's interior with his last meal.

Stepping forward onto the ship's ramp, the Egyptologist began tearing off hunks of tape, affixing them to the Aten's hull and just outside the edge of the opened hatchway. Finished, he came down and asked Peters, "Dr. Peters. Would you like a tour? I can tell you not only where to refuel the Aten, but also how to check if it needs refueling as well."

"How do you know?"

"Classified, Dr. Peters."

"You're joking."

"Nope. Now how about that tour?"

* * *

By the end of the first full week of nosing around, prodding, pulling, and sampling, Roy called a general meeting of his team and the usual suspects. On his agenda were some preliminary findings he wanted to share and some tasks that he wanted taken care of ASAP.

Gathering in the same conference room where he had been made the project's chief investigator, Roy stood before them and cleared his throat. As silence fell, he began.

"Well, folks. It's been a very exciting and busy week. And if it hasn't been that way for you, then you don't have a pulse."

Some good natured guffaws and chuckles broke out.

"But let me say up front, and especially to all of you fine people who helped out on the SNOWMAN project. Well, guess what? The preliminary analysis of the sample taken from the package's outer fuselage shares many, I repeat, many similarities in composition with that of SNOWMAN. I wish to express my deepest thanks to the material sciences team for turning over that analysis so quickly. In fact, even at this early juncture, I am willing to bet the farm that we'll eventually discover an unused SNOWMAN aboard the craft that had yet to be deployed. Now, people, I don't know about you, but that is a very big early win!"

Such a strong preliminary statement from this notoriously introspective and careful mind caused a gale of spontaneous clapping, woof, woofs, and whistling to break out from the audience. And once they settled down, Peters continued.

"But, as you all know, we have literally years of research and investigation still ahead of us and before this is all over, this team will grow considerably and will become far more interdisciplinary in composition. Now why do I say this? Because, and especially for those of you who were there when Dr. Richards first opened the Aten craft, there is a significant organic component to this mechanism."

At this point, Roy purposefully paused to let that statement sink in.

"Currently, we do not know whether that organic component represents the craft's pilot, the actual mechanism's onboard systems, or a symbiotic mix of both functions. However, given the compact nature of the Aten craft, my money is on an organic symbiosis that blended hardware with living software. And for us to figure all of that out means that we really have to think outside of the box. So, beginning next week, three new team members will be joining us. Generally, they will be representing the life sciences, and in particular the fields of genetics, organic chemistry, and physiology. But have no fear, my friends. They're just as geeky as us, and best of all, just as curious. Please grant these newcomers a warm welcome.

"Well, that's all that I have to say. But while we're all conveniently here in one place, I'd like now to open up the floor to any needs or issues."

* * *

By January 15th of the next year, Dr. Roy Peters had his first spiral-bound and numbered preliminary report on the desk of Dr. Paul Young. His copy, the dean noted, was copy number four. That mildly irked him, but decided to let that perceived slight pass – at least for now. He consoled himself that at least he was considered among the upper third of the recipients. The sheer fact that this preliminary report was before him, and so soon, was remarkable enough for the economist.

As for the report itself, it was hardly a first draft as so many items kept popping up and so many hypotheses either came to fruition or fizzled. And then Peters had to address a handful of marginalia that a certain retired colleague in Iowa had so carefully penned. Regardless, in the end, it was "just" a preliminary report, but its cover alone indicated that it was not exactly bedtime reading either.

ALPHA CLASSIFIED MATERIALS

The Aten Spacecraft.
Preliminary Report No.1.
Initial Technological and Physiological Findings.

Copy Nr. 4 of 12.
Edited by Dr. R. Peters, Chief Investigator

ALPHA CLASSIFIED MATERIALS

> Any unauthorized use or reproduction of any of the materials, data, or media contained within this report will result in a prosecution to the fullest extent of the Federal Secrets and Securities Act.

Young had a pet theory that you could tell how good an administrator or project head was by the structure of his written communications, be they simple e-mails or more formal reports such as the one before him. So the economist began to work through this report, all the while building his assessment of Roy Peters.

So, let's see, Young thought, about an inch and a half thick. *Plastic spiral binding. Unpretentious gray stock covers. And what's this? Ah, a laser disk pocketed into the back cover. Most helpful. Well, clearly an inexpensively produced, internal, desktop production. No doubt far more easily controlled and secured. So far so good.*

"Edited by."

So Peters trusts the work of his colleagues and apparently even those of his Russian compatriots as well. Interesting.

Opening up the report, the dean next went to its Table of Contents and scanned its overall organization: Executive Brief, Preface, Introduction, Abbreviations, Preliminary Technological Findings, Preliminary Physiological Findings, Appendices, Video Tour.

Video tour? Now that looks interesting. Well, all in all quite good so far, but where are the indices? For shame!

And the dean made a note to that effect.

Then, without skipping a beat, he turned to the Executive Brief in the mistaken belief that this portion of the report was really written for his consumption only. So he started to scan through it, but soon found that there were references scattered throughout the brief that were clearly of things that even he was not privy to. And the dean's irritation was again tweaked.

For instance, under Preliminary Technical Results:

> Point 3. The material of the Aten spacecraft's outer hull shares similar properties to that of SNOWMAN, excepting that the former has proven to be even more durable than the latter.

Who or what is SNOWMAN? Young wanted to know. And again under Preliminary Technical Results:

> Point 5. Advanced and extremely efficient photonic crystal fibers (PCFs), constructed of stacked silica capillaries with continuous and internally reflective lacunae measuring twenty-five nanometers in diameter, were employed to provide data transfer (?) via laser light throughout the craft's internal systems thus far investigated.

Good God, man! Do or don't you know what being passed via these PCF things?

Miffed, the dean deigned to read one more point under the Preliminary Technical Results heading:

> Point 7. From all appearances, the Aten spacecraft employed a dual-mode propulsion system. Within an atmosphere, a versatile hydrogen/oxygen engine was utilized that could be fueled directly with water, liquid hydrogen, or liquid oxygen. While outside an atmosphere, the craft shifted to some other sort of drive system. As for that secondary drive system, we not only do

> not know what we are dealing with, we do not even know where it is located in the ship. As for what it used for fuel, or what it relied upon, or tapped into, is unknown. However, it is the learned consensus that the coils noted are of some sort of antigravity technology that may have harnessed dark energy for propulsion. This supposition seems reasonable given that approximately 73 percent of the universe's mass is made up of what is poorly understood as "dark matter." Given its abundance, in essence, such a power source could potentially allow the Aten spacecraft to effortlessly surf through the void.

Well now, that I can understand. Well composed. But what's all this speculation about dark energy and dark matter? Almost sounds medieval. I will have to ask, the dean thought as he scribbled a question mark in the margin.

I really liked that last phrase about effortless surfing.

Then the dean paged over to the Preliminary Physiology Results section and began to scan there.

> Point 2. The electroluminescent display located before what is believed to be the command location is composed of an organic film that is very thin, light, flexible, and is capable of displaying images and symbols in 256 colors. Others may be attainable, but further research is required in this direction.

So, big deal, we have liquid crystal displays that can do that, the dean harshly concluded, missing the entire point that the organic display was a thin flexible film and not a piece of laptop hardware. *So let's try another one under Preliminary Physiology Results.*

> Point 5. The organic remains of system controls and perhaps even an occupant were discovered within the Aten spacecraft.

My God! Who ever said anything about a pilot being aboard!

> These remains, after analysis, have been shown to possess many of the same unique DNA constituent parts as those gathered from the Pharaoh Akhenaten. These facts lead us to conclude that the organism contained with the Aten spacecraft could well have been one and the same with the entity known as the Pharaoh Akhenaten. Current speculation as to how that relationship may

> have come about include: direct cell implantation into a human fetus or a budding at an adult organismic level with the former speculation representing the most plausible.

My God! Young thought. *The implantation of alien DNA into a fetus that then grows up into an adult. This is just too much!*

With both eyes now wide open, the dean continued on with the rest of Point 5.

> From all appearances, the occupant of the Aten spacecraft was organically "integrated" into the ship, suggesting that it never had any intention of leaving it nor was capable of an extravehicular excursion. In short, the Aten spacecraft, to borrow an analogy from the insect world, was the occupant's exoskeleton, while the constituent parts of the occupant itself, specifically its internal organs, nervous system and brain were intimately and permanently interfaced into the craft. Such a merger would, in effect, create a perfect symbiosis of organic software with its surrounding and protective hardware.
>
> In summation, it is our preliminary analysis that the Aten spacecraft was much like that of a modern automobile, but without the many onboard management systems and without the entire electrical wiring harness that integrates the whole. In the case of the Aten spacecraft, the occupant itself provided that integration.

His initial qualms about the fitness of Roy Peters had been totally dashed to pieces. His skepticism about his quick request for the additional life sciences people was unequivocally justified. Young, still intellectually staggering from what he had just read, forgot about the laser disk in the back pocket, which contained a narrated video walk around the spacecraft and a tour of its rather, at times, gory interior spaces. He even had to admit to himself that though Peters had not been his first choice for the position of chief investigator, the man nonetheless was far better than his choice would have been.

At this point, Dr. Paul Young, still shaken by the ramifications of what he had just read, sat back and closed the document without having read the next point under the rubric Preliminary Physiological Results.

Point 6. Organically grown crystals seem to have provided the practical means for data storage aboard the Aten spacecraft. The method of data retrieval, however, remains unclear. However, their mere existence alone suggests potentially tantalizing possibilities.

CHAPTER XLVI

Another Spring Break (Cont.)

On the Saturday following the momentous opening of the treasury, while the team's now traditional meeting place before the tourist entrance of the Karnak Complex hadn't changed, roles had. For when the Europeans arrived, they discovered much to their surprise that Richards and Dr. Sharil Moussa were there already waiting for them, both sitting on the curb chatting away.

* * *

Also on that very day, a long newspaper column appeared simultaneously in the *New York Times* and *Times* of London. It was one of those marvelous cultural pieces accompanied with several color pictures that stirred the imagination, if not the soul. The subject was the recent academic publication of a sensational archaeological discovery in Sakkara, Egypt. The principals who were interviewed in these articles were none other than the Director of the Egyptian Antiquities Organization and his assistant, Dr. Sharil Moussa, herself the director of the Cairo National Museum. In the lengthy articles, the discoverer of the tomb, Professor Dr. Willem van der Boek, and his team – all described in surprising detail – were praised for their grit and professionalism that resulted in such a pristine clearance of an undisturbed tomb. Allusions and comparisons, both direct and indirect, to Howard Carter's famous find of Tutankhamen were everywhere. So far so good, but then the Egyptian Antiquities Organization officials dropped what amounted to a media bombshell, when they casually mentioned that the tomb's inscriptions included references to the ancient Egyptian's capacity for glider flight.

Well, that detail positively set the Western media ablaze. The cable news channels went nuts with headline stories like, "Ancient Egyptian Hang Gliders! Can You Believe It!" The networks' talking heads went bananas pontificating on this point and that. Newspaper cartoonists had a field day, with one penning a sketch of the Kitty Hawk piloted by a kilted Egyptian in full eye paint. One quick-thinking southern California hang glider manufacturer swiftly began advertising on the web that their painted glider wings offered "really cool and authentic blue-and-gold Egyptian vulture wings of the Goddess Nekbet." Experts in anything even vaguely Egyptological were paraded before the cameras. Predictably, several of the old guard types parroted a hard-line approach and consequently dismissed all the fuss and feathers as poppycock. Other, far more thoughtful ones – meaning those who had actually gotten their hands on van der Boek's Leiden produced publication and who had read it cover to cover – expressed honest, pinch your bottom, blinking surprise.

Even the Deutsche Museum in Munich got into the act by dragging out and putting on prominent display in their Zentrale Aula their lone photograph purported to be of an ancient Egyptian glider model that was found in a third-century BC context. The model in question can be viewed in the Cairo National Museum in Room 22 on the second floor. Registered in the *Journal d' entrée* as number 6347, it was recovered in 1898 from the tomb of the priest Padiamen found near the pyramid of the Sixth Dynasty Pharaoh Tety at Sakkara. Made of sycamore wood, the glider carries the faint painted traces of "the Gift of Amen" on its tail section, the significance being that Amen was the god of the wind and air. While some have dismissed this model either as a child's toy or a wind vane, those learned interpretations cannot then explain why the obsidian eyes of the bird model were actually the ends of an obsidian rod that provided the model with its critical counter weight.

The media, ever hungry and with a voracious appetite for data, then initiated a run on van der Boek's academic publication itself, which the public quickly picked up on. For the first time in modern history, the publication run of 350 hardcopies of a bookish, academic work with a separate folio, vanished from the shelves in an instant. Then predictably a day later, the title began to appear on Internet auction sites at wildly ludicrous prices. But throughout this entire melee, the media was drooling and chomping at the bit to interview van der Boek and his crew to "get their personal perspectives on this most momentous archaeological find of the century." But to their chagrin, they were nowhere to be found.

Why?

Because they were very, very busy.

* * *

Van der Boek had forgotten how much he hated breathing through a gas mask. While the newer, full-face version allowed him almost full peripheral vision, it still chafed his skin almost raw from its continuous use. Perspiration leaked and gathered at its bottom to the point that his chin seemed perpetually immersed. Then there was the discomfort of that clunky air bottle strapped sidesaddle across his lower back. While it was far better than wearing it scuba-style, one's hips certainly moved differently when shifting all of that extraneous mass.

Ah, Villy, you are clearly no longer a young man. Pace yourself. Pace yourself, the near-retirement-aged archaeologist bemoaned and silently chanted to himself.

But deep down in his heart of hearts, especially as he gazed down upon the ancient glider frame before him, some inconvenience could be put up with. Then Claude, who had been standing next to him, said, "Willy, I have completed all the digital imagery, both black-and-white and color, complete with all the proper scales and numbers in place. It's time, my friend, to begin the clearing of this storage room."

Nodding his head in agreement, van der Boek looked over to the partially obscured mask of Sharil and smiled with emotion that was reflected in his speech.

"Vell, Sharil. I see dhat you already have on your cotton gloves. Are you ready to carry out dhat hawk helmet?"

"Yes," she breathlessly whispered through her mask.

"Okay. Now Claude, take up a position at the treasury's entrance and photograph everyding that is brought out. Remember those *National Geographic* photos of Tutankhamen's clearance? Dhat perspective exactly. Ja. Gut. You understand."

Then turning back to Sharil, who already had the hugely flared helmet cradled in her arms. Smiling again through his mask.

"Okay, Sharil. Valk carefully out, mind the traps, and go make us some history!"

About eight minutes later, Sharil did just that and ascended the long stepped ramp. But to her surprise when she reached the top, Richards with his field log and Claude with his two cameras were not alone. For her father was there as well at the entrance, along with two video camera crews – ones with well-known logos: one British, the other American – which were filming her exit from the treasury with the helmet carefully carried before her. As soon as Sharil had gently deposited the beautiful falcon helmet into a preprepared transport box filled with popcorn Styrofoam, she removed her oxygen mask and shook it out, as Richards extended to her some tissues to wipe her face dry. While still facing the American with the two cameras to her back, she whispered in a stressed, low voice heard only by him, "Joseph, just what is going on here?"

"Long story. Apparently, a news report broke either yesterday or today about Willy's publication of Meryptah's tomb. Since then, the media have been scouring the Earth trying to interview him about the glider references. Your father not only knew where Willy was, but what he was up to, so he called up these two media sources, cut an exclusive deal worth who knows how much, and so now they're here. It was just pure dumb luck that you came walking out first with the falcon helmet. Trust me on that one!"

"Oh, my!"

"Well, Dr. Moussa, what I suggest that you do now is smile, turn around, face the world, and become an instant celebrity."

And with a nervous wink for luck, Dr. Sharil Moussa did just that, while Richards slipped off and entered the treasury unnoticed.

But little did Sharil know that Richards' prophetic words would indeed come true. For when the piece was aired, a certain cosmetics company executive saw this intrepid female archaeologist. The sheer act of her removing her mask and shaking out her thick black hair, only to reveal her regal facial lines and natural beauty made his eyes bulge. Rising from his reading chair before his wide-screened plasma television, he pointed and exclaimed to his wife next to him, who was calming reading *Business Week*.

"Susan! Look! Look at this! That beauty that has just emerged from that tomb, covered head to toe in dust! I don't know who she is, but I've got to have her face for our new cosmetics line!"

Then he reached for his cell phone.

* * *

Meanwhile, as van der Boek prepared to take out the awkward wing of the glider himself, Richards suddenly appeared. A little surprised, the Hollander asked reasonably, “Joey, now just vhat the hell are you doing down here? It’s not your shift yet! Und vher ist your oxygen!”

“I know, Professor Dr. van der Boek, but we have some important company on the surface.”

Richards’ use of his formal title and family name stopped the man in his tracks.

“Vhat do you mean, Joseph, by ‘important company?’”

“The EAO director for one, and two news cable channels for another. Are you prepared to become instantly famous?”

“Do I haf a choice?”

“Well, I don’t think so. To date, Horst has yet to find another way out of this warren, and you are only carrying so much air in your tank. So what were you about to carry out?”

“Die ving here.”

“Perfect. Just make sure that when you emerge, you look surprised.”

“Vhy?”

“Because the EAO director wants to surprise you.”

“But vhy?”

“Willy,” Richards stated with some exasperation. “Have you ever had a surprise birthday party?”

“Vhy no. Besides, they’re silly.”

“Well, guess what, Willy? This is going to be your first surprise birthday party. Now, get your ass up topside with that wing in tow and prepare yourself. You’re about to become really famous.”

“But, Joseph . . .”

“No buts, Willy. Now get your ass moving to the surface!”

* * *

While Sharil was being interviewed by two alien-looking optical lenses, each with a single glowing red eye, and while Richards was informing van der Boek as to what to expect topside, Horst and two of his people were carefully exploring the obscure nooks and crannies of the treasury complex. Their first priority was to rough out a layout of the treasury’s many corridors and side passages, the immediate second was to identify, mark, and record any and all booby traps, which currently were numbered at twenty-six!

The trio, all breathing easy and moving carefully, checked their air supplies every five minutes per Horst's ever-vigilant and beeping watch. Dieter, a longtime friend of Horst, played out a light nylon cord from a plastic reel on his hip in a modern imitation of Theseus' ploy, when he explored the Minotaur's labyrinth. Unlike Theseus, however, this cord was marked with a broad red band every twenty-five meters. While considered overkill, Horst didn't want either an emergency or a sudden loss of air to delay any of his charges getting to the surface. Besides, the cord and its distance markings helped greatly with the rough layout that Marta, one of van der Boek's graduate students, was sketching on a pad of architectural graph paper.

Stopping to note again a distance marker, Horst peeked over Marta's stooped form as she sat cross-legged on the floor.

So far, he thought, *the treasury has an initial main corridor with fourteen isolated chambers on the right, or western, side and thirteen chambers to the left, or eastern, side. Of the western chambers, fully half are booby-trapped with false plaster thresholds, while of the eastern chambers, only three are, and only those that led to the second corridor that we are now exploring. Something is wrong*, he concluded.

"Marta."

"Ja, Horst."

"Are all three of the eastern booby-trapped chambers, here, here, and here, that led off from the main corridor to a second corridor of the same length?"

"I don't know yet. We have only checked the first two, and both of them measure approximately the same, at or around twenty-five meters."

"Ah, you know, I will wager that if we backtrack right now that the third chamber's eastern access will not join up with this one. What do you two think?"

"Well, it's an interesting idea, Horst. Do you want to try?"

"Ja, gut. Let's do it, because this plan just has too much wasted space in this central section."

"My thoughts exactly," Horst confirmed.

And off they went, now backtracking, making one left turn and following Dieter as he cranked away on his reel. As he neared a bright green glowing chemical marker, he announced, "Okay. We're back to the main corridor. Be careful to use the vooden planks to cross this verdammt trap!"

Once all were again in the main corridor without incident, they worked their way left again to the ninth eastern chamber and its planked-over trap. Stopping, Horst said, "Okay, Marta, the other chambers you said ver twenty-five meters in length. Dieter, vhat's now our distance?"

"Right now, it's a little short of fifteen meters."

"Marta, note that – plus/minus fifteen meters. Okay, ve go."

As the intrepid trio creaked their way across the planks, Horst took the lead. Proceeding slowly, four beams of light painted every square meter of that regular and smoothly cut passage in the limestone bedrock. Then after seemingly no time, the explorers came across another broken section of the passage's flooring – a new man-trap that had to added to the survey. Horst, getting down on his stomach, peered into the darkness and saw the mangled remains of some poor soul a good twenty feet down. Then extending his torso through the break in the floor and fanning his flashlight around, Horst announced, "Vell, dis entire section is plaster. Ve'll have to come back with some planks before ve can continue."

Wiggling his way back out and getting up off of his stomach, he concluded, "You know dhat dis is the first time dhat ve have encountered a false floor dhat vas not a chamber's threshold."

Then taking the butt end of his flashlight, he experimentally began rapping it against the flooring. Bang, bang, bang, thump, thump.

"From now on, and especially mit dis passageway, ve must proceed very, very carefully.

"Let's return to the surface and tell Villy about all of this. I don't know about you, but I feel dhat all of dees traps are a very gut sign. Dhey must be hiding someding."

* * *

For the two film crews, it was like something taken right out of an Indiana Jones movie. The American newsman spoke excitedly into his cell phone to his producer in Atlanta.

"Marge, are you sitting down?

"Yes, we're in Luxor with the Egyptian Antiquities people.

"Now, Marge, you just are not going to believe this!

"First, the team's cameraman emerges out of this dark stair-stepped passage carrying his two high-tech Leica's, sweating like a pig, covered in dust, and wearing full breathing gear!

"Yeah, breathing gear, as in like scuba!

"Then, this simply gorgeous, and I mean gorgeous, woman archaeologist comes out.

"Yeah, her name's Dr. Sharil Moussa.

"That's S-H-A-R-I-L M-O-U-S-S-A.

"Yeah, that's it.

"And she's the daughter of the EAO director. You know, the guy who first tipped us off.

"Okay, back to this drop-dead gorgeous archaeologist. She's all sweaty and covered with dust, but she's carrying what looks just like a black motorcycle helmet that's all painted to look like an Egyptian falcon god's head!

"Yeah, no shit! But it gets better.

"Then she tells us, no, it's not a motorcycle helmet, it's a glider pilot's crash helmet!

"Do you believe that!?!"

"But, Marge, hang on. It gets even better.

"Moments later, that head archaeologist, whose name's van der Book or something, comes out carrying, now get this, the entire wing of a glider! And it's all painted to look like a bird's wing with big feathers and everything!"

"Yes, Marge. Marty is here. And yes, he got it all.

"By the way, can you spell Pulitzer?"

* * *

By the time Horst, Marta, and Dieter plodded out of the treasury, its entrance had become a complete bedlam with boom microphones maneuvering for position and hovering about like giant insects. Power cables intruded into the entire area with light stands and reflectors being hurriedly erected. Dog tired, dehydrated, and absolutely reveling in the cooling breeze against their soaked clothing, the three pushed their way through all the media people scurrying around, found their three favorite stone blocks, and literally plopped themselves down with a slight squish. With the outer ring of their faces still deeply creased from their breathing masks, they blankly looked about not saying a word, just observing all the hustle and bustle. They then finally located van der Boek in a crowd facing two video cameras, with Sharil to his right and the EAO director to his left.

"Mein Gott!" Horst blurted out. "Vhat Willy hat told us vas no joke! Let's go find some vater before dhey find us interesting!"

* * *

Following the initial day of media orgy, van der Boek firmly and autocratically put his foot down and told the two crews that they could not go into the treasury.

Period.

Outraged, they threatened to invoke the exclusive filming rights that the director of the Egyptian Antiquities Organization had granted them. To that, the Hollander wisely and openly laughed in their faces.

"First of all," van der Boek sternly lectured them in a low voice, "die director und I are gut friends. So do not threaten me. You vill lose! Besides, you do not have the appropriate safety equipment to breathe in dhat atmosphere. Second of all, ve are still surveying the treasury und already, at least as of yesterday, ve have located twenty-six booby traps."

That detail created some furious scribbling by several of the media crew.

"Third, ve are still finding und clearing avay all artifacts dhat ve find. Und fourth, die passages are too narrow to accommodate both us vhile ve are verking und your film crews. So, until ve are finished, you stay above ground. Und now, I have verk to do.

"Sharil. Vhere's is dhat crate vor die ving?"

* * *

The second day was quieter. Van der Boek had given the two film crews total carte blanche to the makeshift shipping tent that had been erected for Dr. Rashid's restoration people. There, the film crews could endlessly shoot all the spoil that began to emerge from the treasury. They recorded the initial examination of the object, the notation of its assigned catalog number, and careful packing for shipment by truck via a military armored caravan back to Cairo. Not surprisingly, once all the sensational glider gear had been filmed, their continued interest, as van der Boek had hoped and calculated, began to wane. By day four of the media invasion, the film crews had become skeleton crews, who were becoming more and more restive and frankly were more interested in getting home. By day five, the crews began packing up with the promise that when van der Boek was finished clearing the treasury that they and they alone would have first dibs on a tour.

On day six, all had blessedly returned to normal. However, among the team itself, they knew that they were in for a very big challenge. For during the media's *Blitzkrieg*, Horst and his crew had completed their preliminary layout of the treasury and located fully thirty-six mantraps – some of which turned up in rather unexpected locations.

"Vell, Villy," Horst began, "here's vhat ve currently know. Die treasury is made up of not one, but three parallel korridors: the main entrance korridor and two others located zu the east. All tree appear to be excavated at the same level. Of this, ve will not be sure until further, more precise survey work ist completed."

Referring to his notes and Marta's sketches of the treasury's plan, he continued, "The eastern-most korridor – dhat Marta hast labeled here as Korridor C on her plan – can be reached vom the third and sixth eastern chambers off the main korridor. At the back of each of these chambers, there ist a passage of about twenty-five meters in length that konnects dhem to Corridor C. Vhat is interesting about dhis korridor – dhat is about one hundert and ten meters in length – is dhat all of its fifteen side chambers are along its eastern side, with notding opening toward the vest. The reason for dhis arrangement, ve vere soon to discover, is the existence of another korridor between the main entrance korridor und Korridor C, which Marta hast named Korridor B.

"Die only access to Korridor B ist through the back of the ninth eastern chamber of the main entrance corridor, or Korridor A. The passage, while only some fifteen meters long, ist treacherous as it has two mantraps along its short length. Once ve got to Korridor B, ve explored it and ve have found more mantraps, all located in the most unexpected spots – some at thresholds to chambers, others within de korridor itself. In fact, ve discovered one undisturbed trap before the blank vall of its southern terminus. This ve thought was most suspicious. Within the korridor itself," again peeking at Marta's notes on her sketched plan, "vhich measures about sixty-two meters in length, ve found another fourteen side chambers – seven on each side. Und just as mit the other two korridors, Korridor B ends mit a blank vall on its southern end. Dis, ve believe, is a significant observation and one dhat should be investigated as I have already said. Generally speaking, throughout our explorations, Korridor A, dhat is about as long as Korridor C, seems to have been the most plundered of the three, while Korridor B seems the least mit many of its chambers still filled to the ceiling mit artifacts.

"To be honest mit you, Villy, ve all firmly believe that this Korridor B vas the most important one of the treasury, especially given all the unexpected traps und dhat mantrap before its blank southern end. Also, Villy, ve have not looked for any false valls vithin any of the korridors or side chambers. This too ve must do. In short, my friend, the proper klearance of dhis treasury vill take years. The establishment of a sound base survey, at the very least, another veek. Then with dhat plan before us, ve can better see vhere ve should begin probing."

* * *

In light of the news of Horst's and Marta's preliminary survey, van der Boek decided to send the director of the EAO an e-mail.

Dear Dr. Moussa:

I wish to inform you that at our current progress, we should have the main corridor of the Amen Re Treasury cleared within two weeks' time. While this corridor clearly has suffered the most from ancient plundering, nonetheless, the staff of Dr. Rashid has been tireless in their efforts to keep up with the continuous flow of artifacts that we have been able to recover. That it will be literally years before these alone are fully studied goes without saying.

However, the main corridor, Corridor A on the plan attached to this e-mail, is only one of <u>three</u> that we have explored. Corridors C, and especially B, contain far more artifacts, and in some cases, chambers are literally stacked to their ceilings. If you can image a cluttered storage room, many if not most of these chambers are so burdened with material, in some cases, as I have said, even stacked one atop the other to a chamber's ceiling. Fortunately, each has a central access aisle, no doubt established in order to view or get at such and such an *object d'art*.

Consequently, I respectfully suggest that the clearing of this complex become a joint effort, perhaps one shared by multiple foreign institutions, for it is far beyond the capacity of my team.

To this end, and in order to preserve continuity, I am willing to remain on as long as I am able as the excavation's guiding principal.

I thank you for your consideration in this matter.

Sincerely yours,

- vdB

Having read and reread the e-mail, the director called his daughter into his office.

"Sharil, please read this e-mail that I just received from our dear Dutch friend and tell me what you think."

After several moments passed, his daughter said, "Well, considering one stressful week wasted on the media and three intense ones devoted to the clearing of Corridor A, I would offhandedly say that van der Boek knows what his team's limits are, and that he is getting close to exceeding them. In short, he needs help."

"Yes. That's how I see the situation as well. But help from whom?"

Smiling at her father, Sharil diplomatically stated with a tip of her head, "Father, you know as well as I that we have an opportunity, perhaps an unprecedented opportunity, much like the successful UNESCO archaeological salvage of Nubia was, to transform this excavation into a multinational effort. That would mean involving the French, of course, who to date have been positively impossible because of the Dutch-American presence within their traditional preserve, as they call it. Then there are the Poles, the Austrians, the Americans, and the Germans just to name those whose schools are already established in the Theban area. That van der Boek would want to lead such an international effort, even given the proper jurisdictions and support, I seriously doubt, especially given the French mindset. In short, we will need a firm administrator who understands the logistics of the situation and who also has a delicate diplomatic touch."

"Are you interested, my daughter?"

"No, Father, I am not. But I will think of a solution nonetheless. But what really troubles me is the following. What remains to be seen is our practical ability to absorb all the artifacts that will simply pour out of that treasury and into Dr. Rashid's department. To say that he and his staff are burning the midnight oil already would be an understatement. For a brief period, this they can do. But not over a period of months or years. So, in order to make this happen, we need increased transportation, facilities, trained staff, and storage space. It is here that we really need the international effort, in the preservation and storage process, and not in the clearing and exploration of the treasury. In short, Father, either we find those resources, or we must shut down and seal off the treasury. We have done that in the past. The second boat grave of Khufu remains undisturbed and sealed to this day for just those reasons."

A quiet and heady silence passed between the two seated figures that faced one another, eyeball to eyeball.

"You know, Sharil, that as your father, I love you very, very much. But as remarkable as it may seem to you, as my assistant, I love you even more. As our ancestors so often said, 'Speak your heart,' and this you have never, ever, failed to do. What we have before us is a logistical crisis and our friend the Dutchman understands that as well. If you were me, what would you do?"

Sharil closed her eyes in reflection and whispered, "I would first speak with Dr. Rashid as to his limitations, how far and long he and his staff can last. Find out what our storage limits are. Then, on the basis of his projected threshold, close down and seal off of the treasury until such time that the necessary transport, facilities, resources, and museum space would be in place and available. Anything less would be nothing more than the cultural rape of our very own heritage."

Upon opening her eyes, she saw her father's bowed head silently nodding in agreement with her words. Then looking up with a mixture of conviction and pride in his eyes.

"As always, my daughter, you have spoken with your heart. However, this time you have spoken with such wisdom and as one ready for a leadership position of her own."

"Tomorrow, we go to Luxor. I will inform van der Boek of our coming."

* * *

The attendance list was surprisingly liberal. The EAO director and his daughter wanted the entire team in one room, while the future of the treasury's exploration and its clearing was discussed.

"My colleagues," the director began in preamble as he looked around and made brief eye contact with all who were assembled in the hotel's conference room rented for the occasion.

"In so little time, you have accomplished so very much. Currently, the world's media is still trying to grasp the magnitude of what you have found. Currently, your colleagues-in-arms are split in either joy for you or jealous hatred. The entire Egyptian nation is busting their buttons in pride over what you have recovered of their technological heritage. Proof of this is the surge in the Cairo National Museum's attendance by the Egyptian citizenry alone, not to mention their open interest in the weekly radio, newspaper, television, and Internet updates that my department generates out of their hunger to know what you are doing. However, consider and look around you. You're just about finished clearing Corridor A. How big is the backlog for just the sheer processing of those artifacts? How long each day does Dr. Rashid and his staff work trying to keep up with your furious industry? Currently, we are up to three armored convoys a week just to transport all the artifacts back to Cairo where they are rapidly filling up the secured storage docks.

"My friends, the Egyptian Antiquities Organization only has so many resources. Currently, we are understaffed and do not have the facilities to even safely store, much less restore, preserve, and display, any but a small proportion of the artifacts from the Amen Re Treasury. Given this situation, unless anyone here has a better idea, we will have to close down and seal off the treasury within the next two weeks."

To this announcement, van der Boek nodded in clear understanding and even agreement, for he had foreseen this situation coming as soon as he saw how much there was to clear and how overwhelmed Dr. Rashid and his staff had become.

Richards flatly was surprised. For him, coming from a land of seemingly endless resources, such a determination based upon such practical constraints was alien.

Horst shook his head, went on the offensive, and stated flatly, "Herr Director, please excuse my bluntness, but if you close down de excavation and stop its clearing, dhen you vill inherit an immense security issue. Just as in the days of the pharaohs, dhis complex will be broken into, most assuredly. I vould estimate within one month's time, someone vill have successfully tunneled into it. How, Herr Director, vill you prevent dhat? Vhat ist your guess as zo how many tunnels are right now undervay?"

The comment was noted and written down by Sharil, whose eyebrows were raised in alarm.

"At this time, Horst, I do not know how I could prevent anyone from digging within their household and tunneling below. But I thank you for your observation. It raises a very serious security concern."

"What about appealing to the United Nations for assistance?" Richards posed. "After all, you did it in the past with the Aswan High Dam Project. Why not now?"

"Dr. Richards," the director responded, smiling. "I am amazed by how similarly you and my daughter think! She too mentioned that possibility, but it is a possibility that requires much politics, both from within Egypt and without, to work – if at all. Either way, the excavation would have to halt for a time, and as your colleague has so aptly pointed out to us, time we do not have, out of fear of plundering."

"But Mr. Director, what of the monies from the cable news networks?" van der Boek asked. "Vhat of them?"

Sighing sadly, the director responded, "Professor van der Boek, those monies have been already earmarked for the museum's capital budget and are not available to me for a discretionary purpose such as this. In essence, that money has already been spent."

"Well, if it's a quick infusion of funds that you need, then form a nonprofit, research organization specifically for the purpose," Richards opined. "They do it all the time in Canada and the US. What you need is some sort of a charter agreement from your government that would allow the organization to exist and function. All we really need is a sponsor or leader from your government that has sufficient credibility to take on and lead such a task."

A small smile creased the Director's formerly glum and serious face.

"And Dr. Richards, do you have a candidate for this position in mind?"

"Yes, sir, she's sitting right next to you."

* * *

The Egyptian Exploration and Preservation Organization, or EEPO for short, first announced its existence to the world during a special session of the United Nations three weeks later. Its first head, Dr. Sharil Moussa, had been quietly ratified by the Egyptian government two weeks prior to that announcement. The construction of four museum storage annexes and a modern restoration facility, all connected with the Luxor Museum, had broken ground one week prior to Moussa's purely parliamentary rubber-stamping. Seed monies for the organization had been loaned to the EEPO without interest and liability from an anonymous source with extensive land holdings in the American states of Montana, Idaho, and Wyoming. It was fully expected that as the organization's existence and its stated purpose became known that the flow of further donations and grants would begin. And begin they did with a flood that initially surprised and taxed their Geneva bank account's administrators. What fueled this zealous fire of philanthropy was a well-timed campaign that the cable news networks assisted mightily with, when they aired their exclusives, at the end of which the EEPO was mentioned and where donations could be made.

But no one imagined that it would be the EEPO's own Internet site that would generate so many hits (crashing its server twice in the first two days of its existence), and such revenue. Established initially as an academically-oriented share site where van der Boek's latest finds were illustrated and described, the site quickly had become a financial juggernaut of its own.

With the construction of the additional facilities in Luxor underway with a nationalistic frenzy that was truly unusual for Egypt, and the guarantee of sound financial backing firmly in place, the next logical step was the invitation sent to the many foreign archaeological services in-country for their scientific assistance. Predictably, especially given the favorable conditions, all fell into line and pledged their aid – even the French. But what really surprised all of these academics was the assurance that what they restored in full, they were free to publish. All that was required was a dedicatory footnote that acknowledged the EEPO, EAO, and the usual and necessary archaeological source details of the artifact. What a hook! But to ensure that competitive cherry-picking of choice pieces would not occur, a lottery of sorts was established and administered by the EEPO, and Sharil put Dr. Rashid in charge of it.

But it was firmly the EEPO's own head that had sold the world on the preservation of Egypt's past. Realizing the initial need for media exposure, Sharil did just that, beginning with the American and British cable networks with which her government had already made their exclusive arrangements. Once those pleas for financial help, physical, and technical assistance aired, it truly was just a short time before Sharil's exquisite presence and message were broadcast from a very select collection of the world's news and talk shows.

To this very day, despite the fact that Sharil had twice politely put off all of those lucrative cosmetic offers, that very same firm was one of EEPO's first contributors in the rarefied Benefactor category. The cosmetic executive's logic was pure and simple. First, it was a fine tax deduction. Second, it was great publicity. Third, he argued, had not the ancient Egyptians invented cosmetics? But fourth, this same executive reasoned and hoped that Sharil just might someday change her mind and take up his company's offer.

* * *

With so many of the excavation's issues confronted, if not addressed, with an uncommon speed and will, van der Boek and his core team returned to the site after only a two-month delay. To everyone's relief, during that time the treasury had remained unmolested.

During that two-month hiatus, however, van der Boek had returned home for some much needed rest in the care of his loving and now exceedingly proud wife. Horst Willing, upon his return to Germany, found his young business in need of his guidance, but he was back only two days after the clearance had resumed. Even so, once his clients found out that he was the chief architect behind the find, his company's phones rang off the hook. As for Claude Assman, his supervisor at the Royal Ontario Museum was thrilled just to have him there, their man on the ground, "in the thick of it," as she so bluntly put it. So the extended presence of his cameras was assured, although his flat mate in Toronto, while pretending all happiness and excitement for him, was not at all thrilled at the news and his newfound international notoriety. Brigitte Claus thoroughly enjoyed the brief break from Luxor to be with her husband in Amsterdam. But to her amazement and no doubt because of her involvement in the project and all the media hype, she promptly landed a promising teaching and research position at the University of Amsterdam's Department of Linguistics. In the meantime, Dieter Meier and Marta Rosen had been given permission by van der Boek to push on and continue their painstaking mapping of the complex, which they rightly reasoned had to be done regardless. By the time Horst returned, they had produced a colorful 3-D digital ground plan of the complex that could be rotated on all three of its axes. When they unveiled their creation to the entire team, it received a well-deserved and ecstatic reaction.

With everyone still aglow over the plan, Marta then made a bold appeal to van der Boek, one that Horst had previously agreed to but refused to present on her behalf. Arguing directly from the 3-D plan, she requested that a concerted effort be made to investigate the highly suspicious southern terminus of Corridor B. What she boldly called for was nothing less than a bridging of the mantrap before the wall and a probing of its surface. Why? Because she was convinced that something very important lay beyond that wall. As to what that something was, she didn't know, but her argument for a mantrap directly before a wall and the expenditure of energy that it represented remained her single decisive point. Van der Boek, looking to Horst for his opinion, agreed with his teammate.

His supporting argument was so typically Horst.

"Zo, to date ve have found twenty-nine mantraps located before the threshold of a chamber and only five in other locations. And here ve have a mantrap before a vall. I dink dhat Marta is correct and dhat dis vall is false and dhat it blocks just another threshold to another chamber."

So it was decided, van der Boek temporarily divided the core team into two with the surveying team the next day to assault the southern wall of Corridor B, while he supervised. Otherwise, Richards, Claude, and Brigette would begin the recording and clearance of the chambers of Corridor C. Besides, the reduced output would be much appreciated by Dr. Rashid and his staff until such time as the foreign schools had their own staffs in place.

Soon after that team meeting, van der Boek sent an e-mail to Dr. Sharil Moussa about what they were about to undertake. In it, van der Boek suggested that if she was interested at seeing firsthand just what might appear, then she should make some quick travel plans. Otherwise, he would hold the crew back until she could conveniently arrive. About an hour later, the Hollander's laptop chimed indicating that he had an e-mail. Unfortunately, Sharil regretted that she could not tear herself away from the daunting administration of the EEPO in Cairo any time soon. Smiling to himself, he reread her sign off.

"Good hunting, Willy! If you again hit the jackpot, the media will surely hound you again, but for a full two weeks this time!"

She wasn't far off.

* * *

It had been Marta's idea from the very start, so under the harsh glare of two halogen lights, she got to swing the first blow with a pickax, which ripped through the smooth plaster of the wall and buried itself into a mass of firmly packed and plastered debris. Grunting to remove it herself, Marta yanked and a cascade of rubble came free.

To which van der Boek remarked through his face mask with a straight face, "Now, Marta, I did not know that you were so strong that you could pulverize rock into plaster and rubble."

Reaching to his belt and extending his own handpick to her, he said with humor in his voice, "I think that you should now start with this and begin to carefully clear and tease away some of the awesome carnage that you have already caused! Now don't go any deeper," he coaxed. "Just extend the depth that you're at horizontally and vertically. If there is indeed another passage, we have to first find its outline. Dhen ve must slowly remove any of de rubble blocking to prevent a cave-in on the other side.

"Also, Marta, vhat ve are looking vor now is another smoothed plaster layer. If I am correct, ve vill encounter such a plaster layer. Und dhis plaster layer may be stamped with many large seal impressions. Und I vant to recover dhem all intact. Do you understand?"

Shaking her head positively, she repeated, "I vill go slowly, pick away at vhat is loose."

"Precisely, Marta, you vill make a fine archaeologist!"

Nodding her head in understanding, she began again clearing away at the rubble, methodically course by course, starting from the top and proceeding to the bottom, while her colleagues Horst and Dieter dutifully carted it all away, but not before van der Boek inspected carefully each and every piece of rubble or plaster fragment for any evidence of graffiti or significance.

By the end of that first day, van der Boek noted that Marta had fully penetrated the rubble and plaster slurry of the suspicious southern terminus wall of Corridor B by some twenty-four inches. He also noted that the rubble and plaster blocking filled a passage that was nearly the same dimensions as that of the Corridor B itself. In other words, Marta was extending a branch of Corridor B that for some reason had been carefully hidden and filled, and that fact alone strongly supported her theory that something was there – not to mention the planking that they stood upon covered over the plaster camouflaged pitfall before it.

At the end of day one's assault, two two-wheeled push carts were purchased from a local construction firm to aid in the removal of the debris from Corridor B. Since a loaded cart could not be pushed up the treasury's entrance ramp, the debris had to be unceremoniously dumped at its base. From there, several local laborers carried the rock and rubble up the seventy-five steps and onto the flatbed of the old pickup truck of Labib and Naguib, who managed the additional local workers. Once loaded, the debris was dumped in at their previously arranged location to the south of the main temple.

As it turned out, all of these arrangements worked like a charm, and so by the end of day two of Marta's assault on the wall, a full five feet of rubble had been carefully removed under the watchful eye of van der Boek.

CHAPTER XLVII

Wealth Worthy of a God

To everyone's surprise, except the ever-patient van der Boek, Marta's assault on the southern wall of Corridor B took a full week and a half of labor before an encouraging sign was reached. Working at removing all the rock, rubble, and plaster, and guided by the watchful eye of the Dutch archaeologist, Marta and her hardworking colleagues Horst and Dieter had effectively extended the corridor some eighteen feet to the south.

That van der Boek and Willing had allowed this experiment in logic and intuition to continue and for so long was the simple fact that the smoothed walls of this southern extension of Corridor B had continued. Given this passage had been purposely defended with a mantrap spoke volumes. It's heavily plugged access had to be for some good reason.

Besides, the Hollander was stubbornly patient. The idea had been Marta's, and he was not about to stifle such brilliant insight. That both her teammates assisted throughout without complaint was another, albeit silent, tribute, and one that the Hollander did not miss nor would forget.

Marta's "magic moment" arrived around eight o'clock on a Thursday morning. Reaching up with a gloved hand, Marta pulled out a chunk of limestone rubble. With it fell the usual dust and smaller material. But what was revealed in the rock's gap took her breath away. At that moment, Marta stopped. In what van der Boek remembers best as a little girl's voice, he heard, "Herr Professor, I dink dhat I have found someding significant."

Coming closer and noting the smoothed plaster in the gap in the upper right corner of the fill, the Hollander did something very human. He hugged the dusty, dirty, and sweaty young woman and said, "My dear Marta, I can count on one hand how many people in the vorld have done, vhat you have just done. Now quick, go tell the others and get Claude mit his cameras. And," grabbing her by the arm to stop her, "don't forget to bring the meter sticks for scale! Now off with you! Und mind die traps!"

As Marta ran, screaming at the top of her lungs all the way to the treasury's entrance, both Dieter and Horst, who had been dumping the last cartload of rubble, looked around in alarm with wide-eyes.

"Horst!" Dieter gasped. "Do you dink dhat dere has been a cave-in?"

* * *

By lunchtime that very day, Marta had cleared away the remaining plugging material to fully reveal a smoothly plastered surface that was covered with large, palm print-sized seal impressions, most of which were in perfect condition due to the German surveyor cum archaeologist's care. Next, the entire area was hand brushed and eventually judged camera ready by van der Boek. Meanwhile, Claude had decided to set up two sets of lights, one at each side, at roughly forty-five degree angles to the plaster wall. Shooting alternately in both black-and-white and in color, his efforts to capture the seal impressions in their pristine fullness were very successful. With that accomplished, the team ended their busy day on a distinctly high note.

Then Claude offhandedly asked, "Willy, just what do all these impressions say? They all look the same to me."

"Vell, dhat's because they are. I vill have to check, but I believe them to be totally unique, for they seem to be the seal of the High Priest of Amen Re himself, attributed to a certain Meryptah. Sound familiar, Claude?"

As before with the plaster seals of Meryptah's own tomb, van der Boek's first thought was to divide the entire wall into numbered quadrants, and then chisel out and remove each one, so that the entire wall could be later reconstructed. The trick was to accomplish this feat without doing any injury to the seal impressions themselves. But given the fact that these seal impressions were unique to the field of Egyptology, he decided to call up Sharil first with the good news and then Dr. Rashid, for he might have an approach for dealing with such historically unique plaster impressions.

Predictably, Sharil was thrilled at the team's progress and results. Promising to tear herself away from Cairo and make a visit the following day, she then warned that she would not be coming alone. In short, have the team prepared for another media invasion!

Sighing to himself and beginning to appreciate what the cost of notoriety was, the archaeologist next called his overworked, but very happily busy colleague, Dr. Ahmed Rashid.

"Ahmed. I am in need of your formidable wisdom and experience."

Momentary silence.

"You know, Willy, every time that you call me up and say something like that, I begin to worry. What is it now, my friend?"

"Well, Ahmed, the good news is that Marta has uncovered a plaster wall that is covered from floor to ceiling with pristine seal impressions. The bad news is that they are totally unique. Nowhere in my experience has anyone encountered such seal impressions of the High Priest of Amen Re."

"You're, of course, joking with me!

"No, my friend, I am not. Further, this high priest we have met before."

"Meryptah?"

"Precisely, Ahmed. Apparently, he sealed off a portion of this treasury either just before or during the Amarna Revolution and failed to tell anyone about it."

"Willy, what I remember from his x-rays, he was an extremely old man at his death. And from what I suspect, one with a lot on his mind."

"True enough, my friend, but what I need from you is a thought, some inspiration, as to how I can safely remove this plaster wall of unique seals."

"Well, I remember that you segmented and labeled the plaster seals of Meryptah's own tomb. I remember Brigitte delivering them to the museum's dock in pieces. What's wrong with that approach? It worked well in the past."

"Have you ever worked with latex molds, Ahmed?"

"Ah, now I see. Yes, I have. They are very easy to work with, but are only useful with stone inscriptions, making molds of statuary and the like. Latex would be very bad with something as soft and absorbent as plaster. I would not recommend that approach."

"That's what I needed to know. So I guess that you should expect to shortly receive several crates of carefully packed and numbered plaster fragments."

* * *

The following day, under the glare of lights and video cameras of a joint British-American camera crew, Marta and van der Boek, with Sharil in attendance, began their surgical removal of the plaster wall. The process was greatly aided with the use of a cordless drilling tool that jewelers across the world use on a daily basis. With plaster dust flying this way and that, van der Boek had quickly outlined all the sections with neat but very deep incisions. Then came the tricky, ticklish part – the extraction of the first piece.

Much as with the first piece of a warm cherry pie, van der Boek expected trouble, so he started with a section whose seals were not as pristine as the rest. Predictably, the first one broke into three pieces, but pieces that could easily be joined. Now with an easier access to the plaster layer's backing, the second section came away cleanly and uninjured, as did the third. While van der Boek had removed roughly the first third of the plaster, Marta then completed the task, much to Sharil's surprise, which she did admirably and without one break. So the process went on until the entire plaster surface had been removed, each carefully photographed, labeled, packed, and boxed for transport.

Now with the plaster removed, van der Boek, Marta, Dieter, Horst, Claude, Sharil, and the camera crew were confronted with a wall that was clearly laid wet in regular courses and composed of manageable blocks of limestone.

"Now, Marta," the Hollander coached. "Ve must be very careful. It is best to begin as ve have before, in one of the upper corners, and literally tease avay at the material. The idea now is not to bash the vall down, but instead gently break through and dhen pull each piece outwards, so as to lessen anyding from falling back into the chamber beyond." This entire conversation the camera crew caught on tape. The cameraman quipped, "Damn, this is like going to an archaeology class."

Nodding in understanding and feeling like a veteran, Marta took the lead and began in the upper left corner. Soon she had a rock loose, wiggled it, and then out it came. Her ultimate reward was a five-by-five-inch gap of total blackness, for there was nothing behind that shoe box-sized block of limestone.

"Mein Gott!" Marta positively squealed, who was now hopping up and down excitedly on her toes. "I don't believe it! I vas right! Herr Professor! I vas right! I vas right!"

Again the camera crew caught Marta's reaction. "This is gold, pure gold." Never before have more prophetic words been spoken.

She hugged her mentor and just about everybody else in the corridor. Marta's exuberance was indeed infectious, for everyone had to take a peek, but not before van der Boek first allowed Sharil to do so and with his own flashlight.

"Madam," he formally intoned. "I believe you should be the first to see vhat's beyond the vall."

Taking the offered flashlight and stepping toward the gap, the Egyptian archaeologist realized that she wasn't tall enough. So she turned to Marta and said, "No. I will not be the first. Marta. Here. Please tell us all that you can see."

And so, in the full glare of the film crews' twin halogen lights, before the lens of Claude's digital camera, Marta got up on her tiptoes, held the flashlight to the side of her head, looked in, and jerked her head back quite shaken!

"Mein Gott!" she said. "There's someone in there looking back at me!"

Taking the flashlight from her trembling hand, Horst next looked in, smiled, and said, "Marta's correct. Dhere is a guard on the other side!"

The Brit cameraman again quipped, "You just can't make this stuff up." Our producer will be really pleased with just that one very human reaction alone!

* * *

As to what lay beyond that last barrier that separated Marta, her cohorts, van der Boek, Sharil Moussa, and the American and British cameramen was difficult to imagine, much less describe. But take a moment and try: a large, dark rectangular chamber, whose ceiling was supported by fourteen squared columns. Imagine also that it is packed from floor to ceiling, much like a moving truck's interior, but instead of boxes, imagine it neatly organized by item with passable aisles between. Also remember that this is not a funerary deposit. It's an inventory, the portable wealth of a powerful god and his vast temple community. An inventory that was meant to be easily viewed, readily recovered, but at some later undetermined date.

From the film crew's point-of-view, if they chose to pan their video camera's halogen light source over here, they saw literally hundreds of wine and beer jars. Each precisely stacked one atop another, arranged row after row as if they were artillery shells. Their contents and vintages were readily identifiable, because their labels either hung from a string impressed in the clay vessel, or were just painted or stamped on their necks.

Pointing their cameras over there, the bright lights encountered life-sized statue upon statue made from precious cedar wood, gold, bronze, and electrum. All stand like Halloween ghosts, each peering out at the camera's lens from beneath their individual gossamer dust sheets.

The cameras now turn left to peek in the neighboring aisle behind the statues. There six ivory inlaid cedar wood sedan chairs decorated in embossed gold foils wait ready for use. The EEOP representative, Dr. Sheril Moussa, noted what they truly represented, "Glorious statements of wealth and power from another time!"

But next to the sedan chairs and also on the floor, five heavily-built gurney-like conveyances sat, no doubt designed to be lifted by four sturdy backs. Piled atop each, and secured within low wooden frames, raw and crudely formed ingots of gold and silver bullion rested.

Now panning to the immediate right, and stacked right next to the bullion, are tens of thick ox hide-shaped plates of copper and bronze, all ready for smelting, resting in four stacks, each sixteen plates high.

Stunned at all of this wealth, the cameramen now retreat farther to the right and then to the left. There lay cedar wood planks, again in those maddeningly neat stacks, extending almost to the ceiling, left to season in place. They were positively identified by their aroma alone.

Panning now over to the western end of this vast inventory of a god, and again piled neatly row upon row, are hundreds of labeled jars filled with honey and cedar oils. Their identification was sure because their distinctive smells filled the cameramen's noses as the seal of one must have broken open.

Looking now over here, behind this mountain of fragrance is another orderly pile, this time of linen garments. How many? Who knew? The mound was four and a half feet tall by about eight square. Gazing at the pile, one of the Yank cameramen commented, "Makes you simply cringe, Jack. What a typical temple laundry day might have been like."

Carefully stepping over to the southwestern corner, the camera lights now illuminated a pyramid-shaped stack of easily fifty tightly woven papyrus wicker baskets with their lids all securely tied down. An extreme close up shot of a clay seal on one of the baskets, Dr. Moussa read aloud. "Its raw myrrh gum. It's the temple's incense imported from Somalia or Ethiopia."

* * *

And so on and on the inventory went. As with so many things in life, after a fashion, a certain kind of numbness took over. While archaeologists around the world pride themselves in their patient diligence, the graduated sifting and even flotation of soils, all the gleaning of artifacts – no matter how seemingly insignificant or small – here, within this chamber's inventory, one sensed the practical need for a laser RF gun and bar-coded labels. In this sense, one of the American cameraman summed up the scene the best.

"Jesus H. Christ! This place is like Home Depot."

And while all just stood there stunned at what was arrayed before them, let the following be said. The benefactions given to the Great God during the lifetime of a later pharaoh, from a lesser time, easily eclipsed the treasure trove that now stood amassed before van der Boek and his team. And how do we know this? Because the inventory lists of the Papyrus Harris said so. And now the cataloging of this vast hoard was destined to become the subject of Marta's dissertation.

CHAPTER XLVIII

The Recovery of the Hope

What occurred during the waning moments of September 29th and early hours of September 30th will never be fully revealed to the public, even though practically every inhabitant of the world with an electric light or appliance, a car, cell phone, computer, microwave, or television was in some way or another directly affected. In fact, even within the stratified layers of the U.S. government and its military, the "need to know" behind these events was strictly limited to only a few. And of those few, even fewer grasped the entire picture. But within that narrow cadre represented by two national entities, they and they alone knew the context and motivation behind these extraordinary cosmic events. In fact, to these few, the "event" itself was deemed sufficiently "human in logic and sentiment" to be fully justified. One was even quoted as having said, "The recovery [from Wright-Patterson AFB] which occurred, while regrettable, is acceptable, especially if one is willing to consider what the potential alternative could have been."

August–September

The long awaited near-Earth arrivals of the asteroids Toutatis and Poliahu held the rapt attention of the entire planet. These interstellar visitors were scheduled to pass by the Earth at their nearest approach on September 29th at the scant distance of only .01 AU, or about 930,000 miles. The extraordinary imagery provided by the Hubble Space Telescope (HST) made their astronomical details the stuff of everyday breakfast, water cooler conversation, and desktop screen savers. In fact, several rather randy witticisms were abroad about Poliahu's penchant for acquiring small asteroids and debris. As of the most recent HST image of several days ago, Poliahu had captured no fewer than thirteen such orbiting bodies.

Meanwhile, strong emotions regarding the asteroids and their near brush with Earth were expected to be manifested in many and varied ways, but all were predictable, and local, state, and national governmental entities had been alerted as to what they might expect.

Outbreaks of panic, hysteria, and their consequent repercussions were anticipated. Fringe groups of all favors and kinds from Doom's Day, pseudo-religious, Satanists, and other activist-oriented groups were on the rise. That Poliahu had recently attracted to its influence a thirteenth satellite was all the proof some needed that the coming of the Antichrist was nigh.

In the main, peaceful religious and scientifically-oriented events were planned and expected to take place on a global scale. Even a religious summit of sorts had been hastily organized to convene within the confines of Old Jerusalem.

Odds makers in both London and Las Vegas were accepting wagers on several possible scenarios. The most popular one was a horse race as to whether Poliahu, the faster moving of the two asteroids, would indeed overtake and pass by the Earth before the slower moving Toutatis. Another possibility, a dead heat, had current odds hovering around two million to one.

Buy your ticket now!

In short, there was a clear expectancy in the air as the population of Earth waited and held its collective breath to witness the celestial passing.

* * *

The Xoxx's concentration levels were in high gear. His colleagues understood given the gravity of their mission and how close at hand all was about to unfold.

"Well, this species possesses a phrase that encapsulates this moment." The Xoxx piped.

"And what may that be?" cautiously queried the Quimbly.

"IT'S SHOW TIME!"

Silence.

Finally.

"I do not understand," said the Sard.

"Neither do I." agreed the Quimbly.

Now rumbling with emotion that amounted to a belly laugh for the Xoxx.

"You just had to have been there!"

Now with a serious and testy note, the Sard chided, "My dear Xoxx, I do believe that your current juggling act of thirteen satellites and their associated debris has you a bit overextended. Am I correct?"

*   *   *

"You know, Lt. Perry. Something really bothers me about all the imagery that I've seen of Poliahu. Be it radar or those spectacular Hubble shots."

"What's that, Dr. Perry?" The Air Force lieutenant leered from across their shared office in Colorado Springs.

"None gives us one peep at the central mass of Poliahu. Not one!" Becky punctuated with her finger into the air. "For all I know, the core of Poliahu could be a Dodge Ram truck!"

"Ah, Beck, there's no stone in a Dodge Ram truck," her recently minted husband said most reasonably. "Besides, all the spectrographic data indicate that Poliahu is a classic dark S-Class asteroid of a stony-iron composition."

"You're totally avoiding my point."

Brief silence. Then a sense of wonder with a tinge of alarm colored his voice.

"Beck, are you absolutely sure about that?"

"Yep."

"Now that is really weird, as in almost scary. Do you think something's actually trying to hide inside that fur ball of swirling satellites?"

"Well, no. It's just really odd. That's all."

*   *   *

September 27th, 10:37 GMT

As it turned out, Toutatis' very dumb, but very rapid passage past the Sun had caused a wake. This turbulence directly affected the Sun's corona that resulted in a coronal mass ejection in the one billion ton range, not to mention a rather pronounced Yarkovsky acceleration effect accompanied by a solar-gravitational deviation to Toutatis' projected course.

September 27th, 11:12 GMT

Asteroid 1994 BH, Poliahu, cunningly, but very rapidly passed by the same region of the Sun's corona, rending it further. This time, the coronal mass ejection was estimated in the two to three billion ton range, and as with Toutatis, the projected course of Poliahu also subtly changed.

September 28th, 00:55 GMT

In full view of the Hubble Space Telescope's formidable lens, the National Oceanic and Atmospheric Administration's (NOAA) Space Environment Center (SEC) went to full alert. As the United States, prime space weather forecasting bureau, an agency that usually depends upon geocentric satellites and fixed position spacecraft to provide them with data, what they just saw happen via the Hubble's imagery was all they needed to know. A massive space storm was coming Earth's way that would hit in two waves, arriving about two hours apart, with the second being far worse than the first. In essence, what NOAA saw with the multiple passing of the two asteroids was a pulling away of a significant amount of the Sun's corona, the stuff of sunspots.

The "stuff" that was now hurtling out into space and into the Earth's path contained two unprecedented wave crests of particles – electrons, protons, pions, neutrons, and low and high-energy muons. As a result, NOAA began initiating procedures for a phased shutdown of their space-based satellites and ground-based assets.

First to be shut down, as their instrumentation had been pegged at an extraordinary "plus X-20," were two spacecraft parked in a fixed position at the gravitational neutral point between the pull of the Earth and the Sun. These two guardians at the fringe's edge were NASA's Advanced Composition Explorer (ACE) and the Solar and Heliospheric Observatory (SOHO), itself a joint European Space Agency and NASA project. In many respects, these instruments represented Earth's first trip wire that watch for such inconvenient and damaging events that a fluctuation in ionized particles within the solar wind could bring.

The next that were turned off were NOAA's geocentric Earth satellites, the Geostationary Operational Environment Satellites, or

GOES. This second trip wire measures proton flux levels and x-ray levels during solar radiation storms. And before they were turned off, their instrumentation also went off the charts as the maxima for a solar radiation storm of S5, "extreme," and radio blackouts R5, "extreme," had been eclipsed.

The last that NOAA shut down was its ground-based magnetometer installations that measure geomagnetic storm levels in real time, in other words, as they happen on the ground. Their last instrument readings went off the scale as well with a planetary K index of "plus 9."

With all of its assets shut down, NOAA was blind. Also blind by design was the Hubble Space Telescope, as its owners powered it down and closed all of its shutters just in case. NOAA's full alert was noted by other governmental agencies, both domestic and international, all with similar concerns and assets aloft. Then were powered down all the global positioning satellites (GPS) and with them went one's ability to find that hotel or restaurant, or how far away the green was on the seventh hole, soon to be followed by the many television and radio satellite providers as well.

So as one, the entire Earth began turning off its shielded and non-shielded assets. Why? Because the two wave fronts of high-energy particles, these two solar flares, represented an unprecedented threat to anything electrical. For the charged particles of sunspot activity overload electrical systems with extra current, initiating false commands, altering memory files, and outright burn up silicon chips. Turning off such systems in time means that the high-energy particles "pass through . . . without any consequences."

So confronted with this threat, governments began shutting down anything and everything electrical, satellites, their defense grids, even the electrical grids of their cities. They did so advisedly, because the Canadian city of Quebec had lost its entire electrical grid in March of 1989 during a far less intense solar flare up.

But truly at risk were the astronauts aboard the Space Lab, who had to early on take appropriate measures to protect themselves from the hard radiation. Frankly, few thought that they would come out of this unscathed.

* * *

"You know, Xoxx, this plan of yours is truly remarkable," the Sard commented neutrally. "For there has been a very noticeable drop across all transmitting sources and bands of electromagnetic energy. The planet's inhabitants are very wisely shutting down."

"From my photonic sensors," the Quimbly piped up, "even their habitation grids are falling. A self-imposed darkness is falling across their planet."

"By the way," the Sard continued, "have you had any success with those baseball statistics that you were troubled about?"

Pleased at his colleague's concern about its side investigation, the Xoxx said, "Actually, no." The Xoxx almost bristled. "In fact, there appears to be far more to this 'baseball' then I had expected. Apparently some outside variables are involved that I have yet to quantify."

"And what variables are those?" the Sard delicately prodded.

"Two statistical items, really, both apparently controlled by something called a 'curse.' One has something to do with 'The Bambino' and the other with 'The Billy Goat.' To date, I have not been able to make any statistical sense of either."

* * *

What the crew of The Redemption could not see throughout some of the regions of "self-imposed darkness" was the immense weight of uncertainty that hung in the air like a thick, heavy smoke. For a planet that was addicted to 24/7 news and instantaneous communications, all of that was gone. Even cable providers, fearful of frying their networks, had gone black. With television, radio, and cell phones down, people dependent upon their beloved media did not know what to think. And so, perhaps all too predictably, rumors began to spread, which engendered fear, rioting, outright pillage, and general lawlessness across many parts of the planet. For some, this was a purely manufactured windfall opportunity. For others, it signaled the end of the world, only to be witnessed in candlelight.

September 29th, 00:44:32 GMT

At this moment in time, a time of self-imposed darkness across the Earth, an exceedingly bright light was clearly and suddenly seen in the night's sky across half the planet and by a good part of both hemispheres.

Poliahu and Toutatis had collided spectacularly.

September 29th, 02:12 GMT

As a result of that titanic collision of two asteroids, shattered fragments spread in an ever-expanding ripple across space. While some missed Earth, others showered down upon it. Most were harmless, creating in their pyrrhic wakes fantastic displays the likes of which mankind has no historical record. Among those fallen angels was also The Redemption and its crew, one of whom was slightly shaken up.

"Well, Xoxx! I hope that you are pleased with yourself!" a very grouchy Quimbly complained. "Lucky for me that I was fully prepared for that impact, otherwise I would have become so many molecules spread throughout this ship."

"Our colleague sounds a tad shook up," remarked the Sard. "Organics. They're all so fragile. I must really apologize. But I did so want to create a good diversion."

"That you did, my friend. That you did!" prattled on the Quimbly. "And now that we are clear of the initial scatter, I will begin active probing for the Hope, and with luck, no one will be the wiser."

* * *

But as the story always goes, someone stubbornly had not fully shut down their tracking systems. In fact, NORAD fully considered expendable the huge golf ball shaped radar domes at Butler AFB in Aurora, Colorado, and their linked geocentric satellites. They were willing to "waste them" during just this sort of situation. Chalk it up as a practical field test of their "hardening" against severe EMP, or just institutional paranoia, or maybe even a more primal fear of the dark.

But NORAD remained as live as it could be based upon a handful of radar domes and their dedicated satellites. And what their radar operators saw they could not believe. Worse, they were powerless and could do nothing about it, for nothing could launch and nothing could fly through the dense electromagnetic interference to intercept what they detected. For that matter, NORAD could not even call the local police department on a landline! But what they could do was watch and record what was going on outside the Magic Mountain.

* * *

"I have located the Hope and have successfully powered up its emergency beacon!" said the Quimbly with undisguised relief.

"Organics. So unnecessarily emotional," the Xoxx rumbled.

* * *

September 29th, 02:44 GMT

"Sir, we have a bogie vectoring and decelerating. I repeat. Vectoring and decelerating toward North America and in particular the Great Lakes region. It looks like it's going to impact."

"Are you sure about that, Sergeant?"

"Bet my pension on it, sir."

"If you collect it."

So The Redemption disguised as a large meteorite impacted squarely into the deepest portion of Lake Michigan, equidistant between Racine, Wisconsin, and Holland, Michigan, creating as a result a mild tsunami-like wave that was eight feet high and traveling over forty-five miles an hour. Hundreds of millions of dollars later in damaged lakefront property and surface craft, the lake would eventually subside as if nothing out of the ordinary had occurred.

"Well, Sergeant. What did you say about your pension?"

"Well, Commander. I didn't think that it was going for a swim."

And swim The Redemption did, some fifty miles southeast in fact, where it emerged from the lake and flew at a low altitude over the Benton Harbor and Saint Joseph area on a heading directly toward their lost colleague and its scout craft at Wright-Patterson AFB. The emergence of The Redemption from the lake was witnessed beachside by sixteen very drunken teenagers, who from that day refused to ever drink again.

September 29th, 03:15 GMT

The Redemption's low-level flight cross-country was tracked by NORAD's dedicated satellites that had continued to function flawlessly. Its flight path was later confirmed by scores of eyewitnesses, and reputable ones too, of the passage of a dark, faceted, and silent object about the size of a large house.

As one grounded local pilot later recounted, flying conditions over Dayton that early morning were described as "crap." And by "crap," he meant overcast, poor visibility, foggy, and with light rain. For the crew of The Redemption, and after all of what they had already been through, they were oblivious to the very conditions that helped to further cloak their presence.

The extraterrestrial ferry, having passed directly over the intersection of Interstate Highways 70 and 75 and crossing over State Highway 4, beelined over to Hanger P and hovered above it at an altitude of about two hundred feet. When the Quimbly scanned the craft, it found it empty, too empty. With practiced resignation, the organic then remotely sealed the Hope's lone hatch and powered up its atmospheric engine.

Within the empty hanger, the unshielded security cameras were totally fried by the sun spot activity. As a result, they failed to record the closing of the Aten's hatch and a sound that had not been heard on the Earth for over three millennia – the ignition whine of the Hope's hydrogen motor.

Satisfied, the organic lifted the scout craft off of its MPC, since no tie-down attachments had been judged needful due to its weight and bulk. As one of the wrench heads that hailed from New Jersey had so aptly quipped, "Like who's gonna, like, walk off with it?"

In many ways, the initial lift of the Hope, while it was still within the hanger, would have looked to the security cameras like a floating, plastic-wrapped apparition from an emergency room, complete with all of its umbilical cables and cords still attached. However, all of those cameras were inoperable and did not capture the Aten as it went right through the hanger's roof. Now free, the scout craft matched the altitude of the ferry, slid over to its ventral docking strut. The Quimbly deftly engaged The Redemption's latching mechanisms, and only then powered down the scout craft. The docking maneuver now completed, The Redemption's crew automatically compensated their drives to support the additional mass. Then the ferry quite literally rose, kept rising, and did not stop until it broke away into free space.

At first it had been the muffled roar of hydrogen motor's exhaust shortly followed by the rending of the metal hanger's roof that tipped off the local MPs that something was up at Hanger P. But by the time the Humvees got there, all was in disarray with hanger roof material scattered about.

In one soldier's words, "The place looked like a damn yard sale!"

Subsequent investigations would prove that there was no evidence of a ground-level forced entry into the facility. All that remained was the plain and obvious fact that the craft decided to leave on its own accord and the only way that it knew how – straight up.

September 29th, 03:49

"Sir! That bogie that settled over Wright-Pat."

"Yes, Sergeant. Now what's it doing? Refueling?"

"No, sir. But now it's bugging out. Like straight up. Geez-o-Pete's! It's already in orbit and going, going, going, gone. Bye-bye.

"Sir, I've lost it."

* * *

Soon after The Redemption began its dizzying elevator-like climb with the Hope in tow, its eager and relieved crew beamed a message that their mission had been successfully accomplished and without incident. However, they expressed their concern regarding the condition of the Hope. Much was missing from within it, including the organic remains of the First Scout.

```
PARTIAL RECOVERY.
Recovery Craft REDEMPTION.
Surveyors 73, 31, 90.
Scout Craft HOPE secured, but compromised.
Surveyor 1 not recovered.
Redemption enroute to Survey Community.
Are prepared to return. Awaiting instructions.
```

Coordinates 3944.4331.3220.
Relative Time 640901.093.
PARTIAL RECOVERY.

CHAPTER XLIX

Postmortem

Four days after the spectacular cosmic events of September 29th, an extremely encrypted teleconference took place, again courtesy of a U.S. Air Force satellite hookup. As before, the Air Force allowed a select outside few to listen in as well. But this time, the ploy did not work. Their feeds were scrambled in some way that made their viewing and listening useless. Surprised, angry, and finally questioning just what the Air Force was up to, all that the Air Force could do is shrug their shoulders in ignorance. After all, they were just the hookup. Could they help that the users of their hardware had decided to further encrypt their signal's encryption?

Dr. Young stated the obvious, "Gentlemen, thank you for being available so soon after the recent fireworks. We have much to discuss."

"Da," was all that was said by Ostrogorsky on behalf of the entire Russian panel.

"First off," Professor Jung began with a mix of agitation and dismay, "it appears that an unknown – based upon NORAD tracking telemetry and other ground sighting reports during the space storm – entered the Earth's atmosphere, violated United States airspace, maneuvered within it, and paid a visit to our Wright-Patterson Air Force Base facility. Once the unknown reached the air base, it somehow removed the Aten spacecraft through the roof of its secured storage hanger, and took off with it straight up into, through, and out of the Earth's atmosphere.

"Now for my question to the Russian panel. Do any of you have information that may be germane to this remarkable chain of events?"

If one tried to read the three expressions on the Russian faces from half a world away, one might conclude that what they had just heard was either very interesting, very funny and ludicrous, or just plain unbelievable. However, it was the "very funny and ludicrous" face of Drazinzka that responded to the American.

"Professor Jung, let me see if I understand you correctly. You say that, during the two most intense solar flares of recorded history, your NORAD facility and its satellites tracked an unknown in near space, watched it violate your sovereign airspace, then recorded its flight to a heavily secured airbase, saw it steal the Aten craft, and then tracked it as it flew away."

"Essentially, sir, yes. Yes, that's exactly what happened."

"Then, Professor Jung, how could your NORAD still function during the two solar flare fronts, while the rest of the entire world sat by candlelight?"

"Sir, I have a copy of the entire episode, complete with the radar operator's chatter and his commander's heckling. As to why NORAD could still remain functional during the solar flares, that I cannot answer."

Suspicious if not antagonistic silence fell.

"And what of the organic materials, metallurgical samples, and data that were removed from the Aten craft?" Rosovec wanted to know.

Again Jung answered, "All is still safe and sound. For now…"

"Humph!" Drazinzka snorted. "For now."

When Jung continued, he then dropped his bombshell.

"We believe that we know who recovered the Aten craft."

"What!" Ostrogorsky snapped in total surprise.

"First you call the intruder an unknown and now you tell us that you know who it is! What sort of game are you Americans playing?"

Jung, ignoring Ostrogorsky's theatrical bluster, for he saw it for what it truly was, calmly continued on.

"We believe we know who recovered the Aten spacecraft, because we have a copy of their homeward-bound transmission that fractionally reflected off of the upper atmosphere."

Silence was created by that final trump card.

Finally, Rosovec asked, "Well? Are you going to tell us what it said?"

"Academician Rosovec, if I knew what it said, then I would have told you. We are in the process of trying to break it down."

Ostrogorsky then burst in.

"Well then how, if you don't know what the transmission says, do you know who stole the Aten?"

"Academician Ostrogorsky," the philologist Milson said, "It's really only a matter of time before we do. But I can tell you this, parts of the transmission, and in particular several repeated values, most likely represent nouns. These are relatively easy to pick out, especially if they are repeated. For instance, the recovered Aten craft, we're relatively certain, was referenced several times. Further details no doubt will be revealed with study. However, may I suggest one concern about the current condition of the Aten craft. We removed a considerable amount of organic material that most likely represented the Aten craft's pilot. When the recovery team discovers this fact, they may be back for those remains. So, gentlemen, in review, our planet has recently experienced unprecedented natural events spurred on by the desire of an advanced extraterrestrial civilization to recover, under a cloud of carefully premeditated deception, one of their own. Need I say more?"

Milson then paused for effect.

"Additionally, we have full telemetry of this daring and bloodless raid. Now," Milson said with firm conviction and raising his index finger in emphasis. "Just when are we going to start acting as adults toward one another? Just when are we going to start trusting one another? And, most importantly, when are we going to start working together, instead of against one another? Granted, the loan of your three scientists was a nice start. But after conversations with Academician Rosovec, we had frankly hoped for more."

At this revelation, both Drazinzka and Ostrogorsky briefly glanced at their younger colleague with measuring eyes, while Milson continued.

"But specifically, Academician Ostrogorsky, just when are you going to quit with the all histrionics? Frankly, sir, they accomplish very little of substance. In short, gentlemen, I value straight talk."

A belligerent silence broke out.

And then Milson quietly concluded and gestured with open hands.

"Gentlemen, now, please consider this. Look how easily they violated our near space and terrestrial envelope. Note also what extremes they went through in order to cover their tracks and hide their presence. Then they walked right in and took what they wanted – their lost spacecraft. I don't know about you, but that makes me very nervous, especially if they decide to come back, this time looking for the remains of their pilot, and I serious doubt that they will do so without any pretense of subterfuge."

CHAPTER L

A Morning's Coffee Surprise

Professor Emeritus Dr. Willem van der Boek had just finished his first cup of morning coffee. Now looking down at his empty cup, the Dutchman, who loved his coffee, got up from his office chair to replenish it from his Krups coffee maker. An old wedding gift, the now ancient artifact still produced the glorious aromas and sacred liquids that made life ever so much more livable.

Now once again settling into his chair, the emeritus professor checked his computer for any new e-mails and indeed he had several, but one really caught his eye, and so he opened it.

> Dear Professor Dr. van der Boek:
>
> It has been brought to my attention that during the clearing of the Amen Re Treasury, a papyrus was found secreted within the framework of the Horus glider frame. Dr. Rashid, our Chief Conservator, was the one who found it.
>
> Given your intimate knowledge of the Meryptah inscription and your key role in the clearing of the treasury, I thought it most appropriate that the publication of this papyrus should be placed in your hands.
>
> Attached you will find three files of digital imagery from Louis Bando. One is in color, the second in black-and-white, and the third in infrared.
>
> I hope that my decision to entrust this artifact's publication to you is agreeable.
>
> Sincerely yours,
>
> Dr. Sharil Moussa
>
> Director of the Cairo National Museum

Mein Gott! The aging Egyptologist thought.

Then he reread the e-mail just to make sure that he got it right the first time. Then, impulsively perhaps, van der Boek clicked on the first attachment, and his computer's screen filled with two columns of beautifully formed hieroglyphic text. Even without printing out the text, the Egyptologist could read the significance of the papyrus' context, and for the second time that day exclaimed, "Mein Gott!"

CHAPTER LI

"On Mastering the Winds of Amen Re"

In all, the digital images that Louis Bando's cameras so precisely produced almost playfully danced before van der Boek's eyes, for they told a story that was far beyond any Egyptologist's wildest dreams. The papyrus' narrative, while reasonably straightforward in a grammatical sense, nonetheless stretched the known Egyptian vocabulary to its absolute limits. Further, a considerable philological excursus would be required just to cover all the new meanings and nuances that were attributable to this newly uncovered ancient technology.

Without doubt, considered the Dutchman, the publication of this document would firmly establish the aeronautical contribution of the ancient Egyptians to Western Civilization.

Then there was the logical and scientific presentation of the experimental process involved with the development of the falcon glider that threatened to shake the field of Egyptology to its very foundations. In essence, van der Boek's publication of the papyrus and its content in the *Zeitschrift für die Ägyptische Sprache* – Egyptology's oldest journal – would initiate a long overdue floor to ceiling reevaluation of Egyptian technology. Never again could a philologist, historian, or archaeologist use the term *unsophisticated* when discussing ancient Egyptian know-how. When matched with the glider paraphernalia recovered from the Amen Treasury, the glider's fuselage, wing, various harnesses, and helmet, all now had a firmly established context.

As for the physical characteristics of the papyrus, in all it was only fourteen columns long, each column sixteen centimeters wide by thirteen, each fifteen lines long with a seven centimeter space between, recto only, with an extremely smooth surface without blemish. Its modest length was indicated at 3.45 meters, or about eleven feet four inches of absolute, intellectual, dynamite.

* * *

Column I

These are the words of Meryptah, the first falcon flier, acolyte, trainer of falcon fliers, and first prophet of the Great Hidden One of Mighty Thebes! Contained within are the words On Mastering the Winds of Amen Re. As long as men have walked, they have desired to fly upon the warming morning winds that are the very breath of Amen Re. While such has long been men's desire, the means to do so has never been understood. Then arrived near divine inspiration from a *sem*-priest of the god of the Great White Wall. This *sem*-priest was called Piankhotep. He shared the observation that something light, strong, and well-formed could be made to fly. Then, much to my wonder and amazement, Piankhotep demonstrated much cleverness and proof of this fact. How a squared sheet of papyrus, if cunningly folded, could be made to glide through the air much like a bird. Once so demonstrated that a common object, if well-formed, could be made to glide through the air, I began to find other such common materials. Both the woods of the tamarisk and sycamore trees proved to be both light and strong.

Column II

I was not alone in my curiosity for during my youth I was the friend of another equally curious. His name was Neferkheperure. And together we crafted in secret our first wooden falcon glider. Built of the feather-light wood of the tamarisk tree, the body was finely formed as that of a small falcon ending in an upright tail. Joined to the body was a single wing of six palm widths and to its tail a smaller one of four finger widths. As with the proper balancing of an effective throw stick, we reasoned that a small amount of weight was needed. We added the weight, a small, short rod of obsidian, to the falcon's head, its ends cleverly forming the falcon's eyes. With such balance now achieved, a gentle warping of the larger wing allowed for gentle turns. We learned that the gentle warping of the smaller tail wing allowed for faster turns. After many attempts and many failures, the falcon glider was ready. It was to be a royal gift presented on Neferkheperure's fifth birthday, which brought much joy to the hearts of the king and queen. Thereafter, now with our falcon glider no longer a secret to the king, we were instructed to continue our efforts.

Column III

Success can lead to dangerous thoughts and equally dangerous consequences. If a small falcon glider could effortlessly glide through the air, why not then could a larger glider do the same? A glider that could perhaps be commanded by the desires of a man that rode astride it? The understanding of this by Neferkheperure was proof of his divine inspiration, even while he was a young man still with his forelock of youth. What he grasped was that the glider's body could not be formed from the trunk of a tree, for it would be far too heavy. Rather, he reasoned, small branches could be cleverly woven much the same way that a basket is woven. Such a construction would provide the needed strength and lightness required. As with a bird's feathers that catch at the wind and allow the bird to soar, so too did the woven glider body and wings need assistance. Stretched cloth proved capable of catching the wind much as it does when used as a riverboat's sail. But while a sail catches the wind, much wind also passes through the weave. After much thought put to this matter, it was found that a light coating of whitewash sealed the cloth against the wind. But it was also found that the whitewash did not attach well to the cloth, as it easily cracked, and even tore the cloth.

Column IV

We consulted with the temple's tanners of animal hides. We spoke with the temple's weavers and dyers of cloth. But it was from the temple's carpenters that we discovered their way of sealing and water-proofing wood. Using a thin resinous liquid mixed with soured wine, the stretched cloth sealed out the wind and attached well to the glider's wooden frames. The stretched cloth dipped in the resinous wine mixture also tightened the cloth against the glider body's frame and when it dried provided additional strength. As with the glider's body, so also were constructed the glider's wing and tail wing. The reasoning behind the construction of the great wing's length and breadth was based upon observation and the following calculation. If a falcon's wingspan is two cubits in length by one palm and two fingers in width, then that falcon must weigh five deben. The reasoning of the glider's tail size was based upon observation and the following calculation. If a falcon's tail span is three palms in length by two palms in width, then that falcon must weigh five deben. With these calculations, we constructed a flacon glider model that weighed twenty-five deben and three kites. When hurdled from atop the temple's pylon, it effortlessly flew! When hurdled from atop the cliffs above the mortuary temple of the beloved Osiris Makare Hatshepsut, the falcon glider soared endlessly on the warm morning winds of Amen Re himself!

Column V

With the encouragement of Nebmare Amenhotep and the blessing of the first prophet of the Great Hidden One, Amenemhet, we fearlessly began to calculate the measures needed to construct a falcon flier that could carry a man. On agreement, our task was strictly confined to the sacred temple precincts of the Great Hidden One, where materials were readily available, as were skilled craftsmen. Early on, it was decided that I, Meryptah, would be the first to attempt such an undertaking, as the king forbade his son from attempting such a dangerous adventure. Given the weight of my body, the temple mathematician first began with his figures. Since it was my thirteenth inundation, my weight was calculated at 430 deben, 5 kite. From those figures, an estimate was made as to how broad and wide the glider's great wing and the glider's tail must be. Then the mathematician weighed the remains of our model and from it estimated the weight of its soon to be built big brother. This figure the mathematician then added to his figures, his final estimate was calculated, and the construction of the first falcon-flier so began. Because of my great fear of being the first falcon-flier, a test was devised to prove the correctness of both the mathematician's calculations and the construction of the first falcon glider.

Column VI

Because of the great size of the glider's body and its great wing, it was decided that they should be constructed apart. The great wing was to be lashed to the glider body by means of strong leather straps that were found discarded by the temple's chariot builders. As with the falcon glider model, it was decided to test the falcon flier again from atop the western cliffs. Bags of sand and rock, weighing precisely 430 deben, 5 kite, were tied to the front third of the glider's body. Neferkheperure and three *sem*-priests ascended the cliffs with the falcon glider. I, with three *sem*-priests, waited below on the first terrace of the Osiris Makare Hatshepsut's mortuary temple. With the rising of Amen

Re in all of his magnificence, we waited for the warm winds to arise, which Neferkheperure could best detect from his lofty position. At the agreed upon moment, Neferkheperure and the priests held the glider body above their heads and allowed the winds to fill the great wing and tail. They together released the falcon flier into a strong freshening of Amen Re's breath, and the falcon flier at first fell as its wings fought to catch at the air. Then, in a most marvelous moment, the falcon glider no longer fell, but instead rose majestically and began to soar. Then, after a certain time the falcon glider again fell, only to again rise and briefly soar. This occurred four times before the falcon glider hit the ground and was dashed to pieces.

Column VII

While the falcon glider was no more, much was learned from its first flight. First, it was agreed that the great wing had to be made larger if the glider was to soar properly in the warm wind. Second, the great wing and tail required greater strength as they bent far too easily when catching the wind. Third, Neferkheperure saw that when the great wing's tip twisted in the wind, the falcon glider turned in that direction. Fourth, it was decided that the first falcon flier should not be firmly affixed to the glider's body. Instead, the falcon flier should be made to hang within the glider's body. The reason for this Neferkheperure demonstrated while riding in his chariot. Leaning into a turn assisted in the turning of the chariot, so too would the falcon flier be allowed to lean from side to side and from front to back. This meant that padded harnesses, much like that of a chariot's pair of stallions, would have to be devised for the falcon flier and a leather loop made to catch the feet. Fifth, to aid the falcon flier in his movements, a padded crossbar was to be added within the glider's body. Sixth, to assist with the glider's ability to turn, the great wing had waxed lengths of heavy twine affixed from their tips to the padded crossbar. The falcon flier would then pull on the twine to bend the tip of the great wing and thus begin the turn of the falcon glider. With so many new ideas discovered, it was decided to build another falcon glider, which was accomplished readily as the craftsmen were already familiar with the glider's design. And with the second build, the falcon glider became stronger and lighter through a variety of ingenious innovations.

Column VIII

We returned to the cliffs before Amen Re's first appearance once again to test the falcon glider. This time I climbed the cliffs with the falcon glider, and Neferkheperure remained below on the first terrace of the Osiris Makare Hatshepsut's mortuary temple. This was decided as it was believed that perhaps a different view would reveal new ideas. With the sacks of sand and rock firmly tied into the new hanging flier's harness, the appointed moment arrived. This time as the falcon glider fell, it quickly caught the wind with its larger great wing. As the great wing and tail were both strengthened, the glider soared for the first time higher than the cliffs, held aloft by the strong breath of Amen Re! As the glider seemed to for a time hang motionless, it was joined by a true falcon, which no doubt was curious as to who this stranger was that had so intruded into his domain! Then, with the great wing losing the wind, the glider tipped over on its side and fell. But just before it had become one with the ground, it again caught the wind and soared on many times climbing, falling, and again soaring high into the air. While the first test of the falcon glider had lasted perhaps mere moments, the second test lasted four times as long before the glider became undone.

Column IX

We were so satisfied with the falcon glider's ability to catch the wind and soar upon it that we immediately commanded the temple's craftsmen to build yet a third glider. This one they built even quicker than the last as the canny carpenters had made plans and molds, and as with so many things, that which is done often becomes better. Additionally, two chariot craftsmen had become interested in the glider's construction, and as a result this third glider was yet again stronger and even lighter in its form. But before I was ready to attempt to fly this finely built glider, I asked the craftsmen how difficult it would be to fashion two chariot wheels to the glider's frame. Neferkheperure, ever curious as to the workings of my mind, spoke to me with his *sia* as was our habit when we worked alone. Overjoyed with my idea, he agreed to find a fine and level plain over which to pull the wheeled glider with his chariot. The purpose of this test was for the falcon flier to feel the harnesses, to feel what the wind did to the glider, but most of all to calm my fearful heart. With the rope tied with a quick knot to the glider's crossbar, Neferkheperure began slowly to pull the glider along on its wheels. As the speed of the chariot increased, I sensed the glider's wing and tail begin to catch at the wind much like the sail of a boat. As Neferkheperure urged on his horses on to the attack speed, the glider fully lifted its wheels effortlessly off of the ground! I released the rope tether and flew for the first time! After a brief time, I quickly came down hard, breaking both of the chariot wheels and nearly some bones as well.

Column X

After some needful repairs to the falcon glider and several more pulls of the chariot, we found that the falcon glider could fly for some time and with control while tethered to the chariot. I even was able to make gentle turns while being so pulled into the wind by tugging on the waxed twine. But by far the greatest lesson learned was how to slow the glider in such a way as to stop it, as would a duck on the river or a falcon on the ground. To stop the glider and bring it to the ground without injury, first release the tether rope. Next, by leaning far back on the harness so as to raise the head of the glider, this will open the great wing and catch much wind, thereby greatly slowing the glider. If this is done correctly, the glider will practically fall straight to the ground on command. After practicing this stopping many times, I began to understand the glider's many habits. Then Neferkheperure had another one of his ideas. He reasoned that while the glider's body, great wing and tail was one with the wind, I was not. On the following day of our chariot-pulling falcon glider adventures, the noble one presented me with a surprise. It was a magnificently crafted falcon helmet that broadly extended to my shoulders. The purpose of the large helmet, Neferkheperure reasoned, was to cut through the wind. With a broad opening at the throat, I could easily see out and turn my head right and left, as it was so large. Held in place with straps under my arms, the helmet was not comfortable. Again we practiced with the chariot-pulling, and immediately I noticed the great difference with the helmet. My eyes no longer were weeping in the wind. No longer was my head battered this way and that. The helmet became comfortable.

Column XI

Now with many landings successfully accomplished, and now able to gently turn the glider while tethered, and now at peace within the quiet of the helmet, my confidence began to soar like a falcon. Neferkheperure, ever my silent companion, sensed this with his *sia* and so asked the question that was before my eyes. On the appointed day for the first falcon flight, my stomach felt like it was filled with many fluttering birds. As I stood on the edge of the cliff, bent over in the harness with the falcon glider strapped to my back, I was sick with worry. Neferkheperure, standing beside me, quietly whispered his many encouragements and reminders. As the winds warmed before Amen Re's early morning rays, they began to gather and strongly blow. While two *sem*-priests steadied the tips of my falcon glider's great wing, I stepped off at the appropriate angle and plunged to my death! So sure that I was about to go West, I loosened my bowels! Then the great wing caught at the wind, and for the first time of my life, I soared as Horus! How long I was aloft I cannot say so overjoyed my heart was! I soared! I turned this way and then that, following the warm winds. Then suddenly, during one fall, I realized that speed was my dearest of friends, just as it was when a chariot was at attack speed. Speed was not to be feared, because speed created the opportunity to catch the wind in the wings all that more firmly! Then I learned the way of the cresting of the soar, that near hover atop a warm uplift of wind, and the tipping to one side to fall, create speed, and only to soar again. Then I became exhausted. I had to come to earth. And so I slowly began to allow myself to descend lower and soar less. In the end, I was so exhausted that I landed clumsily and much bloodied on the pavement of Osiris Makare Hatshepsut's own mortuary temple.

Column XII

As I lay bruised, bloodied, and befouled beneath the falcon glider's body, I can say with some pride that the glider got the better of me, for it was merely scraped here and there, while I had broken no bones. Neferkheperure was humorous, being both overjoyed and exceedingly jealous at the same time. Lessons learned were as follows. First, the falcon flier must be strong of body and character and quick with his wits. Second, the tethered chariot practice needs several more lessons. Third, much was learned while aloft that cannot be practiced from a chariot's tether. Fourth, speed is good and is to be trusted. Speed provides wind. Wind provides the ability to soar. Fifth, practice in the harness while on the ground will teach many lessons and safely correct many mistakes. Sixth, the waxed tethers must be attached to hinged handles on the crossbar in order to make turns smoother and better controlled. Seventh, a falcon flier needs leather gloves, much as do chariot drivers. Eighth, a falcon flier cannot practice too much. Given the above lessons that were learned on that first soaring flight of the falcon glider, I could not wait to again wear the glider on my back!

Column XIII

I was like an intoxicated man who did not know when to stop drinking his beer! Every day I lived only to soar on the warm winds of Amen Re! I practiced in the harness. I made myself strong. I practiced with the chariot tether. I practiced stopping on the earth. I practiced in the harness again. Immensely pleased with my progress and with several improvements to the falcon glider, Neferkheperure suggested that the cloth of the glider's body, great wing, and tail should be painted with the form and feathers of Horus himself! After all, he reasoned, did I not wear the hawk-headed helmet of that god himself? The reasons why for all of this decoration the young prince did share with me, but I did not fully understand at the time the truth behind his motives. And so even though I was just a lowly acolyte, I became the first teacher of the falcon fliers of the Great Hidden One! And so, perhaps strangely, as I trained others to perform this most marvelous of deeds, I continued to learn as well. The most important thing that I learned was that the winds changed with the seasons. While one can soar from the cliffs on any day at Amen Re's first appearance, how long one can soar and how far away from the cliffs is a very changeable thing. Another lesson that I learned was that one can soar over the sacred mountain that lies behind the cliffs above the Osiris Makare Hatshepsut's mortuary temple.

Column XIV

As I write these words, I, Meryptah, once acolyte and now first prophet of the Great Hidden One, have trained six falcon fliers. It is with a sad and heavy heart that four falcon fliers have gone West, while under my tutelage. Again, many lessons were learned and many more will no doubt be discovered as I have long suspected.

CHAPTER LII

Magic Time

Midway through the first semester of his second year, a very bright lightbulb went off in Dr. Joseph Richards' head. His elder mentor and friend, John Milson, emeritus Professor of Egyptology, had warned him of such personal epiphanies and had told him how to train himself to bring them on almost at will. But while Milson's "magic time" occurred after having worked for a time on a troublesome ancient text or some such, Richards' occurred during the process itself. What Milson had not thought to consider was the freewheeling nature of Richards' young memory, a memory that had been enhanced through hypnosis and drug therapies far beyond what might be described as merely photographic. Richards remembered in near digital detail, meaning that he could remember a general scene one moment, analyze it, and then zoom in on a particular part of it the next.

But the process that kicked off this entire train of thought was the young scholar's preparation for his first advanced philology class in ancient Egyptian. He needed a well-known narrative text for his students to chew on, one that would inspire them, and one that would display Egypt's legacy to the heritage that is Western Civilization. For some subliminal reason, he unconsciously gravitated toward a religious treatise associated with the god Ptah, the patron god of the ancient and sacred city of Memphis. The treatise, referred to by modern scholars as "The Memphite Theology," Richards decided to make it the central focus for his class. But what struck the young academic was something that he remembered the high priest of Ptah say at Meryptah's funeral. The sentiment had remained fuzzy and out of context until he had read the fifty-third through fifty-seventh lines of the "Memphite Theology."

> Line 53:
>
> There took form in the heart [mind], there took shape on the tongue [speech] the form [image] of the god Atum. For the very great one is Ptah, (he) who gave essence [life] to all the gods through his heart [mind] and through his tongue [speech].

Line 54:

Horus came into being in him. Thoth came into being in him as Ptah. Thus the heart [mind] and tongue [speech] rule over all the limbs in order that it [heart/mind] is in every body and it [tongue/speech] is in every mouth of the gods, all men, all cattle, all creeping things, whatever lives, thinking whatever it wishes and commanding whatever it wishes.

Line 55:

His [Ptah's] Ennead is before him as heart, authoritative command, teeth, semen, lips, and hands of Atum. This Ennead of Atum came into being through his semen and through his fingers. Surely, this Ennead [of Ptah] is the teeth and the lips in the mouth, proclaiming the names of all things, from which Shu and Tefnut came forth as him, and

Line 56:

which gave birth to the Ennead [of Ptah].

Sight, hearing, breathing, these all report to the heart [mind], and it [heart/mind] makes every understanding come forth. As to the tongue [speech], it repeats what the heart [mind] has devised. Thus all the gods were born and Ptah's Ennead was completed. For every word of the god came about through

Line 57:

what the heart [mind] devised and the tongue commanded.

Cross-checking the text's critical commentaries by Sethe, Junker, Erman, Breasted, Wilson, and Lichtheim, Richards had to agree with them that Line 56 should have had followed Line 54. Besides, Richards could easily imagine a harried stonecutter mistakenly misplacing the line in the Twenty-Sixth Dynasty inscription that now resided in the British Museum.

But once beyond that philological detail, the clear parallel in meaning between the text of the "Memphite Theology" and that of the "Logos Doctrine" of Biblical *Genesis* seemed unmistakable, for in both texts divinity spoke and things were created. Without a doubt, Richards was intrigued first by the geographical proximity of the two cultures and how such a sharing could occur, but then was surprised to realize that the composition of the "Memphite

Theology" was far older than the Twenty-Sixth Dynasty, or for that matter the Israelites, thousands of years older.

It was then that the light bulb went off.

But that is a story best told at another time.

A Note Regarding Egyptian Priests & Priesthoods

Regarding references to Egyptian priests and their many priesthoods, by the time of the New Kingdom (1567–1085 BC), priestly duties were no longer performed on the behalf of the king by secular officials. Instead this burden was taken on by priesthoods devoted to each god. As one might expect, priestly bureaucracies coalesced in order to manage better the resources of a particular god's estate. Just as naturally, priestly hierarchies developed in order to apportion the many tasks associated with the daily care and maintenance of a specific deity. At the top of this priestly ranking stood those who served the god – the high priest, literally first servant or prophet of the god, who in turn was followed by second, third, and fourth servant or prophet of the god as well. In opposition to these administrative ranks, the vast majority of Egyptian priests, who undertook the drudgery of day-to-day temple duties, were the common priests, the *wab*-priests, literally the cleaners.

In addition to the servants and cleaners of the gods, specialty priesthoods existed as well, especially those devoted to the teaching of hieroglyphics and funerary functions connected with royal mortuary complexes, mummification, *The Opening of the Mouth* ceremony, and the security of the necropolis. One such type of priests, the *sem*-priests, appears to connote a distinct ranking that is unique to them. While certainly not as powerful as high priests nor as lowly as *wab*-priests, the influential title of *sem*-priest most often was associated with specific gods (Anubis, Isis, Osiris, Ptah, and Sokar), funerary activities, and even cultic functions connected within the royal palace itself.

A Note on the Vocalization of Ancient Egyptian

Regarding the vocalization of ancient Egyptian, the fact of the matter is this: the language is a very dead one – meaning that what it sounded like has been long lost. Its closest linguistic cousin, Coptic, is itself a dead language, but at least one that included vowels within its script. On this shirt-tailed basis, Egyptologists have compared the vocabularies of the two languages and have constructed a scientific vocalization scheme to approximate what the Egyptian tongue might have sounded like. But even if the assigned vowel placements are accurate, their quality remains just as uncertain as is where the accent falls on a particular word – not to mention that there is evidence to suspect several regional dialectics during the course of any given dynasty. To add even further confusion, different vocalization schemes have been put forward by the dominant Egyptological schools be they American, British, French, Italian, or German. As a consequence, the vocalization of ancient Egyptian becomes more a matter of one's cultural preference than anything else. In short, just what the language sounded like during a given time period and within a given region is unknown.

With the above caveats and considerations in mind, the author offers the following possible pronunciations for the ancient Egyptian names and words that appear in this manuscript.

Akhenaten – King of Egypt: ach-en-a-ten

Akhetaten – Capital city built by Akhenaten – aa-khet-a-ten

Amen Re – Chief divinity of Thebes: a-men-ra

Ankhmes – Court royal physician: anch-mes

Anubis – Egyptian god of the Necropolis: ah-new-bis

Atum – Egyptian god of creation: ah-tomb

Djoser – King of Egypt: zoser

Hapi – Egyptian god of the Nile: haa-pee

Horemheb – Prince of Memphis: Hor-em-heb

Imhotep – Architect of King Djoser: im-ho-tep

Kia – Nurse of Nefertiti: ke-ya

Maat – Divine order: maa-haat

Mayneken – *Sem*-priest of Ptah: may-necken

Meryptah – High priest of Amen-Re: mary-p-taah

Mutnedjemet – Second wife of Prince Horemheb: moot-neh-gem-et

Nua Wepwawet – Religious tool connected with *The Opening of the Mouth* ceremony: new-a wep-waa-wet

Neferneferru Nefertiti – Queen of Egypt and Chief Wife of Akhenaten: nefer-nefer-roo nefer-tee-tee

Nekhbet – Egyptian goddess of the sky: neck-bet

Osiris – Egyptian god of the Underworld: oh-sir-iss

Paneshy – Stone-cutter and Guardian of the Domain of the Aten – pah-neshy

Piankhhotep – Seer and *sem*-priest of Ptah: pee-anch-ho-tep

Ptah – Chief divinity of Memphis: p-taah

Sekmet – Goddess of war: sech-met

Sia – Divine understanding: see-ya

Smenkhkare – King of Egypt: ss-menck-ka-ra

Thoth – God of writing and civilization: thoawth

Tutankhaten – Same as below, but before he became king: toot-anch-aten

Tutankhamen – King of Egypt: toot-anch-a-men

A NOTE ON THE EDITING OF INSCRIPTIONS

The study of inscriptions, known as epigraphy, possesses well-known philological shorthand for the recording and interpretation of such ancient monuments – be they carved stone inscriptions, painted surfaces, or hastily scratched out graffiti. This methodology was first established by Theodor Mommsen, the founder of the *Corpus Inscriptionum Latinarum*, or *CIL*, in 1853. The *CIL*, which celebrated its 150th anniversary in 2003, is a vast compendium of nearly eighty volumes of inscriptions that relate to the Rome and the Roman Empire. The continued publication of newly discovered inscriptions from this period of history is the patient and laborious task of the Berlin-Brandenburgische Academie der Wissenschaften, *Corpus Inscriptionum Latinarum*'s staff, under the direction of its capable director, Professor Dr. Manfred Gerhard Schmidt.

With such a tool available, historians and philologists of other ancient time periods naturally gravitated to the *CIL* methodology forf philological criticism and commentary and either wholly adopted it or did so with few exceptions.

Consequently, all of the ancient Egyptian inscriptions contained within this book follow the *CIL*'s editorial conventions and use the following symbols to indicate:

a|bc Breaks in the text, usually a line break

a||bc Text located outside of an inscribed field or displaced text

(vac.) The presence of a gap in the text

[[abc]] An ancient erasure of text

<<abc>> Ancient text inscribed on an erased background

abc (!) An ancient grammatical error, misspelling, or philological irregularity of some kind

abc (?) Uncertain reading of the text

(abc) Either the modern explanation of an abbreviation or philological convention

a[bc] A modern editorial addition, explanation, or change to the text {abc} A modern editorial deletion of text

<abc> Letters once read by previous editors, which are currently lost or unreadable

If you liked this book, look out for the next in the series:
Children of Ptah: The Third Manuscript of the Richards' Trust

ABOUT THE AUTHOR

To craft such a tale takes wit, a love of science fiction, and above all a deep reverence for ancient history and archaeology. All of these qualities are stitched together beautifully in his books, because Cherf has been there, dug that. This is a guy who has even seen the sunrise from atop the Great Pyramid. Cherf likes to tell a story about when he was eleven years old and had become bored with dinosaurs. While exploring the Field Museum along Chicago's water front one Saturday morning he discovered Hall N – the ancient Egyptian collection. From that time forward Cherf was terminally smitten as that truly was his life-changing ah-ha moment.

Needless to say, Cherf's books have been generously reviewed by his readers, who have eagerly shared their joy. Recently, *Bow Tie* was rated by the Historical Novel Society as an "Editor's Choice" for 2013. For an author, such sentiments are an embarrassment of riches; precious words like honey deliciously drizzled.

Cherf has excavated in Israel and Greece and toured and photographed many of Egypt's ancient sites firsthand. He is also a big fan of Tom Clancy and Michael Crichton. But Cherf is quick to point out, whenever he can, the four men that professionally shaped him. Rufus J. Fears first lit the fire; Edward W. Kase stoked it; George J. Szemler refined it; and Charles K. Wolfe, Jr., set him free.

With a BA in Anthropology, MA in Egyptian Archaeology, and PhD in Ancient History, Cherf remains current as an elected officer of Denver's Egyptian Studies Society.

Living with his beloved wife, Sue, they keep Foxbat 1 out in the garage. They enjoy playing golf, road racing (that's where the Foxbat comes in), jawing around a fire pit on a cool evening while sampling craft beers, and rooting for the Cubs – clearly Cherf is a hopeless romantic. Bottom line: Cherf just flat makes science fiction, ancient history, and archaeology come alive.

Come visit www.wjcherf.com to access free sample chapters of his eighteen works and continue to follow the temporal adventures of Egyptologist Joseph Richards.

www.ingramcontent.com/pod-product-compliance
Lightning Source LLC
Chambersburg PA
CBHW030544020726
47494CB00005B/1474

* 9 7 8 1 7 3 2 9 7 7 9 8 3 *